Codename Angel

By

Jason Chapman

The Angel Chronicles

Book 1

© Jason Chapman 2012 – 2022

Updated April 2022

All rights reserved

No part of this publication may be reproduced, stored on a retrieval system, or transmitted in any form or by any means without the prior permission of the Author.

This book is dedicated to all those who have spent their lives looking for answers.

The truth still exists.

another fall. Plus, you've been going on about converting it into a bedroom for ages.'

'I promise I will sort that room out this weekend so mum and dad can use it as a downstairs bedroom.' Jones offered.

'When this baby is born Brian we will have to move to Leeds. Dad promised you a job as a clerk at the factory.'

'Don't keep going on about that, you know I'm happy where I am. Mr Adams needs me and Sir Ingles has promised to give me a wage increase. This time next year I'll be earning ten shillings a week.'

'I don't care Brian. We have to move for the baby's sake. We can't live in the middle of nowhere forever.'

'But what about mum and dad? I can't just abandon them.'

'For god's sake Brian we're not moving to the other side of the world.' Edith rolled her eyes. 'It's only twenty miles away. We'll take the baby up there every other weekend.'

A car approached on the opposite side of the road. Jones squinted at the headlights as it sped by. 'Listen, I know I promised you we'd move. I'll speak with Mr Adams tomorrow but I know he will try and convince me to stay.'

'I just said I don't care Brian. Besides it's more money at the factory than what Sir Ingles has offered. We'll be able to put a deposit on that house.'

'Courtesy of your dad.' Jones mocked. 'We'll end up owing him for the rest of our lives.'

Edith glared at her husband unimpressed by his tone. 'No we won't, dad says we can repay him slowly.'

The car radio started to crackle replacing Vera Lynn with static.

Jones reached forward to tune in the radio station.

A long stretch of road lay ahead, climbing a gentle slope ending in a bend at the top of a hill.

'It'll be so much better for the baby and they have some modern shops now in Leeds. We can go shopping every Saturday.' Edith sounded excited at the prospect of moving to

Prologue

Ripley – North Yorkshire – 10:56pm
Friday 27th June 1952

The crystal clear night sky shimmered overhead.

The car drove slowly along the deserted country road.

Brian Jones glanced up, marvelling at the stars that filled the sky. The surrounding landscape consisted of gentle slopes that gave an impressive view of the Milky Way from horizon to horizon. Jones hummed to the voice of Vera Lynn drifting out of the radio.

He had received a telephone call from his mother Knaresborough who had sounded very distressed. Jon father, a World War One veteran had taken a bad fall do the stairs and had not been able to get up. Unable to leave heavily pregnant wife Jones had no choice but to wake and bring her along.

Edith Jones was in no mood for Vera Lynn. She read forward and turned the radio control knob until it clicked 'This is the fourth time in less than two weeks your mo has asked for help. I'm getting fed up Brian why can't Quince next door deal with it?'

Jones reached forward and turned the radio back on you mind I was listening to that.' He stared at the road at 'Sweetheart, you know how mum is. She won't knock d door this time of night.'

'So instead she decides to pull us out of bloody bed.' looked down gently massaging her stomach. 'She does I'm due to give birth in just over two weeks doesn't she

'Don't be like this Edith. You know how dad is wi injury.'

'Too bloody right I do. I seem to remember Doctor J telling him to use the spare room downstairs instead of a bustling city. 'Within two years you could be earning double what you're being paid now. And you know there's a job for life at the steelworks. Those types of places will never shut down. You said last week Mr Adams is retiring next year. So there's no point in keeping you on.'

Jones ignored his wife and kept turning the dial on the radio but the static grew louder. 'Bloody radio I was enjoying that music.'

All of a sudden the car headlights blinked out. The road ahead became pitch black.

Jones pushed the brake pedal and the car came to a gentle halt. The engine spluttered and then died. 'I don't bloody believe this!' He shouted clenching his fist and hitting the steering wheel.

'I thought Frank fixed this car last week.' Edith complained.

'He did.' Jones seethed. 'I gave him two bloody shillings.' He turned the key in the ignition but nothing happened. 'You wait till I see him tomorrow.' He tried the ignition again but still the car wouldn't start.

'Well we can't sit here all night long.' Edith pointed out.

Jones produced a box of matches and got out of the car.

Edith looked out of the window into the star filled sky.

A shooting star streaked across the heavens.

'It's a shame there's no moon or I'd consider walking, it's quite warm.'

'I don't think so, not in your condition.' Jones remarked striking a match across the box.

Although there was no breeze the flame from the match emitted almost no light.

Jones stepped back. 'I can't find the problem. It's like the car has died.' He glanced up the road considering Edith's suggestion.

A bright light appeared around the bend at the top of the hill.

'It's ok love there's another car coming. They'll be able to take you to mum and dad's house.' Jones stepped out into the middle of the road waving his arms in the air.

The light kept coming and showed no sign of stopping. Jones also noted it was moving fast, perhaps a little too fast for a car.

The light showed no sign it had seen Jones who moved to the side of the road. The light then started to grow in size becoming more intense.

'Brian, get in the car.' Edith called out glaring at the oncoming light.

Jones put his hand over his eyes to block out some of the glare of the approaching light. 'Just a second sweetheart.'

'Brian come on!' Edith called out again with more urgency. A familiar fear she was unable to explain began to grow from within.

The light was now a few hundred yards away. It lifted off the road before starting to slow.

'Brian please get back in the car, I'm scared.' Edith's fear peaked as she stared at the approaching object.

The object moved slowly over the car bathing a wide area in a soft blue light.

Jones stood rooted to the spot looking upwards at the intense light.

A low-pitched humming noise filled the air.

Jones could sense the hairs on his arms tingling from a static discharge.

'Brian please.' Edith started to cry. 'Get in the car.'

There was a sudden intense flash of brilliant white light and then instantaneously the road plunged into blackness again.

Jones rubbed his eyes.

The car engine suddenly jumped back to life. The headlights came back on. The static on the radio cleared and Vera Lynn played.

Jones took several seconds to process what he had just

witnessed before running back to the car and getting in. 'Did you see that love. It was bloody amazing.'

The passenger seat was now empty.

Jones climbed back out of the car. 'Edith where are you?'

Vera Lynn continued to play.

'Edith sweetheart stop mucking around.' He walked to the front of the car and peered down the road. 'Edith, where are you? Look I'm sorry ok.' Jones looked up into the clear sky.

A tiny point of light moved across the star filled heavens then in an instant it accelerated away.

Jones screamed at the top of his voice. 'Edith!'

Chapter 1

Downing Street – London – 11:28am
Monday 28th July 1952

Professor Ralph Frederick adjusted his bow tie as he waited patiently outside the Prime Minister's office. He waved his hand through his short brown hair. His wife Elizabeth had gone out of her way to make sure he looked his best that morning.

'It's not every day you get to meet with the Prime Minister Ralph. You have to put on a show here.' She tugged on his tie.

'Careful Liz darling, I need to be able to breathe when I meet with him.'

'I wonder what he wants to speak to you about? Perhaps you're in line for the top job at the Royal Society.' Elizabeth said excitedly.

'Norman already has that job remember love. Besides you act as if this were the first time I have met with Mr Churchill. I was on his scientific advisory council during the war.' He winked at her playfully.

'Yes I remember, the result being our marriage.' Elizabeth finished his bow and kissed her husband on the tip of his nose. 'Say hello for me and Susan please.'

Fresh out of Cambridge, Frederick was handpicked to work at Bletchley Park. He had demonstrated a remarkable gift understanding complex mathematics and coded sequences. As the German army began its relentless march across Europe Frederick was assigned to a government scientific advisory team.

In July 1940 while on official business to the War Office Frederick encountered Elizabeth Greenwood. Elizabeth was one of the Prime Minister's cabinet secretarial staff. After several weeks Frederick plucked up the courage to ask her out to an evening at the cinema. Unfortunately, due to the Third Reich's merciless bombing, Ralph and Elizabeth spent most of the night in an air raid shelter.

Tragically Frederick's parents were unable to make it to one of the many shelters set up around London and were killed that night.

They were married in October 1941 but were unable to enjoy a honeymoon due to wartime restrictions. After the war, Frederick surprised his wife with a trip to Paris. Our long-awaited honeymoon as he called it.

The Fredericks lived 38 Miles outside Cambridge on the Norfolk Cambridgeshire border in a village called Emneth. In September 1947 Elizabeth gave birth to a baby girl they named Susan.

In 1949 Frederick returned to Cambridge to work on a gravitational wave theory. He wrote a lengthy paper that went on to earn him a Nobel Prise in physics in 1951.

Frederick was finishing up for the weekend at Cambridge, when an unexpected telegram from London landed on his desk.

Office of the Prime Minister.
Winston Churchill.
Requesting an audience with Ralph Frederick. Professor of Astrophysics Cambridge University. Regarding matter of a scientific nature.
Monday 28th July 11:30am

Frederick paused before knocking on the door of the Prime Minister's office. There was a short pause before a voice beckoned him in.

Winston Churchill was staring at a newspaper as Frederick approached the large reading desk and stood patiently.

The Prime Minister looked up. 'Sit down please Professor.'

Frederick sat in a chair opposite.

Churchill handed Frederick the newspaper he was reading pointing out an article. 'What do you make of that?'

Frederick reached into his inside pocket pulling out a pair of turtle shell reading glasses. He peered at the newspaper article.

'Flying saucer kidnapped my wife.'

Frederick smirked as he read the article. 'It looks like another silly story about flying saucers sir.'

'Yes, that's what I thought.' The Prime Minister answered abruptly. He put a large cigar to his lips and lit it. He got to his feet and stepped out from behind his desk. 'Unfortunately these stories about flying saucers and men from Mars seem to be all the range these days.'

'Surely Prime Minister you don't think there's any truth to these stories. It sounds as if the press have nothing better to do. It's all a load of codswallop if you ask me.'

'I don't know what to think.' Churchill said taking a drag from his cigar. 'We have been inundated by these reports in the newspapers. Our military pilots are reporting strange objects in our airspace.'

'I'm sure many of these so called flying saucer sightings have a rational explanation.' Frederick said with confidence.

Churchill pointed at a piece of paper on his desk. 'I'm sending a memo to Lord Cherwell at the Air Ministry to look into this nonsense. Henry Tizard has had a team working on this flying saucer problem since the summer of 1950.'

Frederick looked across the desk at the memo.

```
What does all this stuff about flying
saucers amount to? What can it mean?
What is the truth? Let me have a report
at your convenience.
                                      W.C
                          28th July 1952
```

'Well if anyone can get results on this it's Henry.'

The Prime Minister shook his head. 'I'm only doing it to quash any public interest on this matter. The sooner people have an answer the better. Stop any more ridiculous stories being fed to the public. I don't want them thinking we are not in control of our airspace. Besides, I'm not happy with the progress Tizard and his team have made. They've had two years and have yet to produce anything solid. They've had some limited communication with the Americans on this matter but the Yanks are keeping tight lipped.'

'Do you think the Americans could be withholding information?'

Churchill nodded. 'I wouldn't be surprised.'

'If I may Prime Minister. I'm a bit puzzled as to why I have been summoned here today if you already have Henry working on the issue.'

Churchill walked back over to his desk and sat down. 'I want you to conduct a separate investigation away from the prying eyes of the press. Henry's group has attracted unwanted attention. I believe there could be a leak.'

'Then you do think there's more to this.'

'The war has been over seven years. Yet as a result of Hitler and his Nazi rabble there have been major advances in technology. Talk of rocket ships into space and cities on the moon are becoming more common. Added to that we are in the midst of this cold war and we have no idea what the Russians are up to. Both America and Russia are building these atomic bombs at an alarming rate. Tensions in Korea are becoming more volatile every day and we are caught smack bang in the middle of it all.' The Prime Minister shook his head. 'I don't like it one bit.'

'Do you think the Russians or the Americans could be behind some of these flying saucer sightings?' Frederick suggested.

'That's what I want you to find out Ralph. I want to know if it's either the Soviets or the Yanks.'

'I will give it my full attention Prime Minister. However, if I may be so bold as to ask. It's one thing not to trust the Russians. But America, aren't we their closest ally?'

'You know what the Americans are like.' Churchill said with a mocking tone. 'It's like you just said, they may be holding out on us. Besides there have been rumours coming out of America since the late forties. They might even have captured one of these so-called flying saucers. I have spoken to President Truman on this matter but he hasn't been very forthcoming.' Churchill puffed on his cigar. 'We need to get started immediately so I am giving you a free rein on this Ralph. I want regular reports on your progress. I want you to use all methods to find out more about these dammed flying saucers. The sooner we get this matter wrapped up the better.'

'Of course Prime Minister.'

'You're a Cambridge man are you not?'

'Yes sir. I studied there and now teach at Trinity College.'

'Former member of the Cambridge Apostles and now an Angel.'

'Uh, well.' Frederick stumbled over his words.

Churchill waved his hand grinning. 'It's alright Professor your secret is safe with me. My former private secretary Edward Marsh was a member. He did a little digging around for me the other day. I thought it might be useful if former Apostles made up this group given your code of secrecy.'

'That is a very good idea sir.'

'Excellent, as from now you are to head up the science division of The Angel Committee. I have contacted Malcolm Chambers and said you would meet with him an hour from now. I am confident you will be able to find suitable people for your team.'

'I will keep you informed at every turning point Prime Minister.'

'So, how's Elizabeth and Susan?' Churchill asked changing

the subject.

'They are very well. Elizabeth sends her regards.'

'Fine woman you married there Ralph. Proud to have her as a member of staff during the war.'

'Thank you Prime Minister. If there is nothing else to discuss I will get on with the matter in hand.'

Churchill gave a dismissive nod. 'Carry on Professor.'

Chapter 2

Ministry of Defence – Whitehall – 12:32pm

Sir Malcolm Chambers stepped out from behind his desk to greet Frederick. 'Ralph how are you. It's been too long old boy. How's the family?' The World War One veteran smiled broadly as Frederick shook his hand.

'I'm very well thank you Malcolm. Elizabeth and Susan are fine. How's young William, I'm afraid I haven't had time to pop in on him yet at Cambridge.'

'He's settling in fine. He did mention he has yet to see you, but he's been a little busy himself. He's already been accepted by the Apostles.'

'Really, didn't take him long to jump into your shoes did it.' Both men laughed.

'How have you been since last year?' Frederick's tone indicated concern for his friend who he had first met at Bletchley Park. 'Elizabeth was extremely worried when Agnes telephoned and told her about your heart attack.'

'I'm fine, blasted doctor has got me taking all kinds of pills. Can't enjoy as much of the good stuff as I used to.'

'Well I'm sure it's for the best.' Frederick remarked.

'I take it the Prime Minister briefed you on what he wants.'

'He did, but I'm still a little puzzled as to why he wants a separate team working on this. Henry Tizard has already been assigned with the task.'

'Henry doesn't know our team exists and we've been given strict orders not to reveal ourselves. Which means we'll have to do a lot of sneaking around. We also suspect Henry's ship has a leak.'

'Leak?'

'A steady stream of newspaper articles is being fed to the press. Most notably the Sunday Dispatch and The London

Evening Examiner.'

'You think someone from Henry's team has been going to the newspapers?'

'It's a possibility, there are a lot of high-ranking people gossiping about flying saucers Including Hugh Dowding and Lord Mountbatten. There are rumours the Duke of Edinburgh has an interest in Flying Saucers. The Prime Minister feels the Americans haven't been very cooperative sharing information with us. They captured quite a few installations throughout Europe in the closing stages of the war. But aren't very generous when it comes to sharing the spoils of war. Intelligence reports suggest they are busy improving on the V2 rockets they snatched from Germany. The Russians are also well into their atomic weapons development. Churchill feels we are dragging our heels a bit.'

'So what's all this got to do with Flying saucers?'

Chambers leant back in his chair. 'We've been receiving reports of flying saucers for years. Since we first developed radar technology these things have been showing up constantly and quite frankly we are puzzled. The Americans have also had their own little research projects running. As a matter of fact flying saucers have been in the Washington Post this week. Something about a mass sighting over the nation's capital over the last few days. I'm guessing this what has Churchill The Air Ministry is abuzz with rumours. The Prime Minister is pinning his hopes too much on American or Russian experimental aircraft. Given the evidence we have these things have been around for a lot longer.'

'How much longer exactly?' Frederick asked.

'There have been reports of strange objects in our skies stretching back to the First World War and before that. But these accounts were either dismissed or destroyed. No one really took them seriously. As radar continues to advance we are finally realizing there is substance to this flying saucer phenomenon. If we can get one scrap of evidence to prove these flying saucers actually exist it may give us an edge.'

'Well it will be quite a large undertaking of resources. Any ideas who we should recruit for this research team?'

'I've compiled a list for your approval.' Chambers passed a piece of paper to Frederick. 'Feel free to make any changes.'

Frederick looked through the list. 'I'm familiar with all of these men. But I'd like to add my own choice. Professor Richard Wilks of Greenwich. I've known him for years and he's a former apostle.' Frederick looked back at the list. 'Kim Philby is in Washington, you won't be able to pull him away.'

'Kim Philby is rather a sore subject at the moment in the midst of the recent MacLean and Burgess defection. I will replace him with this Wilks you've recommended. I will preside over the committee deciding which casefiles are worthy of our attention. You have been appointed both lead scientist and front man on this committee. You will investigate the cases we receive.'

'As long as it won't interfere with Cambridge or attract attention from the press. I'm a Nobel Prize winning physicist. Norman Hinshelwood at the Royal Society would take a dim view of me chasing after flying saucers. I was going to turn the Prime Minister down but I didn't want to ruffle the old man's feathers.'

'That's what he was counting on. He holds you in the highest regards. The Prime Minister picked you because of your no-nonsense attitude. Any investigation you do for this committee will be under wraps. You won't be appearing on the front pages of any newspapers. We will hold our first meeting in just under a week at Highclare House.'

'How long will this committee run for?'

'Six months should be enough to get to the bottom of this mystery. With any luck we should be finished by Christmas. The Prime Minister is disappointed with the progress Tizard and his team have made. Despite the timescale they have had to investigate these flying saucer reports.'

'Six months is plenty.' Frederick said. 'Most of these flying saucer sightings are most likely hoaxes or have a more down to earth explanation. But I am interested in looking over some of the radar data you have.'

'I'll have to get in touch with Tizard about that.' Chambers offered.

'Tizard.' Frederick said. 'Didn't you just mention something about sneaking around behind his back.'

'I've been acting as go between for Tizard's group and the Prime Minister. I will make sure your paths won't cross. Most of Henry's research comes through me anyway. There's quite a bit of paperwork to trawl through. In the meantime I have your first assignment. I take it the Prime Minister showed you this article.' Chambers held up the newspaper Churchill was reading.

'The mystery of the missing wife.' Frederick nodded. 'If you ask me she just got fed up and buggered off. You know what young married couples are like these days. Probably easier for this man to come up with a flying saucer fairy story than face the truth.'

'You are probably right Ralph. However, the night this woman disappeared radar stations in the North of England picked up a number of unidentified contacts. According to radar operators we have interviewed they came in from the North Sea.'

'I see.' Frederick said thoughtfully.

'I need you to go and interview this man and log everything he says to you. As you say it's probably a load of old cobblers.'

'I'll certainly look into it. But it looks like I'll be gone for a few days.'

'You think Elizabeth might start asking questions about your absence.'

'She does get curious sometimes and she knows I met with the Prime Minister earlier today. In the war years she became quite fond of the old man.'

'I'm sure you'll think of something to quash any interest Ralph. From how well I know Elizabeth, she's very understanding.'

Frederick smiled and looked out of the window. 'Flying saucers, what is this world coming to?'

'You're not a believer I take it.'

'I like a good story like the next man. But some of these tales of encounters with beings from other worlds are just too farfetched. I wouldn't have got where I am today by believing in such nonsense.' He looked back at the newspaper. 'All this flying saucer invasion paranoia could be nerves left over from the war.'

'Well let's hope you're right. I have to admit I want this investigation over and done with quickly.'

Frederick stood. 'Likewise, I'll see you soon old friend.'

Emneth – Wisbech – Cambridgeshire – 8:48pm

'How did it go with the old man?' Elizabeth asked.

Frederick looked up from his armchair. 'He says hello to you and Susan.'

'And.' Elizabeth pursued.

'And he said you were a fine woman and a valued member of his wartime staff.'

'But what did he want to speak to you about?'

'Nothing much, internal matters that's all. Nothing of interest dear.' He glanced at Elizabeth.' By the way, I've been called away on business for a few days later this week.'

Elizabeth smiled at her husband. 'Well at least you were wearing your best bow tie.'

Chapter 3

Trinity College – Cambridge – 9:20am
Tuesday 29th July 1952

'Knock knock.' A voice called out.

Frederick looked up from his office desk to see Professor Chester Osborne.

Frederick and Osborne had known each other for twenty years. They had studied at Cambridge together, worked at Bletchley Park and were now teaching at Cambridge. Frederick never considered Osborne amongst his closest friends. In the past both men had disagreed on many things and had even stopped talking to each other on a number of occasions. One occasion happened when they studied together at Trinity College. Frederick had become quite popular around the campus. Rumours started to spread fellow undergraduates Guy Burgess and Richard Wilks were going to make him an offer to join the Cambridge Apostles. An elite discussion group founded in 1820 by Bishop of Gibraltar George Tomlinson when he was a student. The group initially consists of twelve members and meet every Saturday evening. Topics discussed included truth, God and ethics as well as other scientific debate.

Frederick had been unwittingly invited to a series of dinners which was part of the initiation process into the Apostles. As for Osborne, although a brilliant mathematician he was never given the opportunity to join. Guy Burgess explained to Frederick Osborne lacked what the Americans called spunk. Frederick's acceptance into the Apostles was a source of jealousy for Osborne and he would constantly hound Frederick to reveal the secrets of the Cambridge Apostles. Frederick never yielded any useful information. Despite Osborne coming from a wealthy family he couldn't even buy his way into the secret discussion group.

Osborne stood in the doorway looking at Frederick who was sifting through some notes for a lecture.

'Is there something I can help you with Chester?'

Osborne stepped into Frederick's small office. 'I was just passing and wanted to know how things went with the Prime Minister yesterday.'

Frederick looked up at Osborne. 'How things went with the Prime Minister.' He shook his head and shrugged. 'Is that supposed to mean something?'

Osborne smiled back. 'Don't worry Ralph I know all about it. I spoke to Norman Hinshelwood last night. The Prime Minister mentioned he was forming a new research group looking into the current spate of flying saucer sightings.'

'Really.' Frederick remarked picking up his satchel and putting it on the table in front of him.

'I was wondering if you knew Henry Tizard is running a team investigating these flying saucer sightings. It's called the Flying Saucer Working Party.'

Frederick glanced at Osborne. 'This is all fascinating Chester but why would I be interested in such nonsense?'

'I was wondering if that's what the old man wanted to see you about yesterday. After all you are one of his chief scientific advisors.'

Frederick looked back at his notes. 'I am indeed Chester, thank you for reminding me. I'm afraid you'll have to go on wondering. You know as well as I do Prime Minister's briefings are not to be discussed outside Downing Street.'

'Yes of course Ralph. But if you have been assigned to this task and you're looking into assembling a team on this matter then I would be more than happy to assist you in finding suitable members.'

Frederick gathered his notes and put them into a leather satchel. 'I will see you for lunch Chester.'

Chapter 4

RAF Yeadon – South Yorkshire – 10:09am
Friday 31st July 1952

Frederick walked carefully down the steps from the AS.57 Ambassador aircraft where a man was there to greet him.

'Professor Frederick, I'm flight lieutenant Walter Fletcher. The Air Ministry has provided a car for you. I've been instructed to accompany you to the village of Ripley.' Walter Fletcher towered over Frederick. His Royal air force uniform was immaculate and he had a grip of iron as he shook the Professor's hand.

'Thank you flight lieutenant, If we leave now we can get this over with quickly.'

Fletcher loaded Frederick's bags into a jet black 1940s Jowett Javelin saloon car.

Grey clouds lined the horizon as the car made its way out of the RAF base.

'Have you been up this way before Professor?'

'I've been to Harrogate on a number of occasions but not the surrounding area.'

'The hotel you are staying at is nice. They serve a really good pint of beer.'

'I'm not much of a drinker I'm afraid and this is an official visit.'

'Suit yourself. I'll be staying there as well so if you change your mind.'

'Thanks for the offer but I'm fine.'

'So, you are up here investigating flying saucers.' Fletcher remarked with a grin.

'I take it you've been briefed.'

'Yes sir and I understand the classified nature regarding the radar data. Do you really think this bloke's wife was kidnapped by a flying saucer?'

'That's what I'm here to find out. Although I think it's a cock and bull story.' Frederick glanced at the flight officer. 'What's your opinion on flying saucers?'

Fletcher mused over Frederick's question. 'I like to think I've been around. I flew Lancaster bombers over Germany during the war and saw a lot of strange stuff up there. But I dismissed it as pressure under fire.'

'Did you file a report of any kind?'

'It didn't enter into our heads. It was enough to worry about the Luftwaffe trying to shoot us out of the sky without having to worry about invaders from Mars.' Fletcher hesitated before continuing. 'I remember one night time bombing mission over Germany, we were surrounded by these lights. They changed colours, red, blue, yellow, green. Quite spectacular to look at. We nicknamed them foo fighters.'

'What do you think they were?' Frederick asked.

'Don't know, perhaps some kind of natural phenomena which occurs at high altitude. There's plenty science still doesn't know. They could have been some kind of Nazi secret weapon.'

'Before I return to London do you think you could write an account of what you saw during your missions.'

'As long as it won't get me kicked out of the RAF. I heard a story once about a battle of Britain pilot being locked up because he saw something strange while out on a run.'

'You can remain anonymous. I'm just interested in collecting witness accounts for now. I'm not a believer in flying saucers. I'm just jumping through hoops for the Air Ministry.'

'I fully understand sir.'

The car sped out of the base into open countryside. The grey clouds advanced resulting in rain.

The village of Ripley boasted an impressive castle owned by a family who had lived on the site for about 900 years. The

Boars Head Hotel had a spacious bar and restaurant. Frederick and Fletcher checked in to their separate rooms and then met outside the hotel's main entrance.

The rain had stopped and was now giving way to warm sunshine which quickly evaporated the surface water.

The Jones' lived in the street behind the hotel in a small terraced house. It took less than five minutes to walk the distance.

Fletcher read from the report as the men walked along the street. 'Mr Jones reported his wife missing on June 21st. He claims she disappeared the night before on the 20th. After his car started he headed for the local bobby's house but was unable to wake him. The following morning local police called the main station in Harrogate. They sent out ten police officers to assist in the search. The owner of the castle Sir William Ingles rounded up all his staff and village residents to help look for Mrs Jones. Brian Jones had been questioned by the police but they let him go. They had no reason to suspect foul play.'

When they reached the front door Frederick adjusted his tie and then turned to Fletcher. 'Remember let me do all the talking. You're here as an objective witness.'

Fletcher nodded stiffly. 'Understood sir.'

Frederick knocked on the door and stood patiently.

Inside movement could be heard. After several seconds the door creaked open. A man stood in the doorway in his pyjamas and dressing gown. The man hadn't shaven for several days. A thick layer of stubble wrapped itself around his chin. Scruffy black hair sprayed outwards.

Frederick removed his trilby and smiled. 'Mr Brian Jones.'

The man stared back with a worn expression, blinking at the daylight. The curtains to the house had been drawn throughout the day. 'Yes.'

'I'm sorry to disturb you. My name is Ralph Frederick and this is my colleague flight lieutenant Fletcher. We are here on behalf of the Air Ministry regarding your experience last month.'

'The Air Ministry.' Jones stared blankly at Frederick. 'I'm not sure I understand. You interviewed me three weeks ago regarding my story. Why are you here again?'

Frederick glanced at Fletcher. he'd been caught off guard with Jones' claim that the Air Ministry had already been to interview him. Frederick quickly gathered his thoughts. 'We are here to follow up on our last interview with you Mr Jones. Just in case you have recalled any detail you might have missed out last time.'

Jones nodded and beckoned them in.

The three men walked through a narrow hallway into a small living room. Jones clearly relied on his wife to do the housework. Dirty dishes were stacked up on a dining table. Newspapers had been piled up on the sofa. Piles of clothes had been dumped on the floor and on the living room chairs.

'Sorry about the mess. Since Edith went missing I've let myself go a bit. Would you like a cup of tea?'

'That's alright Mr Jones we won't take up too much of your time so tea won't be necessary. If you could just recall what happened that night.'

Jones relayed his story to Frederick while Fletcher sat on the arm of a chair jotting down notes. Frederick listened as Jones talked about his experience.

Jones sounded sincere but it wasn't enough to convince Frederick there was any truth to his story. When Jones had finished the room fell silent for several seconds.

'I think about it time and time again. The bright flash of light then the darkness. I still can't believe it happened.' Tears welled up in Jones' eyes. 'Where's my wife? Where's Edith and our baby?' He started to sob. 'Please bring her back. Bring them both back, please god!'

Fletcher packed his notepad away and looked at Frederick who signalled for him to leave the room.

Frederick knelt down to console the sobbing man. 'Mr Jones on behalf of the Air Ministry I'd like to say how sorry I am about your wife. We will investigate this matter thoroughly.'

'But you won't be able to bring her back will you.'

'I don't know but I promise you we will do everything in our power to find out what happened to her. Mr Jones can you tell me why you decided to contact a newspaper about your story?'

'It wasn't me who contacted that newspaper it was my employer Sir Ingles.' He wiped his nose on his sleeve.

Frederick recalled Jones' earlier claims. 'You say you had already been visited by men from the Air Ministry. Can you describe the men who interviewed you?'

Jones composed himself. 'There were three of them.'

'Go on.' Frederick encouraged.

'There was something odd. They didn't sound English. They sounded as if they were from the continent. American journalists also visited me Last week. They said they were from the New York Times.'

'Really.' Frederick replied sounding puzzled. 'Did they say how they heard about your story.'

'They claimed the Echo got in touch. The News of The World has also been in contact. A journalist from the London Evening Examiner has also visited me.' Jones searched his memory. 'His name was George Rayman.'

'Besides the newspapers and the Air Ministry, has anyone else called on you?'

'Sir William Ingles was here yesterday with another man who was interested in my story. But that's about all, except for family and friends, and now you.'

Frederick smiled and then reached for his trilby. 'Well I think that is all for now Mr Jones. You have been an enormous help to us.'

Jones escorted Frederick out of the untidy living room.

Fletcher waited outside the front door.

A few neighbours had appeared and looked on chattering to each other as the two strangers said their goodbyes.

'I think I will join you for that drink after all flight lieutenant, say seven this evening.' Frederick offered.

'That would be fine. I'm going to head back to RAF Yeadon and write that report you requested. I will be back later this afternoon if that is alright with you Professor.'

'Yes, I have I have matters to take care of this afternoon.'

Both men parted company. Fletcher jumped into the car while Frederick headed into the hotel to look for a telephone.

'European you say?' Malcolm Chambers expressed his puzzlement. 'I can assure you Ralph you are the first people the Air Ministry has sent to interview this man.'

'Obviously someone picked up Jones' story by way of the newspapers. It's puzzling as to why they would pose as ministry officials.' Frederick explained. 'And then there's the American newspaper men.'

'It does add depth to this investigation. I will speak with Morris Stanford later on today and ask him to try and throw some light on the subject. In the meantime Ralph I want you to pop in on Sir William Ingles and find out about the man he was with yesterday talking to Jones. What's your initial assessment of the situation?'

'He sounds sincere but I'm nowhere near being convinced his wife was whisked away by Martians. I think she just buggered off. Judging by the state of their house I don't blame her.'

'Ok the committee's first meeting is on Monday so we'll discuss this matter further. Hopefully Morris might have something on the Yanks and our so-called European friends. Good luck with Sir Ingles.'

Chapter 5

Ripley Castle – 2:33pm

Frederick knocked on a large wooden oak door. An unusual marking caught his eye. A three-armed spiral pattern made up of individual circles was etched onto the door several inches above the knocker. After a short while the door was answered by a tall thin man who led Frederick through to a large sitting room.

A medium height stout man stood to greet Frederick shaking his hand vigorously. 'Professor Frederick, Sir William Ingles at your service.' Ingles seemed over friendly and reminded Frederick of a character straight out of a historical novel he was currently reading.

Portraits of long dead ancestors hung on the walls of the sitting room. One picture above the fireplace dominated the room. A man wearing a white vest with a red cross stared out from a canvas.

'So what is it that brings Cambridge's finest to my humble dwelling?'

'I didn't say I was from Cambridge.' Frederick said with a puzzled expression.

Ingles chuckled. 'It's a relatively small world Professor. I am a huge supporter of the scientific community. When a Nobel Prize winning scientists visits our humble village news travels fast.'

Frederick nodded. 'I'm here looking into the alleged flying saucer kidnapping of Mrs Edith Jones.'

'Really.' Ingles mused. 'I didn't think the scientific world took the matter of flying saucers seriously.'

'We have an open mind, Sir Ingles. Besides this is more of an Air Ministry enquiry. I understand Mr Jones works for you.'

Ingles nodded. 'He's my game keeper's clerk, a most

efficient young man. We are all missing him terribly at the moment.'

Frederick sipped from a teacup a butler had brought in moments earlier. 'Mr Jones said you visited him yesterday with another gentleman regarding his flying saucer incident.'

Ingles looked down his spectacles at Frederick. 'Yes, I wanted to see how he was coping. A friend of mine came up from London earlier this week and I mentioned the story to him.'

'Would you care to divulge who this friend of yours is?'

Ingles took a moment before revealing his friend's identity. 'Peter Horsley.'

'As in Peter Horsley, equerry to the Duke of Edinburgh.'

'The very same. I've known Peter for many years. He comes up here twice a year to enjoy the trout fishing in the lake.'

'And you took it upon yourself to introduce him to Mr Jones.' Frederick remarked.

'Peter has a passing interest in flying saucers. He is also Air Ministry. I'm surprised your paths haven't crossed since you are both investigating the same thing.'

'I have met Mr Horsley on a number of social occasions but he never expressed his interest in flying saucers. And the ministry doesn't have any official body investigating flying saucers.'

'Yet here you are Professor.' Ingles smiled. 'Peter prefers to keep his interest to himself being a member of the royal household. You know how the press are these days. The Royal family doesn't want the newspapers accusing them of being a bunch of crackpots.'

'Are you saying members of the Royal Family have an interest in flying saucers?'

Ingles smiled at Frederick. 'What I'm saying Professor, is these kinds of matters are best kept behind closed doors. Now if there's nothing else I can do for you I have an estate to run.'

Frederick finished his tea and set the cup down. 'No, you've been most generous in granting me an audience today Sir William.' He stood and offered his hand. 'It's been a pleasure meeting you.'

'Not at all Professor I've enjoyed your little visit. Let me show you out.'

As both men appeared out onto the courtyard Frederick pointed at the symbol on the door he had spotted on arrival. 'That's an interesting marking.'

'It's been there centuries.' Ingles revealed.

'Do you know what it means?'

Ingles thought for a moment. 'I believe it was used to ward off evil spirits. It appears my ancestors were a little superstitious.'

'Thank you again for your time Sir Ingles.' Frederick smiled and walked away.

Ingles returned to the sitting room and walked over towards a telephone picking up the receiver. 'Sarah could you connect me to Peter Horsley at Buckingham Palace please.' Several seconds passed. 'Peter old boy how are you it's William. I have some information that might interest you.'

Chapter 6

Downham Market Railway Station – Norfolk – 9:17am Monday 4th August 1952

After his meeting with Sir William Ingles Frederick returned to the hotel and waited for flight lieutenant Fletcher. The RAF officer had written a full report about his experiences with unidentified flying objects during wartime bombing missions. Over the evening meal Fletcher went into detail about stories he had heard from other royal air force pilots.

Frederick returned home the next day and enjoyed the rest of the weekend with Elizabeth and Susan. He also found time to type out a short summary of the investigation for Lord Chambers.

Engrossed in The Times newspaper Frederick failed to notice the two men approaching his table.

Both men seated themselves opposite. They were dressed in identical grey suits with trilby hats.

'Are you Doctor Ralph Frederick?' One of them asked.

Frederick peered over the top of his newspaper. 'It's Professor actually.'

'I am sorry Professor.' The man replied apologetically. 'My name is Doctor Vincent Rothschild. I am with the East German Academy of Sciences. This is my associate Doctor Androv Alexis also with the academy.'

Frederick folded his paper and stared at both men. 'Really, and how is it you know me?'

Rothschild grinned. 'You are a Nobel Prize winning physicist. Well known at the academy and well respected.'

'I'm honoured, I didn't realise you chaps took the work of western scientists seriously.'

Rothschild stared back at Frederick. 'I believe all scientists are the same the world over. Our drive for discovery is a common purpose is it not Professor.'

Frederick found himself being impressed by Rothschild's guile. 'What is it that brings you to this part of the world gentlemen?'

'We wish to speak to you about a matter of up most importance Professor.' Rothschild answered.

Frederick looked at his watch. 'I'm afraid I don't have much time. I'm due to board a train to London shortly.'

'Your trip is why we wish to speak to you.' Dr Alexis spoke for the first time.

Frederick smiled politely. 'I'm afraid my trip to London is of no scientific value gentlemen. Just another tedious day at the office.'

'We beg to differ Professor.' Rothschild said. 'Myself and Doctor Alexis are very interested in the aspect of science you are going to discuss with your distinguished colleagues later on today.'

Frederick started to feel a little uneasy in the presence of the two men. 'What aspect of science would that be exactly?'

Rothschild looked around the café. A few people were scattered about. A man in a bowler hat and pinstriped suit reading a copy of the financial times. A couple chatting too busy to notice the three men sat in the corner. Two women stood behind the counter gossiping, glancing disapprovingly at the couple.

Rothschild leaned across the table. 'It pertains to your discussions about flying saucers.' He said quietly.

Frederick kept smiling. 'Flying saucers, I'm afraid gentlemen I don't quite follow.'

Rothschild's attitude changed. 'Do not perceive us as being naive Professor. We know about the group your Prime Minister Winston Churchill has established.'

'Then I'm afraid Doctor Rothschild you have been misinformed. I've no interest in such nonsense. As a Nobel prize winning physicist I have to keep my feet firmly on the ground.'

The whistle of an approaching train sounded.

Frederick checked his pocket watch. 'Now if you will excuse me gentlemen, I have a train to catch.'

All three men got to their feet. The man in the bowler hat also stood tucking his newspaper under his arm before picking up his briefcase and heading towards the door. The man and woman stayed seated oblivious of the hustle and bustle of the train station.

Frederick headed out of the door after the pinstripe.

The train slowly pulled into the station. Steam filled the platform obscuring the view for boarding passengers.

Frederick grabbed the first carriage door handle he could find.

Rothschild grabbed his arm firmly.

'Let go of me!' Frederick shouted pulling his arm away from Rothschild's grip.

A train guard further on down the platform heard Frederick's shout and looked in their direction.

Rothschild expressed sincerity. 'I am sorry Professor, but you seem unwilling to listen to what I have to say. You are interested in astronomy are you not?'

Frederick wondered how this man knew so much about him.

Rothschild noted the expression on Frederick's face. 'I have many friends at the Royal Society Professor who speak very highly of you. When you get the chance to peer through a telescope again consider this. The universe is a mathematical constant. If a star is born then the possibility of the process repeating itself is very high. So why do scientists ignore the possibility the same could be true with the creation of planets like ours? Can you be one hundred percent certain we are alone in this vast universe? That our sun is the only star with a planetary system?' Rothschild reached forward and opened the carriage door. 'Goodbye Professor our paths will cross again.' He turned and headed back down the platform.

Frederick stood rooted to the spot watching the two men melt into the wave of passengers leaving the train.

'Excuse me sir, but the train is about to leave, you must board.' The station guard coaxed.

Frederick snapped out of his trance. 'Yes of course.' He apologised before stepping onto the railway carriage.

The train whistle pierced the air as the locomotive slowly pulled out of the station.

Rothschild watched as the train gathered speed disappearing around a bend.

'Do you think he'll accept your offer when you present it to him?' Alexis asked.

'He will accept. Professor Frederick's place in history has been assured.'

'Are you talking about the prophecy?'

Rothschild nodded. 'Professor Frederick is about to embark on a journey that will change his life forever.'

Chapter 7

Whitehall – London – 12:42pm

Morris Stanford and Malcolm Chambers listened as Frederick told them of his encounter at the train station earlier that morning. He also mentioned the conversation with Professor Osborne a few days earlier. 'Someone already knows of our existence.'

Stanford considered Frederick's claim. 'It's possible.'

'How?'

'You mentioned your colleague Professor Osborne questioning you about flying saucers. Churchill may have mentioned it to another member of the Royal Society.'

'Yes Norman Hinshelwood, but he pales in comparison with this Doctor Vincent Rothschild and Androv Alexis I encountered this morning. I don't understand how these men could know we have a meeting today.'

'It is worrying.' Chambers said. 'Have we vetted committee members thoroughly?'

'Yes, all committee members are trusted at the highest levels.'

'Could there be a mole at the Royal Society?' Chambers suggested.

Frederick thought for a moment. 'Scientists come and go all the time. Many do cross the East German border. People discuss all matters of science at the Society. It's possible someone might have overheard Norman Hinshelwood and Osborne discussing the flying saucer phenomenon. Carried on that conversation with someone else and so forth.'

'Chinese whispers.' Chambers stated.

'The possibility foreign agents may have infiltrated the Royal Society is disturbing. Most of our best scientists are members including nuclear scientists. We have our first atomic tests soon in Western Australia. We cannot allow the Soviets to get their hands on any research material. I will have MI6 look over the Royal Society. If foreign agents have crawled into any cracks we will deal with it.' Stanford offered.

'What about the so-called American journalists who interviewed Jones?' Frederick asked.

'Probably CIA but I can't be sure.' Stanford replied. 'With all these flying saucer reports they probably want to know if the Soviets are testing anything over Western Europe.'

Frederick shook his head. 'We may as well publish details of our meetings in The Times since every intelligence agency know we exist. Not to mention what will happen if this gets back to the Royal Society. Norman Hinshelwood will want my head on a silver platter if he finds out I've been running around looking into flying saucers. The sooner this investigation is over the better.'

'Nothing is airtight.' Stanford remarked. 'There will always be leaks; the only thing we can do is control the amount of information leaking out.'

'I don't know about you gentlemen but I suggest we have a hearty lunch before our first meeting this afternoon.' Chambers said changing the mood.

Chapter 8

Highclare House – Surrey – 4:34pm

Frederick looked at the nine other men sat around the large oak table. The room was filled with a pungent smell of cigar, pipe and cigarette smoke which lingered in the air.

'I would like to thank you all for attending this meeting today. Although I can understand your apprehension given the memo you have in front of you.'

All of the men looked down at the information Frederick had prepared.

Unidentified Flying Objects

For a number of years reports have been circulating concerning Unidentified Flying Objects or as they are more commonly known by the press, flying saucers. Both the public in the United Kingdom and throughout the British Empire and highly trained military personnel have reported seeing strange objects in our skies.

Unidentified flying objects were reported after the war in the summer of 1946. There were a large number of sightings over several European countries including Sweden, Finland, Norway, East Germany and France. These UFOs came in all shapes and sizes but the cigar shaped UFO and the disc shaped UFO were the most common description given.

The USA has also had its share of UFO sightings in recent years. In June of 1947 a civilian pilot reported seeing nine UFOs flying at incredible speeds in Washington State over Mount Rainer. As recently as June this year UFO reports have continued to flood in to various defence agencies all over the globe.

To ascertain whether or not these flying saucers or UFOs represent a threat to the security of the United Kingdom a committee of highly trained scientific and military personnel has been established. Its function, to investigate flying saucer observations and reach a logical conclusion. Listed below are possible explanations for such Unidentified flying objects.

Known astronomical or meteorological phenomena.
Mistaken identification of conventional aircraft, balloons, birds, etc.
Optical illusions and psychological delusions.
Deliberate hoaxes.

The following individuals have been picked to chair this committee.

Professor Ralph Frederick – Cambridge University.
Sir Malcolm Chambers – The War office.
Sir Morris Stanford – Head of British Intelligence.
Air Marshall Sir Ian Morgan – Director of Intelligence Air Ministry.
First Sea Lord Admiral Anthony Berkshire – The Royal Navy.
Sir Harold Bates – Former scientific advisor to Lord Chamberlin.
Dr Alan Good – Cambridge University.
Professor Richard Wilks – Astronomer Royal, the Royal Observatory Greenwich.
Dr Arthur Lloyd – Oxford University, Physician to His Royal Highness George VI.
Professor Norman Canning – Bletchley Park.

Frederick drew a breath. 'I leave it to you to come to your own conclusions on what these UFOs could be.'

'It's absolute nonsense!' Admiral Berkshire mocked. 'All this talk about flying saucers and men from Mars. Sounds like something that H.G Wells fellow wrote about.'

'Flying saucers are a popular subject with the press.' Air Marshal Ian Morgan replied. 'Our RAF boys were reporting objects in the skies over Germany during the war.'

'Yes foo fighters, but that doesn't mean they're from Mars. We still don't know the full story regarding German research projects.' Berkshire added.

'You may be right Anthony.' Frederick replied. 'But we still have all these eye witness accounts that cannot be easily explained away.' He turned to Stanford. 'The Prime Minister thinks it could be the Russians or Americans testing some kind of new aircraft.'

'It's possible, we have operatives in Moscow monitoring the Soviet nuclear weapons program. We have managed to recruit a few people from inside the Kremlin but the intelligence we are getting off them is sketchy at best. Talk of research labs in Siberia. Massive factories manned by slave labour, POW's and political enemies of Stalin. We have yet to hear anything about experimental aircraft. The Soviets have a ring of steel around any information regarding research and development of any kind. They're still gloating over MacLean and Burgess at the moment. We will keep digging, something is bound to come up.'

'What about the Americans?' Frederick asked.

'Our lads in Washington have drawn a blank over rumours the Yanks have one of these flying saucers. If they do have one then they're not sharing. The Americans seem to be preoccupied with hunting down foreign agents on their soil. However, we have been able to gather intelligence on a research project being set up at the moment.' He reached into his inside pocket and pulled out a folded piece of paper that he slid across the table towards Frederick. 'Something known as Project Blue Book. Apparently, it's an air force operation headed by a man called Allen Hynek. The Yanks have had two earlier projects, Project Sign and Project Grudge. Blue Book is their third investigation into the flying saucer phenomena. We also have reports the Americans have a storage and research facility out where they're testing their atomic bombs. Somewhere in the middle of the Nevada Desert.'

'Makes sense deter any curious sightseers.'

'What about the Germans?' Dr Alan Good asked. 'I agree with Anthony, they were pretty advanced in their development of aircraft during the war. Could it have been something they built and is now being tested by the Russians or the Americans.'

'It's probably the best explanation.' Sir Malcolm Chambers answered. 'Both the Russians and Americans raided top secret German laboratories during the war and dismantled many aircraft in development before shipping them back to their homelands for study. We had some luck in obtaining a few bits and bobs ourselves. The Americans managed to get hold of most of the scientists who developed the V2 rocket. They're now happily assisting the Yanks in new rocket research and development.'

'Are you saying these flying saucer sightings could be rockets?' Frederick speculated.

'It's possible yes.'

'How far advanced are we with our rocket research?' Ian Morgan asked.

Professor Norman Canning spoke. 'We are coming along with research at Boscombe Down. We have managed to fire off a couple of test rockets. But I'm afraid we're still behind what the Americans are achieving. We are looking at moving our rocket research project to our nuclear research site out in Australia.'

Frederick glanced around the room. 'Well gentlemen, it seems we have our work cut out for us. Has anyone else any theories on what these flying saucers could be?'

'I don't mean to throw a spanner in the works gentlemen.' Professor Richard Wilks said.

Everyone looked at him.

'There is one possibility we haven't discussed yet. What if these unidentified flying objects are not man made?'

'Not man made?' Frederick fixed his stare on Wilks.

'Most of you have made up your minds it's either the Russians or Yanks testing new aircraft, or rockets. But none of you are willing to propose the idea these so-called flying saucers could be from elsewhere.'

'Surely you're not suggesting these flying saucers are actually from Mars.' Berkshire said.

'I have read some of these reports we have been receiving from our pilots. I have to admit some of them do make you think. The Germans did indeed develop advanced aircraft during the war. However, some of these witness reports go beyond what the Nazis were capable of.'

'Why don't you share your thoughts with us Richard.' Frederick invited.

'There are a few astronomers including myself who believe the planets in our solar system are not a unique phenomenon in our universe.'

'Explain.' Stanford invited.

'It's possible there are stars like our own sun which may have planets similar to the ones in our solar system. Planets capable of supporting life.'

Frederick recalled what Rothschild had said to him during their encounter earlier that morning.

'Do you realise what you are saying.' Berkshire snorted.

'I do, and I'm more than willing to stick to my theories.' Wilks shifted in his chair. 'As technology and science progress in unison we discover more about our universe. With every new telescope built we are able to look further out into space which reveals more of itself. I doubt whether it will happen in our lifetime. But perhaps by the end of the twentieth century we may have telescopes powerful enough to detect other planets orbiting distant stars. Once upon a time we believed the Earth was the centre of the universe and that everything revolved around us. We have come a long way in understanding the cosmos. We know we are not the centre of the universe. But inhabit a tiny spec in our Milky Way galaxy. Thanks to developing technology we also know there are other galaxies out there.'

'Rubbish pure fantasy.' Berkshire continued to taunt.

Wilks glared at him. 'You've made it obviously clear Anthony you are unwilling to believe in anything that might challenge your faith.'

Berkshire nodded.

Wilks looked around the table at all the others. 'With the exception of myself and Professor Frederick, most of you are over sixty. Half a century ago we were just beginning to explore the possibility of powered flight. Fifty years later we have the atomic bomb and jet propelled aircraft. Rockets capable of penetrating the boundaries of space. We've developed communication arrays that can transmit across the planet. Mankind has invented new technology such as television and terrible weaponry capable of killing tens of thousands in an instant.' Wilks made eye contact with Berkshire. 'If we would have had the same conversation fifty two years ago, would you have been as quick to dismiss such ideas?'

Berkshire didn't answer.

'I'm sorry if the thought of men from Mars makes you feel uncomfortable. But we cannot rule out the possibility these flying saucers might come from somewhere other than Russia or America.'

Frederick leaned forward. 'Ok, just for arguments sake. If these flying saucers originate from somewhere outside our own solar system. What means of propulsion would they use to get here?'

Wilks shook his head. 'This is an area of science we cannot even begin to imagine. The distances between galaxies are incalculable. They are so vast even light from their stars takes eons to reach us. Perhaps one day we might be able to harness the power of our atomic bombs to create a propulsion system capable of great speeds. But at our current level of advancement we are decades from developing such technology, perhaps well into the next century.'

'Speaking of advancement.' Dr Alan Good said. 'If what you say is true how far advanced would another civilisation be compared to our own? Fifty years, one hundred years maybe.'

'Perhaps.' Wilks answered shakily. 'Perhaps more.'

'How much more?' Good continued.

'Maybe a thousand years or far greater.'

'A thousand years or far greater.' Dr Good repeated with a smile.

'This is all speculation of course.' Wilks explained.

'You say these flying saucers could originate from elsewhere in our galaxy.' Dr Arthur Lloyd stated.

'It's highly likely.' Wilks said. 'Nearly all the planets that make up our solar system are either too close or too far away from our sun to sustain life.'

'The Nearest star is Proxima Centauri about 4.2 light years away. Even if these flying saucers could travel at the speed of light, they would take over four years to get here. Even a more intelligent species would see that as a problem.'

'Yes, I have thought about that.'

'And?' Lloyd pressed.

'It's possible these flying saucers could exceed the speed of light.'

'You realise what you are saying would be classed as bordering on madness. A flying saucer, ship or whatever capable of faster than light travel.'

Wilks composed himself. 'For the past few years I have been in contact with Hermann Weyl. He is a German

Mathematician. I have also been communicating with American theoretical physicist John Archibald. Both have speculated the possibility of being able to fold space itself to create a tunnel or short cut. This would enable a more intelligent species to travel vast distances in a short space of time. Both Nathan Rosen and Albert Einstein have also theorised the possibility of creating what's known as a wormhole.'

Admiral Berkshire jumped to his feet. 'This is ludicrous! Why are we entertaining such preposterous blasphemy?'

'Please Anthony sit down.' Frederick said calmly. 'The very reason this group has been set up is to explore all possibilities no matter how farfetched they may seem.'

Berkshire sat back down.

'Ok.' Frederick said wringing his hands. 'Suppose at least some of what you say is true. What do these flying saucers want?'

'The only conclusion I have reached so far is to study us.'

'Study us?' Chambers queried. 'To find out our weaknesses. Are we talking about a possible invasion?'

Wilks shook his head. 'If they are far more advanced than us then they could have invaded whenever they want. My guess is they are here on some sort of scientific venture. Studying us in the same way we study animals and other elements.'

'So we could be the subject of scientific research?' Sir Harold Bates commented.

'It's possible.' He looked across at Admiral Berkshire and noted the expression on his face. 'I know what I have said here today is difficult to take in. For all we know it could be the Russians or Americans. But we cannot rule out the theory it could be something else, something we haven't yet encountered.'

Frederick glanced around the room. 'I think we need to leave it there for the time being. There's a lot to digest.' He turned to Wilks. 'I want you to prepare a full report for the Prime Minister.'

'I'd love to see the old man's face when he reads it.' Berkshire mocked.

Frederick then turned to Professor Norman Canning. 'I need you to monitor our listening posts. If anything crops up with any reference to these flying saucers, I want it catalogued.'

Canning nodded.

'Another report is being prepared by Henry Tizard.' Chambers said. 'In response to public and Newspaper interest. Ok thank you for coming today. I needn't remind you this meeting is classified.'

Chapter 9

Downing Street – Whitehall – 11:18am
Wednesday 6th August 1952

The Prime Minister puffed on his cigar reading the report Professor Wilks had prepared.

Frederick sat opposite fidgeting nervously.

After what seemed like an eternity Churchill looked up. 'You realise this Professor Wilks sounds like a raving lunatic. Why on earth did you assign him to the committee?'

'Professor Wilks is the most senior astronomer and a trusted friend sir. I know his ideas are unorthodox but I promise you he wouldn't have said what's in his report if it didn't have a foundation of truth.'

'I take it Lord Admiral Berkshire wasn't too pleased with these ideas.'

'No sir.'

'Berkshire is from fine stock. He is not fond of change. This so called brave new world full of technological wonders can scare a lot of people. New ways clashing with more traditional ways.'

'Yes Prime Minister.'

'I've set up funding for your group and a temporary office has been set aside at Bletchley Park in order to collect intelligence on these flying saucers.'

'If I may ask Prime Minister, what do you plan to do about all the press stories and the public interest?'

'Let them run. I've a feeling the public will tire of these stories after a while and go back to their lives. In the meantime you and your group will carry on with your investigation.' The Prime Minister paused. 'I know you're uncomfortable investigating this flying saucer nonsense Ralph. This is why I put you on this team. I trust your judgement and know you will not be easily sucked in by all the hype. I promise you'll be done in a few months.'

'Thank you Prime Minister.'

'What about this chap who claims his wife was kidnapped by a flying saucer?'

'I interviewed the gentlemen in question and a number of other people. The husband seems to be sticking to his story about an encounter with a mysterious object late at night. But like I said to the others it's nothing more than a domestic tiff.'

'And the police what is their view on the matter?'

'They're puzzled, but they are sure he didn't murder her.'

'Good work Professor, at least there's a rational explanation to this man's story.'

Frederick hesitated. 'If you don't mind me asking Prime Minister I would like to know if you have discussed the subject of flying saucers with anyone else.'

'I have discussed the matter with Norman Hinshelwood a few times. The subject has surfaced on a number of occasions with Royal Society members.'

'I see.' Frederick nodded. 'Norman must have mentioned it to a colleague of mine. He briefly questioned me several days ago regarding our first meeting.'

The Prime Minister looked back at Frederick. 'You're worried about leaks.'

'As you can see from my report the man I encountered at Downham Market claimed he knew many people at the Royal Society. I'm already uncomfortable looking into the flying saucer phenomenon. I explained to Malcolm I don't want my reputation damaged by such nonsense. If we are to maintain total secrecy we must discuss committee matters with members only.'

'I understand Professor. If Norman asks me anything else I'll pass him on to Henry Tizard.'

'Malcolm also feels Tizard's team have a leak. There's also the matter of Peter Horsley's visit to Ripley and the Duke of

Edinburgh's interest in flying saucers.'

'I wouldn't worry about the Duke Professor. He will soon tire of all this flying saucer nonsense. If he does pop up I will speak to him further to quash any interest.'

'Thank you Prime Minister.' Frederick got to his feet and headed for the door.

Chapter 10

RAF Yeadon – South Yorkshire – 7:27am
Wednesday 14th August 1952

'Professor I never thought we'd be meeting up so soon.' flight lieutenant Fletcher greeted picking up his suitcase.

Frederick yawned. 'Thank you Mr Fletcher neither did I.'

'A bit too early for you is it.' Fletcher laughed.

Frederick did not share his enthusiasm. Neither did he appreciate being dragged out of bed at two thirty in the morning. The phone had rung several times before Elizabeth pushed him out of bed to answer it.

Morris Stanford apologised for calling at such a late hour. But a matter concerning a number of radar and visual sightings were being reported at RAF Church Fenton in South Yorkshire on two consecutive nights. Stanford explained should any more sightings occur then a man on the ground would be invaluable.

The car drove out of the base heading for open countryside. Fletcher briefed Frederick as they headed towards Church Fenton.

'The objects were first picked up two nights ago around midnight. Radar spotted nine contacts coming in from the North Sea over Hull. I have spoken to a number of control tower personnel who all stuck to the same story. The objects were travelling at alternate speeds. Between five hundred miles an hour to around seventeen hundred miles an hour.'

'Bloody hell that's fast!' Frederick remarked.

'There's no way the Russians have developed anything that fast. Therefore, we have ruled them out of the equation. Quite frankly there are a lot of folks up here baffled by it all. I phoned on ahead, the base Commanding Officer is Wing Commander David Fitzpatrick. He is expecting us and his staff have been informed an official from the Air Ministry will be visiting to talk to them.'

Frederick yawned again 'In the meantime flight lieutenant Fletcher I would like to catch up on my sleep.'

Fletcher smiled. 'There's a bunk house on the base sir. I'm sure they can sort you out.'

Chapter 11

RAF Church Fenton – South Yorkshire – 6:52pm

The officers' mess was quiet when Frederick, Fletcher, and Wing Commander Fitzpatrick sat down to dinner. On arrival at the RAF base Frederick had been introduced to the base commanding officer who was a former World War one fighter ace. Fitzpatrick was a legend in the RAF and well respected. Although just a few years off retirement he showed no sign of wanting to hand in his wings just yet. Frederick managed to get a few hours' sleep before interviewing base personnel about their sightings. He was taken out onto the base and shown around.

RAF Church Fenton was home to the new Hunter Hawker jet fighters which flew regular missions out over the North Sea. Fitzpatrick explained four of them had been scrambled to intercept the unidentified radar contacts on two consecutive nights. The jets were unable to keep pace because of their speed.

'It's frustrating not knowing who the enemy is.' Fitzpatrick complained. 'Back in the day when we were fighting the Huns, you knew who your enemy was. All you needed was a clear shot.'

Frederick looked across the base towards the perimeter fence. 'Last night you say the objects appeared at the edge of the runway?'

Fitzpatrick nodded. 'Bright lights hovering just beyond the perimeter fence. It looked like they were watching us. The minute we scrambled our fighters the bloody things flew off. Dammed if I've seen anything like it before in all my years of flying.'

'I suggest we take a walk out to the perimeter fence so you can show me where exactly these objects appeared.'

'That's a good idea, I'll make sure all aircraft are grounded for the next hour while you conduct your investigation Professor.' Fitzpatrick offered.

After dinner Frederick and Fletcher headed out to the Ryther Arms which was part of a small village consisting of a small group of houses centred around the pub.

'You're getting me into bad habits.' Frederick said as he sipped from his pint glass. 'This is the second time in as many weeks you have dragged me out to the pub.'

Fletcher smiled. 'I find a good pint helps me think better and relaxes the mind.'

'As a scientist I must remind you alcohol gives you Dutch courage.'

'Maybe so but it does feel good.' Fletcher took a swig from his glass before setting it down on the table and looking across the bar.

Several locals were huddled around a table playing dominos while a few others were leant against the bar talking to the landlord. Occasionally they would look across at Fletcher and Frederick. On the opposite corner of the bar, two other RAF officers sat drinking. Like the locals stood at the bar they would both look over at Frederick and Fletcher and chat away.

Fletcher made eye contact with the two flight officers. 'That's strange.'

'What?' Frederick asked taking another sip from his glass.

'I know I'm stationed at Yeadon, but I visit Church Fenton regularly. I like to think I know most of the pilots.'

'And?' Frederick said.

'The two over there in the corner are wearing pilot insignias. But I have never seen them before.'

'Perhaps they're test pilots up here to fly those new Hawker jets.'

Fletcher shook his head. 'I checked the personnel log this

morning when we arrived to see if there were any new pilots on base but there weren't.' He picked up his pint glass and stood up. 'Come on let's go and have a chat with our two pilots.'

Reluctantly Frederick scooped up his glass and followed Fletcher over to where the two men were sat.

'Hello chaps mind if we sit?' The flight lieutenant boldly asked.

One of the two men looked up at him. 'No please pull up a stool.' He had jet black hair which was swept back and held into place with a large amount of hair gel. The other man had brown hair styled in a crew cut fashion.

Frederick and Fletcher sat down. for several seconds no one spoke.

'How long have you chaps been on the base?' Fletcher broke the silence.

'We arrived yesterday.' The black-haired man revealed.

'I take it you are up here flying those new Hawkers?'

'Yeah.'

'How are you finding the Avon 103 engine?' Fletcher asked as he took another swig from his pint.

The black-haired man looked to his colleague for support. 'We haven't had the chance to get in one yet. We make our first test flight tomorrow.'

'I see.' Fletcher pressed on. 'Only I didn't see any new signatures in the log book this morning. It's strict procedure for new pilots on the base to sign in before they get access to any aircraft.'

'We didn't get time. I did mention it to your commanding officer this morning and he cleared it.' The man looked at his watch. 'That reminds me we have to get an early night.'

The two men stood quickly and politely said their goodbyes before heading to the pub entrance.

'What a load of bollocks.' Fletcher stated as they walked out of the door. 'They're not air force.'

'How can you tell?' Frederick enquired.

'Because one of them was smoking Marlboro cigarettes. Most of the pilots on base smoke Woodbines.'

'Hardly a reason to accuse them of anything flight lieutenant.'

'Only the Yank pilots used to smoke Marlboro.'

'But they sounded British.'

'A little too British for my liking.' Fletcher finished his pint glass and looked at the time. 'We better get back to base. I'll ask Fitzpatrick if he has met those two.'

RAF Church Fenton – 11:34pm

Fitzpatrick shook his head. 'I have no idea who those men were and I have strict policy about signing into the base.'

'My thoughts exactly Wing Commander. I know how you are at following protocol.'

'Whoever they were, they're not stationed at this base. You are the only two people who have come back and forth this evening. I will have a couple of extra boys on the gate tonight. If anyone is sneaking about posing as RAF then we'll bloody well nab them.'

Frederick yawned looking at the clock on the wall. The two pints of beer he had at the pub acted as a sedative. 'I think I'll retire for the night. It looks like this visit has been a no show.'

'Yes, good night Professor.' Fitzpatrick replied.

Chapter 12

Friday 15th August 1952 – 2:32am

'Professor, Professor wake up.' flight lieutenant Fletcher shook Frederick's arm.

Frederick opened his eyes feeling disorientated before realising he was still on the base. He looked bleary eyed at the flight lieutenant. 'What's the matter?'

'Sir, you need to accompany me up to the radar tower immediately.'

Frederick got dressed quickly and followed Fletcher.

Fitzpatrick was stood looking out of the window with a mike in his hand. 'Roger that Hawker one. Maintain your speed and let us know when you have a visual.' He turned to face Frederick. 'Radar picked up four objects heading for this position. Our tracking station at RAF Hull called it in first. We've scrambled four Hunters to intercept.'

'Could they be other jets?' Frederick suggested.

Fitzpatrick shook his head. 'They fit the same profile of the objects we encountered over the last two nights.'

'Base this is Hawker one *over*.' A voice crackled over the loud speaker.

'Go ahead Hawker one.' Fitzpatrick responded.

'We now have a visual.' The radio crackled. 'Four brightly coloured objects, *over*.'

'Is that all Hawker one?'

'They are disc shaped, blue in colour, moving extremely fast towards our position. We are altering our course, *over*.'

'Hawker one, maintain a visual but do not engage, repeat do not engage.'

'Roger that base.'

'Sir given their speed the objects should be in visual range within two minutes.' The radar operator announced.

Fitzpatrick picked up a pair of binoculars and peered out of the control tower window. Medium height cloud lay on the horizon with breaks allowing a full moon to cast shadows across the base.

'There!' An excited Fletcher cried out pointing beyond the end of the runway.

Four lights came into view evenly spaced out.

Frederick stared out of the window at the approaching lights.

'Flight lieutenant Fletcher, get a car.' Fitzpatrick ordered.

Less than five minutes later Frederick found himself heading for the end of the runway. Up ahead the perimeter fence could be seen in the moonlight.

A jeep with four armed guards accompanied Frederick's car.

The four lights Fletcher had spotted were no longer in sight. The car came to a stop a few hundred yards from the fence.

Frederick climbed out of the car, scanning the horizon for the lights.

The guards fanned out along the width of the runway.

Fitzpatrick had his binoculars in hand and began scanning the flat horizon which stretched out beyond the air force base.

Frederick suddenly became aware of static discharge. The hairs on the back of his neck stood to attention.

'Look!' One of the guards shouted, pointing towards the opposite end of the runway.

Four brightly blue lights hung motionless in the air.

All seven men stared in the direction of the lights.

The objects suddenly accelerated upwards crossing each other's path performing a strange areal ballet.

Frederick stared at the lights mesmerised by what he was witnessing.

Fitzpatrick adjusted the focus on his binoculars. 'Bloody

things are too fast for me to get a proper look.'

The objects plummeted towards the ground with ferocious speed as if they had heard Fitzpatrick. They stopped instantaneously several feet off the ground.

Frederick watched in astonishment as the lights slowly glided towards the group of men. His heart pounded as he tried to process the sight in front of him.

One of the guards lifted his gun aiming at one of the lights.

'No!' Frederick called out. 'Lower your gun!'

The guard glared at Frederick then looked at Fitzpatrick who nodded.

Frederick slowly walked toward the lights which had stopped moving. He studied each light individually for several seconds. They were glowing circular shaped objects perfectly round with no visible windows. Each object was approximately 25 to 30 foot across. As he got closer Frederick became aware of a humming sound. He held up his hand and noted the static discharge grew stronger the nearer he got to the objects.

The sound of the Hunter Hawkers could be heard in the distance heading back to base.

Frederick was about to touch the surface of one of the objects.

Suddenly the objects accelerated vertically at ferocious speed. Becoming pin pricks of lights indistinguishable amongst the stars in the night sky. Several seconds later the Hunter Jets screamed overhead.

Frederick was still staring at the sky dumbfounded by what he had just witnessed.

Chapter 13

Whitehall – London – 3:20pm
Monday 19th August 1952

All committee members had been called to the debriefing to look over the report Frederick had hastily put together. After the incident involving the unidentified objects he had returned to the base with the other men. Each man filled out a detailed report. All the witnesses including Fitzpatrick were shaken by what they had seen. Frederick took it upon himself to telephone Lord Chambers. Despite the time of the morning Chambers listened with great interest. He instructed Frederick to stay another night. 'Just in case our friends decide to put on another show.' However, the next evening nothing happened so Frederick returned home before heading to London.

'Astounding!' Dr Alan Good commented. 'We're obviously dealing with something that goes way beyond what the Russians or Americans may be capable of. It's such a shame you couldn't have captured any of it on film.'

'We would have needed flood lights to get anything on film. It was too dark unless you count the area where the objects appeared.'

'Sounds too good to be true.' Admiral Berkshire remarked.

Professor Richard Wilks looked across at him. 'You doubt Professor Frederick's eye witness account admiral?'

'No but I still refuse to buy into the notion these objects may be from another planet. I'm sorry Professor but unless I see these things for myself then I'll keep my feet firmly on the ground.'

'You are entitled to your opinion Admiral.' Frederick said. 'But I would appreciate if you would keep an open mind on this. I have trouble believing what I saw but I did see these things first hand.' He recalled the scene in his head. 'To witness something so astounding challenges the laws of physics. The way they moved, there was no displacement of air. This rewrites modern day aeronautical science.'

'Question is, what do we do about this? These objects are able to out manoeuvre our aircraft and are superior in speed.' Norman Canning said. 'We need to adopt some kind of strategy in dealing with these UFOs.'

'I think all we can do for now is observe.' Dr Arthur Lloyd stated.

'Agreed!' Sir Harold Bates said. 'But next time if we get the opportunity to view these things close up we have to have some kind of electronic recording equipment.'

'Tizard's Flying Saucer Working Party has never encountered anything like this.' Chambers remarked.

'At least we have something to go on now.' Ian Morgan said.

'I want all of you to take these reports away with you and read over them and then you must burn them.' Morris Stanford instructed.

'Burn them?' Wilks queried. 'Isn't that a bit drastic.'

'This government is still reeling from Burgess and Maclean last year. British Intelligence believe there are still Soviet spies at large. We will keep the original report which Professor Frederick has written. But under no circumstances must any copies exist. We now have evidence these objects are not American or Russian which makes this above top secret. We'll meet up again next month to discuss any new developments.'

Chapter 14

Ripley – North Yorkshire – 10:26am
Monday 1st September 1952

Michael Smith slammed on the brakes with such force he thought his foot was going to go through the floor of his lorry. The figure in the road seemed to appear out of nowhere. Applying the handbrake the local Farmer jumped down from his cab and briskly walked to the front of his lorry. 'Are you bloody stupid or what?' He bellowed. 'I could have killed you!'

The woman had her back to him and didn't respond.

Smith walked around to face her. 'Did you hear me you stupid..' Smith stopped dead in his tracks and stared at the young woman who was glaring down at her stomach cradling it.

Her blonde hair sprayed outwards and down over her face. There was blood running from her nose and her clothes hung loose around her.

Smith put his hand on her shoulder. 'Are you okay?'

The woman slowly looked up.

Smith stepped back. 'Bloody hell Edith!'

Whitehall – London – 11:06am
Wednesday 3rd September 1952

'You know this is a complete waste of time.' Frederick protested. 'We've already been to this woman's house. It's clear she just buggered off and left her husband. Now she just turns up out of the blue. We are better off discovering the true nature of the objects I encountered at Church Fenton a few weeks ago. Not traipsing all the way up to Ripley to sort out a domestic tiff.'

'I know it seems like a waste of time old boy. But humour me will you. We have to keep all lines of investigation open.'

Chambers coughed and rubbed his chest.

'Are you ok?'

Chambers continued to cough nodding. 'Yes just a bit tired that's all. Probably all these bloody pills I'm taking to keep the ticker going.'

'Well try not to overdo things.' Frederick advised.

Chapter 15

RAF Yeadon – 6:25pm
Friday 5th September 1952

The familiar smiling face of flight lieutenant Fletcher was there to greet Frederick as he stepped off the plane. Frederick telephoned committee member Dr Arthur Lloyd and requested he came along to examine Mrs Jones. Dr Lloyd was a renowned psychologist and former physician to his majesty King George VI.

'If anyone will be able to see this is a waste of time Arthur it's you.' Frederick said.

'I will try my best, but I'm on your side Ralph. This story seems too incredible to be true.'

When they arrived at Ripley all three men checked in to the hotel before setting out to the Jones' house.

As they approached the front door Frederick spotted a police constable standing outside.

The constable approached. 'Can I help you gentlemen?'

'We are here to see Mrs Edith Jones.' Frederick said.

'Really and who might you be?' The constable asked blocking their path.

'I'm Professor Ralph Frederick. This is Doctor Arthur Lloyd and flight lieutenant Walter Fletcher. We were here a few weeks ago interviewing her husband.'

'Well Professor, you will appreciate Mrs Jones needs her rest and won't be seeing anyone for the time being.'

'That's not what you told me yesterday.' Fletcher argued. 'You said we could interview her.'

'That was yesterday wasn't it. I'm afraid things have changed since then.'

'In what way?' Dr Arthur Lloyd asked.

The constable was about to reply when the front door to

the Jones' house opened.

Sir William Ingles and two other men appeared. 'Professor Frederick, how nice to see you again.' Ingles greeted in a cheerful manner. 'And I see you've brought reinforcements.' He stretched out his hand towards Dr Lloyd. 'William Ingles at your service sir.'

'Pleasure Sir William.' Lloyd replied before making eye contact with the man behind. 'Peter, what brings you up here?'

'He is a guest of mine.' Ingles answered quickly before his friend had time to answer.

Peter Horsley remained silent.

The third man was the local doctor who hurried past Frederick and the others.

'If you don't mind Sir William we would like to speak to Mrs Jones.' Frederick said politely.

'That won't be possible Professor. Mrs Jones is resting and won't be seeing anyone for a while.' Ingles explained.

'But she has spoken to you and Mr Horsley.' Lloyd commented.

'Mr Jones has requested to be left alone which includes everyone.'

'When will we be allowed to speak with her?' Frederick asked.

'I'm afraid you didn't hear me Professor. Mrs Jones isn't speaking to anyone. I suggest you head back to London, there's a good fellow.'

'As former royal physician I am requesting access to Mrs Jones to assess her condition.'

Horsley and Ingles looked at each other. 'As you say, former royal physician Doctor Lloyd. Which means you have no jurisdiction here. Besides our own doctor has examined her thoroughly. Now if you'll excuse us gentlemen.' Ingles and Horsley brushed passed the three men.

Chapter 16

Ryther Arms – 6:56pm

'I don't believe the nerve of that man.' Lloyd protested sipping from a glass of whiskey. 'And Peter didn't even acknowledge us.'

'When I first spoke to Sir Ingles he said Horsley has been up this way before. I suspect Ingles has direct contact with Buckingham Palace.' Frederick summarised. 'For what it's worth we need to speak with Mrs Jones to find out what happened to her. Just to end this ridiculous line of investigation.'

A man who was stood at the bar staring at the group in the corner walked over to them. 'Sorry to bother you blokes but are you up here about Edith Jones?'

'No we are just enjoying the scenery now bugger off.' Fletcher snarled.

'Suit yourself, but my brother was the one who found her wandering on the road the other day.' The man turned and started to walk back towards the bar.

Frederick's interest suddenly kicked into gear. 'Really and you are?'

He looked back. 'I'm Dave Smith.'

'Ok then Mr Smith why don't you tell us what you know.' Dr Lloyd said offering the man a seat at their table.

'It'll cost you a pint.' He held his glass out to Fletcher who looked across at Frederick.

Frederick smiled back at him. 'Would you accommodate this gentleman flight lieutenant.'

Fletcher snatched the glass off Smith and headed for the bar.

'Mr Smith why don't you tell us what your brother told you?' Frederick asked.

'Did you know she was pregnant before she disappeared?'
'Yes, about eight months I believe.'

Fletcher returned with a full pint glass and set it down in front of Smith. He scooped it up and drank half immediately. 'When my brother found her she was screaming about her baby.'

'Go on.' Lloyd said.

'She wasn't pregnant anymore. My brother said she just kept screaming her baby was gone.' He took another swig. 'Rumour has it she was sent away to a convent to have the baby because it wasn't her husband's.'

Lloyd drew a disappointed breath. 'Really Mr Smith and who's baby was it?'

'Old man Ingles of course. They reckon while her husband was managing the books at the castle, Ingles was sneaking out and managing Mrs Jones if you know what I mean.' Smith smiled to reveal a toothless mouth. 'Sir Ingles has always had a way with the local ladies.'

'Thank you for that important bit of information Mr Smith.' Lloyd said with sarcasm.

Smith got up and finished the rest of his pint. 'No problem gents, glad I could help.'

'That was a waste of a perfectly good pint.' Fletcher complained glancing at Smith as he walked away.

Frederick thought for a moment. 'Well that settles it. We're heading back to London tomorrow. I knew there had to be a simple explanation.'

'It doesn't make sense. If what that yokel just said is true. Why make up such an elaborate story about a flying saucer kidnapping his wife?' Fletcher questioned. 'Surely it would have been better for her to have the baby and keep quiet about who's it was.'

Frederick glanced at Fletcher. 'I hope you are not suggesting she was actually kidnapped by a flying saucer.'

'After what I witnessed at Church Fenton a few weeks back

Professor I'm willing to believe anything at this point.'

'There's only one way to find out what happened to Mrs Jones. We need to question the local doctor who was with Peter Horsley and Ingles earlier this evening.' Lloyd suggested.

'Am I the only rational one here.' Frederick sighed. 'There is nothing to investigate.'

'All I'm saying is we go and interview the doctor to settle any doubt.'

Frederick and Fletcher glanced at each other. 'You know that's going to annoy Ingles.' Frederick warned. 'Besides there's no guarantee the doctor will even speak to us.'

Lloyd smiled. 'Let me worry about him.'

Chapter 17

8:26pm

After the hotel Landlord had drawn Frederick's group a crude map the three men found themselves outside the surgery of one Dr Charles Williams.

Dr Williams yanked open the door. 'Who is it?' He barked blinking into the fading daylight.

Lloyd stepped forward and took off his hat. 'Doctor Williams my name is Doctor Arthur Lloyd. My colleagues and I wish to speak to you about Mrs Edith Jones.'

'I'm afraid I cannot comment on Mrs Jones to anyone but her and her husband. You as a doctor are aware of patient confidentiality.'

'I am aware of the regulations.' Lloyd responded. 'However, I could call the Home Office and send an order for you to hand over medical records and have you struck off.'

Frederick and Fletcher glanced at each other impressed by Lloyd's guile.

Dr Williams rubbed his forehead and nodded before beckoning them in.

Across the street two men watched from their car.

'Those are the two guys we bumped into a few weeks back.' One of the men said with an American accent.

'It has to be this Professor Frederick Jacob Barnes briefed us about.' His companion stated.

'We need to be on our toes. I'll break into the surgery and steal the information.'

'Be careful the doctor could be one of them.' The brown-haired man advised.

When the front door to the house slammed shut one of the men got out and ran across the road.

Doctor Williams brought a tea tray in and set it down on a large coffee table.

'I appreciate you talking to us Doctor Williams.' Frederick said picking up his cup.

Williams looked across at Lloyd. 'I don't see I have much of a choice in the matter.' He sat down in a large leather armchair. 'This whole thing with Edith Jones is getting way out of hand if you ask me.'

'We understand Mrs Jones was eight months pregnant when she disappeared. But when she was found the other day she was no longer pregnant.' Lloyd explained.

'That's correct.' Williams said.

'Is there any explanation as to what could have happened to the child?'

Williams shook his head. 'I examined Mrs Jones and could find no evidence she had even been pregnant. This is despite the fact I examined her two days before she vanished.'

'Did you examine her thoroughly?' Lloyd asked.

'I did yes, she was in perfect health despite losing the child. I found no marks to indicate she might have given birth prematurely. It's a dammed mystery as to what happened to her and her child. Her husband said she suffers from constant nose bleeds and is sick on occasion.'

'There are rumours circulating amongst the locals the baby could have belonged to Sir William. Is there any possibility this could be true?'

Williams shook his head rigorously. 'Absolute rubbish. The locals at the pub have too much time on their hands. Gossip mongering and spreading rumours that simply aren't true.'

'I take it you have a record of Mrs Jones' pregnancy.' Lloyd enquired.

Dr Williams nodded before getting up and leaving the room for a few minutes to look for the records.

'What do you think?' Frederick asked Lloyd.

'I don't doubt his story but until I look at her records for myself I cannot.' Lloyd stopped in mid-sentence.

Doctor Williams could clearly be heard shouting at someone in the surgery. Fletcher jumped to his feet and removed his sidearm from its holster. All three men heard the Doctor's scream for help then another muffled cry followed by a loud crash as if someone had fallen.

Fletcher moved stealthily down a narrow hallway.

The door to the main surgery was open.

Dr Williams' body lay sprawled on the floor face down.

As he stood in the doorway Fletcher caught sight of a figure. The air force officer instinctively jumped out of the way as a chair hurtled passed his head into the hallway. He waited a few seconds before launching himself through the doorway. Fletcher fired off two rounds.

The bullets drove into the wall behind the intruder.

The doctor's assailant drew a pistol from his inside holster and pointed it at Fletcher.

Frederick cautiously stepped through the doorway to see a startled Fletcher locked in a Mexican standoff with the other man.

'Gentlemen.' The man said with a bold tone and a broad American accent. He backed towards the door and then vanished into the fading light.

Fletcher wasn't finished. He sprinted out into the street spotting a car speeding away. The flight lieutenant fired his weapon in the direction of the car as it sped down the street. However, within seconds the car had vanished from sight.

Lloyd entered the surgery spotting Dr Williams. He knelt and checked for a pulse. 'He's dead.'

Frederick pointed to a mark on the back of the doctor's neck. 'What do you make of that?'

Lloyd pulled down the doctor's collar which revealed what looked like an incision approximately half an inch running vertical down the back of Williams' neck. 'I'm not sure, it looks like a surgical procedure of some kind.' Lloyd hauled the body of the doctor onto his back. 'He hasn't been shot, or hit with anything.'

Fletcher entered the surgery out of breath. 'Bastards scampered off.'

'Why did I recognise that man with the gun?' Frederick asked.

'He was one of the blokes in the pub several weeks back. The ones at Church Fenton who said they were testing the new Hunter Hawkers.'

'The fake RAF pilots.'

Fletcher nodded and then looked at the corpse of the doctor.

Lloyd stood. 'Better call this in.'

Chapter 1 8

Whitehall – London – 1:34pm
Tuesday 9th September 1952

Following the death of Doctor Williams Frederick and his companions had been interviewed by Harrogate police.

Lord Chambers and Air Marshall Morgan listened as the two men gave their account of the last few days.

'Doctor Williams must have disturbed the intruder as he entered his surgery.' Lloyd explained.

'Plus the medical records of Edith Jones had vanished. Everything including the report on her condition after she returned.' Chambers mentioned.

'Yes.' Frederick answered. 'We did request an interview with her but Sir Ingles wouldn't let us near her. He's even moved Mr and Mrs Jones into his castle for safety.'

'I tried to talk to Peter Horsley This Morning.' Morgan revealed. 'But he just stonewalled me. Buckingham Palace will want to keep this quiet. They won't want a member of the royal household at the centre of a murder enquiry. There's definitely more to this woman's experience than meets the eye.'

'Now we can't get anyone near her with Ingles protecting her.' Frederick Pointed out.

'You are positive the man from the doctor's surgery was American?' Chambers asked.

'Yes, both myself and Fletcher recognised him from the incident at Church Fenton. My guess is the other one must have been driving the getaway car.'

'Why would Americans be poking around Ripley?' Chambers mused.

'More importantly what was worth killing that doctor for?' Morgan added.

Lloyd shook his head. 'He wasn't killed by the American. When I briefly examined the body I couldn't find any sign that he had been attacked.'

'There must have been something in that report.' Frederick suggested. 'But until we are able to talk to Mrs Jones we won't know.'

Chambers looked at Frederick. 'Do you still have doubts about this woman's story?'

Frederick considered the question 'I was convinced this story was just a hoax. I'm still not willing to accept she was kidnapped by a flying saucer. My experience at Church Fenton a few weeks ago has swayed my opinion on flying saucers. But we need physical evidence. As it stands, we have none.'

The door to Chambers' office opened and Morris Stanford walked in. 'I've just received a phone call from RAF Yeadon. The body of the doctor that was murdered has vanished.'

'Vanished?' Frederick questioned.

'Your friend flight lieutenant Fletcher said a local police constable had telephoned him last night. According to the report the body was reported missing on Sunday night.'

'What the hell is going on here?' Chambers questioned. 'First the missing wife and now a murdered doctor who happens to disappear himself.'

'When we examined the doctor's body, we discovered a small incision on the back of his neck. But there was no other visible evidence to suggest he had met a violent death. That's why I don't think he was murdered by the American.'

'There are many pieces to this puzzle.' Morgan remarked.

'We'll bide our time.' Chambers said. 'Ingles will eventually let them return to their home and then we'll look into it further.'

Chapter 19

St James' Park – London – 11:42am
Friday 12th September 1952

Frederick checked his pocket watch for the fifth time swearing under his breath. He had been waiting in the same spot for about forty minutes. He cast his mind back to the day before when he had received a note from Dr Vincent Rothschild. The man he had encountered a few weeks earlier at Downham Market train station. The Note had been delivered by courier.

St James' Park, main entrance 11:00am
Come alone if you want answers about Edith Jones
V Rothschild.

Frederick's first reaction was to pick up a phone and call Morris Stanford to brief him about what was going on. However, he did have questions for this man and MI6 watching him might jeopardise any information Rothschild might be willing to give.

After checking his watch again Frederick decided he had been stood up and started to walk towards Buckingham Palace. He then caught sight of Rothschild who was walking towards him.

'Professor Frederick, thank you for agreeing to meet with me. I was expecting you to stand me up.'

'And I thought you were about to.' Frederick complained. 'I'm not in the habit of just loitering around parks. I have more important matters to tend to.'

'You must forgive me Professor but I am just as distrustful. I wasn't sure you would bring company.'

'Should I have?'

'I am no threat to you Professor, I merely wish to discuss matters of a scientific nature and come to a mutual understanding. And hopefully make you an offer which you might find interesting.' Rothschild sat down on a nearby bench and invited Frederick to sit next to him.

'And what matters would they be?'

Rothschild smiled. 'Still trying to hide the truth Professor.'

'I thought I had explained to you and your colleague. I have no interest in flying saucers.'

'But you still chose to meet me. Plus your experience at Church Fenton a few weeks back must have changed your mind.'

Frederick said nothing.

'First let me assure you, although I am on the east side of the border in Germany I have no allegiance to Stalin or his regime. Although I do have to work under their watchful eyes.'

'Why not just come over to us?'

'To do that would tip the scales too much in the west's favour. I believe great minds should be equal on both sides.'

'So what is it you want from me?'

'What I just said mutual understanding.'

'Why don't we start with how is it you know about Church Fenton?'

'Nothing is as classified as you would like to believe Professor. Secrets have always been shared. Not freely of course, there is always a price to pay. But I would like to know if you still think flying saucers are nonsense.'

Frederick recalled his experience at Church Fenton. 'To tell you the truth I don't know what to think. I saw what I saw but can't explain it.'

'I remember my first experience.' Rothschild recalled.

Frederick looked at him. 'You've seen these things?'

'On many occasions.' Rothschild rubbed his hands together. 'Each experience left me spellbound.'

'Are these objects some sort of Russian military experiment?'

Rothschild shook his head. 'No Professor, neither are they American. No power on this planet can construct what we have witnessed.'

'Where are they from?'

'As the Americans like to say, that's the sixty four-thousand-dollar question. I can tell you both the Soviet government and the Americans are locked in a race.'

'What kind of race?'

'A race to develop technology captured or found over the years. Technology that is far beyond human capability.'

'Are you saying the Americans and Soviets have flying saucers in their possession?'

Rothschild nodded. 'Which is why I have come to you Professor. Your group needs to be aware you are lagging behind in this race. The Americans have many secrets they are not willing to share. The Soviet Union is just as secretive. There are also other countries with secrets as well as religious sects who have kept certain truths hidden from mankind for centuries.'

'Hidden truths.'

'The world is not as black and white as you might think Professor.'

Frederick thought for a moment unwilling to get sucked in by Rothschild's words. 'What exactly is your role in this Doctor?'

'For now, I am an observer part of a group the Soviet government have established. But I have no allegiance to them.'

'In other words, you don't have access to information that might be useful to the British Government. And I'm certainly not going to give you any information that might give you the upper hand.' Frederick stood. 'You've come all this way for nothing I'm afraid.' He started to walk away.

'Is that what you think?' Rothschild said. 'You disappoint me Professor.'

'Then tell me what you want!' Frederick demanded turning to face Rothschild.

'To make you an offer.'

'Offer.' Frederick shrugged.

'To become part of an elite scientific body that operates outside of any government jurisdiction.'

'What kind of scientific body?'

'A group that has existed for centuries yet remains a great secret.'

Frederick shoved his hands into his pockets smiling at Rothschild. 'So you just decided to reveal it to me. Sorry Doctor but so far you haven't been very forthcoming with any kind of information. And this cloak and dagger act you like to put on is becoming tedious.' Frederick started to walk off towards the Palace.

'Don't you want to know what happened to that woman's child? Or who that man was you encountered in the doctor's surgery.' Rothschild called out.

Frederick stopped and spun on his heels. Frustration began to take hold. 'I regret not bringing British Intelligence along. Stop playing mind games Doctor either you do or you don't have access to information that might be useful. You obviously have access to information we have. Who was responsible for the doctor's murder? And what has happened to his body?'

'Why don't you ask the Americans?'

'Why?'

'Because they know more than anybody what went on in Ripley.' Rothschild answered. 'As for what happened to his body. Let's just say he got up and walked away.'

'Why steal the medical file of Edith Jones?' Frederick asked.

'Because of the information it contained. At first she was

pregnant, then she wasn't. Most puzzling wouldn't you say. And it wasn't the first time this woman has been reported missing.'

Frederick's patients hung by a thread. 'Not the first time. What exactly are you getting at?'

'What I'm trying to make you understand Professor is you need to go back and interview this woman. You need to find out everything before it's too late.'

'Too late.' Frederick stated shrugging his shoulders. 'What's that supposed to mean?'

Rothschild stood. 'I think Professor I have given you enough to go on with for now. Whether you want to go on meeting with me is your choice. The group I represent needs men like you. Everything you've discovered about flying saucers so far isn't even the tip of the iceberg.' Rothschild stood up. 'Goodbye Professor we shall see each other again soon enough.'

Chapter 20

Ripley North – Yorkshire – 1:12pm
Monday 15th September 1952

Frederick felt anxious about returning to Ripley and not telling the committee what he was up to. He hadn't even contacted flight lieutenant Fletcher to tell him he was returning. Frederick looked around before knocking on the door of Mr & Mrs Jones' house.

The door opened a little way.

Frederick peered through the narrow gap. 'Mr Jones, we met a few weeks ago, my name is Ralph Frederick. I'm from the Air Ministry.'

'What do you want?' Jones barked from behind the narrow opening.

'If it's possible I would like to speak with you and your wife regarding her flying saucer encounter.'

'Look I'm fed up with people calling around here. Just leave us alone will you.' The door slammed shut.

Frederick stood for a few moments wondering what to do next. He knocked on the door again.

'Piss off we don't want to talk with you!' Jones shouted from behind the door.

Frederick produced three one pound notes from his wallet. 'Mr Jones I have travelled all the way from Cambridge to speak with you. I am willing to pay you for your story.'

The door opened again. Jones stared at the money Frederick held in his hand before opening the door wider.

Frederick sat down on the sofa opposite Mrs Jones who sat in the main armchair.

The woman looked thin and had pale skin. Her eyes were blood shot from hours of crying.

Her husband entered the room with a tea tray he placed

on a small coffee table. 'I'm sorry I swore at you Mr Frederick. It's just so many people have been around here wanting to take the piss. People calling all hours of the day. We're getting so fed up of it now.'

'I can understand your frustration. I thought Sir Ingles had put you up at the Castle.'

Jones shook his head. 'I don't work for him anymore I was given the sack yesterday.'

'Oh dear I'm sorry to hear that.'

'I'm not, we got fed up of him and his friends. All they wanted to do was question us over and over. In the end I moved us back here. We were going to be interviewed by The News of The World but Sir Ingles stopped them from coming up here. They were going to pay us fifty pounds for our story. I had an argument with the old man a couple of days ago about it.' Jones looked at his wife. 'That was that, he ended up sacking me.'

Frederick looked across at Edith Jones.

'She's hardly said a word since her experience.' Jones walked over to her and stroked her hair. 'But she has terrible nightmares.'

'Nightmares.'

'She keeps screaming about terrible black lifeless eyes staring at her through the window. It takes a lot to calm her down.'

'If you don't mind me asking Mr Jones, is this the first time your wife has gone missing?'

Jones shook his head. 'She went through a phase with sleep walking last year. Edith got out of the house one night and vanished for nearly a day. We eventually found her wandering in the local woods.'

'When was this?' Frederick asked.

Jones thought for a moment. 'It must have been towards the end of last October.'

'And shortly after you found out she was pregnant.'

Jones looked at his wife. 'We thought it was a miracle because Edith was told she was unable to have children.'

Frederick thought back to what Rothschild had told him. He looked back at the couple. 'What will you do now you have lost your job?'

'We're moving to Leeds to be close to her parents. Her dad has offered me a job in a factory he runs. I wasn't looking forward to going there. Now I cannot wait to get out of this shithole. Besides Sir William owns this house and he wants us out.'

Frederick decided he had spent enough time in their company.

Mrs Jones wasn't going to reveal anything. The poor woman was in a state of shock.

'Thank you for speaking to me Mr Jones I hope you and your wife can find peace with all this.'

Jones showed Frederick to the door.

Chapter 21

Cambridge University – 4:52pm
Wednesday 17th September 1952

'Good afternoon Professor I trust your little visit up north bore knowledgeable fruit.'

Frederick was just about to get into his car. He glared at Rothschild and then glanced around to see who was in the vicinity.

'Please Professor do you think I would come here if I knew we were being watched.'

'That's not very reassuring Doctor.' Frederick snapped. 'I took a great risk going up to Ripley.'

'And what did you discover?'

'The woman was extremely traumatised. Her husband said she's hardly spoken a word since the incident.'

'What else did the husband say?'

'He admitted it wasn't the first time she had gone missing.' Frederick revealed. 'She disappeared for nearly a day last year. He also mentioned she was unable to have children before her first disappearance.'

'Yet shortly after she came back this woman became pregnant.' Rothschild added.

'Yes, but something tells me you already knew that.' Frederick said.

'I can tell you this case is not new. Similar incidents have happened all over the world.'

'Ok then Doctor humour me. How is it a woman unable to give birth suddenly became pregnant after a short visit to the local woods?'

'I thought that would be obvious to you by now Professor.' Rothschild replied.

'She became pregnant by a flying saucer.' Frederick

restrained from laughing. 'Do you have any idea how absurd that sounds?'

'Several weeks ago Professor you told me flying saucers were nonsense. But now you have seen these things for yourself. Is it so hard to go one step further and speculate these craft are being piloted by creatures from another world?'

Frederick remembered what Jones had said about his wife's nightmares. 'Mr Jones did mention his wife was having nightmares. Large black lifeless eyes staring through an open window.'

'Yes, a common description of the occupants of these craft.'

Frederick shook his head. 'The notion that this woman became pregnant as a result of contact with a creature from another world is too incredible to believe, despite what I have seen.'

'I understand your scepticism Professor but consider this. Our world is filled with technological wonders. The invention of radar helped protect these shores from Hitler's marauding armies. But it has also revealed new mysteries. In the past people mistook unidentified flying objects as visions or falling stars. Now technology has demonstrated these things are anything but. They are as real as you and I standing here. Believe me when I say this Professor. Encounters with flying saucers and beings from another world are nothing new.'

Frederick stood looking at Rothschild feeling like a young boy again being lectured. 'What now?'

'The offer is still open to join our group.'

Frederick looked out across Trinity College. 'I'll need a little time to make my decision. I cannot suddenly jump into something I might regret.'

'Wise words Professor Frederick.' Rothschild replied with a thoughtful tone. 'We have no interest in your government's secrets if that is your main concern. Our interests lay beyond the realm of petty government decision making. We had plans to approach you last year, just after you were awarded your Nobel prize in physics. Our group feels your knowledge is best served to advance mankind peacefully not through the development of modern warfare. I promise you if you decide to join our group you will get the opportunity to talk freely with us about any scientific theory you have. No prejudice and no restrictions. We will find answers to every question you have. That's what our group is about. Until next time Professor.' Rothschild tipped his hat before walking away.

Chapter 22

HMS Illustrious – Norwegian Sea – 1:42pm
Thursday 25th September 1952

Frederick wiped his brow before flushing the toilet. It was his fourth trip but it did nothing to calm his stomach. Frederick was never fond of boats. He tried his best to convince Chambers to send another committee member. However, Chambers refused to budge on the matter and insisted Frederick should join Admiral Berkshire on a naval exercise.

A number of UFOs had been reported by Royal Navy personnel operating in the North Sea.

Despite Frederick's reluctance and busy schedule at Cambridge he was eventually persuaded into going. Chambers had also acquired a film camera which he insisted would be used if any major sighting took place.

Lord Admiral Anthony Berkshire stood on the command deck of HMS Illustrious scanning the horizon with his binoculars. The Illustrious and her escorts were a small part of a massive naval exercise codenamed Mainbrace. Amongst the nations taking part were the United States, Canada, France, Denmark, Norway, Portugal, Netherlands, and Belgium.

The entire fleet was spread out over an area of 30 square miles. The military flotilla consisted of ten Aircraft Carriers with fighter support. Two Battleships, six Cruisers, ninety six escort ships, and thirty three submarines as well as several dozen other ships which had been committed to this enormous fleet.

Vampire jets were parked up on the flight deck of the Illustrious and naval personnel hurried about the ship performing their day to day duties.

Frederick returned to the bridge to join Admiral Berkshire who delighted at seeing the pale colour in his face.

'Don't worry Professor you will soon grow some sea legs.'

'I'd rather stay on dry land thank you Admiral.' Frederick replied trying not to swallow.

The weather was cloudy with good visibility and despite Frederick's unsettled stomach the sea was a calm battleship grey. The American Aircraft Carrier USS Franklyn D Roosevelt was visible on the horizon.

The Illustrious had just taken part in a mock battle in which a simulated attack was carried out by the Americans.

Berkshire smiled as he looked out to sea. He had never been fond of promotion and always felt his place was on the deck of a ship not stuck behind some bloody desk in Whitehall. He missed the sea and always jumped at the chance to step aboard any ship.

Standing at the Admiral's side was commanding Officer Timothy Mayflower a World War Two veteran. The ship's communications personnel sat at their posts talking and coordinating battle drills with other sea traffic.

A loud squawk sounded over the main speaker and the voice of a pilot could be heard.

'Illustrious this is Golf Alpha Sierra, *over*.'

'Roger golf alpha.' A young communications officer replied.

'I'm twenty-seven miles out and tracking five unidentified contacts heading towards your location, *over*.'

Berkshire and Frederick took up position behind the communications officer and peered into the radarscope.

'Roger that golf alpha I'm tracking you and the contacts, stand by.'

Frederick looked at Berkshire. 'Do we have anything else in that area?'

The Admiral shook his head. 'Besides that lone vampire all other aircraft have been recalled.' The communications officer handed him the microphone. 'Golf alpha how far away are the contacts *over?*'

'I'd say about fifteen hundred feet above me, *over*.'

'What can you see, *over*?'

'They're flying in formation similar to the spots on a dice. They are circular in shape. The object at the centre of the formation is very large. I would say about a hundred and fifty feet in diameter maybe more. The smaller objects look as if they're flying escort, *over*.'

'Roger that Golf Alpha stand by.' Berkshire looked at another communications officer. 'Scramble four of our vampires.'

The officer acknowledged the order.

Less than ten minutes later four Vampire jets screamed off the flight deck heading out to sea.

Another communications officer handed a sheet of paper to Commander Mayflower who joined Berkshire and Frederick. 'The Americans have just scrambled six of their fighters and the USS Midway is heading for our area.'

Berkshire moved to the command deck window and peered through his binoculars. The outline of another aircraft carrier could be seen heading towards the position of the Roosevelt.

'Contact our escorts, have them form a tight formation around us. What's the position of the HMS Eagle?'

'She's deployed at the outer edges of the fleet.' Mayflower replied.

'Contact her and brief her on the situation. Tell her to have her vampires on standby.'

Berkshire continued to peer through his binoculars mulling the situation over in his head. He thought back to the committee's first meeting and his defiance with what Richard Wilks had suggested. 'Huh, pure fantasy.' He muttered to himself before looking at Frederick. 'Professor may I have a word please.'

Both the Admiral and Frederick retreated to the captain's office. Berkshire shut the door behind them. 'I need to know if you have any thoughts about what could be heading for our position.'

Frederick shrugged. 'I have no idea what we are about to face.'

'Given your experience at Church Fenton. I thought you might be able to lend some insight on what we could be up against.'

'I trust you read the report I submitted.'

Berkshire nodded. 'I just want to know if you have anything extra to offer this moment in time.'

'I'm afraid I don't Admiral.' Frederick said. 'I do not think we are in any immediate danger if that's your concern.'

'No, but I am relieved to know you are confident we are not in any kind of peril.'

Both men returned to the bridge and Berkshire resumed looking through his binoculars. He looked out across the grey ocean in the direction of the approaching Vampire. An object came into focus. Berkshire felt an icy cold shiver race down his spine. The object was circular in shape, but what disturbed him was its size. Four smaller objects then came into view.

The command crew of the carrier continued to talk to the aircraft that had been scrambled. The lone vampire had joined them and were now keeping pace with the five craft.

Frederick had been handed a pair of binoculars and stared at amazement at the sight on the horizon. For the first time since coming on board he forgot about his sea sickness.

'Good lord!' Mayflower exclaimed as he looked out of the window.

Some of the command personnel also looked mesmerized by the approaching objects.

Within a few minutes Berkshire, Frederick, and Mayflower were on the flight deck of the Illustrious.

A junior bridge officer was already on the flight deck with the film camera which was pointed in the direction of the approaching objects. Six escort ships had pulled up on both sides of the aircraft carrier.

The four smaller UFOs had broken away from the larger UFO and fanned out heading towards the two American Aircraft Carriers.

Berkshire looked at Mayflower. 'Set a course for the Roosevelt then order our escorts to do the same. Send a message, we are on our way to assist in any way we can.'

Mayflower scurried back towards the command deck.

A short time later the Illustrious started to turn her bow towards the American Aircraft Carrier.

Frederick couldn't help smiling at the irony the situation presented. He glanced at Berkshire. 'Still think it's a load of old cobblers?'

Chapter 23

1:56pm

Admiral Berkshire glared at the enormous object which had manoeuvred between the HMS Illustrious, the USS Roosevelt, and the fast approaching USS Midway.

The object hovered approximately 200 feet above the sea and was accompanied by a low pitched humming sound. Static electricity crackled all around.

A frigate lay underneath the shadow of the craft. Its size made the frigate look like a model boat.

The four smaller objects were hovering just above the flight deck of the Roosevelt.

The Illustrious was still too far away for Berkshire to get a clear view of what was going on.

'This static interference is what happened at Church Fenton. It doesn't seem to be affecting our instruments.' Frederick revealed.

'I don't know whether to take that as good or bad news Professor.' Berkshire said still peering through his binoculars.

Several minutes past as the Illustrious sped towards the US Carrier.

The objects still hung over the Roosevelt's flight deck. The larger object had moved off and hung motionless at the edge of the fleet.

Berkshire and Frederick returned to the bridge to get a higher vantage point. Whilst on the flight deck Frederick had used all the film in the still camera he had brought with him.

'Sir I'm receiving a message from the Roosevelt. They're ordering us to change course and remain at a distance of seven miles.' One of the communication officers relayed.

'Ask them why.' Berkshire ordered.

The com officer shook his head. 'I'm not getting a response

sir. They just keep repeating the message maintain a distance of seven miles.' The colour drained from his face. 'Or they will open fire on us.'

Berkshire stared at the carrier in the distance. 'Maintain our speed and course.'

'With all due respect sir.' Captain Mayflower said.

'I said maintain our course and speed!' Berkshire barked cutting Mayflower off in mid-stream.

Frederick glanced at Berkshire remaining silent.

The Illustrious carried on its course for a few minutes before the communications officer spoke again. 'They're still repeating the warning sir.'

Berkshire grabbed his binoculars and scanned the horizon. Five US navy jets were approaching the Illustrious and her escorts.

Another bridge officer approached handing a piece of paper to Mayflower.

'According to this, sonar is tracking three objects in the water.'

'Subs.' Berkshire stated.

Mayflower nodded. 'But they're ignoring all attempts to contact them.'

Berkshire sensed his stomach tighten.

The US jets were now on top of the British fleet.

Frederick looked on as they fanned out.

Without warning the lead jet screamed by the Illustrious strafing the water with its machine gun.

Berkshire cursed under his breath; he was hoping the Americans were just bluffing. 'All stop!' He ordered.

'All stop!' Mayflower repeated. 'Contact our escorts and tell them to take up defensive positions.'

'Sir off our port bow submarine surfacing!' A bridge officer shouted.

Berkshire glared at the surface water breaking as the top of a submarine glided silently from beneath the calm sea.

Everyone on the bridge could make out the unmistakable Red Star visible on the submarine's side.

'I'd say things have got a little more interesting.' Frederick remarked.

Chapter 24

2:27pm

Admiral Berkshire picked up the small shot glass of vodka which had been placed in front of him taking a sip. Shortly after the Russian submarine had surfaced, the HMS Illustrious had received a message requesting a meeting with the senior ranking officer on the carrier. Despite Mayflower's protests Berkshire and Frederick decided to meet with the sub's commander.

Berkshire and Frederick boarded a small boat with an armed escort and headed over to the Soviet Foxtrot Class submarine. They were greeted by the sub's commanding officer. Both Frederick and Berkshire were informed a high-ranking Soviet military officer was on board ready to greet them.

Colonel Yuri Konev gripped his glass and swallowed the contents in one gulp before pouring out another glass.

The compartment Frederick and Berkshire were shown to was cramped and the heavy smell of diesel hung in the air.

Konev stared hard at the Admiral.

Unlike admiral Berkshire Frederick declined a glass of vodka. He noted the way the Colonel bolted his glass. 'I like a tipple every now and then Colonel but the way you consume that stuff. It will be the death of you.' He said politely.

Konev smiled. 'This submarine will be the death of us all if we remain on board too long.'

Berkshire sipped from his glass again.

Konev stared at Berkshire. 'I must say Admiral, I am surprised to see such a high ranking officer on a naval exercise. Who is your companion?'

'This is Professor Ralph Frederick; he is a guest of mine and an expert in international affairs. As for me being here

Colonel, you know how it is. I like to stretch my old sea legs every now and then. I thought this little exercise of ours would be a perfect opportunity.'

Konev poured another glass. 'Since when does a naval exercise include visitors from another planet?'

'We don't know what's going on yet. I think it's unwise to jump to any outlandish conclusions don't you Colonel.' Frederick stated.

Konev slammed his glass down hard on the table glaring at Frederick. 'I take it you have seen what is taking place on the deck of the Roosevelt.'

'We have.' Berkshire replied unmoved by the Colonel's dark tone.

'Are you also aware of who's on board the carrier?'

'I don't quite follow you Colonel.'

Konev poured another glass. He put it to his lips and looked at Berkshire. 'Former allied Commanding Chief, General Eisenhower.'

Berkshire glanced at Frederick then looked back at the Colonel. 'And how is it you know this Colonel?'

'The Soviet Union is not as backward as you assume. I have been given direct orders from Comrade Stalin himself to intervene in this meeting. Surely it's no coincidence the former commander of allied forces in Europe is aboard that aircraft carrier. And is now making contact with an intelligent species from another planet.'

'As I've just stated Colonel it's a little too early to go jumping to conclusions.' Frederick added.

'And yet Professor Frederick it's happening as we speak. Plus US navy jets just opened fired on your carrier.'

Berkshire stared at Konev taking another sip from his glass.

'How we came across this information is not important. What I can tell you Admiral is this so-called naval exercise NATO has put together is more than just a jolly jaunt. The

Americans knew exactly what was going to happen and now they're playing you for fools.'

Frederick admitted to himself the Colonel was right and time was also passing quickly. 'What do you expect us to do about it Colonel?'

'We form an alliance.' Konev replied.

'I beg your pardon.' Berkshire could barely stop himself from laughing.

'We blockade the Americans from leaving the area and demand they tell us everything.'

'You realise the Americans will see this as an act of aggression. With all what's happening in Korea at the moment, I'm not sure that's a good idea.' Berkshire said.

'What is your suggestion Admiral? We sit here while America conducts negotiations for its own interests.' Konev stood. 'Come, let us see what is happening up top.'

Berkshire set his glass down and followed Frederick and Konev through the cramped submarine. Their armed escort followed close behind.

The three men stood on the submarine deck looking over at the US aircraft carrier. The objects still hovered over her flight deck. US jets could be heard in the distance as they patrolled the fleet looking for signs of any approaching ships.

The HMS Eagle had moved closer to the Illustrious.

Berkshire looked over at the activity on the Roosevelt.

The four objects started to move away quickly, accelerating across the bow of the Illustrious at breakneck speed. They headed towards the huge object which sat motionless the whole time to regroup. In a blink of an eye all five objects accelerated vertically and disappeared into the cloud layer.

Berkshire thought for a few seconds before speaking. 'Colonel how many subs do you have at your disposal?'

'We have three which you have probably detected plus five more at the edge of your fleet.'

'I want you to contact them and deploy them in a circle around the fleet. Under no circumstances are your subs to take any further action.'

US Navy jets screamed overhead heading back to the Roosevelt where they landed on the flight deck.

Berkshire peered through his binoculars. 'It looks like they're getting ready to go.' He lowered his binoculars and looked at Konev. 'Send that order then join me on the Illustrious.'

Chapter 25

3:43pm

'Are you sure this is a good idea?' Frederick asked when he got the chance.

'What do you suggest we do Professor? You just witnessed what happened. What's your take on this?'

Frederick pursed his lips. 'We will have to tread carefully. Relations between America and the Soviet Union are not exactly Rosie. We cannot afford an incident.'

'Your concern is noted Professor.'

The Illustrious had turned her bow towards the Roosevelt which was now heading out of the exercise area.

Captain Mayflower glared at Konev and the two Russian officers flanking him.

Berkshire looked out over the ocean at the stern of the Roosevelt. 'Have you contacted the HMS Eagle?'

Mayflower looked away from Konev and the two men. 'Yes sir, she's standing by.'

'Good.' Berkshire replied. He glanced over at Konev who was looking around the bridge. 'Taking everything in are we Colonel.'

Konev smiled. 'I have to admit this carrier is very impressive.'

'The best in Her Majesty's fleet.' Berkshire boasted. 'I take it your subs will be in position by now.'

'Yes they should be.'

'Captain Mayflower, contact the Eagle and have her and her escorts move into position.' Berkshire ordered.

'Sir we're getting a message from the Roosevelt.' A com officer called out. 'They're ordering us to break off pursuit and re-join the fleet.'

'Maintain our course and speed.' Berkshire commanded.

'Then send a message to the FDR. This is Admiral Berkshire of Her Majesty's Royal Navy. You are to come to a complete stop and your commanding officer is to come aboard immediately.'

The Roosevelt continued her course. The HMS eagle came into view with four frigates cutting across her bow.'

'Sir the FDR is sending another message ordering the Eagle to move aside.'

Berkshire walked over to the com officer and grabbed the microphone. 'This is Admiral Anthony Berkshire of Her Majesty's Royal Navy. I'm ordering you to come to a complete stop.'

No answer.

The Illustrious sped on flanked by the frigates. In the distance American jet fighters could be seen taking off from the FDRs flight deck.

Berkshire spoke again. 'I repeat this is Admiral Berkshire of Her Majesty's Royal Navy. You are ordered to come to a full stop.

Still no answer.

Berkshire looked at Konev and signalled him over. He handed the Colonel the mike who leaned over and flicked a switch and slowly turned a dial. A few seconds of silence followed before the Colonel gave an order in Russian.

Frederick looked on, unsure whether to believe what he was witnessing.

The HMS Eagle was now blocking the path of the FDR which cut through the grey sea. Her fighters screamed towards the British carrier.

Suddenly the water in front of the Eagle began to churn and two black Russian submarines surfaced.

The admiral peered through his binoculars and smiled. 'They're slowing.'

Chapter 26

4:25pm.

Rear Admiral Sidney Souers glared at Konev who sat across a large table. Souers had come on board the Illustrious with a heavily armed escort and had protested the minute he boarded.

'You realise what you have done can be considered as an act of war.' He continued to glare at Konev.

'And so can firing on one of her Majesty's aircraft carriers Admiral.' Berkshire remarked.

Souers looked at Berkshire. 'We were never going to fire directly at your carrier.'

'But you did fire across our bow.' Frederick pointed out.

'A warning shot.'

'I've never heard such nonsense even from an American.' Konev scoffed. 'This is ridiculous; just tell us what happened on your carrier earlier this afternoon. And why Eisenhower is not here instead of you.'

'Just who invited you to this party Comrade?' Souers seethed. 'I don't recall the Soviet Navy being part of this exercise.'

'Neither were those creatures from another world you made contact with.'

Souers remained silent for a few seconds before answering. 'What you saw Colonel was a highly classified military project involving a new kind of aircraft we're developing.'

'As you Americans like to say Admiral, horseshit!' Konev stated. 'We know Eisenhower is on board. Like I have said to the British, Russian intelligence is not that backward.'

'Let's not let things get out of hand here gentlemen.' Frederick interrupted. He looked at Souers. 'Admiral Souers we all witnessed what just transpired and now have the events on film. There are thousands of witnesses on board the ships in the fleet. It would be beneficial for us all if you share what you know with us.'

Souers glanced at Konev. 'I'm afraid Professor I am under strict orders not to reveal anything about what you witnessed.'

'Huh, typical American selfishness.' Konev barked.

'Fuck you, you commie prick!' Souers shot back.

Konev jumped to his feet. 'You are treading on thin ice Admiral. I have eight submarines at my command. I could sink your carrier in a heartbeat.'

'And risk all-out war. Go ahead we both know who will come out on top.'

Berkshire slammed a clenched fist down on the table causing both men to jump. 'That's enough! I will not have this sort of behaviour aboard a ship of Her Majesty's Royal Navy. Colonel sit down please.'

Konev slumped down in his chair like a sulking child.

'If you are not willing to share vital intelligence on what these objects are then take this message back to your superiors. Both the governments of the Soviet Union and Great Britain will be launching a full enquiry into the events that have transpired here today. A very public enquiry with film reel and all.'

Souers smiled at the Admiral. 'I'm afraid you're not a very good poker player Admiral. We know both your governments have covert projects involving flying saucers. By exposing us you will be exposing yourselves.'

'Then you admit they are not of this world!' Konev announced triumphantly.

Souers smiled then got to his feet. He put on his officers cap. 'It's been a real pleasure gentlemen.' He then headed towards the door.

Konev also stood and glared at Berkshire. 'This isn't over

admiral.' He then strolled towards the door.

'Colonel.' Berkshire called after him.

Konev turned to face Berkshire.

'He's right you know. We cannot afford another world war. Not after what we went through with the last war.'

Konev took in a lung full of air and nodded before disappearing out of the door.

Chapter 27

Whitehall – London – 12:13pm
Wednesday 1st October 1952

All committee members sat in silence staring at the projector screen which displayed the film which was taken a few days earlier. After the incident with both the Americans and Russians Berkshire ordered the Illustrious home.

Despite being without sound the film spoke volumes to the men in the room.

'What do you suppose we do about any witnesses?' Dr Alan Good asked. 'With all those ships in the immediate area news of this encounter is bound to get out.'

'We are dealing with the matter in regards to Royal Naval personnel and monitoring the press for any unwanted publicity. As for other countries taking part in the exercise it's still unclear. Our listening posts throughout Europe have been monitoring news broadcasts and printed news. So far nothing has turned up. I think other governments are as keen as we are to keep a lid on this.' Morris Stanford explained.

'What disturbs me about this film.' Norman Canning said. 'Is the part the Americans played. Firing on one of Her Majesty's warships shouldn't go unpunished.'

'It certainly undermines this so-called special relationship the Prime Minister likes to refer to.' Sir Harold Bates said. He looked at Stanford. 'Any news from the US Embassy.'

Stanford shook his head. 'Not a peep I'm afraid. Given the information Anthony and Ralph supplied I think this was more of an embarrassment for the Yanks.'

'You mean we caught them with their trousers down.' Chambers said.

'And given the very nature of this film, it points towards the possibility this was not their first meeting with these creatures.' Stanford said.

'But why the public display?' Richard Wilks asked. 'Surely the Americans have as good as any reason to keep this a secret.'

Frederick considered Wilks' statement. 'Do you suppose the Americans had prior knowledge Soviet subs were patrolling the area?' His question was directed at Admiral Berkshire who had been quiet during the meeting.

'It's possible.' Berkshire replied.

'What are you suggesting Ralph?' Chambers asked.

'Perhaps the Yanks did plan that meeting on purpose. Not so much for our benefit but as a display for the Soviets. A warning, they not only have allies on this planet but beyond. Colonel Konev speculated the Americans might have put on a show.'

Richard Wilks shook his head. 'Surely a more advanced civilisation would be above trivial matters such as planet superiority.'

'Who's to say the Americans didn't lie to whoever it was they met with. A cock and bull story about bringing many nations together to witness the event for the sake of peace. But in reality, a propaganda stunt put on for the Soviet elite to witness. An incident like that would have wide reaching political implications and could affect the outcome of any conflict. Russia might think twice about attacking the US if they know these beings or whatever you want to call them are keeping a watchful eye on what's happening.'

'It's a good suggestion Ralph.' Chambers commented. 'But until we have solid evidence the Americans have some sort of relationship with these creatures, I'm afraid we are still at square one. And the longer the Yanks stay silent the longer we will be stuck there.'

Other members nodded in silent agreement.

'This film is startling and would suggest the Americans have some sort of relationship.' Chambers looked at Stanford.

'How much do we know about this Rear Adm. Sidney Souers and this Colonel Yuri Konev.'

'Souers was appointed as the first Director of Central Intelligence by President Truman back in 1946. Before that, he was with naval intelligence. As for Konev he's much more interesting. He was head of the Russian Army and science research division. His job was to gather whatever technology the Nazis left behind. He has two children who are prominent scientists. Although no one in scientific circles has seen or heard from his daughter in a few years.' Stanford looked at the document in front of him. 'Her name is Anna Vilenko.'

The name jogged Frederick's memory. 'I have heard of Doctor Vilenko. She was an up and coming physicist. Unfortunately, because she is a woman the Soviet Scientific elite have made her life extremely difficult. I read some of her work, remarkable stuff.'

'Where exactly does this put the subject of God?' Berkshire interrupted.

All the other committee members looked at him.

'What are you trying to say Anthony.' Chambers asked.

Berkshire indicated to the projector screen. 'This film goes far beyond the political and military landscape. We have to consider the impact this has on religion. I don't know if any of you are familiar with the bible but it doesn't exactly mention creatures from another world. There are hundreds of millions of people around the world who have a strong belief system. Are we just going to abandon teachings which have been passed down for thousands of years?'

Berkshire's words were greeted with a wall of silence.

'A revelation such as this would decimate many of the main religions.' Richard Wilks said.

'Something you would be more than happy with I suppose Professor Wilks.' Berkshire remarked bluntly.

'Not at all Admiral, I fear it could tear this world apart if religion was suddenly brought into question. Disclosure of this nature could set the religious world on fire. This is something I am not eager to see.'

'I think gentlemen we need to leave the philosophical debate for another time. We have more pressing matters, no disrespect to your faith of course Admiral. We have to decide whether to trust the Americans concerning their involvement over this affair.'

'I'd like to know what the Prime Minister is going to make of this film.' Frederick asked.

'I don't think the PM needs to see this film yet.' Stanford replied. 'No sense in getting the old man's feathers ruffled. Besides he's not in the best of health at the moment, both physical and political.'

'Are you suggesting we lie to him?' Dr Arthur Lloyd said.

'Not at all, I'm merely suggesting we don't show him this film straight away. We'll just give him the report on paper so he can read it in his own time.'

'It sounds as if you want to break away from government leadership.' Frederick stated.

'It's a course of action which could be beneficial to our group. The less people involved means it's unlikely secrets get out. The defection of Burgess and Mclean only highlights the need for absolute secrecy.'

'But Churchill established this group on the condition we report directly to him while he is Prime Minister.' Frederick said.

'And we will honour that agreement to a certain extent. Nevertheless, we must think of the future. The Prime Minister's enemies are gathering. He will not be in office much longer. His leadership during the war was invaluable, he gave the nation hope. The world has changed dramatically since the war. As a peacetime Prime Minister he doesn't fit in. After he is out of office, we cut all ties with government bureaucracy.' Stanford noted the look on Frederick's face. 'It's for the best Ralph. I'm as fond of the old man as everyone else in this room. But given the evidence displayed here today we have to act in a positive manner. If the Americans are sneaking behind our backs then I suggest we do the same. Cutting government ties would minimise the risk of exposure.'

'As much as I hate to admit it Morris you are right.' Air Marshal Ian Morgan said. 'I hate keeping anything from the old man. However, if there is a greater good in taking this course of action then so be it.'

Stanford gave a satisfied nod. 'We will keep this film under lock and key and make time to study it further. Until then I suggest we adjourn for now until further notice.'

Chapter 28

Trinity College – Cambridge – 1:23pm
Friday 3rd October 1952

Frederick looked up and smiled at Norman Hinshelwood who had just knocked on his open door. 'Norman what a pleasant surprise.' Frederick greeted.

Hinshelwood entered the room and sat down opposite Frederick. 'I haven't seen you in a few months Ralph and since I was in town I thought I would catch up with you. See what you've been up to.'

'I've been keeping busy. You know how Cambridge life is.'

'Yes, Chester has been filling me in on events.' Hinshelwood remarked dryly.

Frederick recalled the brief conversation he had with Professor Osborne a few months earlier. He was about to say something but Hinshelwood beat him to it.

'I also spoke to the Prime Minister a few months back at the Royal society. He told me about the group he was setting up and your name was mentioned.'

'Really.' Frederick replied.

'We both know what the old man is like Ralph. I wouldn't get entrenched in this ridiculous notion concerning flying saucers and men from Mars.'

'Thank you for the advice Norman.'

'I wouldn't call it advice Ralph, more of a warning. You are in line for the chair at Cambridge. A respected member of the Royal society, not to mention a Nobel Prize winning physicist. Your involvement in a group which investigates flying saucer sightings could jeopardize all that.'

Frederick glared at Hinshelwood. 'Thank you for the warning Norman I shall take it into advisement.'

Chapter 29

RAF Topcliffe – North Yorkshire – 10:15pm
Saturday 4th October 1952

Corporal Patrick Summers stretched out his arms and let out a yawn that seemed to go on forever. The radar operator hated the night shift. A four month old copy of Picture Post kept his mind ticking over.

'Topcliffe this is Charlie Alpha victor, *over*.'

Summers grabbed the radio mike. 'Go ahead alpha victor.'

'We are tracking a target about five miles out from your position, *over*.'

'Say again Charlie Victor.'

'We've got a visual on another aircraft, *over*, what's on your radar?'

Summers stared into the radar tube. His face bathed in an eerie green glow. 'Stand by Charlie victor.' He stared at the tube again confused by what the pilot was claiming. 'Charlie victor I see only you, *over*.'

'Topcliffe there's definitely something up here. It's about two thousand feet above us at our two o'clock position, matching our speed and course, *over*.'

'Can you describe the aircraft, *over*.'

The radio crackled. 'It's rectangular in shape with rounded edges. It seems to be emitting green and blue lights, *over*.'

Summers knew there was a full moon that night as he had sneaked outside for a cigarette earlier. 'Charlie alpha can you see any markings on the aircraft, *over?*'

'There are no markings to identify the aircraft.'

'What's the size of the object, *over?*.'

'it's big.'

'How big, *Over?*'

The crackling grew more prominent. 'About one hundred

feet long.'

Summers stared at his radar screen again. 'Did you say one hundred feet, *Over?*'

'Roger that Topcliffe requesting further instructions *over.*'

Summers continued to scrutinise the radarscope.

'Repeat Topcliffe requesting further instructions. The object should be closing in on your position within seven minutes.'

The young corporal looked around for the telephone receiver. He picked it up and dialled quickly.

Sergeant Frankie Williams grabbed the ringing telephone. 'Williams!'

'Sir this is Corporal Summers up at the tower. Two of our Vampire jets report they have a visual on an unidentified object.'

'I'll be right there.'

Summers was still hypnotised by the radar tube when Williams marched in and looked over the corporal's shoulder.

'Topcliffe you should now see the object heading from a northerly direction.' The Vampire pilot advised.

Both men looked out of the window. The full moon made it possible to see down the runway and a tree line in the distance. As both men looked, they could see a single light approaching fast from the direction the pilot had said. It descended just above the pine treetops.

The sound of the two jet fighters could be heard closing fast.

The object however was faster.

As Summers and Williams looked on in amazement the object sped down the runway and past the tower at incredible speed before climbing into the moonlit sky. Several seconds later the two jet fighters screamed down the runway and also climbed into the sky in pursuit of the UFO. The radio continued to crackle.

'Tower do you have a visual?'

Williams grabbed the mike. 'Charlie Victor do not engage the target. Repeat do not engage the target. Break off your pursuit, *over*.'

Static came back over the radio. Summers walked to the window and looked straight up. 'Look!' He shouted out.

Williams dropped the mike and rushed to his side. The UFO plummeted in a straight line and then stopped instantaneously hovering around thirty feet off the runway. Both Summers and Williams backed away from the window.

As the pilot had described, the object was around 100 feet long by about 30 feet in height. Cylindrical in shape with two bright green lights at each end.

The UFO dwarfed the radar tower. The object glided to the left illuminating the control room.

Summers and Williams stood rooted to the spot. Suddenly the object released an intense burst of light. Both men shielded their eyes. After a few brief seconds the room returned to normal and the object was gone.

Williams returned to the mike. 'Charlie victor do you still have a visual *over*.' Static was the only thing that made any sound. 'Charlie victor what's your position, *over*? Charlie victor come in. Charlie victor where are you, *over*?'

Chapter 30

Air Ministry – Whitehall – 11:34am
Sunday 5th October 1952

Wing Commander Ian Morgan glanced around at the assembled committee members who had managed to attend at short notice. 'There was an incident last night at RAF Topcliffe in North Yorkshire involving two vampire aircraft and the pursuit of one of these UFOs. The result being the loss of both aircraft.'

'Where did they go down?' Doctor Alan Good asked.

'They didn't crash, they vanished.' Morgan revealed. 'Radar at Topcliffe tried to regain contact but they were gone. This is definitely something new. Jet fighters being snatched out of thin air doesn't bear thinking about.'

All eyes fixed on Professor Wilks who drummed his fingers on the conference table.

'Professor Wilks.' Morgan asked. 'Do you have any theories on what could have happened to those aircraft?'

'I've been reading the report from the ground crew at Topcliffe. The object they describe is large enough to swallow two jets.'

'In my book taking two aircraft is a hostile act.' Lord Anthony Berkshire said. 'I think we should implement a shoot on sight policy.'

'That is not a good idea.' Wilks replied. 'These craft have the ability to take our aircraft, they are obviously more advanced. Our weaponry might not be capable of bringing down one of these craft.'

'So you suggest we just let these things take our military hardware at will.' Berkshire responded scornfully. 'Find out our weaknesses.'

'I'm merely suggesting we do not engage these objects in

any manner. We collect all radar data and witness accounts so we can come up with an effective defence strategy.'

'According to the report nothing was picked up on radar which suggests these objects can elude detection.' Morgan said.

'We can't let these UFOs just invade our airspace it makes us look weak.' Berkshire stated.

'I don't see that we have any choice.' Wilks replied. 'These craft are way beyond anything we have. Studying them will give us a chance to learn more about their capability.'

'And in the meantime, they're just free to fly about our airspace taking whatever they want.'

Wilks looked at Berkshire. 'I know it may be hard for you to deal with Ian. But at our current state of technology there is nothing we can do. I am convinced whatever took our aircraft last night is not planning an attack on the UK.'

'How can you be so sure?'

'We are talking about advanced technology here. Way beyond anything we have. I think whatever these UFOs are they could have quite easily taken us over already. I will go up to Topcliffe with Ralph to collect intelligence.'

Chapter 31

Trinity College – Cambridge – 10:31am
Monday 6th October 1952

'Dead, what do you mean dead?' Frederick demanded to know. He scribbled furiously glancing up as Professor Wilks entered the room. 'Ok thank you flight lieutenant Fletcher, I will look into it.' He put the phone down and momentarily pondered over the notes he had just scribbled.

'Something the matter Ralph?'

Frederick took a moment to answer his friend. 'The woman I investigated at the centre of the flying saucer kidnapping died last week.'

'Good lord!'

'That's only half of it. Her husband Brian Jones apparently committed suicide. He was found hanging in the local wood yesterday morning. I'm flying up there to see if I can get to the bottom of this matter. We'll also interview the tower personnel at Topcliffe regarding their encounter.'

'I am willing to tag along if you don't mind the company.' Wilks offered.

'Not at all.' Frederick said. 'The more people we can expose this mystery to the better.'

Ripley Castle – North Yorkshire – 1 56pm
Thursday 9th October 1952

After a brief spell at RAF Topcliffe interviewing two air force officers Frederick and Wilks met up with flight lieutenant Fletcher who drove them up to Ripley. Frederick decided he would speak to Sir William ingles about the Jones'.

Sir Ingles' butler showed them through to the drawing room of the castle where the old man was waiting for them.

'Sir William thank you for meeting us today.' Frederick

stepped forward offering his hand.

'You can dispense with the pleasantries Professor, what is it you want?' Ingles barked glaring behind him at Professor Wilks and flight lieutenant Fletcher.

'We are here to offer help regarding the recent deaths of Mr and Mrs Jones.'

'Really, would you care to explain since you and the Air Ministry showed up three people have died.'

'The Air Ministry is just as shocked as everyone else and wish to get to the bottom of this matter.'

'You just want to know more about their UFO encounter which is why you have come to see me.'

'Well you did have the most contact with them. And with all due respect Sir William you did throw them out of your castle when Mr Jones refused to cooperate any more with your questioning. You also fired him from his job.'

'What are you suggesting Professor, I was responsible for their deaths?' Ingles said in a raised voice.

'No I'm not, but perhaps if you would have given them a bit of a respite from your constant prodding then they would have stayed in the safety of your castle.'

'How dare you, get out immediately!' Ingles exploded.

Wilks stepped forward. 'Gentlemen that's enough! Playing the blame game will not get us anywhere.' He looked at Ingles. 'Please Sir William we need the keys to the Jones' cottage so we can conduct our own investigation.'

'The police have already been over the place thoroughly. It's obvious what happened. Mrs Jones collapsed last week and died as a result of some kind of haemorrhage. Overcome with grief her husband took his own life on Saturday.'

'I'm sure the police have been thorough in their investigation. But it won't hurt if we have a look as well.' He smiled at Ingles who eventually nodded.

Chapter 32

2:32pm

Frederick turned the key in the front door of the terraced cottage. The door creaked open and both men slipped quietly through.

Fletcher had returned to the hotel to order ahead for a late lunch.

The hallway was dark, Frederick tried a light switch. 'The electric has been cut off.'

'Charming landlord Sir Ingles.' Wilks remarked.

Both men made their way to the living room which had been left undisturbed by the investigating police.

'At least the people are honest around here.' Wilks said pointing to a small carriage clock on the mantelpiece above the fireplace.

Underneath were the three pound notes Frederick had given Jones.

Wilks looked down at a small table at a folded piece of paper sat on an envelope. 'It looks as if a national newspaper was interested in the Jones' story.' He handed the letter to Frederick.

'It's from Reg Cudlipp editor at the News of the World.' Frederick recalled what Jones had said to him.

A loud thud caused both men to look up towards the ceiling. 'Looks like we have some company.' Wilks said.

As they turned towards the living room door Frederick and Wilks came face to face with a tall man standing in the doorway pointing a small pistol. He held out his hand. 'The letter please Professor Frederick.' His American accent was clearly evident.

Frederick hesitated staring at the man before recollecting where he had seen him before. It was one of the two men posing as RAF officers he and flight lieutenant Fletcher had encountered several weeks earlier.

'The letter now Professor!' He demanded holding out his hand.

Frederick stepped forward and reluctantly handed over the letter.

'Who are you?' Wilks asked.

'Someone who gets what they want Professor Wilks.'

'And how is it you know us?' Frederick questioned.

The man smiled as he slipped the letter into his inside pocket. 'Let's just say I'm in a position to know quite a lot of things.'

His accomplice appeared by his side.

'You realise our government will not stand for this nonsense.' Frederick protested. 'You have no right to go traipsing all over the place invading people's lives.' Frederick made eye contact with the man who killed the doctor. 'Murdering whoever gets in your way.'

'Check your facts Professor.' The American said.

'What exactly is that supposed to mean?' Frederick replied.

Both men remained silent and stepped backed towards the door. They fled down the hallway and ran out into the street jumping into a jet black Ford Galaxy which sped off.

Wilks watched as the car disappeared from sight. 'We have to report this to the committee.'

Chapter 33

Whitehall – London – 11:37am
Saturday 11th October 1952

Lord Chambers looked out of the window towards Parliament Square.

Frederick had caught a train into London early that morning and found Professor Wilks was already outside Chambers' private office.

Ian Morgan and Morris Stanford were also there ready to greet Frederick and Wilks who gave a detailed account of the weekend's events.

'My guess is they were CIA agents poking their noses in our business.' Stanford suggested.

'I'm getting a little tired of the arrogance of the Americans.' Frederick said. 'The events at Operation Mainbrace proved they are purposely withholding information from us. Now secret service agents are traipsing all over the country stealing intelligence. Murdering innocent people, something must be done about this.'

'Check your facts.' Wilks said. 'That's what the American said when Ralph mentioned the doctor who was murdered.'

'There's nothing to check, the doctor's body went missing.' Chambers remarked.

Frederick thought back to his meeting with Rothschild and what he had revealed concerning the doctor. *'As for what happened to his body. let's just say he got up and walked away.'*

'If the Americans are running a secret project investigating UFOs then sooner or later they will reveal themselves.' Chambers remarked. 'What disturbs me is they knew you two by your names. This alone indicates we still have a leak. We need to find out how information is being fed to them. I suggest we keep an eye on who is coming and going at the US Embassy.'

'You realise if discovered it could cause a stink.' Stanford said.

'I don't think the Americans will complain if they want to keep their operation a secret.' Chambers replied.

'I'll organise some bodies to watch over the Embassy.' Stanford offered.

Chapter 34

RAF Topcliffe - North Yorkshire – 2:15am
Wednesday 3rd December 1952

Corporal Summers glanced towards the radio. For several seconds the speaker crackled and hissed before dying down again. Summers paid no attention and went back to writing out his nightly report.

Sergeant Frankie Williams entered the main control tower room with two hot mugs of coffee. 'There you go, that should keep you awake for the rest of the night, it's strong as hell.'

'Thank you sir.'

The radio started to crackle and hiss again. Williams looked over at it before glancing at the report Summers was writing.

'Repeat Topcliffe do you have a visual?' A loud voice suddenly boomed over the radio.

Summers and Williams both looked towards the radio.

'Topcliffe are you receiving, *over*? Do you have a visual on the target?'

Williams cautiously picked up the microphone.

Summers looked at the radarscope and saw two blips were clearly visible.

'Unidentified aircraft you are in UK airspace please respond *over*.' Williams called out.

'Topcliffe say again.' The voice asked.

'Repeat you are in restricted airspace state your identification, *over*.'

'Stop pissing us about Topcliffe this is Charlie Alpha Victor we are tracking an unidentified target heading for your position.' The pilot stopped. 'Topcliffe the object is no longer in range what does your scope show *over*?'

Summers and Williams glared at each other in complete

amazement.

Ministry of Defence – London – 12:47pm

Sir Malcolm Chambers and Sir Ian Morgan walked briskly down the corridor. 'This is an incredible turn of events.' Chambers said excitedly. 'Where are the two pilots now?'

'We have them confined to quarters at RAF Topcliffe. I've ordered they are to speak to no one until our team arrives.' Morgan explained.

'Good we'll keep them there and send Ralph. Professor Wilks and Doctor Lloyd will accompany him and make a full psychological assessment of these men.'

Chapter 35

RAF Topcliffe - North Yorkshire – 1:42pm
Friday 5th December 1952

Squadron Leader James Finch and flight Lieutenant Andrew Barker sat patiently in a small interview room which had been hastily prepared. Dr Lloyd looked at their flight report. Frederick and Wilks sat either side.

The committee members had been bundled into a refitted English Electric Canberra aircraft and flown straight to Topcliffe. Malcolm Chambers had instructed them to interview the two pilots. Then they were due to be taken to a larger base for a debriefing.

'So Squadron Leader Finch why don't you tell us exactly what you remember.' Frederick asked.

The pilot composed himself before speaking. 'We were on a routine patrol, flying at approximately eight thousand feet when my wingman Lieutenant Barker spotted an unidentified aircraft a few thousand feet above us.'

'What did you do?'

'We took immediate action and increased our height to match the aircraft's altitude.'

'Then what happened?' Lloyd quizzed.

'The aircraft increased its height so we levelled off and called it in to Topcliffe.'

'What did this unidentified aircraft look like?'

Finch seemed hesitant in answering.

'It's ok squadron leader we are not here to persecute you in any way. We just want to know what you saw.' Professor Wilks said reassuringly.

'It was big, a hundred feet in length with a pulsating light, green and blue if I recall correctly. I advised the control tower. It was heading in their direction. It started to pull away from us at incredible speed.'

'Any guesses to what sort of speed it was doing?' Lloyd enquired.

'I would say over one thousand miles per hour.' Finch looked at the other pilot who nodded agreeing with him.

'What happened next?'

'We continued to pursue the object as it flew over the base. The aircraft then started to climb.' Finch paused. 'We continued to give chase, then.' Finch stalled shaking his head. 'The next thing I knew the object just vanished. We headed back to base. I'm sorry I don't remember anything else.'

'That's ok you've provided us with more than enough.' Lloyd said. 'One more thing gentlemen do you know what today's date is?' He asked looking down at the flight report.

'Yes it's the twenty forth of September. It's on my flight report in front of you.'

'Oh yes of course it is.' Lloyd replied pretending just to notice. He smiled at both men. 'That will be all for the time being gentlemen. You will be escorted to Church Fenton for a debriefing then you should be allowed home.'

Barker spoke for the first time. 'Are we in some kind of trouble sir?'

'No not at all.' Lloyd smiled back at the men.

'It's just we hear all kinds of rumours regarding RAF boys seeing UFOs.'

'You've nothing to worry about Flight Lieutenant it's just routine questioning.'

'Thank you sir.' Barker said getting to his feet.

Frederick watched as the two pilots left the room accompanied by two military policemen.

'Opinions please gentlemen.' Lloyd invited.

'It's incredible.' Wilks stated. 'They have no awareness of the passage of time.'

'And they look in perfect health despite being missing for over two months. How is that even possible?' Frederick questioned.

Wilks shook his head. 'It's not, they should be dead through malnutrition.'

'I noticed the pilot hesitated when he tried to recall part of the incident. It's possible there could be some kind of suppressed memory hidden deep within the subconscious. They could start to remember in time. Hypnosis can help bring back suppressed memories.'

'What happens now?' Wilks asked.

'We will accompany them to Church Fenton for their debriefing, then it's straight back to London.' Frederick replied.

'How do you think they will react knowing they've been missing for over two months?' Wilks asked Lloyd.

Lloyd shrugged. 'We are in uncharted territory. They could either take the news very well or they could both suffer a complete psychological breakdown.'

What about their families? Both men have been missing for over two months. Their families have already been told they're dead.' Wilks pointed out.

'We need to come up with a strategy to deal with situations like this.' Lloyd replied.

Frederick looked at his watch. 'I suggest we get moving.'

A few minutes later Frederick and Wilks were driving an air force car behind an ambulance containing Dr Lloyd and the two RAF pilots.

Two lightly armed military police officers drove in the front of the ambulance.

'What do you think happened to them?' Frederick asked.

Wilks considered his question. 'They obviously went somewhere for over two months.'

'The woman I was investigating Edith Jones, was pregnant when she disappeared. When she came back the baby was gone.'

'Yes a most intriguing case.' Wilks commented.

'Do you have any theories?'

'Her child was obviously of interest to whoever or whatever took it. Some kind of breeding program perhaps.'

'It's too much to get my head around.' Frederick said. 'Even for a theoretical physicist. Creatures from another world just randomly taking civilians and air military personnel for experimentation.'

'Agreed, it's a lot to digest even for me. Which is why I'm keeping my opinion to myself at the moment Ralph. Can you imagine what Berkshire would say if I suggested the same thing to him.'

'I think admiral Berkshire is somewhat more open minded since the incident in the North Sea.' Frederick remarked.

Up ahead the ambulance braked sharply and stopped. Frederick and Wilks got out of their car. The doors to the ambulance opened and Dr Lloyd jumped out.

'What's going on?' Wilks asked.

Frederick peered into the back of the ambulance spotting the bodies of the two air force officers. Blood ran from their noses and eyes.

Lloyd looked visibly shocked. 'They both started to have some sort of seizure.'

'Seizure.' Frederick said.

Lloyd nodded. 'One minute we were talking about their experience. The next they both started to convulse. I tried to help but they were gone in an instant.'

Wilks climbed into the back of the ambulance and examined the bodies. Blood continued to pump out of their eyes and nose. He reached felt the wrist of one of the men.

Lloyd wiped his brow. 'I've never seen anything like it in my entire medical profession.'

'This man still has a pulse.' Wilks revealed.

'What?' Lloyd exclaimed looking at Frederick.

Wilks stared at the bodies. 'It's odd, they've all the signs of being clinically dead. Yet they still have a heartbeat. We need to get them back to Church Fenton for examination.'

Church Fenton – 4:23pm

An examination room had been prepared at the RAF base. Frederick and Wilks waited patiently outside while Lloyd examined the bodies. When he finally appeared Lloyd looked exhausted.

'What did you find?' Frederick asked.

'Total blood loss. Every drop of blood has literally been pumped from their bodies.'

'Is this even possible?' Wilks questioned.

Lloyd shook his head. 'It's not, after death the heart stops pumping. Yet even now those men still have an active pulse and heartbeat. Even though there is no blood to pump around the body, those men are clinically dead. It's scientifically impossible. I also found a small incision on the back of their necks. It's similar to the doctor in Ripley.'

'You think this is connected with the Ripley incident.'

'It's too much of a coincidence not to be.'

'Obviously an effect of being taken by those creatures.' Wilks suggested. 'If we had the medical records of Edith Jones we could see if there is a link to what happened to her.'

'Well there's nothing left to do but head back to London and report our findings to the committee members.' Frederick said.

Chapter 36

Downing Street – London – 10:04am
Monday 15th December 1952

The Prime Minister slowly looked around the table at the assembled committee members who were sat in the cabinet room around a large boat shaped table.

'Gentlemen I have read the report Professor Frederick has submitted. I have to say I am shocked at the events of the last six months.' He picked up the report. 'Particularly recent events concerning the two airmen who were snatched by forces unknown and were missing for two months. What I also find disturbing is the Americans have had secret service agents running all over England investigating flying saucer related cases.'

'We are still trying to trace whoever these men might be.' Morris Stanford explained. 'However Prime Minister we have yet to come up with anything significant. Plus, the Americans haven't been forthcoming with information.'

Churchill looked back at the file. 'I have to admit I was doubtful whether or not this committee would be fruitful. However, because of the events which included the incident that happened during Operation Mainbrace it proves this flying saucer phenomenon is very real. Not only that but the Americans seem to think they can come over here and do what they bloody well please. Mr Stanford, I want an extra man assigned to the British Embassy in Washington. His key role will be to monitor all newspaper, radio and television broadcasts relating to flying saucers. I also want an extra agent in Moscow to monitor the situation over there. We must be vigilant and on our guard from this moment on Gentlemen.' The Prime Minister paused for thought. 'This whole flying saucer issue leaves me uneasy to say the least.

During the war we knew what we were up against. We fought to overcome a dark tyranny that would have engulfed the planet. God only knows what we are up against now. We can only hope the events of the past six months are not part of something bigger. From this moment on anything relating to flying saucers will be classed as above top secret. All Material will be filed away for analysis. We will meet up again in the new year to discuss a strategy regarding American incursions on the British mainland. I'm afraid gentlemen this investigation into flying saucers is ongoing for now.' Churchill looked at Frederick. 'I know you were only expecting to be part of this group for several months Professor but it seems we are going to need your services for a lot longer.'

'Given my experiences Prime Minister, I wouldn't want it any other way.'

Chapter 37

St Peter's Church Gardens – Wisbech – Cambridgeshire – 2:04pm
Friday 19th December 1952

Frederick glanced over at the nine-hundred-year-old Norman church which dominated the local landscape. After the briefing with the Prime Minister Frederick returned to Cambridge and took his final lectures of the year. The day before had been packed with final meetings and endless goodbyes from the students he taught. Late in the afternoon he had received a telegram from Rothschild who he had not seen for a while. Frederick spent the evening wrestling with the offer Rothschild had made.

Rothschild approached from the town centre dressed in a grey suit and matching trilby. 'Professor good to see you again. I'm sorry I have not been in touch sooner. Rumour is rife Comrade Stalin's health is failing. As you can imagine crossing from east to west is getting a little difficult.'

Frederick nodded. 'Well I won't keep you for long Doctor I'm here to accept your offer to join your organisation.'

Rothschild nodded. 'That is good to hear Professor we were hoping you would accept.'

'It's been quite a year.' Frederick commented.

'And it is just the beginning Professor. There are wonders in our cosmos we are only now discovering. Life elsewhere is just a small part of the splendour which makes up our universe. The more science pushes the frontier the more we learn.' Rothschild looked towards the town centre. People rushed by going about their day to day business. 'I'm afraid my time is short Professor I must leave immediately for Berlin.'

'What happens now I have accepted your offer?'

'We will be in touch very soon Professor. Some of my colleagues are anxious to meet with you.'

Frederick nodded. 'Is there a way I can contact you.'

'That bottle of unopened brandy you keep in your office at Cambridge. When you need to contact me leave it in the window in plain view, then I will be in touch. In the meantime, I suggest you learn all you can from your experiences of the past year. It will prepare you for what lays ahead.' Rothschild tipped his hat. 'Merry Christmas Professor.'

Chapter 38

Whitehall – London – 12:08pm
Friday 16th January 1953

'Take a look at these.' Chambers handed Frederick four photographs.

'A wartime colleague of mine took them a week and a half ago.' Explained Doctor Arthur Lloyd.

Frederick rifled through the photos of a cow. Parts of its upper body and head had been stripped clean of flesh leaving the bone exposed. Parts of its jaw had also been removed.

'A newspaper in Hereford reported a number of UFO sightings around the time of this event. The chap who took these photos claims the animal was found in a field with a locked gate. No tracks were leading away from the animal which also suffered complete blood loss.'

'I want you and Doctor Lloyd to go and investigate this mystery and find out what exactly happened to that animal.' Chambers instructed.

'You're not suggesting this has anything to do with flying saucers are you.' Frederick said.

'Those photos are disturbing enough to warrant an investigation. It is better to be safe than sorry.' Chambers remarked.

The Litchfield Vaults – Hereford – 11:53am
Monday 19th January 1953

Dr David Mitchell swigged down half a pint of beer and set it down on the table. 'Dammed if I've seen anything like it before. I've shown these pictures to other vets in the area. They are as mystified about this as I am.'

Frederick had the photographs in front of him. 'Where is the animal now?'

'The farmer who found the animal destroyed it before I could make another examination.'

'How long did you have to examine the animal?'

'I received a telephone call from another vet who asked me to go over to the farm to examine the cow. I examined it for about an hour.'

'What did you find?'

'First of all the animal was in a field with a locked gate. There was no way anyone with a vehicle could have got in. The first thing I noticed when I examined it was the total loss of blood. I looked around the immediate area but there was no spillage.'

'All the blood was gone?' Lloyd said.

Mitchell nodded.

'What about the wounds?' Frederick asked.

'I gave them close attention but could not find signs that any kind of cutting tool had been used. The edges of the animal's wounds were smooth like nothing I have ever seen. The cut on the jaw bone was also smooth. The bone was bleached but the most puzzling aspect was the heart.'

'How so?'

'It was still beating for one thing. No blood, the liver had been removed, yet the heart was still functioning. It's scientifically impossible; the heart shouldn't have been beating.'

'Where exactly is this farm?' Asked Frederick.

'Near a place called Stoke Lacy about eleven miles out.' Mitchell revealed. 'If you are going out there I should warn you the locals don't like outsiders.'

'Are there any boarding houses in the area?' Lloyd asked his friend.

'Try the Plough Inn, but like I said don't expect anyone to roll out the red carpet.'

Chapter 39

The Plough Inn – Stoke Lacy – Herefordshire – 2:36pm

The pub landlord glared hard at Frederick and Lloyd who had just knocked on the main door of the pub.

'Good afternoon sir.' Frederick greeted politely. 'Do you have any rooms available?'

'Nicholson Farm is a few miles down the road I suggest you try there.' The man barked.

Frederick shoved his foot in the door before the landlord could shut it. 'I'm afraid we've already been there but they've no spare rooms so they suggested we come here.'

The door opened wider. 'You better come in.' The landlord sighed.

'Thank you.' Frederick replied as he stepped through the door followed closely by Lloyd.

'You can have the double room, there are two single beds. Dinner is at seven thirty, we have two other guests. I will tell you what I told them. We are simple country folk around here. We don't want any trouble makers or do-gooders. We would be grateful if you kept to yourselves and leave as soon as possible.'

'We won't be any bother.' Lloyd reassured him as the landlord led them to their room.

'I'm afraid there's only one bathroom so you'll have to share with the other guests. There's a chamber pot in your room. If you need the main toilet then it's located the other side of the farmyard.' The landlord turned the key in the lock.

'Thank you for your hospitality.' Frederick smiled as the landlord handed him the key.

'Don't be late for dinner.' The landlord grunted.

'Friendly chap.' Lloyd remarked.

Frederick surveyed their room. Two single beds were set

out in the middle of the room with a chest of drawers. The chamber pot was just under the window which looked onto the farmyard at the back of the inn. Frederick walked over and peered out.

The landlord was below talking to another man who wore priest's robes. Two women were also present. The group of people looked up at the window Frederick was standing by. They stared at him for several seconds before walking across towards the farmyard entrance.

'I don't know about you Arthur but there's something definitely off about the people in this village.'

'We'll keep on our toes.' Lloyd advised. 'If we need to get out quick then we better be ready. The last thing we need is a bunch of country bumpkins turning on us. We'll track down the farmer tomorrow; see if he is willing to give us more information.'

Chapter 40

6:52pm

Frederick glanced at his watch. He'd been waiting outside the bathroom for about five minutes. Whoever was in there was making plenty of noise.

Finally, the door opened.

Frederick glared at the bathroom's occupant. 'You!'

The man seemed completely surprised to see Frederick.

'What the hell are you doing here?' Frederick demanded to know raising his voice.

'Professor Frederick.' The American greeted. 'What an unexpected surprise.'

Two of the guest room doors opened and Lloyd and another man stepped out.

'I demand you answer my question.'

'Calm down Professor, you don't want to draw attention to yourself. If you want answers then we need to speak privately.'

Frederick closed the door of their guestroom. The two Americans he had encountered at Ripley four months earlier sat side by side on one of the single beds. 'So why don't we begin with your names.'

The two Americans glanced at each other.

'Look either you tell us who you are or we'll ring the police. Since you are wanted for the murder of that doctor in Ripley last year and impersonating two Royal Air Force officers.'

'The man you say I murdered last year wasn't exactly an innocent bystander. Besides I didn't murder him, all I did was push him over.'

'Explain.' Lloyd stated.

'Did you bother to examine the body Doctor Lloyd? Was there an incision on the back of his neck?' The American asked.

Lloyd thought back to the strange mark he had discovered. 'I did, there was some kind of surgical procedure evident yes.'

'So you called the cops and the ambulance just carted him away without any further investigation.'

Both Lloyd and Frederick exchanged glances.

The American smiled. 'Don't tell me the doctor's body mysteriously disappeared.'

'We are not sharing any information at this moment.' Lloyd said.

'You don't have to, your looks say enough. If you're not willing to share information then we better leave.' Both men stood up.

'What exactly are you getting at?' Frederick blocked their path.

'What I'm saying Professor, is the doctor in Ripley along with that woman Edith Jones are part of something we've been investigating for a few years.' He paused looking at the other American who nodded. 'Since you have stumbled on to our little operation, we've no choice but to let you come along for the ride. I take it you are here because of the cattle mutilation?'

'How do you know about that?' Frederick asked.

The American smiled back. 'Very little escapes our attention Professor.'

'All right then, if you are in the mood for sharing information is there anything you could tell us about this incident?' Lloyd asked.

'This phenomenon is nothing new. Although this is the first time it has happened on British soil. There have been a number of incidents in France, Germany, and the Soviet Union. We have also had cases in the mid-west United States.'

'Why is US intelligence interested in mutilated cattle?' Frederick asked.

'Because all incidents come hand in hand with UFO

sightings.'

Frederick smiled at the dark haired American. 'You seriously believe these cattle mutilations have something to do with flying saucers.'

'What's your reason for being here then Professor?' The American smiled back.

Frederick said nothing.

'Look either we can sit here and argue all night or we can find out what's going on in this village.'

'Which is what exactly?' Lloyd asked.

'We are not sure but we have managed to make a friend of one of the locals. Which if you haven't already noticed aren't the talkative type.' The black haired American looked at the clock. 'It's almost seven thirty gentlemen I suggest we go down for dinner.'

'Do you both have a name?' Asked Frederick.

'I'm Frank Cones this is my partner Jack Baker.'

'CIA.' Lloyd said.

Cones smiled. 'Sort of but let's not sit here and speculate shall we.'

'Are you going to tell us how you know our names?' Frederick asked.

'Sorry Professor but at this moment we are bound by our government not to reveal anything to you.'

'Typical!' Lloyd sighed.

Chapter 41

7:52pm

Frederick savoured the last mouthful of mashed potato which made him think about Elizabeth's wonderful cooking. Although the bar of the public house was quite busy, the first thing Frederick and his companions noted was the silence. This made it difficult to have a conversation.

The locals sat quietly playing cards and dominoes. Four men were playing darts in the corner of the bar. Occasionally they would look over at the four strangers sat in the dining area.

The main door to the bar opened and in walked the priest Frederick spotted earlier. He walked to the bar and talked to the landlord for a few minutes. Eventually he headed for Frederick's party.

'Good evening gentlemen.' The priest spoke softly.

All four men looked up and greeted the man.

'I trust the food is to your liking.'

'It's excellent thank you. I was just thinking how much it reminded me of my wife's cooking.'

'I'm sure the landlady will be pleased to hear that.' Several seconds of silence followed. 'What brings you to our little village?'

'We're just passing through.' Lloyd said.

'To where exactly?'

Frederick gathered his thoughts summing up an answer. 'We're surveyors mapping out a new road atlas. We're logging all the towns and villages in this area.'

The priest stared at Frederick making him feel uneasy. 'I see.' He said before looking at Cones and Baker. 'But you're not all surveyors.'

Cones shook his head. 'No, myself and my companion are

humble servicemen exploring your beautiful countryside.'

'You are American.' The priest noted.

'Yes.' Baker answered. 'Just enjoying some leave and sampling the wonderful ales you Brits like to brew.'

The priest nodded slowly staring intensely at Cones. 'Very well gentlemen I'll leave you to your business.' The priest started to walk back towards the bar.

'Thank you.' Frederick said politely. 'Father?'

The priest turned and stared at him. 'I'm Father Janus.'

Cones looked over at the bar and noticed everyone was staring in their direction. The priest joined the rest of the locals who remained silent. 'Man, he is one creepy guy.' He whispered.

8:38pm

Frederick shut the door behind him and sat down on the bed. 'I don't know about you chaps but I'm glad to be back upstairs. The silence in that bar was deafening.'

'It was like that last night. The locals aren't exactly the friendly type.' Baker said.

'What did you make of that Janus fellow?' Lloyd asked.

'That's the first person who has had a decent conversation with us since we got here.' Cones said. 'He was in the bar last night but didn't speak to us. The locals seem to view him as a key figure. We have never seen him alone. He always has two or three people with him. The guy gives me the creeps.' Cones shuddered.

'The villagers seem to be his bodyguards.' Frederick speculated.

'What do we do now?' Lloyd said looking at his watch. 'I would have been quite happy propping up the bar all night if it were not for the locals.'

'We wait.' Cones said grinning.

'For what exactly?' Frederick asked.

'You'll see Professor.'

Chapter 42

8:59pm

All four men stood at the window of the guest room. Cones had instructed Frederick to turn the light off. The American stood looking up into the crystal-clear sky.

'What exactly are we looking for?' Lloyd asked.

Cones scanned the sky without answering. A wall clock in the hall outside the room started to chime nine o'clock. 'There!' He stated pointing low on the horizon. The clock continued to chime. 'Right on schedule.'

Frederick and Lloyd stared in the direction where Cones had pointed.

A single light came into view growing in size.

Frederick watched as the light took the shape of a disc which had a soft blue glow. It was similar to the objects he had witness at RAF Church Fenton several months previous.

The object glided across a field about half a mile beyond the farm buildings, stopping behind some trees.

'We need to get over to where that object is.' Frederick said turning and walking towards the door. Doctor Lloyd followed closely behind.

'I wouldn't do that if I were you Professor.' Cones called out watching as Frederick and Lloyd disappeared out of the door.

Frederick stopped dead in his tracks.

Lloyd failed to notice and slammed into the back of Frederick shoving him forward.

The landlord of the pub stood in the hallway glaring at the two men. 'Get back in your room please gentlemen.' He ordered.

Frederick stared at the double barrel shotgun the man was pointing at him. 'What's going on here?'

'I said get back in your room now!' The landlord demanded cocking the gun.

Frederick locked eyes with the man for several seconds before stepping back through the doorway of his room.

'I warned you.' Cones said. 'We tried that last night.'

'Look there they go.' Baker announced.

Frederick and Lloyd returned to the window and looked out towards the farmyard entrance onto the main road. Torch lights could be seen making their way up the road in the direction of UFO.

'Looks like a god damn town meeting.' Cones remarked.

'How did you know the light would show up at this time?' Lloyd said.

'This is our third night here.' Baker revealed. 'It's happened every night we've been here. We did the same thing you just tried but were confronted by the farmer.'

Cones looked towards the door and started to whisper. 'We have a plan to break out of here tomorrow night.'

'In the meantime, we just sit here and do nothing.' Frederick said.

'I don't like it any more than you Professor. But unless you want that guy to start blasting at you with his blunderbuss, there's not much we can do. We have a man on the inside. He has promised to help us bust out of here tomorrow night.'

'How many villagers live here?' Lloyd asked watching the procession of torch lights head up the road.

'We're guessing about fifty maybe more.' Baker answered. 'They don't usually come back until eleven o'clock. So I suggest we make ourselves comfortable because the guy outside the door doesn't move until then.'

Chapter 43

Stoke Lacy – Herefordshire – 12:34pm
Tuesday 20th January 1953

Frederick and Lloyd accompanied the two Americans to a deserted farm building about a mile beyond the boundaries of the village. The landlord of the pub seemed oblivious to the previous night's events and served them breakfast without an explanation.

After they had eaten the group headed out to where the mysterious object had landed. They examined the area for an hour before deciding there was no trace of whatever it was that had landed the previous evening.

As they approached the barn a young man in his early twenties appeared out of the main door.

'Hey Jimmy!' Cones called out.

Jimmy held up his hand. 'Hello Mr Cones.'

Cones shook hands. 'How you doing pal?'

'Very well thank you Mr Cones.' Jimmy replied in a slow voice.

Lloyd studied the young man smirking. 'This is your man on the inside. He looks more like the village idiot.'

Cones ignored the doctor's cruel insult. 'Jimmy, why don't you tell these nice folks what you told me and Mr Baker.'

'The blue light comes every night.' He replied. 'The blue light comes and everyone goes.' He sniffed and wiped his nose. 'I don't go though. He doesn't like me.'

'Who doesn't like you Jimmy.' Lloyd asked.

'The nasty man, he says I'm not clever like the others.'

'Nasty man?' Frederick coaxed.

'The nasty man who lives in the church.'

'Father Janus.'

Jimmy nodded. 'He calls to them. He calls to them every

night to stand under the blue light.'

'Tell them what happens to them when they stand under the blue light.' Baker said.

'They go to sleep. They close their eyes and go to sleep holding hands.'

'Jimmy do you remember what we discussed yesterday. Are you ready for your big adventure?'

'Adventure?' Frederick quizzed.

'Jimmy says he used to play at the back of the guesthouse which overlooks the farm. He can climb in through the guest bathroom window and create a distraction for us.'

'Can you remember what time to meet us Jimmy?' Cones asked.

'When the blue light comes.'

'That's right buddy, when the blue light comes.'

'James!' A voice called out from several metres behind the group.

Frederick and his companions turned to see Father Janus with three other men.

'What are you doing here? Why aren't you helping Mr Diggle with the painting?'

'I was talking to my friends.' Jimmy replied staring at the ground. He seemed unwilling to look at Janus or the other men.

'You've finished talking to your new friends, go back to work!' Janus ordered firmly.

Jimmy ran off back towards the village.

Janus stared at the four visitors. 'I think you've worn out your welcome in this village. First thing tomorrow morning you are to pack up and leave.'

'Says who.' Cones replied in an equally firm tone.

Janus stepped up to him. 'Since you are American I'll excuse your arrogance for not knowing our customs.' He then turned to Frederick and Lloyd. 'As for you two, I suggest you conduct your road map survey elsewhere and stop bothering the villagers.'

'We were just talking to the young man.' Baker stated. 'What's wrong with that?'

Janus glared at the American. 'As you can see James has an overactive imagination. Now I would appreciate it if you would return to the guesthouse and remain there until you leave. Or I'll have you escorted from the village this very moment.'

Chapter 44

9:00pm

All four men looked out of the guesthouse window and watched as the object came into view. It took up the same position as it did the night before. Frederick spotted a dark shadow sprinting across the farmyard.

'That's my boy Jimmy.' Cones said smiling.

'Are you sure this is a good idea.' Lloyd said.

'Do you have a better one Doctor?'

The four of them looked back out of the window. The villagers were already making their way up the road.

'Taking his time isn't he.' Frederick said.

Suddenly the landlord could be heard shouting outside the guest bedroom door. 'What are you doing here Jimmy.' He growled. 'Go back home now!'

Cones picked up the empty chamber pot before creeping towards the door. He opened it slightly peering through the narrow gap. The pub landlord was further down the hallway shouting at Jimmy. The landlord had his back to Cones.

'I said go home Jimmy!' The landlord ordered.

Cones pushed the door open hoping the landlord wouldn't hear the creak.

Jimmy stood at the bathroom door laughing.

Cones lifted the pot above his head before hurtling down the hallway.

The landlord barely had time to turn and face his assailant before the chamber pot came crashing down on the side of his head. The man was sent stumbling backwards before hitting the floorboards with a loud thud.

Frederick, Lloyd and Baker joined Cones who was man handling the landlord.

'Give me a hand will you I want to show you something.'

They hauled the unconscious landlord onto his front. Cones pulled up his shirt and pointed out a small blemish at the base of his spine.

'Looks like an identical incision to the one we found on the doctor in Ripley.' Lloyd said taking a closer look. 'The wound is perfectly straight.'

'Along with the two air force pilots a few months back. Plus that doctor in Ripley' Frederick mentioned glancing at Cones.

'I would have tried to explain. But that air force guy tried to shoot me.'

'What is this mark exactly?' Frederick asked.

'We are not sure but we have discovered a number of people with these marks.'

'I don't mean to rush you guys.' Baker interrupted. 'But there are other things to see tonight.'

Cones stood picking up the shotgun the landlord had dropped and walked over to Jimmy. 'Thanks buddy now you stay here and keep an eye on this guy.'

'Yes Mr Cones.'

Chapter 45

9:23pm

Frederick could feel his heart pound as the four men made their way up the road. A blue glow illuminated a field up ahead.

The gate to the field was wide open. A large oak tree stood guard at the entrance giving the group ample cover.

The villagers had assembled in the field stood to attention in a perfect circle holding hands. A craft hovered about twenty feet off the ground emitting a blue aura that reached out to the circle of people. Frederick noted what Jimmy had described earlier that day. Each villager had their eyes shut but seemed to be mumbling something.

At the exact centre of the circle was the priest who was stood directly under the UFO with his arms outstretched in a cross formation. His eyes were open and were glowing white.

'What do you suppose they are doing?' Lloyd said.

'Looks like their communicating with that craft.' Baker answered.

'What do we do?' Frederick stated.

Cones cocked the shotgun. 'We crash this party.' He stepped out from behind the tree and fired off a round into the air.

Immediately all the villagers let go of each other's hands turning to face the American. They opened their eyes which also glowed white.

Boldly, Cones walked towards the circle pointing his shotgun at the priest. The villagers remained in a circle formation. 'Everyone stay exactly where you are!'

Janus stared at the man with the shotgun smiling as he stepped into the circle of people.

Frederick, Lloyd and Baker walked stealthily behind

watching the villagers who remained motionless.

The static electricity the craft emitted was intense.

Cones stood several feet away from Janus pointing the barrel of the shotgun at the priest's head. 'Just who the hell are you?'

'Someone you've encountered many times before Agent Cones.'

'Trust me pal I'd know if we already knew each other.'

Janus laughed. 'You've no idea the destiny that awaits you Agent Cones.'

'How the hell do you know my name?'

'I know everything about you Agent Cones including the future that awaits you.'

'I know what awaits you, asshole!' He squeezed the trigger but nothing happened.

'Your arrogance is compelling Agent Cones.'

Cones stepped back. He looked at the shotgun before pointing it again and pulling the trigger, still nothing happened.

'Did you honestly think you could just turn up and put an end to this? I can see your thoughts gentlemen. I knew your plan was to come here tonight.' Janus stared at the American pointing the gun at him. 'Agent Frank Cones, champion to kings of old and history's protector. Always rushing in where angels fear to tread. It's a shame you couldn't do that on the beaches of Omaha. Instead of cowering under the corpses of your fallen comrades. Watching helplessly as your younger brother was cut down.'

Cones dropped the shotgun backing away. Fear took hold as the memory of that day suddenly became clear in his mind.

Omaha Beachhead – Normandy – France – 3:34pm Tuesday 6th June 1944

The artillery shells rained down on the small band of soldiers who had taken cover in an impact crater. Machine gunfire seemed never ending clattering around them. Screams of injured and dying men filled the air crying out for help. Other soldiers advanced up the beach but were being mowed down by the machine gunfire.

'Sir we cannot stay here, we have to push forward!' The young private screamed.

'We're pinned down private. If we move then we're all dead. It's a fucking shooting gallery!' Cones yelled back. 'Get on the radio and see where that fucking air support is!'

'If we stay here we're all dead anyway. It's only a matter of time before those German bastards make our position.'

'Frank he's right, if we can take that German gun position further up the beach then we can pave the way for more of our troops.'

Cones looked at his younger brother Mike, eventually nodding. He looked around at the eight other soldiers. 'Ok if we do this then we go all the way. We don't stop until we reach that gun emplacement. Then we light it up with grenades!'

A shell exploded close to their position throwing sand into the crater.

'Ok get ready, Higgs, Hutchinson, when there's a break in the machine gunfire lay down covering fire. The rest of us will make a break for it.'

The two soldiers held their breath looking out over the edge of the crater. The machine gunfire suddenly stopped.

'GO! GO! GO!' Cones screamed.

The group of men hurled themselves over the edge of the crater and started scrambling up the beach clambering over the corpses of fallen comrades. Cones tried to shield himself from the sight of broken and dismembered bodies.

A burst of machine gunfire spewed from directly in front. The man behind Cones stumbled and fell forward.

Cones tried to avoid the falling body but it was too late. The weight of the dead soldier smashed into the back of

Cones' legs causing him to trip and fall forward.

A volley of machine gunfire streaked over his head. Cones looked up and saw his younger brother sprinting towards the gun emplacement. A shell came down hammering the area. Bodies were sent flying through the air. Heavily concussed Cones started to lose consciousness. The last thing he saw was his younger brother being cut down by a volley of machine gunfire.

Cones suddenly found himself back in the field. Janus' eyes burned into his mind. He dropped to his knees.

Janus then looked at Jack Baker. 'You still live as that young boy who witnessed such horror. Seeing your own mother's dead corpse with your father standing over her before he killed himself in front of you.'

Baker tried to look away but Janus' words brought a memory long buried back with frightful vengeance.

New York City – United States of America – 11:45pm Wednesday 30th October 1929

Twelve year old Jack Baker had been awake for about twenty minutes trying to shut out the noise of his screaming parents.

'Don't you get it, it's over!' Charles Baker shouted. 'We've lost everything; the bank has collapsed along with the markets. Millions in stocks and shares gone down the pan.'

'There must be something we can do. Is there no one you can call.' Janet Baker suggested.

'No, we are all in the same boat, everything is gone. I should never have made that investment. Tomorrow Freeman is going to come here with his goons and toss us out onto the streets.'

'You can start again.' Janet said. 'Surely there must be someone who owes you a favour.'

Baker's father shook his head. 'There's no one. Tom and Alan have been arrested for fraud. If Freeman doesn't get to us first the feds will. I'll be slung into jail. You and Jack will be heading for the soup kitchens in Brooklyn.'

'I'll call dad he'll know what to do.' Janet said walking over to the phone.

Charles Baker laughed. 'Your dad won't touch me with a barge pole. He'll be too busy bailing his own boat out before it sinks. Besides he never liked or trusted me.' He walked over to a chest of drawers opening the top drawer looking inside. He reached in and picked up a thirty eight revolver.

Janet started to dial.

Jack climbed out of bed and opened his bedroom door. Slowly he inched along the apartment hallway. He could hear his mother talking on the phone. Through the narrow gap Jack saw his father's outstretched arm gripping the gun.

A single gunshot rang out reverberating throughout the Central Park apartment. Janet Baker's lifeless body fell forwards onto the floor face down.

Jack reached the living room door and pushed it open. His father stood over his mother's body sobbing. Jack stood staring down at his dead mother. Charles Baker looked at his son pointing the revolver directly at his head. 'I'm sorry.' He sobbed.

Jack stared into his father's eyes who pointed the gun away. Charles Baker put the barrel into his mouth and pulled the trigger.

Baker was flung back to the present. Tears welled up in his eyes and he began to sob.

'Your life will end abruptly Agent Baker and you will give it willingly.' Janus then focused his attention on Dr Lloyd. 'Tell me Doctor how long can you deny the truth? How long can you keep your secret from Mary?'

Lloyd started to shake as Janus' words hit home.

'Even now I can see the cancer ravaging your body. Time to face the truth Doctor, your end is closer than you think.'

Finally Janus turned to Frederick. 'Professor Ralph

Frederick your thoughts are as clear as day. I can see why he chose you, such a rare gift in a young species.'

An image of Rothschild suddenly appeared in Frederick's mind.

'So many happy memories with Elizabeth and Susan, but it won't last. The path you are on will lead to great loss. Tell me Professor are you prepared for what's ahead.'

Frederick suddenly found himself in a church or cathedral. He could hear his daughter Susan crying. Slowly he turned to face the little girl who looked slightly older than she was now. She was on her knees next to a hunched figure. 'Susan.' He called out.

'Your colleagues will abandon you Professor.' Janus continued.

Frederick suddenly found himself in front of a group of people. Royal Society members Norman Hinshelwood and Chester Osborne sat at a long table. Looking towards another man seated alone in the middle of a large room.

'And you will lose those whom you hold most dear.' Janus continued.

Frederick's mind was thrust back into the Cathedral. He looked down at his sobbing daughter and then the other figure who was himself, cradling the dead body of Elizabeth in his arms.

'This is your future Professor.' Janus said.

Frederick closed his eyes desperately trying to scrub the image from his mind. He opened them again and walked forward past Cones who was still kneeling. Picking up the shotgun he pointed it at Janus.

'You cannot kill me Professor.' Janus boasted. 'I am never ending. I am your past, your present, and I am humanity's future.' A short intense burst of brilliant light lit up the surrounding countryside before the darkness returned.

Frederick looked into the clear night sky and watched a light streak away. 'Is everybody ok?'

Cones got to his feet feeling disoriented. 'What the hell just happened?'

'I'm not sure.' Frederick answered.

Lloyd looked about. 'Where are all the villagers?'

All four men scanned the field but everyone had vanished along with Janus.

'Mr Cones, Mr Cones!' A voice shouted from the field entrance. Jimmy ran up to the secret service agent. 'It's Mr Andrews come quickly.'

Dr Lloyd knelt as close as he could to the body of the pub landlord. Blood continued to bleed out of his eyes and ears. 'It's similar to the two Royal air force personnel last year.' He looked a Frederick. 'We have to call Malcolm; this village needs to be cordoned off.'

'We'd love to stay around and help out fellas but we cannot be here when the cavalry arrives.' Cones said.

Frederick looked at the American. 'What did he mean when he said you have encountered him many times before?'

'How the hell should I know?' Cones shrugged.

'No offense Agent Cones but Janus seemed to be very familiar with you.'

'I'm telling you that's the first time I've encountered that guy.'

'Fair enough if you are going to continue with this charade. When you get the chance to speak with your superiors tell them the British government will not tolerate rogue US intelligence agents sneaking around rural England.'

Cones and Baker left without saying goodbye.

Chapter 46

Stoke Lacy – Herefordshire – 1:23pm
Wednesday 21st January 1953

Malcolm Chambers, Ian Morgan, Morris Stanford and Professor Wilks sat around the large kitchen table in the guesthouse. Frederick and Lloyd spent the last hour relaying the events of the last few days.

'The big question is, who is this Janus?' Chambers said.

'Or what.' Professor Wilks added.

The other committee members looked at him.

'It's obvious from what both Ralph and Arthur have told us this Janus fellow wasn't human.'

'Despite his appearance.' Lloyd said. 'He looked perfectly human to me Richard.'

'Maybe so but his ability to not only read your minds but also to project images directly into them suggests otherwise.'

'What do you suppose this Janus chap wanted with all the villagers.' Ian Morgan said.

'They were obviously part of whatever plan he was hatching.' Replied Wilks.

'An invasion.' Stanford suggested.

'If so where are their invading armies?' Chambers questioned. 'These creatures are obviously more advanced than us why not just send a fleet of spaceships.'

'Janus also made another claim about Agent Cones. He referred to him as hero of kings of old and he had met him on many occasions.' Frederick revealed. 'He also mentioned something about the future that awaits this Agent Cones.'

'Do you suppose the Americans may know about this Janus fellow?' Chambers asked.

'Agent Cones seemed adamant he had never met Janus before.' Frederick said.

Chambers inhaled. 'There are many pieces to this particular puzzle.'

'What happens now?' Frederick asked turning to Chambers.

'This village will be quarantined for the time being. A cover story is being prepared for the press.'

'What about Jimmy?'

'The young man will be transferred to a secure facility. He obviously has some kind of mental illness and will be well cared for. The body of the landlord to the guesthouse will be taken away for analysis. Porton Down is the best place, it's out of the way and we can arrange for a building to be cleared.' Chambers looked at Frederick and Lloyd. 'How are you two holding up after your experience?'

Lloyd recalled the events and what Janus had told him. 'It is true I do have cancer.' He revealed.

The others looked on.

'Too much passion for the good stuff I'm afraid.' He said staring at the glass of whiskey in front of him.

'How long do you have?' Morgan asked.

'Four months maybe more.' Sighed Lloyd. 'Funny, I was planning to tell Mary this weekend.'

Chambers looked at Frederick. 'How about you Ralph what did you make of what you saw?'

'He claimed to have shown me my future. I saw myself holding Elizabeth in my arms with Susan beside me.' Frederick analysed the image in his head. 'It's impossible to say where I am. I'm familiar with many of the cathedrals in England. There was something vaguely familiar about the surrounding but I cannot put my finger on it.'

Chambers nodded. 'Well I'm sure you will want to get back to your families. Why don't you both take a few weeks out and carry on with your normal working lives.'

'We'll track down information regarding our American friends.' Stanford offered. 'It shouldn't be too difficult now we have their names. We'll also look into their claims about that doctor in Ripley you encountered last year.'

Emneth – Norfolk
9:04pm
Frederick walked up to Elizabeth sweeping her up in his arms and kissing her.

'What's got into you?' She asked smiling back at her husband.

The image Janus had projected into Frederick's mind burned through his thoughts. He smiled back at his wife. 'Nothing I just thought you deserved a bit of attention.' Holding Liz in his arms the image began to fade a little.

Hyde Park – London – 11:56am
Friday 23rd January 1953
Bill Mirren glanced at his watch before wrapping his coat tightly around him. A man approached and sat down next to him.

'You're late.' Mirren grumbled.

'I know.' The man replied. 'I am rather busy you know.'

'What have you got for me?'

The man passed Mirren a folder. 'An incident that occurred recently in the Herefordshire area.'

Mirren opened the casefile.

'The military has cordoned off the village and issued a statement about a smallpox outbreak.'

'Smallpox.' Mirren said.

'It's the best they could come up with at short notice.'

Mirren studied the casefile in front of him. 'Janus, why am I not surprised.'

'The time of the prophecy draws near.'

'Are you sure.'

The man nodded. 'Agent Cones has taken is place on the board. It's only a matter of time before he is partnered up with Frederick.'

'All we can do is wait and watch events play out.' Mirren said.

The man got to his feet. 'I have to go.' He said walking away.

'What do you want me to do about this?'

The man turned. 'You are editor of the London Evening Examiner Mr Mirren. I'll leave it for you to decide.'

Whitehall – London – 9:34am
Saturday 24th January – 1953

Morris Stanford marched into Chambers' office and slammed a newspaper down onto the desk. 'We have a bloody leak!'

Chambers looked at the article for a few moments. 'I'd hardly call this a leak Morris. From here it looks like the Examiner is reaching.'

Stanford pointed at the newspaper. 'They're questioning the whereabouts of the villagers.' He started to pace up and down.

Chambers read the article in full. 'It doesn't say anything here resembling what happened.'

'But it does mention a number of UFO sightings in the area.'

'Probably to make the story sound more interesting than it already is.' Chambers handed the newspaper back to Stanford. 'You know what the press is like. They blow everything out of proportion. There was an article in the Hereford Times about a number of UFO sightings. That's why we sent Ralph and Arthur out there remember. No one will pay any attention to this Morris.'

Stanford glanced at Chambers. 'I wish I had your confidence.'

Chapter 47

St James Park – London – 9:38am
Thursday 29th January 1953

Rothschild approached Frederick flanked by two other men whom he was familiar with.

'Professor Frederick good to see you.' Rothschild offered his hand noting the look on his face. 'You needn't worry Professor you are in good company. I know you are familiar with my colleagues.'

Well known and highly respected physicists Nathan Rosen and Werner Heisenberg shook Frederick's hand.

'I need to speak with you concerning an incident a few weeks ago.' Frederick said.

'The incident in Stoke Lacy. I'm sure it was an experience that left you with a lot of questions.'

'Something tells me that you're familiar with this Janus.'

'Our paths have crossed many times. The Order has records of him stretching back hundreds of years.'

'Who is he, or rather what is he?'

'We do not know.' Rothschild replied. 'We do know that he's been spotted more regularly. Infiltrating society and taking people at random.'

'Does he have the power to show me the future?'

'Perhaps but nothing is written in stone Professor.' Rothschild said. 'You as a physicist should know this. Janus' plan was to scare you into not making decisions that might upset his agenda.'

Frederick stared at all three men. 'You mentioned something called The Order, what is that?'

Nathan Rosen began to speak. 'The Order of Galileo is a group of scientists and engineers who operate outside the boundaries of governing bodies.'

'Our group.' Heisenberg continued. 'Was founded in 1600 by Galileo Galilei who rumour has it was given knowledge by a much older organisation. This organisation supposedly stretched all the way back to the third century BC. Doctor Rothschild has probably told you about our goal which is to learn as much as we can from the observable universe around us. To enhance scientific knowledge, understanding and advancement.'

Rothschild took over. 'The twentieth century has been a leap forward in scientific understanding. Now that we have certain technology we can accelerate our knowledge. We own land on the outskirts of Geneva and several European governments are collaborating in setting up a nuclear physics research laboratory. Our goal is to persuade them to use the land we own in order to establish this research facility.'

'We are on a threshold Professor Frederick.' Rosen continued. 'To unlocking the very secrets that bind our universe. We believe that the creatures that pilot these UFOs have harnessed an incredible energy source. If we can understand and harness that energy ourselves then we can pave the way for the human race.'

'Which is why we are interested in flying saucers.' Rothschild said. 'These creatures possess the technology to not only travel between star systems, but entire galaxies. It is the holy grail of science. To be able to travel to another planet. But we cannot do this alone which is why we have recruited prominent scientists like yourself, Heisenberg and Rosen. Placed around the world influencing governments to push the boundaries of discovery. There are more planets in the heavens than we can count Professor. If the human race has any hope of surviving then it's out there among the stars.'

'It's an inspiring speech Doctor Rothschild but you know as well as I do that politicians call the shots at the end of the day. It doesn't matter if you're in the United Kingdom, USA or the Soviet Union, our leaders will always have the upper hand.'

'Something that we are working on I can assure you Professor.' Rothschild smiled.

'What about the mainstream scientific community you still have to contend with? Many scientists are unwilling to embrace the notion that we are not alone. We have yet to develop the technology to build telescopes capable of seeing other planets.'

'In time Professor Frederick We will achieve things only science fiction can imagine.' Rosen said.

Frederick's thoughts returned to why he had requested a meeting. 'How much of a threat is this Janus.'

'We're not sure. If you are fearful of an invasion rest assured he doesn't seem to be interested in anything like that. Janus is an enigma who has been around for a long time. Your encounter with him a few weeks back won't be the last. If he has accessed your thoughts then he has something in mind.' A gentle breezed carried the distant chimes of Big Ben. 'I suggest we part company for now Professor. My time is more limited because of Comrade Stalin's paranoia. His security services keep a watchful eye on the border. Many of us will be very grateful when he meets his maker.'

'Choice words for someone so dedicating in proving things that will unravel religion.' Frederick remarked.

Rothschild smiled. 'There are many kinds of faiths Professor.' He said tipping his hat and walking off towards Buckingham Palace with the two other men.

'You have yet to tell him your little secret.' Rosen remarked.

'No need to reveal everything yet. Professor Frederick has a long journey ahead of him.'

Chapter 48

**Moscow Suburbs – Soviet Union – 10:53pm
Friday 6th March 1953**

The two men huddled around the dying coal fire trying to draw what little heat they could to warm their freezing hands. The coal scuttle lay empty on its side. One of the men reached for a dirty shot glass and bolted it down. 'Where is he for god's sake. He should have been back hours ago.'

The men had been waiting several hours for their comrade to return. The room in which they waited was sparsely furnished. An old sofa, a cupboard and a table. Three chairs had been pulled in front of the dying fire. A flickering electric light provided dim illumination.

'Perhaps the rumours are false and he's been caught by Stalin's secret police, they are everywhere.' The man's eyes darted towards the window nervously. The light outside cast a shadow from two people trudging through the deep snow in the narrow street.

A faint tapping alerted the two men who looked in the direction of the door. One of them stood and picked up a Russian TT-30 pistol off the table. When he reached the door he pressed his ear against it and called out as loud as he dared. 'Who is it?'

'It is me Comrade. Please open the door.' A voice answered.

The man hesitated and looked back at his counterpart who nodded.

'Comrade it is me. Please open the door.' The voice called out again.

The door creaked open and the man quickly stepped inside. He glanced at the pistol that greeted him.

The man who had answered the door lowered the gun.

The visitor walked over to the table and grabbed a bottle of vodka taking large gulps until the bottle was empty. He wiped his mouth and sat down glancing at what was left of the fire. The man with the pistol sat back down.

The visitor took a few moments to let the vodka settle. 'I have just spoken to Comrade Bulganin. The rumours are true my friends. Comrade Stalin is dead.'

The man with the pistol leant back in his chair and smiled. 'This is a joyful moment; the veil of darkness which has lasted over thirty years has now lifted.'

'We will be able to proceed with our work without the threat of Comrade Stalin and his paranoia. The Tunguska Project has floundered. Stalin's death will bring new life to the Siberian project. I will inform Doctor Anna Vilenko. She will get a chance to redeem herself.'

The visitor stood and walked over to the cupboard. He opened one of the doors and pulled out a full bottle of vodka. He walked back towards the other two men and poured vodka into the two shot glasses.

The man with the pistol leaned forward placing it on the table. He picked up the shot glass

'To Comrade Stalin's death.' The visitor said holding up the bottle. 'And to a new era of scientific understanding.'

The two men knocked back their shot glasses. Without warning the visitor grabbed the gun with lightning speed. He pointed it at the head of the man who had answered the door and fired. The man was thrust backwards. The back of his head exploded, splattering the fireplace with brain matter.

'What are you doing!' The other man cried out.

'Killing you.' The visitor answered before pulling the trigger.

Moments later the door opened and three men stepped inside. Two wore Russian army uniforms and the other was in a plain black suit.

'You have done well Comrade Lakatos.' The man in the suit

said glancing at the bodies. 'Your service will be rewarded.'

'Thank you Comrade Bulganin.'

'You are to make contact with your informant in the United Kingdom and begin intelligence gathering.'

'I will do so immediately Comrade.'

'The Tunguska project will now receive priority.'

The two soldiers picked up the body of one of the dead men and carried him outside to a waiting truck before returning for the second body.

Chapter 49

Emneth – Wisbech – Cambridgeshire – 8:36pm
Sunday 8th March 1953

Frederick gazed lovingly at his young daughter who peered through the telescope he had set up in the back garden. The night sky was crystal clear and the stars glistened overhead.

'Daddy.' Susan said with the enthusiasm only a child could display.

'Yes sweetheart.'

'Do you think there are other people up there? Who live on other planets.'

Frederick looked up into the night sky pondering his daughter's question. For a moment he wanted to tell her everything he knew and everything he had seen. The image of Susan crying over the body of her dead mother flashed in his mind. Sadness washed over him knowing that he could not reveal the nature of his work. He drew breath taking in the cold night air. 'There are lots and lots of stars up there. So there could be many more planets.'

'Are they like us daddy?' Susan enquired.

'Who knows, they could be. Then again they could be very different from us.'

'Do you think we will ever meet someone from another planet Daddy?' Susan continued to question.

'I don't know there are so many stars in the night sky. Some of these planets will be very far away.'

Susan stepped back from the telescope and looked up at her father. 'When I grow up daddy I want to be a scientist just like you. Then I will build a rocket ship which will take us to other planets.'

Frederick knelt down smiling at his daughter. 'I'm sure you will young lady.' He took her in his arms and hugged her.

'Hey you two are you finished gazing at the stars.' Elisabeth said peering out of the back door.

Susan ran towards her mother. 'Mummy when I grow up I'm going to build a rocket ship so that you daddy and me can go and visit other planets.'

Elizabeth laughed as she scooped up her daughter. 'Well young lady before all that you need to go to bed and get a good night's sleep.'

The telephone in the hallway began ringing. 'I'll get it.' Frederick offered marching towards the back door. 'Hello.' He said picking up the handset.

'Professor Frederick it's Vincent Rothschild.'

Frederick looked down the hallway. His wife had taken Susan upstairs and could be heard tucking her in. Fredrick cupped his hand over the receiver. 'How did you get this number Doctor?'

'It is not important, what is Professor is that Joseph Stalin is dead.'

'Dead.' Frederick repeated.

'Yes Professor. I'm telling you this because the wheels of espionage are about to turn and there are those in the Kremlin who are eager to accelerate information gathering. Believe me when I say this. Guy Burgess and Donald Maclean were just the tip of the iceberg.'

'Are you saying there are more foreign agents inside the British government?'

'What I can tell you Professor is that the new Soviet regime will stop at nothing to get their hands on intelligence that you and your team have gathered.'

'I should inform the committee immediately.'

'You could do that if you wish. However, the finger of suspicion will be pointed at you. For now Professor you must carry on as normal. Whoever will be activated to gather intelligence will be careful not to be discovered. The Soviets have learned their lesson with Burgess and Maclean. The only piece of advice I can give you for now is to keep your friends close but keep your enemies closer.' The line went dead.

Whitehall – London – 11:23am
Monday 9th March 1953

'Should we be celebrating the demise of Comrade Stalin?' Malcolm Chambers asked thoughtfully.

'It's hard to tell.' Morris Stanford replied. 'Our operatives in Moscow have heard rumours of a power struggle in the Kremlin. However, it's too early to say who will be the top man.'

'Who do you think will replace him?'

'There are a number of candidates. They seem so intent on stabbing each other in the back. It's hard to know what's going on.' Stanford explained. 'Georgy Malenkov, Nikolai Bulganin, and Nikita Khrushchev are in the running. But as I just said all we are getting are whispers at the moment.'

Chambers sipped from a glass of brandy. 'What do we have on the UFO scene?'

'It's been a relatively quiet month. A report came in last week regarding a sighting by two military pilots. I've spoken to both Ralph and Arthur, they are ready to return after their experience at Stoke Lacy. Although I do fear for Doctor Lloyd. He kept his illness from us all.'

'Doctor Lloyd is a proud man he never likes to bother anyone with personal issues. Still I dread the day when we receive the terrible news.'

Chapter 50

Heathrow Airport – 11:42pm
Wednesday 18th March 1953

Alan Smith stared bleary eyed into his radar scope. Working nights did not agree with the 24 year old. Despite sleeping for much of the day he still felt like sleeping for another day. As he stared at the scope Smith became aware of several unidentified targets coming in from the south east. He glared into the scope intensely trying to figure out what they could be. Terry Hoskins the senior supervisor noticed the look on Smith face and marched over to his position.

'Problem Alan.' He stated bluntly.

'You tell me.' Smith replied gesturing towards the radar scope. 'We have eight unidentified aircraft coming from the Channel.'

Hoskins stared at the radar before looking across the control tower at a young woman. 'Iris call Northolt, ask them if they have anything in the air.'

The young woman picked up a telephone.

Smith shook his head. 'I don't think it's anything military. They're moving way too fast and erratically to be jets.'

Northolt RAF base/radar station
11:54pm

'Sir we have just received a call from Heathrow. They want to know if we have anything on exercise coming from over the Channel.'

flight Group Captain Douglas viewed the young airman with a mocking suspicion before he lifted his overweight body from a creaking chair. 'Better get up to the radar tower and see what's going on.'

Heathrow Airport
11:57pm
'Heathrow this is BEA flight 212 *over.*'
Hoskins grabbed the mike. 'BEA 212 this is Heathrow *over.*'
'Heathrow we're on route to you from Paris *over*. We're currently tracking eight unidentified aircraft at our two o'clock position. They are approximately five thousand feet above us *over.*'
'Roger that BEA 212 we have these aircraft in our scope now. We are currently waiting on Northrop to confirm if they have anything in the air *over.*'
'Heathrow these aren't military *over.*'
'Say again BEA 212.'
'I say again these are not military aircraft.'
'BEA can you describe the aircraft *over.*' Hoskins requested nervously.
'To be honest Heathrow I'm not sure what I'm looking at. All I can say is they're eight spherical balls of light, blue in colour *over.*'

RAF Northolt – 12:07am
Thursday 19th March 1953
Group Captain Douglas and the young radar operator both gawped at the cluster of objects which were present in the radarscope. Douglas had been silent for a few minutes contemplating the image in front of him. Finally he reached for a telephone receiver and dialled a number. 'Scramble Foxtrot one, Foxtrot two, scramble scramble.'
A few minutes later two Vampire jets taxied onto the runway and thundered past the control tower, climbing into the inky blackness of the night sky.

Heathrow airport – 12:17am
'Heathrow the aircraft are descending *over.*'
Terry Hoskins wiped the sweat off his brow with a

handkerchief. 'Roger that BEA 212 be advised Northolt have scrambled aircraft heading for your location *over*.'

Static crackled through the tower speaker. 'Roger that Heathrow, objects are still descending request instructions *over*.'

'BEA 212 drop to a height of eight thousand feet *over*.'

'Acknowledged Heathrow descending to eight thousand feet.' Static continued to crackle. 'Heathrow the objects are now keeping pace. They are at our one o'clock position.'

Hoskins breathed in. 'Roger BEA 212 maintain your height.'

'Acknowledged.'

Several seconds of intense silence followed before the pilot spoke again. 'Heathrow the objects are now running parallel with us at three o'clock. They look more like flat discs..' The pilot's voice became distorted by static. 'Jesus...!' The pilot called out. 'Heathrow the objects have split and are now on all sides of our aircraft *over*. There are two above two below and two each to our left and to our right. We are boxed in repeat, we are boxed in.'

'BEA 212 maintain your course *over*.' Hoskins instructed; his voice cracked under the strain.

'Bloody hell.' Smith yelped. 'They're gone.'

Hoskins dropped the mike. *'What?'*

'The objects no longer appear on the scope.'

'Heathrow the objects just accelerated away. Jesus they were fast.' The pilot called out.

Hoskins grabbed the mike he had just dropped. 'Roger BEA 212 glad you're still with us. Continue your course *over*. A ground crew will meet you when you land.'

'Roger that Heathrow.'

RAF Northolt – 12:19am

'Shit.' Group Captain Douglas cursed. 'Recall the Vampires and tell them to stand down.'

The radar operator couldn't stop himself from smiling. 'Those objects were fast.'

'You can wipe that stupid smile off your face corporal.'

'Yes sir sorry sir. It's just I have never seen anything move that fast.'

'My boot will be up your backside faster if you even mention the word flying saucer to anyone, do I make myself clear.'

Heathrow Airport – 1:56am

Alan Smith swallowed hard as he looked at the radarscope. He glanced over at Terry Hoskins who was mulling over the report he was now having to write concerning the earlier incident. The Vickers Viking aircraft had landed safely and had been met by a ground crew before reporting to Hoskins. The pilot and the co-pilot gave a detailed account of what had happened.

Finally Smith spoke. 'Mr Hoskins sir.'

Hoskins slowly looked in Smith's direction. 'What!' He barked.

'I'm sorry to bother you.' Smith checked the radarscope again. 'I think they're back again.'

Hoskins rose to his feet and then strolled over to the radar operator. 'You better not be pissing around Smith or it's the labour exchange for you.' Hoskins looked into the radarscope at the eight objects. 'Shit.' He seethed. 'Call Northolt again tell them what's going on.'

RAF Northolt – 2:12am

For the second time Group Captain Douglas watched two Vampire fighter jets scream past the control tower. The objects on radar were directly over London and a concerned Smith could only look on as the planes headed for the area.

'Sir shouldn't we alert the Air Ministry.' His junior officer asked.

'I'm not telling them anything until we have something to tell them. Knowing our luck this could be a flock of bloody geese.'

'Yes sir.'

Several minutes passed before the radio crackled into life. 'Northolt this is Foxtrot Tango one *over*.'

'Go ahead Foxtrot Tango.'

'Northolt we have positive contact with the aircraft *over*. You should be able to see them yourselves from the tower *over*.'

Smith squinted out at the night sky trying to focus through the darkness. Here and there were breaks in the cloud allowing Smith to see pinpricks of starlight. But his attention was soon drawn to the eight circular shaped lights which were fast approaching the air force base.

He picked up a pair of binoculars. The lights flew in a v formation. The two jets could be heard in the distance. But the approaching objects made no sound at all.

'Tower do you have a visual on the aircraft *over*?'

'Roger that Foxtrot Tango we have a visual stand by *over*.'

The objects slowed to a full stop and hung motionless at the edge of the airbase. The two jets were closing fast.

'Sir what do we do?'

Smith didn't answer he just stared at the objects. Then in an instant they accelerated vertically into the sky and were gone. The two Vampire jets came into view and overflew the control tower.

London Evening Examiner – Fleet Street – 12:13pm

George Rayman and Bill Mirren listened enthusiastically as Alan Smith relayed his story to them.

'Are you sure what you witnessed last night wasn't another aircraft?' Mirren asked.

'Positive.' Smith replied. 'There were a number of objects. At one point the pilot shouted over the radio that the objects had surrounded his plane.'

'It's a bloody good story.' Rayman said. 'If we can get other newspapers interested it could cause quite a stir.'

Mirren looked at Smith. 'Mr Smith would you excuse us for a moment.'

'Smith got up and left the room.'

'What?' Rayman said as he noticed the look on Mirren's face.

'You are right it is a good story.'

'But!'

'George we can't just print every UFO story that comes across our desk. The London Evening Examiner has a reputation. Our esteemed owner Sir Alfred Bradshaw would boot us both out of the door.'

'We have a credible witness Bill, he's a radar operator at Heathrow. How much more reliable can you get.' Rayman argued.

Mirren thought for a brief moment. 'Tell you what we'll do. We will bring Smith back in here. Get a full account, then I will give Sir Alfred a ring. He'll probably give me a right earful, but I might be able to persuade him to let us run with the story.'

'And then?' Rayman said.

'And then we'll see if we can hook someone from the government.'

Rayman smiled. 'I will bring Alan back in and we can begin.'

Chapter 51

Whitehall – London – 10:33am
Monday 23rd March 1953

Frederick sipped from the cup of tea that had been set down in front of him a few minutes earlier. The committee members were gathering for the first major meeting of the year.

'Good morning.' Malcolm Chambers greeted as he entered the room. 'First off let me begin by saying that Dr Lloyd is unable to attend this meeting. He is undergoing treatment for his cancer so we all wish him well with that.'

The other committee members nodded.

Chambers tossed a copy of the London Evening Examiner onto the table. It slid along the smooth surface before coming to rest in front of Frederick who looked at the headline printed in large letters.

Flying Saucers Buzz Heathrow and RAF Northrop

'Right I'll get straight to the point I have just returned from a short briefing with the Prime Minister who is furious about this story. As well as extensive newspaper coverage there have been interviews with the two vampire pilots, the tower crew and air traffic control staff at Heathrow. Everyone has given a detailed account of what they witnessed. Which incidentally Professor Frederick mimics your encounter last year at Church Fenton. The BBC have been running this story all weekend and now the American network ABC News has also got in on the act.' Chambers paused to take breath. 'I am inclined to agree with the Prime Minister on this matter. We have to control the flow of information by both civilian and military aviation personnel. The Prime Minister is determined to crack down on any information leakages. I want to know what we plan to do about this?'

Air Marshall Ian Morgan reached over and picked up the newspaper.

Chambers looked at him. 'As Air Marshal you should have been on top of this.'

'We have no protocol for these UFO encounters so our airmen are free to talk to whoever they want.' Morgan explained.

'Well I'm afraid it's got to bloody well stop. It's all very well members of the public going to the newspapers and rambling on about flying saucers, it's easier to dismiss. But when members of the RAF start giving interviews it's taken far too seriously.'

'So what do you suggest we do?' Frederick asked.

'For a start we clamp down on information concerning UFO encounters and our military pilots. From now on any pilot witnessing any UFO incident is to be grounded and submitted for a psychological evaluation.'

'Psychological evaluation.' Professor Alan Good stated. 'Isn't that a bit harsh. Surely you don't think our pilots are seeing things.'

'I think we have to consider the bigger picture here.' Professor Norman Canning said glancing at the newspaper. 'Commercial airline flights are becoming more popular. We have to consider the possibility of a mid-air collision with one of these UFOs. We have to implement some sort of policy regarding civilian airline pilots.'

'It's going to be a little more difficult to dismiss a plane full of passengers.' Explained Wilks.

Chambers shook his head. 'Not so Richard, it is far easier to dismiss a member of the public. As for civilian airline pilots, we can use methods a little more persuasive.'

'Which are?' Frederick enquired.

'Any civilian airline pilot who talks to the press about a UFO encounter is grounded for good. I suggest we draw up guidelines for both military and civilian airline pilots concerning UFO encounters. I also want to monitor the press. It would be useful if we knew how they come by these stories. I've set up an interview with the BBC. It will be part of the main evening television news. Professor Frederick and Wilks will attend. The interview will only last a few minutes. Hopefully It should be enough to convince people that the recent newspapers stories are nonsense.'

'Didn't we agree to keep my name out of the public domain regarding UFOs.' Frederick pointed out.

'We did indeed Ralph, I am not asking you to admit flying saucers are real. Quite the opposite actually. Make up some fancy statement regarding the laws of physics. Professor Wilks will be our front man for denying UFOs exist.'

Wilks looked at Chambers. 'I don't feel comfortable going on television and denying the existence of flying saucers. So much has happened since the Angel Committee was established. We are no longer dealing with a figment of the imagination.'

'I'm afraid Professor Wilks that you are going to have to get used to it. You are the country's most senior astronomer. You will be interviewed by a colleague of yours, Patrick Moore.'

'I know Patrick very well. He is an up and coming astronomer who has just written a book about the moon.'

'Ok this meeting is adjourned.' Chambers declared.

Chapter 52

BBC Broadcasting House – London – 5:23pm

'One minute gentlemen.' The producer announced.

'I must say Patrick I'm surprised to see you at the BBC.' Wilks said.

'I'm only doing a favour for someone.' Replied Moore. 'I couldn't imagine myself doing anything for the BBC long term. Books to write and all that stuff Richard.'

'Ten seconds.' Reminded the producer. 'Three... two... one...'

'Good evening viewers.' Moore greeted. 'Over the past few days the newspapers have been abuzz with talk of flying saucers and visitors from mars. The question we are here to ask, are these UFOs real. Joining me this evening is the country's most senior astronomer Professor Richard Wilks of Greenwich Observatory. And Professor Ralph Frederick, Cambridge Lecturer in astrophysics, Nobel Prize winner and scientific advisor to her Majesty's Government. Good evening gentlemen.'

'Good evening.' Wilks and Frederick said together.

'Now let's get right down to the brass tacks shall we. Are flying saucers or visitors from mars real? Professor Wilks what is your take on this phenomenon.'

Wilks drew breath before answering. 'There is no evidence to suggest UFOs or visitors from Mars are real. Some of the most common explanations for these flying saucers are meteors, planets, conventional aircraft or simply hallucinations. We even have had people who misinterpreted the moon as being a UFO.'

'In essence Professor you're saying that some of these people are barking mad.' Moore asked.

Wilks shook his head. 'No I'm not saying that at all. What

I'm saying is that most if not all of these sightings have rational explanations.'

Moore turned to Frederick. 'There has been talk and speculation of life on other planets and that they could be advanced enough to come and visit us. Professor Frederick is any of this possible?'

'No.' Frederick replied. 'You have to understand the distances are immense. It would take hundreds if not thousands of years to navigate interstellar space. Faster than light travel is mere science fiction. Moving on to life on other planets. Science has yet to determine whether there are any other planets out there. At this moment in time we are the only planet which harbours life.'

'Gentlemen thank you for coming in to quash any rumours of invaders from mars.'

'Our pleasure.' Wilks said.

Moore looked directly at the camera. 'So there you have it viewers. These UFOs and invaders from Mars all have rational explanations, good night.'

London Evening Examiner – Fleet Street – London – 5:31pm

Bill Mirren turned the control knob of the television until it switched off.

'What do you think?' George Rayman asked.

'I think they're talking out of their backsides.' Mirren replied.

'What do we do?'

Mirren thought for a moment. 'I want you to go to Cambridge tomorrow. Track down this Professor Frederick and see if you can rattle his cage.'

5:43pm

'Well that was relatively painless.' Wilks remarked as he and Frederick drove away from the BBC building.

Frederick sat in the back of the car watching the streets of London streak by.

'Something the matter Ralph.'

'I was just thinking about something my daughter said to me a while back. She asked me if there could be life on other worlds.' Frederick thought before correcting himself. 'In her own little way.'

'Children can be so inquisitive sometimes.' Wilks remarked.

'Are we doing the right thing Richard?' Playing down the flying saucer phenomenon. Trivializing it to make people think that those who have witnessed something are mad.'

'Considering what we have discovered over the past several months Ralph I would have thought you of all people would know the answer to that question.'

Frederick caught glimpse of a group of people waiting outside a theatre. 'Those people over there have no idea what lies beyond the boundaries of their everyday life.'

'Perhaps it's for the best. Your encounter with Janus should tell you that. In time people will adjust to the possibility that we might not be the only life in our universe.'

Frederick closed his eyes briefly as the image of Elizabeth and Susan appeared in his mind. 'I suppose for now we keep our little secrets.'

Chapter 53

Trinity College – Cambridge – 11:23am
Tuesday 24th March 1953

'Excuse me Professor but there's a young man to see you. He says it's urgent.' Frederick's secretary announced.

Frederick looked up from the paper he was marking. 'Did he say what it's about?'

'Something to do with your television appearance.'

Frederick thought for a moment before nodding.

'Professor Frederick it's a pleasure to meet you.' The man said offering his hand.

Frederick leant back in his chair. 'Is there something I can help you with, Mr?'

'George Rayman from the London Evening Examiner. I was hoping you would give a follow up statement regarding your interview with Patrick Moore last night.'

'What is it you wish to know Mr Rayman?'

'Basically why you think flying saucers are not real.'

'I think Mr Rayman the evidence speaks for itself. As I said during that news bulletin, there is absolutely no reason to believe that flying saucers have any scientific merit.'

'What you are saying Professor is that anyone who claims to have seen a flying saucer is nuts.'

'That's about the size of it yes.'

Rayman scribbled furiously. 'Even people such as aircraft pilots.'

'What exactly do you want Mr Rayman?'

'The truth.'

Frederick thought for a few moments. 'The truth is Mr Rayman there are many things that can't easily be explained. But labelling things as being ghosts, fairies at the bottom of the garden or flying saucers does not mean that they are.'

Frederick looked back at the paper he was marking. 'Good day to you Mr Rayman.'

Rayman remained seated for a few moments before getting up. 'I'll see you around Professor Frederick.'

Chapter 54

The Royal Society – London – 11:36am
Friday 27th March 1953

Norman Hinshelwood and Chester Osborne sat glaring at Frederick who had received a request to attend the Royal Society the day before.

'Thank you for coming in today Ralph.' Hinshelwood said.

'My pleasure Norman what is it I can do for you?'

'We wanted to pull you up on your television interview on Monday night. And also a recent newspaper article that also mentions you.' Osborne answered. 'Regarding flying saucers.'

Frederick thought about the journalist who turned up at Trinity College three days earlier.

'We are a bit puzzled concerning your comments.' Hinshelwood remarked.

'How so?'

'We were under the impression that the group the Prime Minister established last year was to prove the existence of flying saucers. Yet here you are denying that they are real.'

Frederick shifted in his chair.

'It's pointless denying membership of this group. What we want to know Ralph is have you learnt anything about flying saucers.'

'At this moment in time we merely analyse reports that members of the public and military send in.'

'But isn't that what Tizard's team do?' Osborne asked.

'Not exactly. Their job is to file away UFO reports for future analysis.'

'I'm going to make this very clear to you Ralph as you failed to take in our little chat last year. We will not tolerate such nonsense within these walls.'

A loud knock on the door interrupted Hinshelwood.

'Come in!' He barked.

Winston Churchill and Malcolm Chambers marched into the room.

'Prime Minister this is an unexpected honour sir.' Osborne greeted.

'Stop your grovelling man.' Churchill growled. 'This meeting is to cease immediately.'

'With all due respect Prime Minister..' Hinshelwood tried to say.

'With all due respect Mr Hinshelwood.' Churchill interrupted. 'Professor Frederick is one of my top scientific advisors which means he answers directly to me is that clear.'

'Yes of course Prime Minister.' Hinshelwood replied.

11:56am

'We are sorry you had to go through that Ralph.' Chambers said. 'We got wind of your meeting only an hour ago. We had no idea they were going to pull you in and subject you to a Spanish Inquisition.'

'Thanks for pulling me out. I suspect Professor Osborne put Hinshelwood up to it after watching my television interview the other night. I was also questioned by a journalist on Tuesday from The London Evening Examiner.'

Chambers had a copy of the Examiner in his hand. 'I acquired a copy this morning. They were just fishing, must have been a slow news day for them. The Prime Minister has assured me that they won't be bothering you any time soon.'

Frederick glanced at the article. 'That's good to know Malcolm but you know as well as I do once the press sinks its teeth into something they tend not to let go.'

'Rest assured Ralph your reputation remains intact.'

Chapter 55

Leominster – Herefordshire – 3:05pm
Sunday 29th March 1953

'The daffodils are blooming early this year.' Igor Lakatos said as he looked at the other man sat on a park bench.

'Yes they're always early in this part of the world.' The man replied looking up at the Russian.

Lakatos smiled as the man stood and approached. Both men embraced each other. 'It is good to see you Comrade. It has been far too long.' Lakatos said.

'I thought I would never see this day Comrade.' The man replied triumphantly.

'All thanks to Comrade Stalin's death.'

'Nothing like a bit of political upheaval to reunite old friends.' Both men laughed and then sat on the bench.

Lakatos looked across the park at children playing on swings in the distance. Their joyful cries carried across on a cool breeze. 'We had doubts you would answer the call Comrade.'

'With what happened to Burgess and Maclean I thought it would be a good idea if I kept a low profile. How are they by the way?'

'They are fine. Maclean is fast becoming a respectable member of the Soviet Union. However Burgess is finding it a little more difficult. The fool insists on ordering his suits from Savile Row in London. And his exotic taste in partners is frowned upon by the state.' Lakatos looked at the man. 'Which is why you are better off over here given you share Burgess' tastes. As for keeping a low profile, a wise move old friend. With all that is going on in the Soviet Union we need every ally we can get in the West.'

'Which is why I have been working hard to gain the trust

of the highest government officials.'

Lakatos smiled. 'Our superiors at the Kremlin are impressed with your standing. However they are a little disappointed with the amount of information regarding this Angel Committee Prime Minister Churchill established last year. Your messages have been vague at best. The project out in Tunguska has been stepped up.'

'I'm afraid Comrade Lakatos any intelligence gathered by the committee is kept under lock and key. If I may be so bold Comrade, what kind of information are they after?'

'Technical details.' Lakatos replied.

'Technical details.' The man shrugged. 'The Angel committee has nothing technical. Just reports and film footage from the incident in the North Sea last year. I thought the Tunguska crash would have provided you with all the technical details you need.'

'Tunguska has provided us with much. We have operatives in the USA who have provided us with materials recovered from Roswell.'

'Perhaps your decision to remove Doctor Vilenko was a little premature. She has discovered many things about the Tunguska crash. Whether you like it or not, her knowledge and understanding of the technology has been invaluable.'

'Doctor Vilenko has been a thorn in my side. The murder of her brother has persuaded her to stay in her current position. Jacob Barnes seems to be obsessed with double agents at the moment so we have instructed our people to keep a low profile until it is safe to communicate with Moscow.'

The informant nodded. 'We have an extensive casefile on a flying saucer kidnapping last year.'

'Kidnapping.' Lakatos said with a raised eyebrow.

'A young couple claimed they had some sort of encounter. The young woman involved disappeared for several weeks before being returned. I trust you have also read my message on this Janus whom Professor Frederick and Doctor Lloyd encountered.'

'A most interesting case. This Janus is clearly someone who is not of this world. If he is caught he could be valuable to our research.'

'That isn't going to be easy. This Janus seems to be invulnerable to bullets and the committee is clueless as to where he disappeared.'

'These kidnappings you mention, we have had similar incidents in the Soviet Union. But with Stalin's regime a lot of these people who claimed such encounters were sent to a Siberian Gulag or a mental hospital.'

Several moments of silence followed.

'So Comrade tell me about your colleagues which make up this Angel Committee.'

'The committee is made up of a collection of scientists and military officers.'

'All loyal to your new queen no doubt.'

'Of course.'

'Can any of them be persuaded to turn.'

'Maybe, I have been thinking about one individual. Professor Ralph Frederick.'

'The Nobel Prize winner.' Lakatos remarked. 'Do you think he will defect?'

'Frederick is a family man. However, I get the impression he's disappointed with how things are run within the committee.'

'How close are you to him?' Lakatos asked.

'He trusts me.'

'Are you able to gain access to his personal life?'

The informant looked at Lakatos. 'Any sexual advances on my part would only make him suspicious. Besides I have a family of my own. I must maintain this charade if I am to acquire information in the future.'

'Then we must find another method of recruiting him,

appeal to his scientific nature. The research project in Tunguska would be of great interest to this Professor Frederick. You are to contact Comrade Modin and arrange for him to bump into Frederick and make him an offer.'

'I'll see what I can arrange.'

Lakatos got to his feet. 'My time is up I have to get back to Moscow. Comrade Stalin's shadow still hangs over the Soviet Union I'm afraid. A lot of his close supporters are fighting to step into his shoes.'

The other man stood and embraced Lakatos. 'It is good to see you again old friend. Let's not leave it so long next time.'

Both men walked away in opposite directions.

Chapter 56

Trinity College – Cambridge – 12:13pm
Monday 13th April 1953

Frederick sipped from the cup of tea his secretary had just brought in. It was her last task of the day as Frederick had given her the afternoon off. He sat at his desk mulling over the events that had occurred at Stoke Lacy in Herefordshire a few months earlier. Along with the report, on the incident Frederick decided to keep a personal diary of all his experiences. Stoke Lacy was certainly one of the most disturbing incidents. Although Frederick could push aside the image Janus had planted in his mind, it didn't stop them haunting his dreams. The cathedral, Susan sobbing and Frederick himself cradling Elizabeth in his arms. He'd wake up suddenly and look to see if Elizabeth was beside him.

Frederick looked up from his desk alerted to a knock on the door. 'Come!' He called out.

The door opened revealing a large man with white hair and a white beard. He wore a grey suit and a long black overcoat. The man marched in and sat down opposite a bewildered Frederick. He lit up a cigarette and puffed on it contently for several seconds.

'Is there something I can help you with?'

'Actually Professor I was thinking the same thing.' The man replied revealing a broad Russian accent.

Frederick leaned back in his chair folding his arms. 'Really!'

'I am here to make you an offer of service.'

'I'm flattered but I am not interested. Now if you'll excuse me I have work to do, Mr?'

The Russian shook his head. 'Names are not important Professor.' He reached into his inside pocket and pulled out a photograph sliding it towards Frederick. 'This may change your mind.'

Frederick looked down at the photograph which depicted a desolate landscape where trees had been blown over in all directions.

'This picture was taken by a Soviet scientific expedition in Siberia.'

As Frederick studied the picture, he noted an object directly at the centre. Comparing the surrounding countryside and the distance from the object, he estimated it to have been several hundred feet across. The Russian picked up the photograph and slid it back into the envelope before Frederick could study it further.

'We currently have a research project in the area analysing this craft which we believe crashed in 1908. Our scientists have speculated that this craft is from another part of the galaxy. We have salvaged a lot of technology from the crash site as well as many bodies.'

'What is it you want from me exactly?' Frederick asked.

'Nothing much Professor Just a little exchange of information which the Soviet Union would pay handsomely for.'

'What kind of information?'

'We know that your government is conducting secret investigations into these flying saucers and that you are head of one of these teams.'

Frederick remained silent.

'Technical information regarding these flying saucers could benefit mankind Professor.'

'Or give the Soviet Union a tactical advantage.' Frederick replied.

'You would have unprecedented access to the Tunguska crash site and all of Russia's scientific community would be at your disposal.'

'Well thank you for the most generous offer but I am satisfied where my loyalties lie.'

The Russian stared at Frederick for several seconds before standing. 'So be it, but you are missing out on an opportunity few scientists like yourself rarely get.'

Whitehall – London – 11:12am
Tuesday 14th April 1953

'We have no one on our records fitting your description Ralph.' Stanford said. 'But one thing is certain he'll probably be a Soviet handler. He could even be the same one who dealt with Burgess and MacLean. He is obviously familiar with the layout at Cambridge. Now that we have a detailed description of this man British Intelligence can begin a search. If he's operating in the United Kingdom we'll nab him sooner or later.'

'What did you make of the photograph he showed you?' Chambers asked.

'He said the craft crashed in 1908 and that a team of scientists have been salvaging the technology it contains. He also mentioned bodies.' Frederick replied.

'Bodies!' Chambers remarked.

'I have read an account of a meteor or asteroid that came down in Siberia around the time this man mentioned. But no western scientific teams have been near the area.'

'If the Russians do have the remains of a craft from another world it ups the stakes.' Chambers said.

'It also levels the playing field with the Americans who rumour has it also have crashed Flying saucer technology.' Stanford added.

'I suggest we sit tight. Now that we know the Russians are sniffing about for information we'll try and keep an eye on the Soviet embassy. The man you encountered yesterday is bound to turn up sooner or later.'

Chapter 57

The Chequers Guesthouse – Enswell – Suffolk – 11:14am Monday 25th May 1953

Frederick picked up the small brass bell and shook it gently.

A tall thin man with dark hair and chiselled features appeared from a side door smiling broadly at him.

'Good morning sir.' The landlord greeted with a clear cut American accent.

'Good morning to you.' Frederick replied with a little surprise evident in his tone. Behind him stood Professor Alan Good who had agreed to accompany Frederick to investigate repeated UFO sightings in the area. Professor Norman Canning had also accompanied them and was unloading the car packed with fishing equipment which was to be their excuse for being in the area.

Enswell was situated between RAF Lakenheath and RAF Mildenhall. These bases located on the east coast of England also served as American air force bases.

Despite the fact that nothing had been detected on radar, the national press had been running a story about local residents witnessing strange lights in the sky. One witness even claimed to have seen one of these lights land and strange creatures appear dressed in silver spacesuits. Although Frederick had argued the story was probably a hoax he eventually accepted the task of finding out what was going on. And if it did turn out to be a hoax at least home wasn't very far away.

'We would like three single rooms please for two nights.' Frederick asked politely.

'Certainly sir we will be able to accommodate you.' The Landlord replied.

A young woman appeared and smiled at Frederick and Good.

'I'm must say it's unusual to see an American running a traditional English guesthouse. Do you get many locals frequent the pub?'

'Not as many as we would like to.' The American smiled.

'We mostly get the boys from Mildenhall and Lakenheath airbase. Occasionally the odd local or travellers like yourselves come in.' The woman explained also showing that she was American.

'How long have you been running this establishment?' Frederick asked.

'Oh let's see now.' The woman thought for a few seconds. 'My father was stationed here in December last year. I flew over here in January.'

'Your father.' Frederick said.

'Yes he's Mildenhall's base commander.' She looked at the man. 'My fiancé Tom decided to take a short spell from campus and join me. This place was up for lease so we thought what the hell. This will be our ninth week here now.' The woman looked at her fiancé. 'I'm forgetting my manners, I'm Janet Stacy and this is Tom Winchester.'

'I'm Ralph.' Frederick said gesturing behind him. 'My colleague Mr Alan Good and our other comrade in arms is sorting out our rods.'

'Oh I see, you're up here for the fishing. Well if you catch anything, our chef will be more than happy to cook it for you.' Janet offered.

'Thank you very much.' Professor Good replied signing the guest book.

'Listen fellas since you are our first proper English guests, the first pint of beer is on the house. I'll sort your luggage and Janet will escort you to the bar.'

'That's very kind of you.' Frederick remarked. 'But it's a little too early.'

'Nonsense.' Norman Canning snorted. He had just appeared in the doorway laden down with luggage and fishing gear. 'It's never too early, especially if these nice people have offered us a free pint.'

Tom stepped from behind the small reception area. 'Let me help you with that.'

'Thank you young man.' Canning clapped his hands together and rubbed them. 'So how about that free pint of beer then.'

All three men sat patiently at the bar while Tom dealt with their luggage. Professor Good took a large gulp from his glass and set it down on the bar.

'What do you think of our quaint little village?' Janet asked.

'It's very nice.' Professor Canning replied. 'Although while I was unloading the car there were two oddballs watching me.'

Janet smiled broadly shaking her head. 'They're not locals.'

'Really.'

'I'll let you in on a little secret. Over the past few weeks we've been invaded by men from Mars.'

'Good lord!' Canning replied glancing quickly at Frederick who was already rolling his eyes.

Janet finished pouring her second glass and picked up a third one.

'No not for me dear.' Frederick gestured putting up his hand. 'As I said it's a little too early.'

'Would you like some tea?' Janet asked.

'No I'm fine thank you.'

'So who are those two chaps?' Canning asked.

'They're a couple of investigative reporters apparently.' Tom said as he entered the bar. 'I take it Janet has been filling you in on our claim to fame.'

'This gentlemen just commented on those two guys hanging around outside.'

Tom smiled. 'Oh yes our resident Martian hunters. They've been snooping around for a week but they've yet to come in.'

'Well I suppose there are those who take these things seriously.' Frederick commented candidly.

Tom nodded. 'We have plenty of them in America. Flying saucers are a big thing over there to.'

'What sparked off all this flying saucer nonsense?' Professor Good asked.

'A local farmer's son claims he saw something in the sky and that it landed and two Martians appeared. Not one to gossip but he had quite a few beers in here. Lord knows why he decided to go to the press about it.'

'Any other witnesses.' Frederick asked.

'Just a few locals but I think it's more drink talking than anything. Nearly all of them come in here and get tanked up if you catch my drift.'

'I take it you don't believe in such nonsense.'

'No sir.' Tom replied. 'I like to keep my feet firmly on the ground. If you ask me it's too much of an active imagination.'

Canning finished his pint and put it down on the bar. 'Well I don't know about you but I'm here to hunt some fish not Martians.'

Tom laughed. 'I hear you on that one.'

Chapter 58

2:43pm.

After a light lunch of ham and mustard sandwiches and another round of drinks all three men decided to head out for the afternoon.

'I don't see why we can't make use of this equipment. Besides that sweet young lady promised their chef will cook whatever we catch.' Canning said with enthusiasm.

The group walked for about a mile before coming across one of the many waterways which crisscrossed the county of Suffolk.

As they began setting up their equipment Frederick noticed two men watching them from a few hundred yards away. 'Are those the two you spotted earlier Norman?'

Canning looked to where Frederick was pointing. 'Yes that's them.'

The two men started to approach.

Frederick, Good and Canning carried on setting up their fishing rods pretending not to be too bothered about the approaching strangers.

'Good afternoon gentlemen.' The shorter of the two men greeted. He quickly surveyed their fishing equipment and looked almost disappointed that there was nothing more.

'Good afternoon.' Frederick replied.

'I take it you gentlemen are here for the fishing.'

'You don't miss much do you.' Norman Canning remarked sarcastically.

The man glared at him for a few seconds before focusing his attention on Frederick. 'Are you planning to stay long?'

'A few days, it depends what we catch.'

'I see you gentlemen are staying with the Americans at their guesthouse.'

Frederick began to tire at the man's pointless questioning. 'Yes.'

'And what are they like?'

'I don't quite follow you.' Frederick replied.

'What I mean is how is it a couple of Yanks are running an English boarding house.'

Good began to lose patience. 'Look gentlemen is there something you wish to know or are you going to continue to babble on?'

'He was only asking a few questions that's all.' The other man said firmly.

'Let me introduce myself.' 'The shorter man said holding his hand out. 'Fred Barnet, this is my associate Albert Atkins.'

'And what brings you to this part of the world?' Asked Frederick.

'We are here on a matter of a scientific nature.' Barnet replied.

'Are you scientists?'

Atkins shook his head. 'No but our organisation has its roots based in scientific theory.'

'And what organisation might that be?' Professor Good enquired.

'We run the British UFO Bureau of Investigation.' Barnet said proudly. 'We are in the area investigating a number of sightings. Perhaps you gentlemen may have read about this. It's been all over The News of The World.' Barnet reached into a small satchel and pulled out some A4 sheets of paper which were fastened together with a paperclip. 'We have a monthly newsletter that goes out. Our circulation is over eighty now and some of our subscribers are very distinguished.'

Frederick read through the newsletter which was made up of four pieces of paper 'These distinguished subscribers you have just mentioned, who are they?'

Atkins smiled broadly. 'None other than his Royal Highness the Duke of Edinburgh and Lord Mountbatten. We wrote to the palace last year to ask if they would be interested in subscribing to our newsletter. Can you imagine our surprise when we got a letter back from the royal Equerry Peter Horsley.'

'That is impressive.' Canning remarked.

Frederick handed back the newsletter. 'Well good luck with your search gentlemen.'

'One can only hope.' Barnet replied.

'I tell you what, why don't you gentlemen join us for a drink later this evening. We would love to hear stories about your organisation. You must have some fascinating insights into what these UFOs are.' Frederick suggested.

'Oh we do.' Atkins replied enthusiastically.

Barnet stood silent for a few moments contemplating Frederick's invitation. 'We'd be delighted to join you gentlemen for a drink, say about eight thirty.'

Frederick smiled as the two men walked away chatting to one another excitedly.

'I hope you don't think we are going to sit with those bores tonight.' Canning groaned.

'I just wanted to know more about the duke's interest in UFO's that's all.'

'Providing they're not stringing you along.' Canning remarked. 'For all you know they could have made a cock and bull story just to reel you in.'

'Maybe but it still doesn't explain the fact that he mentioned Peter Horsley. I encountered him last year in Yorkshire.' Frederick explained.

'I suppose it is a bit of a coincidence.' Professor Good commented. 'But I'm not talking to them all night long.'

Canning felt a tug on his fishing rod. 'That was quick, looks like fish is on the menu tonight gentlemen.'

Chapter 59

8:23pm

That afternoon all three men managed to land four trout and a large carp. When they arrived back at the guesthouse, they presented their catch to Janet who fulfilled the promise she had made. After dinner the three of them sat at a table in the corner of the bar waiting for the two men they had encountered earlier that day.

'I still say this is a waste of time.' Canning grumbled as he lit his pipe.

'We will see.' Frederick answered.

The bar had filled with American servicemen from Mildenhall. The jukebox that Tom had imported specially from the US spewed out a list of Hank Williams hits.

Atkins and Barnet appeared at the main entrance and looked around nervously. No one paid them any attention as they made their way through the bar towards Frederick and his two companions.

Frederick stood and stepped forward. 'Gentlemen you made it.'

Canning stood. 'I'll get the next round.'

Barnet looked nervously around him at the other drinkers.

'You needn't take any notice of these chaps Fred they're just out for a drink.' Frederick reassured.

'I don't want anyone else listening in on our conversation that's all.'

'I doubt whether these airmen are interested in things such as flying saucers and men from Mars.' Professor Good stated.

'We are not here just for the flying saucer story.' Atkins said. He quickly scanned the bar to make sure no one was looking in their direction. Leaning forward he spoke in a low voice. 'We are also here investigating the possibility that the Yanks could be using Mildenhall as a testing ground.'

'Testing ground?' Frederick enquired.

'For highly advanced experimental aircraft.'

Canning returned with a tray of drinks and set it down on the table. 'Here we go chaps.' He sat down and scooped up a glass taking a large swig from it. 'What are we discussing?'

'Albert was just telling us that the Americans could be testing experimental aircraft out of Mildenhall.' Frederick explained.

'Really what kind of aircraft?'

'We are not sure but we believe that it could be something capable of great speed. Using jet engine propulsion and capable of flying at great height. We believe that these aircraft are being launched from the belly of a modified B-50 American Bomber.' Barnet revealed. 'The aircraft they are testing is based on a German design which was being tested by the Nazis during the war.'

'Forgive me gentlemen.' Good interrupted. 'But that sounds as fantastic as the flying saucer story you said you were up here investigating.'

'Myself and my colleague.' Atkins said. 'No longer believe that any UFOs have been spotted in the area. We believe that it's a cover story for what's really going on.'

'And what is that precisely?' Canning asked.

'We think they're using these aircraft to probe Soviet territory.'

'Nonsense!' Good exclaimed. 'I don't believe the Yanks are that far advanced yet.'

'How do you know?' Atkins shot back.

'My dear man I worked with Frank Whittle during the war and I can assure you that the Americans are yet to develop anything that could penetrate Soviet territory.'

Barnet reached into his inside pocket. 'This is a sketch drawn up by a witness who said he had sneaked into the airbase.'

Good studied the crude diagram that depicted a small one man aircraft with a slender body and swept back wings.

'Of course that's not an accurate diagram but it does match the description of an aircraft the Americans have been testing over the Nevada desert for the past few years.' Barnet revealed.

Good handed the piece of paper to Frederick. 'And how is it you know all this Mr Barnet?'

'We have an American section of the Bureau. He is an aircraft enthusiast. I managed to have a full telephone conversation with him last month. He described an aircraft similar to the one in that drawing. He believes that the Americans have built an aircraft capable of reaching over one hundred thousand feet and flying at speeds of up to Mach two.'

'Impossible.' Good dismissed.

Barnet glared at him. 'Oh really and when exactly was the last time you spoke to Mr Whittle?'

Good found himself on his back heel. 'Well actually.'

'Go on.' Barnet interrupted.

Good gave a nod of defeat. 'It is several years since we last spoke.'

'Exactly, are you familiar with the latest aircraft designs?'

Frederick decided to ask a question. 'Who is the witness you mentioned just now?'

'He's a local lad, goes by the name of William Davies; he's a farmer's boy.'

Canning rolled his eyes remembering what Tom had mentioned earlier that day.

'Have you spoken to him first hand?' Frederick enquired.

'We have.' He pointed at the diagram. 'This is how we were able to get a description of the aircraft.'

Canning looked across the bar and spotted a small group of servicemen hovering around a dart board. He clasped his glass and stood. 'I think I will show those chaps how to play a decent game of darts.'

Good looked in the same direction and also stood. 'Mind if I join you Norman?'

'No not at all.' Canning replied.

'Your friends don't seem to believe us.' Atkins said.

'I have to admit gentlemen your story does sound a little farfetched.'

'We intend to expose the Americans and prove to the world that their testing experimental aircraft out of Mildenhall.'

'And how do you plan to do that?' Asked Frederick.

'The farmer's son showed us a way into the base. There's a hole in the fence the Americans haven't found.'

'Isn't that a little risky trespassing on a military airbase?'

Atkins shook his head. 'The risks are minimal if we manage to get hold of evidence.'

'When exactly do you plan to break in?'

'Tonight just after one o'clock.'

Frederick looked at Atkins unsure as to how to proceed with the conversation.

'We could do with an extra witness.' Barnet said. 'The more witnesses the harder it will be for the Americans to cover up the truth.'

Frederick remained silent. He glanced over at Professor Good and Canning who were instructing the American servicemen in a game of darts.

Chapter 60

10:05pm

'Have you taken leave of your senses?' Good complained.

'I'll only accompany them to the hole in the fence.' Frederick said.

'If you are caught then you could expose us. I thought we had agreed to leave tomorrow. Not follow those two idiots on some wild goose chase.'

'He's right Ralph.' Canning added. 'If you are caught you could expose the committee.'

'I won't be exposing anything.' Frederick put on a defensive posture.

'Maybe not but the Americans will want to know what a prominent Cambridge Professor is doing breaking into an American airbase with a couple of flying saucer nut jobs. And you have mentioned you don't want to draw attention to yourself.'

'Gentlemen.' Frederick stated holding up his hand. 'No one will be getting caught. I will only be escorting them to the perimeter fence. After that they're on their own.'

'Why are you so eager to believe those two?' Canning asked.

'Because of the things I have seen. Look I know you two haven't had the first-hand experience that I have. But if the Americans are testing experimental aircraft on British territory then we need to know.'

Good puffed on his pipe pondering Frederick's words before eventually nodding. 'Ok but I suggest we contact Malcolm back in London. We need a backup plan just in case your little adventure goes belly up.'

'Thank you, all I ask is a bit of faith.' Frederick said.

Mildenhall Air force base – Suffolk – 12:56am
Tuesday 26th May 1953

Frederick parked the car as near as he dared to the base perimeter fence. He managed to find a muddy track leading into a small wood so the car couldn't be seen from the road.

Atkins and Barnet chatted excitedly as they neared the airbase. 'This will increase the circulation of the newsletter if we get hold of evidence.' Atkins said.

'Why did the farmer's son tell the newspapers he saw a flying saucer with Martians coming out?' Frederick asked.

'He didn't go to the newspapers.' Barnet replied.

'So who did?'

'We don't know. All we know he was caught on the base and escorted off. The next thing he knew the News of the World came calling.'

'And no one knows who called the newspapers.'

'No, the moment William told us he didn't tell any newspapers what he saw we knew there must be something more to the flying saucer story.'

'But it still doesn't explain why the News of the World claimed he said that he had seen a flying saucer.'

'We believe that the News of the World was deliberately fed false information. Someone on the base was trying to cover their tracks.' Barnet explained. 'We attempted to interview the editor but he turned us down. Wasn't very pleasant either.'

The three men made their way through the wooded area by torchlight. The distant lights of Mildenhall airbase came into view. Because of a full moon the visibility was remarkably good. Atkins broke into a jog. 'Come on the hole is just up here.'

Frederick found himself strangely exhilarated by his actions. Distant memories as a boy flooded his mind. Adventures scrumping apples from the local farmer's orchard and getting caught. His father looking down at him waving his finger furiously.

When they reached the hole in the fence Atkins and Barnet didn't hesitate climbing through it. Frederick hung back. Both Good and Canning sat on his moral shoulders warning him about the dangers of getting caught.

Atkins turned and looked at him through the fence. 'Aren't you coming?'

Frederick shook his head. 'I'm afraid I'm going to have to chicken out of this one chaps. I'm not as light on my feet as you two. Got a dodgy cricket knee and all that. I'll wait here until you get back.'

'Ok suit yourself we'll be back shortly.' Barnet held up the camera he had brought with him. 'With lots of good pictures we hope.' Both men bolted off across the base and despite the full moon soon melted into the darkness.

Frederick thought best if he headed back to the car to wait for their return.

2:36am

The thunderous noise shook Frederick from his sleep. He shone the torch onto his watch and cursed Atkins and Barnet. 'We'll be back shortly.' He muttered to himself impersonating one of them. For a full minute Frederick sat mulling over the situation and surmising that they must have been caught. Eventually curiosity overwhelmed him and he got out of the car taking with him a pair of binoculars. Frederick mumbled to himself about how pointless this whole venture had turned out to be.

After several minutes he reached the spot in which he had left Barnet and Atkins. Frederick looked out a cross the base and could see the silhouette of a plane on the runway several hundred yards away. The moon reflected off its long slender silver fuselage. There was a flurry of activity around the aircraft. Frederick peered through his binoculars and could see the pilot of the aircraft climbing down a small ladder. The man was dressed in a silver boiler suit and wore a very large helmet. A glass visor covered his entire face. A pipe ran from the back of his helmet and was attached to a small cylindrical tank mounted on his back. The aircraft itself matched the crude sketch Atkins and Barnet had presented earlier. A long slender body several meters in length with swept back wings and a tail.

Frederick's attention was diverted to shouting coming from the side of the runway. He quickly scanned with his binoculars and spotted the light of a torch dancing furiously in the darkness. Both Atkins and Barnet were sprinting towards Frederick's position followed closely by several men who were screaming at them to stop. A gunshot rang out in the darkness and Frederick watched in horror as one of the two men tumbled onto the grass.

It was too dark to see if it was Barnet or Atkins who fell. The other man had stopped dead in his tracks flinging his hands into the air.

It only took a fleeting moment for Frederick to decide he had seen enough. As he turned on his heels a blinding light shone into his face.

'Do not move!' A voice ordered.

Chapter 61

Mildenhall Air force base – 6:57am

Frederick looked around the small room. He rubbed the lower part of his back.

After his apprehension at the perimeter fence of the air base, he was taken away on a jeep before being hauled onto the back of a US army lorry for a few hours. Two heavily armed military police kept a watchful eye on him.

He had been made to wait for at least half an hour in the small room when the door finally opened to reveal Tom from the guesthouse. Frederick didn't know whether to feel relieved or apprehensive. It only took a few seconds for the decision to be made for him as agent Frank Cones walked in behind Tom.

Both men sat down opposite Frederick and glared at him for what seemed to be a long time before Tom spoke first. 'Professor Ralph Frederick, renowned astrophysicist, Nobel Prize winner, university lecturer, father of one and now it would seem a trespasser.'

'I think you will find I wasn't trespassing. I was not on the base when your men arrested me.' Frederick fought to maintain a calm posture. 'Now if you gentlemen don't mind I would like to go. You have no right to keep me here.'

'On the contrary Professor we have every right. You may not have been on the airbase but your friends were. They will be charged with spying.' Agent Cones revealed.

'That's preposterous and you know it, they were just there to.' Frederick found himself stopping in mid-sentence.

'Go on Professor.' Tom pressed.

'Where are they? And what happened to the man who was shot?' Frederick asked.

'We have them in custody. The man who was shot, Mr

Atkins is well enough to answer questions.'

'I want to see them now.' Frederick demanded.

'I'm afraid that's not possible.' Cones stated. 'What I would like to know Professor is what you were doing with these guys snooping about our air base.'

'We were bird watching.'

'Really, at two o'clock in the morning.' Tom said.

Frederick shrugged. 'We were on the lookout for tawny owls. They are nocturnal you know.'

'Cut the bullshit Professor just tell us what you were looking for.'

'Why, so you can have me on some false allegation, I don't think so.'

'Ok then, tell us what those two UFO freaks were doing with a camera.'

'UFO freaks!' Frederick reacted as if surprised by what Tom had just revealed. 'They told me they were bird watchers.'

'I'm glad you think this is funny Professor.' Tom said in a dark tone. 'Because if you don't tell us what you were doing sneaking around in the middle of the night then we will charge you with spying.'

Frederick shrugged for a second time. 'But I didn't see anything, so how can you say I was spying. And I am sure you have taken away the camera those chaps had on them. So you have no grounds to hold them either.'

Both Tom and Cones glanced at each other.

'Exactly what is your role Tom? I'm guessing you are not a humble pub landlord.'

Tom broke into a smile. 'Like you Professor I profess my ignorance in all this.'

'Ok Professor.' Cones took over. 'Tell us what you think you saw tonight.'

Frederick shook his head. 'I don't quite follow.'

'We know what those two guys were up to Professor. We

know they run some kind of organisation investigating flying saucers. What we don't understand is what a top UK government scientist is doing with them. Plus you and your colleagues Professors Good and Canning decided to turn up for a fishing trip. In a village that has been the subject of a number of newspaper articles relating to flying saucers.'

'Like this man.' Frederick replied looking at Tom. 'I must profess my ignorance. I see that you are still traipsing all over the country agent Cones. Where is your partner Jack Baker?'

Cones was about to continue with his questioning when the door to the interview room opened.

Frederick felt relief wash over him at the sight of Malcolm Chambers and Ian Morgan. Cones looked at the base commander who accompanied them.

'This man is to be released immediately.' The base commander ordered.

'We haven't finished questioning him.' Cones protested.

'This interview is over Agent Cones.' Chambers said calmly.

Cones glared at the base commander who nodded silently.

Frederick stood. 'Thank you gentlemen it's been a pleasure. Now if you don't mind I'd like to see the other two men you have detained.'

Ian Morgan looked at Frederick and shook his head.

7:23am

As the car sped through the main gates of the air force base Frederick felt like a free man and breathed deeply. Thoughts of Elizabeth and Susan gave him comfort.

'You're a bloody lucky man Ralph. We had to tug pretty hard on some diplomatic strings to get you out of there.' Malcolm Chambers said. 'You know they were planning to keep you there for a very long time.'

'I appreciate you coming to my rescue.' A grateful Frederick said. 'But I'm more concerned for those two chaps who were caught on the airbase.'

'I'm afraid there's not much we can do.' Ian Morgan revealed. 'The Americans are free to hold them as long as they want.'

'But they will be charged with spying.'

Chambers shook his head. 'They will be released eventually. The Americans won't want any kind of publicity over this, especially what they're testing at that base.'

'I saw something. It didn't look like any aircraft I have seen before.' Frederick said.

'You did see something Ralph and that's what the Yanks were so upset about.' Morgan said. 'It seems they're testing a top secret spy plane and flying it over Soviet territory.'

'Spy plane.'

'Yes it's a later model of the Bell X-1 that broke the sound barrier in forty seven. However this plane is capable of flying much faster and has an altitude of well over a hundred thousand feet.'

'That's what one of the Flying saucer activists claimed last night.' Frederick explained. 'I don't understand how they are able to fly top secret spying missions from the UK mainland. Does the Prime Minister know about this?'

'He does now.' Chambers said. 'And I can tell you the old man was furious. He had a rather heated discussion with the new President Eisenhower. That's how we managed to pull you out of there. Eisenhower didn't want to expose what was going on at that base.'

'I don't understand what that chap Tom was doing there from the guesthouse?'

'He's CIA, recruited out of MIT. This little spy plane project of theirs is a CIA run operation.'

'So the CIA are testing aircraft at Mildenhall.' Frederick commented. 'I wonder what else they haven't told us. And what was Frank Cones doing there? From what we learnt in January He only investigates UFO sightings.'

'We have learnt that Frank Cones and Jack Baker are part

of Project Blue Book. But since they are also CIA I suspect that they're on loan to oversee this operation.'

Frederick thought for a moment. 'The CIA could be responsible for feeding information to the News of The World.' He suggested.

'It's highly likely.' Chambers remarked. 'A game of disinformation to hide the real truth of what's going on at the base.'

'Well I for one am glad to be out of there.' Frederick sighed turning his thoughts to Elizabeth and Susan.

Chapter 62

Highclare House – Surrey – 3:09pm
Friday 29th May 1953

'Has the old man taken leave of his senses?' Professor Good Protested. 'Why should we trust the Americans? Especially what we have learned about Mildenhall and the incident during Operation Mainbrace last year. Not to mention this agent Frank Cones running all over the place. And to top it all off those UFO investigators are still being held at Mildenhall.'

'I'm sure that most of us are reluctant to side with the Americans on this matter Alan.' Chambers explained. 'But the Prime Minister is adamant that we team up with the Yanks. And quite frankly I'm inclined to agree with him. On the flipside I think the Yanks are running damage control after the events at Mildenhall.'

'How exactly will this alliance benefit our committee?' Frederick asked.

'From what the Prime minister told me President Eisenhower is eager to combine resources so that both groups will learn more about the UFO phenomenon. It also gives us the opportunity to find out what the Americans know. Apparently Eisenhower has pledged full disclosure on all materials the Americans have collected over the past decade on flying saucers. This is an opportunity we cannot ignore gentlemen. The Prime Minister believes it will help cement our special relationship.'

'It will also give us the opportunity to know the inner workings of the CIA.' Morris Stanford said. 'I for one am interested to know more about this Agent Cones.'

'Nevertheless we must be cautious.' Professor Wilks advised. 'We must limit the information we share with them.'

'That will be easy considering we've very little information to share in the first place.' Chambers remarked. 'I am very interested to know if the rumours that the Americans have captured one of these flying saucers is true.'

'When do we meet with the Americans?' Frederick asked.

'They're flying in tomorrow so our first meeting is scheduled for Monday.' Chambers replied.

'Has the Prime Minister given any more details about who these Americans are?' Norman Canning enquired.

Chambers shook his head. 'For now everything is being kept under wraps. I can tell you that whoever they are they will be flying in under assumed names. The Americans seem to be obsessed with the spread of Communism lately so they're taking no chances.'

The Kremlin – Moscow – 4:46pm
Saturday 30th May 1953

Igor Lakatos started to get impatient with Kremlin security. Since he had entered the building he had been stopped on every floor and had been asked to present his papers. For a seemingly long while the soldier scrutinised his identification papers before glaring at him and handing them back. Lakatos snatched his papers away from the guard and hurried down the corridor which was filled with many people. He had to say excuse me a dozen times before he got to his destination.

He stood at a large oak door realising that only a few months earlier Comrade Stalin's name had been on the door. Finally Lakatos knocked loudly and waited for a few moments before it opened.

Ivan Volkart stared at Lakatos before asking what was so important to be disturbing Comrade Bulganin.

'I must speak with our new president immediately.'

Volkart opened the door wider for Lakatos to step inside. 'Comrade Bulganin is extremely busy at the moment Comrade Lakatos. If you tell me what is so important I will be happy to pass on any information.'

Lakatos looked Volkart up and down and grinned. 'I see our new leader has already made you his lap dog so I won't waste my time. I'll speak to him directly.'

'Comrade Lakatos, you are one of many people who has requested to see our leader. So far no one has had that pleasure. I may be a lap dog but I am now on the inside and you are still shivering in the freezing political wasteland which has been left in the wake of Comrade Stalin's demise. If I were you I would be careful who you make an enemy of these days. Now if it's that important I suggest you relay the message to me. Then I will decide whether or not it is worthy enough for the ears of Comrade Bulganin.'

'This is outrageous does he not know the sacrifice I made for him?'

'Sacrifice for you maybe, but betrayal to other members of the Russian science academy. Now you can give me the message or you can stand there crying like a small child. In which case I will have no choice but to call security and have you thrown out of this building. Your papers will be confiscated and you will never set foot in the Kremlin again.'

Lakatos grimaced. 'Very well tell him that my informant in Great Britain has told me of an important meeting between the Americans and the British regarding matters of a cosmic nature and that I am flying to London immediately to meet with my informant personally over this matter.'

Volkart shrugged. 'That's it, you went to all that trouble to come down here and tell him that.'

Lakatos smiled. 'He will understand what I mean. Then he will want to speak with me personally. And then Comrade I will also be on the inside. So if I were you I would be careful who you make an enemy of.'

Chapter 63

Whitehall – London – 10:01am
Monday 1st June 1953

Frederick felt nervous as he waited for the Americans to enter the meeting room in which all but two of the committee members had gathered. Lord Chambers and Morris Stanford had gone to the Savoy Hotel where the Americans were staying.

Frederick smiled briefly at Wilks who was sat next to him.

'Don't look so nervous Ralph we have to show the Yanks a united front. We don't want them to get over bearing.'

Frederick slowed his breathing and sipped from a glass of water. 'My experiences with the Americans over the past year haven't been the most enjoyable I'll tell you that.'

The door opened and Lord Chambers marched in followed by three men and finally Morris Stanford. All five men seated themselves.

'Good morning gentlemen.' Chambers greeted. 'We are honoured today to have with us three of America's top authorities on the flying saucer phenomenon. Prime Minister Churchill and President Eisenhower have set out plans for a joint effort focused on dealing with this phenomenon. I am sure that this new partnership will be beneficial to both our countries. Joining us today are Roscoe Hillenkoetter director of the Central Intelligence Agency. Renowned scientist Doctor Vannevar Bush and finally Doctor Donald Menzel of Harvard. Mr Hillenkoetter will brief us on intelligence that the Americans have gathered.'

Hillenkoetter stood and placed a briefcase he was carrying on the table. 'Good morning gentlemen. On behalf of myself my colleagues and the President of the United States I would like to thank you for receiving us.' He paused and looked around the table making eye contact with the committee members. 'First of all we will begin by telling you that myself and my two colleagues with me today and nine other men make up a group known as Majestic 12. This group was formed by President Truman in 1947 prior to an event which happened in the summer of that year which we are about to brief you on.' Hillenkoetter paused for a moment of thought. 'So why are we all here today we may be asking ourselves? We are here because there is a new threat in the skies above us. Namely what we call flying saucers or as they are becoming more commonly known UFOs. Unknown objects are operating under intelligent control. It is imperative that we learn where UFOs come from and what their purpose is. Our government like yours believe that this is by no means a new phenomenon and that these UFOs have been with us for a long time. It is only because of technological advancements made during the war that these UFOs have become visible. Although we understand that there have been reports regarding UFOs for quite a few decades. The earliest report we have was made by a pilot in 1913. Mr Dan Watson was flying his aeroplane over Sothern California when he encountered a large glowing spherical object just outside San Diego.'

Hillenkoetter opened his briefcase pulled out a file and began reading. 'The object appeared above me and was moving very fast. I estimate its size to have been over one hundred feet long. It wasn't long before the object was completely out of sight. At first I thought I had seen a falling star but a few minutes later the object became visible again. It was on a parallel course to me. I tried to change direction but it maintained its heading matching every manoeuvre I made. When it was only a few dozen feet away the object banked sharply and shot away. When I finally managed to turn my plane around the object was no longer visible.' Hillenkoetter handed the report to Chambers who looked at it briefly before passing it on to Frederick. 'Doctor Donald Menzel will now share with you his thoughts on this subject.'

Menzel leaned forward pressing his knuckles against the oak surface of the table before standing. 'I can tell you one thing we are certain of. These UFOs do not originate from our planet. Although I'm sure you are all fully aware of this given your experiences with the phenomenon.'

The committee members exchanged looks.

'Like you British we were hoping for some kind of earth bound explanation. We were hoping perhaps that it was the Russians working on some kind of new experimental aircraft. But all that changed less than six years ago. What I am about to tell you has been classified above top secret. And I'm sure that when you see what we have brought with us today you will all understand that upmost secrecy must be maintained.' Menzel drew breath before continuing. 'In the summer of 1947 the Midwest was plagued by a spate of UFO sightings. Washington was aware of these sightings and had placed our forces on standby should any event happen. At the time we were convinced that the Soviets had begun some kind of new weapons research program and were testing experimental aircraft in the skies above us. In late June we received a report of nine UFOs over the state of Washington in the mount Rainer region. A pilot called Kenneth Arnold had made the report, stating that he had sighted these objects flying at extremely high speed. The newspaper that published his story stated that he described their flight pattern like a saucer skipping across water. Hence the term flying saucer was born. Less than a week later our people in Washington received a telephone call from an Army air force base just outside a small town in the state of New Mexico called Roswell. General Frank Ramey reported that some sort of aircraft had crashed and that a local farmer had found wreckage strewed all over his land. Myself and Mr Hillenkoetter visited the area immediately to find out if reports by local radio and newspapers were true about the army having the remains of a flying disc. We were taken to the location where this disc reportedly crash landed.' Menzel reached into the briefcase and pulled out a large photograph. He then placed it on the table for all the committee members to see. 'It was when we viewed this aircraft we realised we were dealing with something out of the ordinary. We then informed the President.'

'Good lord!' Norman Canning exclaimed.

Menzel smiled. 'Yes gentlemen what you are looking at is a craft from beyond our planet.'

Chapter 64

10:23am

All the committee members stared in disbelief at the photograph Menzel had just laid out in front of them. The object in the image appeared to be embedded in the side of a small hill. 'This craft.' Menzel began again. 'Came down approximately seventy miles North West of Roswell. We believe that it collided with the balloon and lost control after also being struck by lightning during a violent storm that had blown up.'

'Have you managed to access its interior?' Wilks asked excitedly.

Menzel put his hand up. 'Please there'll be plenty of time to ask questions when we finish this briefing. Doctor Vannevar Bush will now explain a few things regarding this craft.' Menzel sat.

'Well as Doctor Menzel pointed out.' Vannevar Bush said as he stood. 'This craft is not from our world, neither does it originate from our solar system. We believe the on board systems malfunctioned after it was struck by lightning. We managed to transport the main bulk of the craft to White Sands Missile range in New Mexico. Debris from the ship was transported to Wright Patterson air force base in Ohio and a facility at Dugway proving grounds in Utah. However, as you can imagine we are having trouble understanding the technology that this craft contains. It's way beyond anything we have and this is why we have decided to set up a joint scientific research committee. You Gentlemen are the first to know anything about the crash. In time we plan to inform other top military and scientific minds from other allied countries.' Bush paused. 'On to the main event as they say.'

Hillenkoetter pushed the briefcase he had with him over

to Bush who reached inside and lifted out a flat object wrapped in black cloth. He placed the object on the table in front of him and unwrapped it. At first glance the object appeared to be a rectangular piece of glass with the corners rounded off. It was approximately eight inches in length by six inches in width and a thickness of less than a quarter of a centimetre. On closer inspection there appeared to be a metallic disc approximately one inch in diameter embedded at the centre of the object. At the centre of the disc was a small hole about half a centimetre making it look like a washer. Crisscrossing the device were rows of thin metallic strips that were barely visible.

'When we gained access to the craft.' Bush continued. 'We were able to remove a lot of the technology. One of the most common items found were these flat looking devices. At first our scientists ignored them believing they were redundant. Then one day out of the blue we discovered they could do this.' Bush reached forward and simply tapped the surface of the object directly above the central disc.

Less than a second later light emanated from the disc projecting in a vertical direction. To everyone's astonishment they found themselves staring at a glowing sphere which spun slowly floating in the air several inches above the alien device. The immediate area was filled with a pale blue light.

'Astounding!' Frederick stated. 'Is that what I think it is?'

Bush nodded. 'It's earth.'

'How is this possible?' Wilks asked.

Bush smiled. 'We have no idea but if you like that watch this.' He reached out and tapped the area of the globe which represented the United Kingdom. In an instant the globe stopped spinning and the familiar outline of Great Britain appeared. To the side of the floating image strange symbols appeared. Bush reached forward again and tapped one of the symbols. Without warning the room filled with sound. The noise consisted of radio broadcasts. Winston Churchill's voice could be heard along with Vera Lynn and jazz music. Bush reached out again and this time tapped the object twice. In an instant the image and sound were gone. 'Our scientists believe that this object is some kind of storage device capable of holding massive amounts of information. We have studied this one in particular and have found it contains a detailed record of our planet. This device has the capacity to store all radio and TV broadcasts as well as movies from every nation on our planet. We have found information on every country's military capabilities including the Soviet Union and China as well as Great Britain and the United States of America. All this information has led us to one startling conclusion. We are being studied and that the creatures which piloted the craft that crashed have been monitoring our radio and TV broadcasts since we first started to transmit.'

'I'm sorry to interrupt Doctor Bush.' Professor Wilks said sheepishly. 'But what do you mean by creatures.'

Bush reached into the briefcase and pulled out a photograph which he looked at briefly before tossing it onto the table in front of him. The black and white photograph showed a humanoid looking creature which had been placed on an examination table. The creature's head was large compared to the rest of its body and had a small opening on each side of its head. The creature's eyes were the most distinguishing feature. Large almond shaped. No pupil just a black iris.

Frederick found himself thinking about the incident in Ripley and what Brian Jones had said concerning the nightmares his wife Edith had experienced. *'She keeps screaming about terrible black lifeless eyes staring at her through the window.'*

'There were six of these creatures at the crash site. Four of them died on impact. Two were still alive although one of the creatures died shortly after the crash.' Bush explained making eye contact with Hillenkoetter.

'So you are still holding one of these creatures.' Frederick said.

Bush shook his head. 'No the creature was able to communicate with its home planet.'

'Are you saying more of these creatures came?'

Bush hesitated before nodding. 'Yes.'

Frederick's tone turned dark. 'Let me get this straight, the United States Government has had contact with beings from another world?'

Hillenkoetter held up his hand. 'I wouldn't go as far as actual contact. Professor you must realise that we are dealing with a matter of huge significance here. To discover that we are not alone in the universe is as profound as when people discovered the world was round and not flat. You have to understand we acted in everyone's best interest.'

'You mean the interest of America.' Wilks added.

Hillenkoetter glared at Wilks. 'Just in case you haven't been keeping up with current affairs Professor Wilks we are in the midst of a cold war. Things may have calmed down in Korea but the Russians are still the greatest threat since the Nazis.' He gestured towards the object. 'If the Soviets ever got their hands on this kind of technology then it could be devastating.'

'Operation Mainbrace.' Admiral Berkshire stated.

'I beg your pardon.' Hillenkoetter said.

'You said that the creature had returned to its home planet. That's what the incident was all about last year during the naval exercise. Those craft we witnessed were part of some sort of exchange program.'

A reluctant Hillenkoetter nodded. 'An exchange was made yes.'

'The Russians were right you have been conducting negotiations with these creatures.' Frederick added.

'No, we have yet to actually have any direct contact. The creature that we had in custody wasn't exactly chatty. Look I know we're a little late but we're here now sharing what we know.' Dr Menzel said. 'We could have kept this from you, and believe me there are those who did not want this meeting to take place.'

'It's very noble of you to come clean Doctor Menzel but it still doesn't excuse your lack of trust.' Malcolm Chambers said. 'The question is where we go from here.'

'I guess we establish a level of trust.' Hillenkoetter said.

'Trust Mr Hillenkoetter is something you have to earn.' Frederick pointed out. 'Over the past year you Americans have proven to be untrustworthy. There have been a number of incidents we need to talk about before any kind of trust can be established. First of all I would like to talk about the two men you are holding at Mildenhall.' Chambers enquired.

'Those two UFO nutjobs will be charged with spying.' Hillenkoetter replied.

'Nonsense.' Frederick snorted. 'You act as if they're working for the Russians. They're just a couple of researchers.'

Hillenkoetter remained silent.

'If you want to establish trust then you are to release those men immediately. Then we can discuss the use of British airspace to test an experimental aircraft over Soviet territory. Which incidentally you failed to tell us about.' Ian Morgan said.

Hillenkoetter thought for a moment. 'Ok, we'll release those guys. But we will keep an eye on them for a while to make sure they don't have any contact with Russian operatives.' He glanced at Morgan. 'Which incidentally we know are operating in this country. As for the X2 aircraft we are testing. We wish to continue with the project. We will share any information we gather on the Soviet Union.'

'And detailed information on the aircraft.' Morgan added.

After several seconds Hillenkoetter nodded reluctantly.

'Tell us more about what happened during Mainbrace.'

Frederick asked. 'Why put on that display in front of so many witnesses.'

'We knew the Russians would be in the area monitoring the exercise. The Alien visitor in our custody had made contact with its home planet. Although the communication equipment on its ship had been damaged during the crash. It was able to fashion a crude communication device using parts from the crashed ship and items which we supplied. It was first suggested that a handover should take place in the Nevada desert. But with tensions reaching fever pitch in Korea President Truman thought that a more public display might make the Russians think again about starting another war.'

'Which is what we thought.' Frederick added.

'What did you learn from the creature while it was in your custody?' Chambers asked.

'The creature was able to communicate by means of telepathic thought transfer. It had the ability to plant images in the minds of our researchers. We were able to learn that the creature's home planet was sixteen thousand light years out from our own planet. The solar system which it originated from contains thirteen planets which orbit a star very much like our own. Three of the planets in their solar system are capable of supporting life and have been colonised by their species.'

'Do you know why they are visiting our planet?' Wilks asked.

'They're basically explorers.' Vannevar Bush took over the conversation. 'We learnt that they developed the ability to travel vast interstellar distances approximately nine hundred years ago.'

'Nine hundred years!' Norman Canning exclaimed. 'The time of the Norman invasion, the crusades, plus the dark ages. America and Australia weren't even on any maps.'

'How long have they been visiting Earth?' Professor Wilks

asked.

'The creature claimed that they have known about us for about three hundred years. At first all they did was catalogue our planet as containing life. But as the Industrial Revolution kicked into high gear they started to show more interest. The Human race was starting to develop technology. Now that we have managed to harness the power of the atom our species is now of great interest to them.' Bush paused. 'And to others.'

'Others.' Frederick queried.

'We've learnt that there are other space faring species out there that have been around much longer than our friends that crashed at Roswell. Thousands, tens of thousands and hundreds of thousands of years more advanced. The creature also told us that their species had observed hundreds of civilizations like our own who have destroyed themselves through conflict. Perhaps it was fate that delivered them to us considering our level of technology.' Bush looked at Frederick. 'This is why we made the decision concerning Mainbrace last year. A public display for the Russians to observe.'

'And when you handed the creature back, was any other exchange made?' Norman Canning asked.

'Not really just a friendly handshake so to speak. They told us they would continue to monitor us and that we had potential and further contact will be made.'

'Has any more contact been made?' Frederick asked.

Hillenkoetter hesitated before shaking his head.

Wilks rubbed his forehead. 'As an astronomer I can barely grasp what we have learnt here today. Our current knowledge and understanding of our universe is practically nothing compared to the other species that we now know to exist out there.'

'I think Gentlemen we can leave it there for the time being.' Chambers announced. 'I suggest we have an early lunch.' He looked at the three Americans. 'I trust you gentlemen are planning to stay for a while. Unfortunately we cannot continue until the day after tomorrow. There's a little matter of Her Majesty's coronation.'

'We'd be delighted to stay for a few days.' Hillenkoetter said. 'Wouldn't miss this little shindig for the world.'

Frederick and Wilks stayed behind while everyone left the room.

'I take it you do not trust the Americans.' Wilks said.

'No I do not, after everything they have done over the past year. For them to just come out now and admit to everything suggests that they still have an agenda. What they have revealed is startling to say the least but something tells me we're still not getting the whole picture.'

Wilks sighed. 'That maybe so but what they have told us today as still been one hell of an eye opener.'

'Yes it's certainly given me a lot to think about.' Frederick glanced at his watch. 'But as William pointed out tomorrow is a big day and I have to get back to Emneth.'

'Say hello to Liz and Susan for me.' Wilks said.

'I take it you're having a day off like everyone else.'

'Oh yes, but I have business to attend first before heading to join in the festivities with Pam and the boys.'

'Well say hello from me.' Frederick said.

Chapter 65

The Mall – London – 10:38am
Tuesday 2nd June 1953

Igor Lakatos caught sight of the smiling princess who waved at the cheering crowds as she passed by in the Royal Golden coach. The sound of dozens of royal horses could be heard as they escorted the future queen to Westminster Abbey to be crowned queen. The Mall was a dazzling sea of red white and blue. Tens of thousands of people waving flags and cheering as the royal procession passed them by. Many people had camped out overnight to catch a glimpse of the royal procession.'

'Brings back a lot of memories does it not Comrade.' Lakatos' informant said.

'What do you mean?' He snapped.

'You were part of the household guard for the Tsar were you not?'

'That was a long time ago, during the dark days before the revolution.' Lakatos replied as another royal coach passed. 'You British should have done away with your royal family a long time ago.'

The informant glared at the Russian. 'Sometimes Comrade it's the simple things that keep us strong. Come let us walk.'

The two men made their way through the throng towards Green Park. Although there were still many people celebrating the day they managed to find a secluded spot. The informant produced a small brown envelope. 'I managed to acquire the names of all Majestic 12 members. The American seem very forthcoming with information.'

Lakatos slid the envelope into the inside pocket of his jacket. 'This is old news, we already know what the Americans are in possession of. What about this new aircraft they're testing?'

'They are keeping tight lipped about that but promised to share technical details. The Prime Minister has agreed to let them continue their tests. There is another meeting tomorrow. Vannevar Bush is to demonstrate part of the technology recovered from the Roswell crash.'

'What is the likelihood of you obtaining this piece of technology?'

The informant shook his head. 'The Americans are running the show at the moment.'

'Well it doesn't matter we have similar technology recovered from Tunguska. We also obtained a piece of technology several years ago when the craft came down in the New Mexico desert. Unfortunately Comrade Modin's efforts to persuade Professor Frederick to turn were unsuccessful.'

'I told you Frederick wouldn't come over so easily. Burgess thought about recruiting him back in Cambridge but decided against it. Besides MacLean made a much more tempting target.'

'Speaking of Comrade Modin, he will handle you from now on. This will be my last trip out for a while. The Tunguska project needs my full attention I must return immediately.'

The informant nodded. 'I understand old friend. I will make sure Moscow is kept in the loop.'

Both men parted company without a handshake.

Chapter 66

Bletchley Park – 1:23pm
Wednesday 3rd June 1953

Vannevar Bush stood in front of the examination table. 'Gentlemen, welcome to the future.' Bush tapped on the object he had shown them two days earlier which immediately projected a spinning globe. The light from the globe lit up the immediate area bathing everything in a blue light. 'First of all how does it work.' Bush smiled and let out a nervous laugh. 'Truth is we haven't a damn clue.' He shook his head. 'Our scientists haven't even come up with any theories what powers it. All we have learnt is how to access its basic functions.'

Sir Harold Bates leaned forward and studied the object. 'It seems to be capable of projecting light directly into the space in front of us.'

Like a film projector on a flat surface.' Frederick added.

'Yes but this doesn't need a flat surface to function. It can project light particles directly into three dimensional space thus giving the illusion of structure.' Bates waved his hand through the floating sphere which did nothing.' He rubbed his fingers. 'There seems to be a static charge emanating from this image.' He tapped the surface of the device twice. The glowing sphere vanished in an instant.

Frederick reached forward and picked the object up. 'It has no weight.' He noted with surprise.

'Drop it on to the table.' Bush invited.

Frederick looked at him.

'Go on.' Bush encouraged.

Frederick held the object flat over the table and then let go. The object did not move. It remained where it was. Frederick, Bates and Canning could only look on in wonder.

'I thought you'd like that.' Bush reached forward and flipped the object on its side, before tapping it once. The transparent material changed colour turning to black masking the inner components. An image of earth appeared on the surface of the object. 'This not only has the capability of projecting light into three dimensional space but you can view information in two dimensional space.'

'Like a television screen.' Norman Canning said.

'But this has a flatscreen.' Bush pointed out.

'What makes it just float in the air?' Frederick asked. 'It shouldn't be doing that. Gravity should pull it down.'

'But it doesn't. Our scientists have theorised that it generates some kind of antigravity field.'

'For what purpose?' Bates asked.

'We believe that different gravitational strengths on different planets may create a problem for beings capable of interstellar travel. These creatures have devised a technology to overcome this.'

'Different planets.' Norman canning stated.

'When we were able to access the craft found in the New Mexico desert we found about thirteen hundred of these devices.'

Canning pointed at the device. 'Thirteen hundred of these.'

'Yes and we have been through all of them. Every one contains a detailed record of other planets and solar systems. What's more, all these devices contain planets that harbour life. We have also learnt that they are all within close proximity to our solar system.'

'How close.' Bates asked.

'Within a hundred light years, we believe that's just a tiny drop in the ocean compared to how many planetary systems there are in our galaxy alone.'

Frederick thought back to the conversation he had with his daughter Susan. 'This is incredible we are talking about billions upon billions of planets. Do you know what this could do for science on this planet. To know that we are not the only planet with life changes everything. It's a shame Professor Wilks isn't here to see this.'

'I agree with everything you say Professor. But let's not get carried away and make any announcements just yet. There are scientists out there who are not ready to accept such knowledge.'

'That's absurd.' Frederick stated.

'Nevertheless, it's true. The fact that we may not be alone in our universe makes a lot of the scientific community nervous.'

'Why?' Frederick asked.

'Professor Einstein's theory of relativity states that it's not possible to travel beyond the speed of light.' Bush indicated to the device. 'Yet the creatures that piloted the craft found at Roswell seem to be capable of faster than light travel.'

'There are scientists that have based their life's work around Einstein, most notably myself. To disprove relativity could throw the scientific community into disarray.'

'Which is why we need to keep things to ourselves.' Bush stated.

'For how long?'

'As long as it takes. Our main goal is to figure out how this technology works so that we can kick start science. It's our first day at school Gentlemen.'

'Kick start science, it sounds as if you have plans to utilize this technology.' Norman Canning said.

'We have some bold plans being drawn up on how we can duplicate this technology.'

'What would you hope to gain from doing that?' Harold Bates asked.

Bush looked at the object which hung motionless in the air. 'Imagine a world where information is available in an instant.'

'What kind of information?' Frederick interrupted.

Bush shrugged. 'Anything you want.' He indicated to the object. 'One day it may be possible to build devices like this for everyday use. An electronic device that can hold enormous amounts of information. Perhaps they will be like this, capable of storing sound and moving images. I have theorised such a device I have called the Memex. Which is capable of storing information on microfilm which the user can access using a series of commands. I have also theorised that it could be possible to build several of these machines and link them.'

'Link them.' Frederick said.

'Yes, several of my devices could be constructed and designed to communicate with each other.'

'How exactly?'

'Through a series of telephone exchanges. I believe it is possible to station a Memex in Washington and link it up to another machine in New York via a telephone line. Each machine would be able to transmit information such as photographs and perhaps one day moving images as well as documents. It's all theoretical at the moment; there is a lot of work to do.'

'But what use would people have for such a device. Surely they have got better things to do than stare at images or moving pictures all day long.' Frederick said.

'But people do.' Bush Stated. 'Television is vastly popular in the United States. We have discovered that people will sit in front of it from dawn till dusk. We believe this device could give birth to all kinds of new technologies.'

'How long do you propose we will be able to build devices like this?' Norman Canning asked.

'I couldn't even begin to guess when we would reach this level of technology. The computers that are being built today fill a large room and can only perform mathematical calculations.' He pointed at the device. 'This technology can manipulate energy in ways we can't yet grasp. But saying that I believe that development of knowledge is the key to understanding how this works. Imagine if we sent a modern day car back in time to Henry Ford. He would have little understanding of how it works. But in time he could duplicate it. Perhaps by the end of the twentieth century we may be advanced enough to build devices like this. I predict computers will be much smaller and many times more powerful. A computer small enough to fit in the palm of your hand may sound like science fiction. So would things like cars, aeroplanes and television if we would have had this conversation a hundred years ago.'

'The end of the twentieth century.' Canning said. 'Isn't that being a little too optimistic?'

'Not at all, it's taken us less than fifty years to go from man's first powered flight to the jet engine. And now we are beginning to build rockets capable of reaching space itself. Who knows what we will be capable of in another fifty years?'

'It's a bold plan.' Bates said. 'But if we are suddenly thrust into the midst of all this technology won't people start to question where it came from.'

'Not if they're reliant on it. No one questions how it's possible to drive cars around, fly aeroplanes, or watch moving pictures on a little box in our living rooms. Technology is already starting to dominate our lives. The development of technology such as this would benefit mankind in ways we cannot begin to imagine. The financial gains it would bring to both the United States and United Kingdom would be enormous. Baring in mind any new technology developed from the Roswell crash would be developed for military applications before it found its way into the public domain. We have a number of research projects up and running looking into how we can advance our own technology. The plan is to patent different products and announce them to the public from time to time. Give different people credit for inventing different technologies. While in reality the technology being developed stems from the crash at Roswell.'

Canning thought about Bush's ambitious plan. 'Military application is a good way of testing new technology. This device demonstrates that it could be possible to gain advanced information on one's enemy, a key goal in any battle.'

'One more reason for keeping this under wraps gentleman.' Bush said. 'I have to admit I had to do a lot of convincing to let you Brits in on any of this. Some of my people feel that you are a leaky ship so to speak.'

'You have had your fair share of spies Mr Bush. The Rosenbergs and their network caused a significant amount of damage regarding US nuclear secrets.' Canning added.

Bush couldn't help smiling. 'That is true which is why we have to work together to intercept anyone who might be working for the Soviets. Rest assured this technology is far more valuable than all our nuclear technology combined.'

Canning nodded. 'I'll start making plans to beef up security around Bletchley.'

'We'll have to set up additional research facilities.' Frederick added. 'There is just so much to do now.'

'But before all this is possible we have to understand this technology more.' Bush said. 'This device contains detailed information on our planet. These creatures have been collecting data on everything about our planet.' He reached forward and grabbed the object placing it flat on the table before tapping it. The glowing three dimensional representation of Earth reappeared. He tapped the outline of the United Kingdom. A larger map appeared with five symbols one above the other at the side. 'Our scientists have yet to decipher the language but we have determined that the symbols have a function.' He tapped the bottom symbol. Immediately hundreds of red and green dots began to appear on the map.'

'What do these glowing dots mean?' Canning asked.

'We are not sure, but we think they maybe landing sites for flying saucers.'

Frederick studied the glowing map in front of him. 'One of these red dots is flashing.' He pointed to a region in the north of England.'

The other men looked at the map.

Frederick reached out and tapped on the flashing dot. The map enlarged itself and focused on the area where the red flashing dot was. Frederick shook his head slowly. 'I don't think these are landing sites, more like markers.'

'Markers for what Professor?' Bush asked.

'People.'

'People?' Bush said bemused.

'Where is that?' Canning asked.

'If this map is accurate, it's Ripley in North Yorkshire the place where Edith Jones lived.' Frederick stated.

'Who is Edith Jones?' Bush asked.

'A woman we investigated last year regarding a flying saucer kidnapping.'

Bush studied the flashing marker.

Bates noted the look on his face. 'Is there something bothering you Doctor Bush?'

The American nodded tapping on the bottom symbol again. The view changed and a map of the continental Unites states appeared. 'If what you say is true Professor then we have a serious problem on our hands.' The four of them stared at the map which was covered with thousands of red and green markers.

Canning looked at Frederick. 'You must go to North Yorkshire to the place where that marker represents.'

Chapter 67

All Saints Church – Ripley - North Yorkshire – 11:12am Thursday 5th June 1953

Professor Frederick, Vannevar Bush and Dr Lloyd were flown up to RAF Yeadon on the orders of Sir Malcolm Chambers and CIA director Hillenkoetter to investigate the information shown on the Roswell device.

'Are you sure you are up for this Arthur.' Frederick asked looking over at the frail man.

'There's no need to fuss Ralph I'm fine.' He coughed.

Vannevar Bush held the device over the grave of Edith Jones, the red dot flashed ominously. 'We exhume the body.' He suggested.

'I'll go and get the local vicar he should be able to locate a grave digger.'

4:03pm

Frederick looked around the doctor's surgery which had been the setting for the previous year's events. Two men had been assigned to dig up the grave. The coffin had been wheeled into the surgery on a makeshift trolley.

Vannevar Bush nodded giving the signal for the two gravediggers to prise the coffin lid open which came up quite easily. 'That will be all gentlemen.' He said placing one hand on the lid.

Frederick and Bush stood at each end of the coffin.

'I should warn you gentlemen this isn't going to be pretty.' Dr Lloyd said.

'On three Professor.' Bush instructed. 'One, two, three.' Both men lifted the lid and put it on the floor.

'This is incredible!' Lloyd remarked. 'It's nearly a year since this woman died, yet her body is perfectly intact.' He prodded the dead woman's cheek bone. 'It's almost as if she's asleep. There is no sign of decay or rigor mortis or any deterioration of the body.' He put his stethoscope on her chest. 'She still has a heartbeat.'

'How the hell is that possible?' Frederick asked.

'I have absolutely no idea.' Lloyd replied.

Bush took the device out of a small satchel and held it up in front of the coffin. Tapping on it once a symbol appeared on the surface.

'What is that?' Frederick asked.

'I have no idea.' Bush replied. 'But there's only one way to find out.' He tapped the symbol and the room filled with sounds while the device displayed all kind of images. 'This is incredible.' Bush stated.

'What's it doing?' Lloyd asked having to raise his voice over the noise.

'It's somehow collecting information.' Bush studied the images on the device. 'Every memory this woman has had is being collected.'

The device seemed to be displaying images of the woman's childhood seen through her eyes. Her parents playing with her and other children running around a school playground. Bush tapped the object and the images speeded up. For several minutes the three men watched the entire life of Edith Jones unfold. Frederick looked on as moving images of the incident which had brought him to Ripley a year earlier played. He saw himself visiting the Jones' months before and then the device stopped suddenly.'

Another symbol appeared on the screen.

Frederick recognised the spiral pattern displayed on the screen. 'I don't believe it!'

'What?' Bush said looking at Frederick.

'I've encountered this symbol before.'

'When?'

'Last year, it's carved onto an oak door at Ripley Castle.'

'How can that be?' Lloyd asked.

'I have no idea but it's definitely the same symbol.'

Bush hesitated before tapping the symbol. All three men jumped back from the coffin as Edith Jones opened her eyes and sat up right.

'What the hell is going on?' Frederick said.

The woman slowly looked around before lifting herself out of the coffin and standing up right. She seemed totally unaware of anyone else's presence.

The device Bush held displayed dozens of symbols that shifted diagonally and vertically around the screen.

Edith Jones located the door and walked towards it.

The two gravediggers outside the room backed against the wall as the dead woman walked past them.

Frederick, Bush and Lloyd gave chase.

Edith Jones walked out of the front door of the building and onto the street. She sprinted down the road and was soon out of sight.

Bush looked at the device shaking his head. 'She no longer shows up.'

Frederick looked over his shoulder. The screen on the device was now blank.

After an hour of searching, the three men decided to give up and return to the hotel. Bush had ordered the startled gravediggers to return the coffin to the grave and bury it.

'Where do you think she is?' Frederick asked.

Bush studied the device looking for clues as to where she might have gone. 'I can't even find the images it displayed earlier. It's like they were there and now they're gone.'

Dr Lloyd entered the guest room and closed the door behind him. 'Just been speaking to the local bobby. One of the villagers reported their car missing about twenty minutes ago. Claims he saw Edith Jones getting in and driving off.'

'We need to close the road in and out of this village.'

Frederick suggested.

'You know that's only going to alert Sir Ingles.' Replied Lloyd.

'A pointless gesture anyway.' Bush remarked. 'She's mobile; she'll be twenty miles away by now.' Bush held up the device. 'And this thing isn't giving us any clues as to her whereabouts.'

Frederick looked across at Lloyd who sat down on the bed clutching his chest. 'Arthur what's the matter?'

Doctor Lloyd groaned in pain before falling off the edge of the bed. Frederick rushed to his side.

Chapter 68

Whitehall – London – 2:45pm
Monday 9th June 1953

Agent Frank Cones sat opposite Professor Frederick smiling at him. Hillenkoetter, Bush and Menzel were also present as well as Morris Stanford and Ian Morgan. The door to the meeting room opened and Sir Malcolm Chambers marched in.

'How is he?' Frederick asked.

Chambers shook his head. 'Not good, his doctors say the cancer has totally ravaged his body. It's only a matter of time now before he succumbs to it.' He sat down at the head of the table. 'I have just received some disturbing news concerning the two air force pilots that were taken late last year. Both their families have reported that their graves have been disturbed and the bodies gone.'

'What do you suppose is going on with these people?' Ian Morgan directed his question towards Dr Menzel.

'They obviously serve a purpose.' He shook his head. 'But what that is, we have no idea.'

'I'd say we were under some form of attack. It's obvious whatever's controlling these people is using them to infiltrate the general population.' Hillenkoetter suggested.

'We have no defence against this.' Ian Morgan stated.

'No we don't.' Hillenkoetter admitted.

'Given the information your device has shown us there are hundreds of people living amongst us who are under the control of these creatures.' Morgan added.

Chambers looked at Vannevar Bush. 'Before you return to America Doctor I want you to get as much information on those markers which show up on the device. I want to know where they are so that we can identify who's been in contact with these creatures.'

'I'll get started immediately.'

'Professor Wilks will assist you. I want a map of where these people are.'

'In the meantime.' Hillenkoetter said. 'I'm loaning you Agent Cones. He will work closely with you in tracking down some of these people. It will be a temporary measure until we assign a more permanent team to investigate this matter.'

'Good idea.' Replied Chambers. 'The more men we can get on this the better chance we have of combating the situation.'

'What about the symbol on the device that brought Edith Jones back from the dead. It can't be a coincidence that it's etched onto the door of a Castle in Ripley.' Frederick pointed out.

'You think Sir Ingles maybe holding something back.' Chambers suggested.

'There's only one way to find out. I could speak to him, see if he knows anything else about what happened to her.'

Chambers nodded.

Chapter 69

Ripley Castle – North Yorkshire
Wednesday 11th June 1953

Frederick walked across the courtyard towards the large oak door. He took a few minutes to study the spiral pattern etched into the oak panelling. It was definitely the same symbol that appeared on the Roswell device.

Frederick became aware of the sound of approaching horses. He turned to see Sir Ingles and another woman on horseback.

'Professor Frederick, I would have thought concerning recent events you would not be bold enough to show your face around here.'

Frederick remained silent.

'You think something like a woman rising from the dead could be kept a secret in these parts? My family founded this village Professor. Nothing escapes my attention.' Ingles dismounted.

Frederick pointed at the symbol on the door. 'Then perhaps you might like to tell me what that means.'

Ingles looked at the symbol for several seconds before looking up at the woman on horseback smiling. 'Would you excuse me Lady Elinor.'

The woman turned her horse which trotted out of the courtyard.

'What is it you wish to know?'

'What this symbol means.'

'I told you the first time you were here. It was used by my ancestors to ward off evil spirits.'

'Is that it?'

'Yes that's it!'

Ingles led his horse away to the adjoining stables. 'If

there's nothing else please leave.'

Frederick glanced at the door before walking after Ingles. 'How many others are there Sir Ingles?'

Ingles stopped. 'Others?'

'I think you know what I mean. How many other people are there like Edith Jones in this village?'

Ingles turned to face Frederick. 'I don't know.'

'Or just don't want to tell me.'

A stable hand walked up to Ingles and led his horse away.

'I'm not lying Professor I swear.' He pointed at the oak door. 'This symbol you are so interested in was brought back from Jerusalem nearly nine hundred years ago.'

'Jerusalem?'

Ingles took a deep breath. 'Come with me Professor.'

Frederick was led through to the sitting room. Ingles looked up at a large portrait of one of his ancestors. 'The man who carved that symbol was this fellow, Sir Thomas Ingles.'

Frederick stared at the white vest the man was wearing. It displayed a red St George's Cross. A shield was also present in the portrait.

'He was a member of the knights Templar, sworn to protect the holy land from Turks. He accompanied Richard the Lionheart on his crusade.'

'And survived.' Frederick added.

'Barely.' Ingles replied. 'It is said that on his return he carved out the symbol in the door. The crusade had changed him. The servants said that he would wake up in the middle of the night screaming about unearthly creatures attacking the holy city of Jerusalem. Led by what he called The Dark Ones.'

'The Dark Ones?' Frederick stated.

'His wife tried her best to comfort him but he slowly began to lose his mind. One morning a servant entered the bedchambers and found sir Ingles huddled in the corner. His wife lay dead on their marital bed. With her throat slit and her eyes gouged out. He was screaming something about his wife being one of these Dark Ones. He claimed that she could change shape at will.'

Frederick found himself transfixed as Sir Ingles told the story.

'Sir Thomas was hanged a few days later. The local clergy said that the devil had possessed him. Before his death Sir Ingles told his son about his time in Jerusalem. At the height of King Richard's crusade a disease swept through the holy city. People were overcome by what became known as the maddening death. He said that these Dark Ones were responsible. Richard and his knights barricaded themselves into a small church and prayed to god to save them from this maddening death.'

'Obviously it worked.' Frederick said. 'I know enough about history to know that Richard returned.'

Ingles nodded. 'Sir Thomas claimed that a mysterious stranger appeared out of a heavenly light. A great battle occurred between Richard and his knights and those inflicted by the disease. This stranger along with a beautiful woman helped King Richard and his knights defeat the maddening death. I know how the story sounds; talk of heavenly lights and beautiful women.'

'A bit fanciful.'

'Yes.'

'What has all this got to do with Edith Jones?'

'When Sir Thomas returned from the crusades the dreams began almost immediately.'

'Dreams.'

'Sir Thomas claimed that demons would descend and take him. They would violate his body before returning him. Poor fellow eventually went mad. The rest I have already told you. Since then there have been sightings of these demons for centuries. People locally have nicknamed them the Grey.'

'And Edith Jones claimed to have seen these creatures.'

'She was just one of many women down the years who have had encounters with the Grey. A while back Edith disappeared for a few days. After she was returned she came to see me. She told me about her pregnancy before she told her husband. She said that her relationship with Brian was starting to break down. They were unable to have children before she was taken.'

Frederick reminisced about what Jones had said to him a year earlier. 'And when she returned she was expecting.'

'Yes, I advised her to keep the child and stick with Brian. He was her best chance of a normal life. This is the first time that this has happened, the Grey returning to reclaim a child. Over the centuries many women in the village have given birth to children because they have come into contact with these creatures. The children were either taken away and killed by the local clergy or died at birth often taking with them their mothers.'

'It still doesn't explain why they visit this area in particular.'

'There is a legend relating to a standing stone which is located in a field at the back of the castle. It is said that god had placed it there as a signpost for his angels.'

'Can you show me?'

Ingles hesitated before nodding.

Several minutes Frederick found himself staring up at a stone monolith which stood alone in a field. Approximately fifteen foot in height and four foot across the stone was covered with strange etchings. Five circles in a straight line with a line pointing up from the forth circle to a series of dots near the top of the stone.

'This field is part of my estate.' Ingles revealed. 'Although it's never used.'

'Why?' Frederick asked looking around.

'None of my cattle will graze here. I have never seen a bird fly overhead or seen a rabbit or fox.'

Frederick looked back at the stone. 'You think it has something to do with this.'

Ingles nodded. 'When a child was born belonging to a woman who had been taken by the Grey this is where the children were taken to be killed. The clergy believed that this stone would ferry their souls to heaven. It's known locally as the dead stone.'

'How old is this stone?'

'It was here before my family arrived. I believe it is thousands of years old.'

Frederick looked towards the base of the stone spotting the same three armed spiral pattern.

Ingles inhaled. 'And that concludes your history lesson and tour of my family's past.' Ingles looked at Frederick. 'When you return to London Professor tell your superiors that you will never stop them. They will keep on coming. They will keep taking women from this village long after you and I have gone.'

Frederick nodded. 'Thank you Sir Ingles.'

'Professor Frederick!' Ingles called out as Frederick started to walk away. 'Once you have knowledge of what has transpired here you will be drawn back time and time again. This village will call you back.'

Chapter 70

St Mary the Virgin Church – 2:56pm
Shipton-Under-Whychwood – Oxfordshire
Wednesday 17th June 1953

The sombre group of people watched the coffin of Dr Arthur Lloyd being lowered into the ground. The vicar recited from the bible as the crowd looked on. Dr Lloyd's wife sobbed while her two sons did their best to console her.

All committee members had attended Dr Lloyd's funeral.

After the vicar had finished his reading the mourners made their way to the cars. Chambers and Frederick stayed behind.

'Such a proud man.' Chambers said. 'I wish he would have told us earlier perhaps we could have done more.'

'But there is nothing you could have done.' A voice said from behind.

Both men spun on their heels.

Frederick's heart skipped a beat as he realised who he was looking at.

Janus glanced down at the grave. 'I warned him about his impending doom.' He said callously before looking back at Frederick. 'I also warned you Professor about your future.'

The image that Janus had exposed Frederick to several months earlier burned through his mind.

'What do you want?' Chambers barked.

Janus looked at him smiling. 'Sir Malcolm Chambers hero of the Somme, or should I say butcher.'

Chambers stepped back trembling, anchoring himself to a gravestone. The surrounding landscape became a swirling mass of colour. Turning to a mixture of grey and crimson red of soldier's blood whose bodies were strewn across a desolate landscape. Shells exploding all around and the smell of death invaded his nostrils.

**The River Somme - Northern France
July 23rd 1916**

'You are the King's men!' Captain Chambers shouted. 'Which means you are fearless men, men with honour and valour in your blood. You will show those Hun bastards that they will not win this war. You will show them that Britannia still rules the waves.'

His men cheered.

Chambers looked into the eyes of the young men in front of him. He then turned and saw Janus glaring back at him.

'The guilt overwhelms you to this very day.'

Chambers lost his grip on the gravestone.

Frederick rushed to his side. 'Malcolm what is it.'

Chambers grasped his chest, taking in huge quantities of air. 'My heart.' He gasped.

Frederick glared at Janus. 'I believe my friend asked you a question, what is it you want?'

'What I want Professor Frederick is for you to stop meddling in affairs you have no control over.'

'Forgive me but if as you say we have no control then what are you doing here?'

'If you think joining up with the Americans is going to make a difference then you're very much mistaken.'

Frederick thought about the last few weeks. All that the Americans had shown him particularly the Roswell device. He smiled at Janus. 'I think Janus, it is you who should stop meddling in our affairs.'

'Remember what I have shown you Professor.'

The image of Elizabeth's limp body stabbed at Frederick's mind. He shut his eyes conjuring up the image of a brick wall. When he opened them, Janus was gone.

Chapter 71

Whitehall – London – 9:56am
Friday 19th June 1953

'How is he?' Ian Morgan asked as Frederick entered the room.

'He's resting for now.' Frederick answered. 'Janus took a heavy toll on his heart.' He paused and looked at the other committee members. 'It seems gentlemen that we may have this Janus fellow on the back heel. Our encounter with him the other day proves this and now we must take advantage.' He then looked at Professor Wilks. 'How many locations did you manage to get from that Device Doctor Bush showed us?'

'Around eight hundred and fifty different locations up and down the country. Although I am unable to determine why some of the markers were flashing red and why others were just a stable green colour. If the Americans had left the device for us to study then I might have been able to come to a conclusion on the information the device displayed. I'm also convinced there could be more people who have had contact with the creatures.'

'I don't think the Americans trust us.' Lord Admiral Berkshire said. 'This Majestic 12 group that President Truman established has kept secrets from us for years. How do we know they're not telling us the whole story.'

'We don't.' Morris Stanford replied. 'But the fact they have now decided to come out and reveal their true nature indicates that they're as much in the dark on the whole UFO situation as we are. And this Janus fellow ups the whole game. If there are creatures from another world already here then we need to know what their plan is. I say we locate one of these markers and snatch whoever is affected.'

'I'm not sure that's a good idea.' Frederick said. 'From my

experience in Ripley last year and with the two airmen these people have very little idea something has happened to them. You cannot just start abducting people off the streets.'

'What do you suggest we do?' Stanford asked shrugging his shoulders.

'We need to study these people and track their movements.'

'I'm sorry Ralph but there are only ten of us.' Ian Morgan reminded. 'We cannot track down all eight hundred individuals and keep an eye on them.'

'I'm not saying that we keep an eye on everyone. We'll select them one by one. As much as I hate to admit it but Agent Frank Cones will be our man on this as well as me.' Frederick explained. 'We will need a few weeks to select our target then we move in.'

'Make it so.' Morgan instructed.

Chapter 72

**British Embassy – Vienna – Austria – 8:34am
Tuesday 7th July 1953**

'I wish to seek political asylum.' The smartly dressed man appealed to the corporal stood outside the sentry box behind the tall iron gates.

The young army officer reached inside the window and telephoned through to the main building. The man looked around nervously as he waited for the soldier to finish on the telephone.

After a minute or so the soldier replaced the receiver. 'I'm afraid you will have to wait a few minutes sir.'

The man looked down the main street nervously. Although it was deserted, it did not ease his anxiety. He looked back at the soldier taking off his wristwatch. 'Look I have this expensive watch. Swiss high quality, it is yours yes.'

The soldier shook his head. 'I'm sorry sir but I cannot accept anything from you.'

The man produced a handkerchief and wiped his brow. He peered through the bars at the main embassy door that opened. He smiled at the sight of the approaching embassy official flanked by two other armed soldiers. His smile soon faded as he glanced back down the street. A jet black Volga car screeched around the corner and sped towards the man.

A figure was leaning out of the back window pointing a gun. Shots rang out as the car raced towards the gates ricocheting off the iron bars narrowly missing the man who dropped to the floor cowering. He looked frantically around for any cover, but there was none.

On hearing the first shots the soldier at the gate drew his weapon and looked cautiously through the bars at the oncoming vehicle.

The other two soldiers sprinted towards the gate.

More shots rang out echoing around the street, and then a painful gasp. A bullet had found its mark tearing through the man's shin, blood sprayed onto the street.

The soldier pushed the barrel of his rifle through the bars and returned fire.

The front passenger window on the Volga exploded causing the car to swerve. The driver regained control and sped towards the injured man.

The man on the ground clasped his shin and glared on in painful terror as the man leaning out of the car window aimed at his head.

A single shot rang out.

The man in the car recoiled after being struck in the shoulder. The iron gates to the embassy swung open. One of the soldiers fired on the car while the other two helped the injured man.

'Thank you, thank you.' He gasped looking back as the Volga roared by before disappearing from sight.

The tall Iron gates clanged shut and the man was helped across the courtyard by the two soldiers. More soldiers appeared and mingled around the main gates. The embassy official approached the injured man, who was clinging onto a leather satchel.

'My name is Dmitri Kirov, I wish political asylum. I need to speak with Professor Ralph Frederick of Cambridge University and The Angel Committee.'

Trinity College – Cambridge – 11:17am
Wednesday 15th July 1953

Frederick looked up as Lord Chambers and Morris Stanford entered his office.

Frederick smiled at his friend. 'Malcolm, nice to see you up and about again, how are you feeling?'

'Oh you know me Ralph like a bad penny always showing

up.'

Frederick chuckled. 'Can I offer you gentlemen some tea?'

'No thank you.' Stanford shook his head. 'I'm afraid we are here on official business.'

After Stanford explained the reason of the visit Frederick mulled over what they just revealed to him. 'He asked for me personally.'

Chambers nodded. 'And he referred to The Angel Committee.'

Frederick shook his head. 'I have no idea who this Dmitri Kirov is. I have never heard of him. Where is he now?'

'We've managed to sneak him out of the embassy although it took over a week. Soviet agents are swarming on Vienna. If we had left it any later we would have had to abandon him. The Russians haven't shown any indication that one of their own may have defected. We think this Dmitri Kirov is part of something outside the mainstream.'

'But how the hell does he know about The Angel Committee?' Frederick asked.

Stanford shook his head. 'We have no idea.'

'What about the Yanks. Now that we've teamed up there could be a leak at their end.'

'It's a possibility.' Stanford answered. 'But I don't want to rock the boat we need the Yanks at the moment. But I suggest we keep this from them for the time being.'

'How do you know he won't play us for fools. You know what the Russians are like.'

'This Dmitri Kirov has information. We have him tucked away at Bletchley Park. Since he asked for you by name it must be you who leads the interrogation which is tomorrow afternoon.'

'Interrogation is a bit strong isn't it.'

'We need to cover our backs. You could be right the Soviets could be trying to put one over on us.'

Chapter 73

Bletchley Park – Bedfordshire – 1:09pm
Thursday 16th July 1953

Dmitri Kirov looked up on seeing the door to the interview room open. He immediately stood as the four men and an armed guard walked into the room. The guard took up position by the door while the other four seated themselves opposite Kirov. 'Professor Frederick, it is an honour to meet you.' Kirov offered his hand. 'I saw you in Munich four years ago when you accepted your Nobel Prize. I did try talking to you about your theory on gravitational waves. But you were being mobbed by the scientific community.'

Frederick glared at the man refusing to shake his hand.

Kirov withdrew and sat down a little nervous at not being able to break the ice. He winced in pain from his injured leg. 'I can understand your apprehension Professor. But let me assure you I am here as an ally not a spy.' The leather satchel which Kirov had with him in Vienna lay on the table.

Ian Morgan was the first to say something. 'Why don't you start by telling us why you decided to come out of the cold?'

'Believe me I didn't make this decision on a whim Mr Morgan.'

'Have we met?' Morgan asked puzzled as to how Kirov knew who he was.

Kirov reached forward and released a strap on a pocket on the front of the satchel. He pulled out a pile of photographs and handed them to Morgan. 'These are photographs taken by Soviet agents who have been assigned to follow you.'

Stanford looked through the photographs. One of the photos showed all the committee members at the funeral of Dr Lloyd.

'Are you saying there are soviet agents operating within

the United Kingdom?' Chambers asked.

'What I'm saying gentlemen is that your group is of great interest to the Kremlin especially in your time of need.'

Frederick looked up from the photographs he had been handed. 'Our time of need?'

Kirov pulled out a folder and then pushed it towards Frederick who eyed it cautiously before reaching forward and opening it.

The folder contained more photographs and a thick pile of documents. Frederick displayed a look of amazement as he looked at the first photo in the pile.

Kirov put on a confident smile. 'Yes I thought that might get your attention Professor.'

The photograph displayed a group of Russian soldiers in a wooded area standing in a semi-circle. They all looked down at what appeared to be a body placed on a white sheet. Frederick immediately noted the corpse was much smaller than a human. He estimated the body to have been about three and a half feet tall. Its arms lay vertical by its side at the end of which was a hand containing three fingers and what Frederick guessed to be a thumb. The head seemed too large in proportion to the rest of the body. The creature's eyes were almond shape, black with no pupil. In the chest area an injury was clearly visible. The body was slightly different from the one the Americans had shown the committee. Frederick looked up at Kirov who had a genuine look of disgust on his face.

'Unfortunately the creature had survived the crash and was found wandering about in the vicinity of the crash site. One of the soldiers took it on himself to shoot the poor thing. The Kremlin has a standing order to fire upon any unidentified target which enters its airspace, which was how this object was brought down.'

The next photograph was of an object which was egg shaped with ridges around the base. The object lay inside what appeared to be an impact crater that Frederick guessed was about thirty feet across. An opening in the side of the craft clearly looked like some sort of escape hatch. Frederick then looked at the next photograph that showed another body with some high ranking Soviet army officers. Kirov was also in the photograph. The group looked straight at the camera smiling as if they were part of some bizarre wild animal safari. The next two photographs displayed the craft being lifted onto the back of a flatbed truck. Frederick turned to the next photograph and spent several seconds staring at it. It showed a desolate landscape of what once looked like a forest. Every tree had been flattened as if a steam roller had driven up and down. It was similar to the photograph the Russian had shown him several weeks earlier at Cambridge.

'That is Tunguska in Siberia. The trees had been flattened by a powerful blast.' Kirov explained.

'I am familiar with the great Tunguska fireball.' Frederick said. 'It has been speculated that an asteroid or a meteor was responsible.'

'That is what our scientists theorised. However, in 1930 Joseph Stalin had ordered an expedition out to the Tunguska region. There had been rumours coming from the area. Witnesses seeing strange things.'

'And how is it you know this Mr Kirov?' Chambers asked.

The Russian looked at Chambers. 'I was part of the expedition team. The project head was a Doctor Marcus Schwimmer.'

'What persuaded Stalin to mount an expedition?' Asked Stanford.

'He was anxious to accelerate Russia's scientific knowledge. For ten years we studied the area until the war. When Germany broke their non aggression pact Stalin halted the project. In 1947 we received information regarding a crash that had occurred in the state of New Mexico.'

Chambers and Frederick threw each other a glance.

'What kind of crash?' Frederick asked.

Kirov smiled at Frederick. 'I know your committee is familiar with the so called Roswell saucer crash.'

Frederick, Morgan, Chambers and Stanford remained silent.

'The Soviets had a spy within the highest ranks of America's scientific elite. In 1949 he defected over to us and managed to bring with him technical data concerning the details of what crashed in the New Mexico desert.'

All four men exchanged glances provoking another smile from Kirov.

'The Soviet Union is not as backward as you have come to believe. They are well organised with a network which reaches into every area from Scientific to financial institutions.'

Frederick drew breath focusing his attention on Kirov. 'Your first expedition to Tunguska, did it reveal anything new about the event?'

Kirov nodded. 'At first we stuck to our hypothesis that an asteroid or meteor had hit the ground. However with the absence of an impact crater the theory started to crumble. On close examination of the soil we found huge amounts of glass fragments on the ground. Whatever it was which exploded in that area gave off an intense burst of heat. Possibly hotter than the bombs that destroyed Hiroshima and Nagasaki. After three days in the area we noticed the lack of animal life. Radiation levels were higher than natural background radiation. Then we started to find other elements which were not part of the landscape.' Kirov reached into his satchel again and pulled out what looked like a chunk of steel which looked as if it had been smelted. He handed it to Frederick. 'As you can see it has almost no weight.' Again he reached into his satchel and pulled out a single photograph handing it to Frederick who studied it.

Frederick looked puzzled at first, but quickly realised what he was looking at.

'At first we thought it was some new type of rock formation until we got near to it. My research team then came across the metal.' Kirov indicated to the piece Frederick had handed to Chambers. 'It was strewn all over the place for miles. From initial research I believe that the structure or craft must have been anywhere between eight to one thousand feet in diameter. I believe that whoever was piloting this craft attempted to execute some sort of emergency landing but failed resulting in a critical failure within its engine. This picture is part of the Hull. When we acquired knowledge regarding the Roswell crash we were able to make great strides with our research project. One of our lead scientists Doctor Anna Vilenko came up with the hypothesis that the craft exploded before it was able to touch down.'

'You're saying that some sort of explosion caused this devastation.' Frederick summarised. 'I find it hard to imagine that an explosion of that magnitude could have occurred in 1908.'

'I can understand your reluctance to believe such a hypothesis' Kirov stated. 'I was sceptical that anything could be so powerful. However I started to think about our efforts to create powerful explosions through atomic research. The Soviets have accelerated their nuclear program and are working on new advancements including the yields of which our bombs are capable. New research into hydrogen bomb detonation is taking place now. The Soviet government is eager to demonstrate to the world that they are leaders in nuclear weapons development.'

Frederick shrugged. 'What does Soviet nuclear weapons research have to do with the Tunguska event?'

'Part of your Nobel Prize was awarded to you because of your theory on Antimatter was it not?'

Frederick nodded slowly. 'It's widely accepted by physicists as the opposite to ordinary matter. Capable of yielding tremendous bursts of energy when the two elements collide. My theory suggests that if harnessed, this type of energy could end our reliance on fossil fuels.' Frederick paused mulling Kirov's words. 'Are you suggesting that what happened at Tunguska was the result of an antimatter explosion?'

Before Kirov could answer Ian Morgan held up his hand. 'I'm sorry to break up your little science seminar here gentlemen but not all of us were born inside a laboratory. Why don't we get back to more practical questions shall we. Such as why Mr Kirov decided to come to us with this information and not the Americans?'

Kirov swallowed. 'I believe that all mankind should benefit from this technology. Both the Americans and the Soviets are working on top secret research projects to develop the technology taken from grounded flying saucers and adapt it for their own purposes. The Americans are developing extreme altitude aircraft capable of flying to the edge of space, way beyond the distance of Soviet radar and rockets. We also know that the Americans are using the United Kingdom as a testing ground for one of these aircraft. The Soviets have also conducted similar experiments. But they believe the key lies in the conquest of space itself which will determine who has dominance on this planet.'

What do you mean by that?' Lord Chambers asked.

'Whoever can launch the first artificial satellite into Earth orbit would be seen as the dominant force on this planet. The Soviet government is eager to win this race. Especially if we are being observed by beings from another world.'

A short silence followed as the other four men considered what Kirov had just said.

'Right now at a place called Kazakh located in the Soviet Socialist Republic scientists are working on the first artificial satellite. They hope it will be ready to launch within three to four years.'

'I must say Mr Kirov you have taken a huge risk coming here revealing this information to us.' Stanford remarked.

'Risks are part of life Mr Stanford.'

'Well it seems that you have much to offer.'

'And much more I can assure you.'

'We will find a safe place for you Mr Kirov but until then you are a guest of her Majesty.' Chambers nodded at the guard who stepped forward.

'I understand, I hope you find the information I have provided helpful.' He stood up and was escorted out of the room.

Frederick continued to look at the photographs. 'Well this is a turn up for the books.'

'It is.' Stanford said thoughtfully.

'What did you make about the Russians efforts to reach space before the Americans.' Asked Morgan.

'It's highly possible they could have some sort of program in operation.' Frederick suggested. 'The question is do we tell the Yanks about this.'

'No.' Chambers said abruptly. 'They've been keeping secrets from us for years. I suggest we don't get too friendly. In time we will let them know about Kirov. But for now we keep everything under wraps and see what else he has to offer.'

Chapter 74

The Kremlin – Moscow – Soviet Union – 4:56pm Saturday 18th July 1953

Igor Lakatos swallowed hard realising the situation he was in.

Both Bulganin and Volkart stared intensely at Lakatos.

'We have heard from Comrade Modin concerning the defector.' Bulganin explained.

'Defector?' Lakatos said.

'Dmitri Kirov.' Volkart replied.

'I have heard rumours but I never thought they were true.'

'Well these rumours you heard are true Comrade Lakatos. Which begs the question, why didn't you suspect this man would defect?'

'I assure you gentlemen I had no idea.' Lakatos said.

'It seems to us Comrade Lakatos that you are not in control of your own staff.' Volkart remarked.

Lakatos glared at Volkart. 'Kirov kept his deception hidden very well. I make sure all my team are regularly scrutinised for signs of betrayal.'

'Well I suggest you find out how this man managed to defect to the west taking with him valuable information regarding the Tunguska event.' Bulganin stated in a sharp tone. 'You are to make contact with Comrade Modin in Great Britain and find out where they have Comrade Kirov so that we can deal with this situation.' Bulganin picked up a glass of vodka and swigged it down.

Lakatos stood. 'I will proceed immediately.'

Chapter 75

**Vallance Road – Bethnal Green – London – 11:23am
Monday 9th August 1953**

Frederick looked down the narrow street at a group of children playing football. At the end of the street lay a derelict landscape of bombed out buildings on which more children were playing amongst the ruins.

'I don't know if this is the right place.' Frederick said.

'The information which your Professor Wilks pulled off the Roswell device is pretty accurate.' Agent Frank Cones said. 'I guess we'll have to start knocking on doors.'

Frederick looked at the American. 'Let me do all the talking will you Agent Cones. The people who live in this part of London can be very wary of outsiders, especially if they are foreign. Just remember our cover story.'

'Don't worry Professor you won't know I'm here. Besides I know what these people are like. I grew up in Brooklyn.'

Both men got out of the car and started to walk down the street. The group of children playing football stopped and watched as the two strangers approached them.

A young boy ran into one of the terraced houses.

Frederick glanced from side to side noting twitching curtains as people stared out of their windows. A door to one of the terraced houses opened and a woman stepped out with two young men. Frederick glanced at them as they approached noting they were twins.

'Hey you two.' The woman said loudly and in a broad cockney accent. 'If you're looking for my husband you're out of luck he's been dead ten years.'

'I beg your pardon madam.' Frederick said innocently.

'Oh don't come over all shy, you're from the war office still chasing after my other half for not signing up.'

'Well actually.' Frederick said before the woman cut him off.

She folded her arms and smirked at Frederick. 'Oh I know, you're here to see fanny Adams on the end there.' The woman said indicating to the end terrace house. 'I hope you're here to evict her. Filthy trollop up the poke again. Probably another dock worker, she gets about you know.'

Frederick and Cones glanced at each other. 'Do you have a name for this woman?' Frederick asked.

'Rosemary Smith.' The woman replied. 'If you need a hand just give my door a knock, my boys are pretty handy.' She indicated to the two young men flanking her.

'I'm sure they are, thank you Mrs?'

'Violet, Violet Kray.'

'Thank you Mrs Kray.' Frederick tipped his hat politely.

The two young men glared back menacingly as Frederick and Cones continued to walk down the street.

Both men stood in front of the door of the end house and looked back up the street. The woman they had just talked to had been joined by other street residents.

'If what that woman said is true this should be the right address.' Cones commented.

Frederick knocked on the door.

The door eventually opened to reveal a short blonde haired woman wrapped in a black shawl. 'Can I help you?'

'Good morning madam.' Frederick greeted. 'We are from the ministry of health. We're in the area conducting a survey on the effects of living near bombsites.'

'I see.' The woman replied glancing up the street at the crowd of people who stared back gossiping amongst themselves. 'You better come in.' She offered.

Frederick did his best to ignore the smell of dirty nappies which were piled up in a small basket in the tiny kitchen. A young boy of about ten years old ran down the stairs towards the front door. 'Don't go too far Johnny.' His mother warned.

'Stay away from those Kray brothers. They'll do nothing but get you into trouble. Also, stay away from Charlie Osbourne. He'll expect you to steal apples from the greengrocer.' The young woman's Irish accent was clear but soft.

Another boy approximately six years old and a young girl a few years younger stood at the top of the stairs looking down at the two strangers.

Frederick and Cones were led through to a small sitting room which was sparsely furnished. Both men sat next to each other on an old sofa which had been salvaged from the bombsite. Frederick noted the woman's pregnancy. 'When's the baby due?'

The woman looked down at her stomach shaking her head. 'I don't know.'

'Well you must be pretty close now.'

'I guess so.'

'Is your husband around?'

'No, he was killed during the war.'

'I see.' Frederick said. 'May I enquire who the father is?'

The woman continued to stare at her heavily pregnant stomach, she started to sob.

'I'm sorry.' Frederick said pulling a handkerchief out of his pocket and getting up. 'I didn't mean to be nosy. Its just unmarried mothers are so rare in this day and age.'

The woman blew her nose. 'I'm sorry.' She sobbed. 'The truth is I don't know who the father is. I know it sounds ridiculous but it's like I woke up pregnant one day.'

Frederick and Cones exchanged glances. 'Well I think we can help.'

The woman looked up. 'How?'

'It's obvious you cannot live in these surroundings. I shall contact my superiors tonight and have you moved to more suitable accommodation.'

'What about my children?'

'They will be accompanying you.'

The woman managed a smile. 'You won't be taking my children away from me.'

Frederick shook his head. 'No, in fact we feel it's important for you to remain as a family. I want you to pack as much as you can and we will be back tomorrow to pick you up.'

Both men stood and said their goodbyes.

Whitehall – London
3:45pm

'Are you sure this woman is who we are looking for?' Chambers asked.

'She says she cannot remember how she became pregnant and her story is similar to Edith Jones last year. Plus the information from the Roswell device is very accurate.'

'We have a number of safe houses. There's one in Surrey, it's quiet, and no one will bother her.'

'She is only weeks away from giving birth. We'll have to send a doctor to examine her.'

'I'll send Alan Good.' Chambers offered.

'I take it we're not thinking of replacing Arthur just yet.'

Chambers shook his head.

'I will start making the arrangements for moving Rosemary Smith.' Frederick got to his feet.

'Ok Ralph this is your show but remember this. If this woman turns out to be some floozy from the East End then back she goes.'

Chapter 76

Vallance Road - Bethnal Green – London – 9:39am Tuesday 10th August 1953

'Huh, you're too late gents someone has already beaten you to it.' Violet Kray called out from her front door.

Frederick and Cones looked down the street towards a large black Daimler Empress which was parked outside the house of Rosemary Smith.

The two men quickened their pace and spotted a man dressed in priest's robes exiting the front door with some bags. Mrs Smith's three children were sat in the back of the car crying.

'What's going on here?' Frederick demanded to know.

The priest looked at him as he threw the bags in the boot of the car. 'And who might you be?' He asked slamming down the boot.

'I asked first.'

Rosemary Smith appeared at the front door with two men dressed in black cassocks with red sashes around their waists and rosaries hung around their necks with red cloth caps. The young woman was crying as the two men led her out of her house. Frederick blocked their path. 'Where are you taking this woman?'

'That is none of your concern!' The priest stated.

'I demand to know where you are taking her.' Frederick fired back.

'This woman is now in the custody of the church and will remain there until her child is born. Now get out of my way or I'll send for the police.'

Frederick reluctantly stepped aside and looked on as Rosemary and her children were driven away. 'I don't understand who were those men?'

Agent Cones looked on as the car turned a corner. 'If I were to hazard a guess Professor I'd say they were Vatican officials.'

'What an earth would they want with Rosemary Smith and her children?'

'That's what we need to find out.'

Whitehall – London – 2:43pm
Thursday 12th August 1953

'It took a couple of days of digging around but you're not going to like it.' Morris Stanford said.

Frederick and Cones were sat at either ends of a large Queen Ann sofa.

'On Monday intelligence got wind of two high ranking Vatican officials passing through Heathrow.'

'But they didn't raise any flags.' Frederick commented.

Stanford shook his head. 'We saw no reason to suspect them of anything. Besides it's Russian operatives we are on the lookout for. 'They passed through Heathrow again early yesterday but this time they had a young woman in tow. Their flight was bound for Rome.' Stanford revealed.

'And still our boys didn't detain them.' Frederick stated.

Again Stanford shook his head.

Frederick shrugged. 'Where are the children?'

'There were no other children.' Stanford revealed. 'Just the woman and the Vatican chaps.'

'It would seem we have a new player on the field.' Cones said. 'The Vatican may be aware of what's happening to these people.'

'Whatever the Vatican is up to, it certainly adds depth to the whole flying saucer mystery.' Frederick commented.

The Vatican – Rome – 2:01pm
Friday 13th August 1953

Cardinal Michael Portis knelt down in front of Pope Pius kissing his hand.

'I take it your recent assignment was a success.'

'Yes your Holiness, the woman is now in our care. We await the birth of her child.'

'And her other children?'

'The children are being taken care of.' Portis hesitated before continuing. 'While in London I encountered Professor Frederick.'

The Pope closed his eyes in brief prayer for a moment.

'The prophecy is starting to play out, Agent Cones was with him.'

Pius nodded. 'We must gather the Brotherhood and discuss these latest developments. The fact that Professor Frederick and Agent Cones have been introduced to each other demonstrates that events are about to unfold. They will face many challenges before the prophecy comes to pass.'

'And the Dark Ones?' Portis questioned.

'The Dark Ones have yet to reveal themselves. Frederick is yet to encounter the creatures which threaten our world. I will instruct the Brotherhood to keep an eye on the obelisk under the Temple mount.'

Chapter 77

Bletchley Park – 10:09am
Thursday 19th September 1953

'I've been looking through the documents you brought with you from Russia Mr Kirov. I am particularly interested in something called Project Orion. Why don't you enlighten us as to what this is?' Frederick asked.

Morris Stanford and Professor Richard Wilks were also present in the interview room.

Dmitri Kirov took a long drag on his cigarette staring at Frederick. 'With all due respect Professor Frederick I have been a prisoner here for weeks and now you just march in here demanding answers.'

'Mr Kirov you must be aware that your comrades will be very eager to get their hands on you. Preparations are underway for you to be moved. For now you will remain here. If you choose not to cooperate with our investigation then you will be here for a long time.' Stanford explained.

Kirov took another drag. 'Orion is an extension of a secret research project started by the Nazis during the war. Hitler was obsessed with obtaining artefacts which he believed contained mythical properties which would help him win the war.'

'Artefacts?' Wilks questioned.

'He believed that there was knowledge which had been lost for thousands of years throughout Europe. Knowledge relating to technology not of this world.'

'Not of this world.' Frederick interrupted.

'The Nazis believed that we had been visited in the past by creatures from another world. The ancient civilisations that built great monuments acquired this knowledge off these beings. When the tides of war started to turn against Hitler he sent teams all over the globe looking for this lost knowledge. In the last days of the war Russian troops gained access to a vault which contained documents relating to all kind of Nazi projects.' Kirov smiled.

'Something amusing you Mr Kirov.' Wilks asked.

'The Americans believe that they had the upper hand capturing rocket research facilities. But what we found was far more valuable. Hundreds of locations all over the world where the Nazis had been, including America and Great Britain.'

'I assure you Mr Kirov there were no Nazis in this country during the war.' Stanford said with confidence.

'Are you sure? Just because you won the battle of Britain doesn't mean you kept the Nazis at bay. The Nazis had teams of archaeologists all over the UK mainland digging for what they hoped would win them the war. They also had teams in North America.'

'So Comrade Stalin decided to carry on the research.' Frederick added.

'Until his paranoia started to dominate him.' Kirov stared at the wall in front of him. 'Two colleagues of mine were ruthlessly murdered earlier this year because of infighting over Project Orion. A scientist called Igor Lakatos is the man behind their murders. He believed in Orion but he wanted it for himself and has been head of the Project since March. I started to fear for my life.'

'Why?' Wilks asked.

'Because I was former head of Project Orion.'

Frederick sat back in his chair thinking about what Kirov was telling them. 'I take it there are teams of Russians all over looking for this lost knowledge.'

'Yes.'

'What about the British Mainland? Are there any Russians on the loose looking for artefacts?' Stanford asked.

'If I tell you.' Kirov said. 'I want better accommodation.'

Stanford glared at the Russian for several seconds before eventually nodding. 'Very well Mr Kirov.'

'There is a team in Scotland.' Kirov revealed.

Frederick could barely stop himself from laughing. 'Scotland, don't be absurd man. What could possibly be there which is of interest to the Soviet Union? Not to mention the fact that you have been with us for a good several weeks. Any information provided by you will be useless.'

'Mjölnir.' Kirov replied.

'I beg your pardon.'

'It's a Viking word Professor.' Kirov said. 'Translated it means the Hammer of Thor. As we speak there is a team of archaeologists looking for this artefact. They have been in Scotland since June and have been given orders to stay there until they found something. The Nazis believed it to be some kind of weapon capable of levelling entire cities. That's why the Soviet Union is so interested. It's highly possible the team is still there.'

Chapter 78

Western Scotland – 11:56am
Friday 25th September 1953

A gust of wind howled in from the sea. Although the sky was crystal clear and the sun blazed down Frederick wrapped his army issue coat tightly around him. Stood next to him was Professor Norman Canning who was dressed identically. As he was the only member of the committee who mastered in geology and history he volunteered to go with Frederick. At sixty six years old Frederick had to admit he was very agile.

'I still say Kirov has sent us on a wild goose chase. For all we know they could have left weeks ago.' Frederick complained.

'Well at least we're out in the fresh air.' Canning remarked surveying the landscape beyond the beach.

Accompanying both men were six soldiers attached to the Special Air Service led by Captain Rodney Crewe, a world war two veteran. The group had been dropped off by HMS Sheffield which admiral Berkshire had ordered to the area Kirov had claimed the Russian archaeological team were. The Sheffield had been ordered to sail further up the coast and return in two days to pick the men up.

Frederick looked across the beach towards the landscape beyond which consisted of a rugged terrain with mountains off into the distance.

Professor Canning studied a geological survey map he had with him. 'If memory serves me correct this area is one big extinct volcano.'

An old ruin of a stone cottage stood where the beach met grassland. 'Not exactly the ideal holiday home.' Frederick remarked.

'Probably abandoned during the highland clearances.'

Canning speculated.

'Ok then chaps.' Captain Crewe trudged past with the five other men close behind. 'We've got a bit of a walk ahead of us so I suggest we get going.'

The group of eight men walked off the beach and followed what appeared to be nothing more than a goat trail. After about two hours the team reached the foot of a mountain which marked the outer rim of the extinct volcano Canning had mentioned.

The group finally rested on a flat piece of grassland on which stood an ancient stone circle consisting of thirteen monoliths. Twelve of the stones were rectangular, approximately nine feet in height by three foot in width.

Frederick noted that the space between each stone was not equal like other stone circles he had seen. The thirteenth stone towered above the rest at twelve feet in height by four foot across. Each stone was approximately a foot in thickness.

Crewe and his men broke out some army rations while Frederick and Canning examined the standing stones. Both men could easily make out all kinds of strange symbols etched into the stones.

Frederick examined the stones one by one. 'There is a similar standing stone on Sir William Ingles estate in Ripley. He told me his cattle refuse to graze anywhere near the stone.'

'Looks like someone's been here before us.' Canning remarked pointing at the stone in front of him. 'The stone has been cleaned. These markings stand out more.'

Frederick stood in front of the largest stone staring at a series of circular symbols. 'Take a look at this.' He beckoned Canning over who looked at the symbols etched on the stone. 'What do you see?'

Canning stared at the nine circles on the stone which were marked out in a straight line and consisted of several different sizes. In between the fourth and fifth circle there was another group of smaller circles overlapping each other varying in size. The sixth circle had a diagonal line through it. Scattered above and below the main circle line were more circles, again varying in size. 'From what I know these stones date back to the first century and before that. No one has been able to decipher them. I know someone at Oxford who has spent a good deal of his life studying stones like these.' Canning removed his rucksack and took out a camera.

Frederick pointed at the sixth circle with the diagonal line through it. 'Saturn.'

'Saturn, are you sure Ralph?' Canning said.

Frederick then pointed at the first circle in line. 'Mercury, Venus, Earth, Mars, Jupiter, Saturn, Uranus, Neptune and Pluto.'

Canning shook his head looking doubtful. 'Impossible, the people who erected these stones were highland tribesmen. They had no social structure like the Romans. No detailed knowledge of the planets or stars.' He pointed at the other circles on the stone. 'What about these other circles just randomly scattered about and the group of circles in between where you say Mars and Jupiter are.'

Frederick thought for a moment. 'Dwarf planets.'

'Dwarf planets, that's a bit of a stretch Ralph.' He said with doubt in his tone. He held up his camera and snapped a picture.

'But we know there are dwarf planets within the solar system.' Frederick remarked.

'Ralph the people who made these markings were simple tribesmen. They were hunter gatherers not stargazers like the Greeks or the Romans.' Canning said. 'And even the Romans and Greeks didn't have knowledge of dwarf planets. They didn't start showing up until the invention of the telescope, not to mention planets such as Pluto haven't long been discovered.'

Frederick stepped up to the stone for a closer look. 'Were

they hunter gatherers?' He said rubbing at one of the etched circles. 'This circle is perfect. It doesn't look like it's been carved out by any stone tool.'

Canning stared at the markings raising his eyebrows nodding. 'Yes they are quite intricate.' He remarked.

'We still know very little about our past and the people who inhabited this planet before modern man. Science itself is partly built on knowledge handed down to us through the ages. We still use basic mathematical principles that the Greeks invented. For some of us everything we learn as we go through life is either based on what we've been told in school or through self-discovery. But for most people all their accumulated knowledge has been handed to them.'

'Ok Ralph, what's your point.' Canning asked.

'My point is Norman, how do we know we are right about half the things we teach.'

'We don't.' Canning replied. 'But it's all we have to guide us.'

'Exactly.' Frederick looked at the upper half of the next stone and noted that there were several indentations marked out in a pattern all connected by intersecting lines. A smile appeared on his face as he realised what he was looking at.

'What's the matter?' Canning asked.

Frederick just pointed. 'Orion.'

Canning studied the markings. 'You're right, that is the constellation of Orion.' He sounded genuinely surprised.

Frederick moved on to the next stone and stared at the markings on the top. 'Andromeda.' He moved to the next stone. 'Aries.' And the next. 'Canis Major, Cancer, Draco, Cassiopeia, Libra, Leo, Pegasus, Sagittarius, finally Virgo.' By the time he had named all the constellations he had returned to the Orion stone. He looked at the constellation and noted the middle star that made up part of Orion's belt had a perfectly straight line pointing down to a line of four circles. He quickly glanced at the tallest stone with the representation of our solar system. The third planet along had a vertical line leading to an indentation which was part of a group. Frederick then focused on the Orion stone staring at the line of four circles. 'This can't be.' He said.

'What?'

'If I'm not mistaken this is another planetary system.'

'Impossible.' Canning stated.

Frederick quickly scanned the other stones that all had a line of circles on them. Each stone had one circle with a line pointing toward a star in each constellation.'

Canning pointed at the tallest stone. 'But what about this stone here? Where you say our solar system is.'

Frederick stared at the group of indentations. 'I have no idea. I'm not familiar with this constellation.' He stepped back and stared. 'Unless, this could be a constellation our own sun could be part of.'

'I am impressed Professor Frederick. We have been studying these stones for weeks but have not been able to come up with answers!' A voice shouted from behind clapping his hands.

Chapter 79

3:06pm

Frederick, Canning, and the six soldiers sat with their hands tied in the middle of the stone circle.

The twelve Russian soldiers had appeared out of nowhere surprising the group.

Norman Canning glared at the ground. 'So much for the SAS.' He scoffed.

Captain Crewe glared back at Canning. 'And your point being Professor.' He growled.

Canning looked up at him. 'You should have had a man on watch otherwise we wouldn't be in this predicament.'

'With all due respect Professor Canning, my men and I were ordered to escort you and Professor Frederick on some jolly highland jaunt. We were not expecting to bump into a small contingency of Russian soldiers. Now would one of you boffins please tell me what the bloody hell's going on?'

Frederick ignored the argument brewing between the two men. He stared over at Colonel Yuri Konev whom he had encountered the previous year during the Operation Mainbrace incident. Konev was stood next to another man who was taking rubbings of the symbols on the stone. The Colonel looked back at Frederick and smiled; he said something to another soldier and indicated at Frederick. The soldier walked over and hauled him to his feet.

'I'm impressed with your ingenuity regarding the meaning of these stones Professor. My team had all but given up. We assumed these stones were unimportant.'

Frederick remained silent.

'Don't be bashful Professor you were more than happy to team up last year during the incident with the Americans.'

'What exactly do you intend to do with us Colonel?'

Frederick asked.

'For now Professor I would like you to assist my colleague and answer some questions he has.'

A soldier walked up to the Colonel saying something in Russian before leading him away outside the stone circle.

The man taking the rubbings watched Konev until he was out of sight. 'Professor Frederick, it is an honour sir.'

'I wish I could say the same.' Frederick said with sarcasm indicating to his tied hands.

The man checked to see Konev was still out of earshot. 'I don't have much time to explain Professor but I can assure you, you are in good company. Doctor Rothschild sends his regards.'

Frederick stared at the other man. 'You are part of the Galileo Order.' He whispered.

The man nodded. 'Professor Alex Pavlov at your service, Russian archaeological academy.'

Frederick scanned the immediate area. Four soldiers guarded Professor Canning and the other men. Five more were dispersed around the stone circle. A distant sound of a two way radio could be heard. 'What exactly is going on here?' Frederick asked.

'We have been here for a few months excavating a site about two miles from here.' Pavlov indicated to the centre of the ring of mountains. 'It is an old Viking burial site complete with longboat and all the wealth this Viking had. But we also discovered something else.' Again Pavlov checked to see the Colonel was out of sight. He bent down and reached into a leather satchel pulling out what looked to be a perfectly square stone tablet. 'We found this buried with him.'

The tablet was approximately ten inches on all sides. On it were symbols that Frederick instantly recognised. 'I have seen these before.' He said.

'Where?'

'The Americans demonstrated a piece of technology from

a crash site in New Mexico.'

'Roswell.' Pavlov stated.

Frederick nodded. 'It displayed symbols similar to these.' Frederick studied the tablet that contained thirteen symbols. Three rows of four with the thirteenth on the top centre. 'I couldn't tell you what they mean unfortunately.'

Pavlov pointed at the base of the rock which was overgrown with fern. He kicked it away with his foot to reveal a symbol that Frederick instantly recognised. 'I have yet to show Colonel Konev this.'

Frederick stared at the symbol. 'I know this symbol. I've seen it before. It's etched onto a door at Ripley castle and a similar standing stone which is located at the back of the castle. It was also displayed on the Roswell device when we were in Ripley.'

'I have also seen this symbol.' Pavlov revealed. 'Many times in Russia and other parts of Europe.'

'Do you know what it means?'

'I have heard a theory that it's somehow connected to humans. It's a theory put forward by a brilliant young physicist Doctor Anna Vilenko.'

'I am familiar with that name.'

Pavlov nodded. 'She was one of our rising stars, until she embarrassed another leading physicist. Since then she has not been seen.'

Frederick looked around. 'Do you know what they plan to do with us?'

Pavlov nodded. 'You will be freed eventually, but at a price.'

'A price.' Frederick said.

'Professor we don't have much time.' Pavlov indicated to the largest stone they were stood next to. 'Before we interrupted you, you were saying about our sun being part of a constellation.'

Frederick looked at the monolith. 'It's only speculation.'

He said finding it difficult to focus. 'The constellations we see in the night sky have been given names by ancient civilizations like the Greeks and Babylonians. The International Astronomical Union divided the sky into eighty eight specific regions for the eighty eight constellations in 1922. They assigned Latin names for the traditional constellations. Except for those named after Greek mythological figures.' Frederick looked up at the pattern of stars. He then looked at the stone directly opposite with the constellation of Cassiopeia. 'Unless.' He stated marching over to the stone followed by Pavlov. Frederick looked at the constellation on the stone then turned to face the tallest stone.

Pavlov noted the expression on his face. 'What is it?'

'It's a star map.' A smile appeared on his face as he looked at the other stones one by one. 'I couldn't understand why these stones are not evenly spaced but now it's simple. It's all about their position in the sky and relative distance.'

'But which sky?' Pavlov asked.

Frederick looked at the line of circles on the stone he was stood next to. The fifth one had a vertical line pointing towards Cassiopeia. 'This sky.' He revealed.

Konev stepped back into the circle marching up to the two men. 'We are to rendezvous at eleven tonight.' He informed Pavlov before turning to Frederick. 'Has he revealed anything significant?'

Pavlov hesitated for a few seconds. 'No, he has revealed nothing of any use.'

'Very well we stay here until nightfall then make our way back to the rendezvous point. In the meantime we set the charges.'

'Charges.' Frederick said.

'You didn't expect us to leave you to decipher these stones did you Professor.'

Four of the Russian soldiers produced explosives from their rucksacks.

'Colonel you cannot do this. These stones are of historical significance. To destroy them would be like knocking down the great pyramid.'

'Professor you have a choice. Either we destroy these stones.' Konev glared at Frederick. 'Or we leave them standing and their secrets die with you and the rest of your party tonight. It's your choice.'

Frederick's thoughts suddenly shifted to Elizabeth and Susan. For him to die in this spot and his family not knowing what had happened to him was a terrifying prospect. He eventually nodded before being led back to the main group.

'Enjoying yourself I see.' Canning remarked with sarcasm. 'You were rather chatty with that chap.' He indicated to Pavlov.

'They are planning to destroy the stones.'

'Well I didn't think they were planning a bonfire with those explosives.'

8:34pm

The sound of the explosion crackled across the landscape like thunder. Frederick and the rest of his team could only look on as the stone circle was reduced to a pile of rubble.

Konev looked across the landscape towards the sea and the fading light on the horizon. 'Once again it's been a pleasure Professor.' He said before looking at Crewe. 'I advise you not to try and follow us Captain.'

Crewe just glared back.

Pavlov looked at Frederick who had been untied. 'You will be contacted by Rothschild in due course Professor.' He spoke softly.

Chapter 80

Whitehall – London – 12:38pm
Wednesday 30th September 1953

'After sunrise we trekked across to Kilchoan where we managed to find a farm which had a telephone. On the way we discovered the remains of a burial site the Russians had excavated.' Frederick shook his head. 'They had taken everything of value and reduced the rest to a cinder.'

'The bloody Russians are everywhere.' Chambers grunted.

'I'll have the Royal Navy patrolling that area regularly from now on.' Admiral Berkshire offered.

'What about the stone circle?' Stanford asked.

'Total destruction.' Canning sighed. 'There's nothing left worth retrieving and they took my camera.'

'We'll keep our eyes peeled for signs of Soviet incursions.' Stanford said before standing. 'I'll get over to MI6 to see if we can prize more information out of Kirov.' Stanford got up.

'What's your analysis on what you discovered?'

'As incredible as it sounds there could well be evidence that ancient civilizations may have had advanced astronomical knowledge.' Frederick said.

'We should mount our own project looking into this.' Canning suggested. 'There are hundreds of ancient sites throughout the United Kingdom which could give us a wealth of undiscovered information. I know someone at Oxford who could do a bulk of the work. He doesn't have to know the real purpose of what we're looking for.'

'Agreed, get in touch with your colleague and come up with a plan on how to proceed.'

Chapter 81

71 – 77 Pall Mall – London – 1:51pm
Friday 23rd October 1953

Frederick stared up at the entrance to the Oxford and Cambridge club feeling somewhat apprehensive about going in. And it didn't help matters that Rothschild had sent him an invite to join him and a distinguished guest for a meeting. Frederick climbed the steps and entered the building. A tall man dressed in a grey suit stood guard just inside the main door. He smiled at Frederick as he walked in.

'Professor Frederick.' He greeted. 'This way please sir.'

Frederick followed the man down a large hallway which acted more like a portrait gallery displaying pictures of past and present members including a picture of Frederick himself. Frederick never considered himself as photogenic and hated having his picture taken.

They stopped in front of a large oak door that led to one of the grand reading halls which occupied the building. The man then knocked on the door before opening it.

Rothschild stood by a large bookcase browsing through the volumes of books. He turned and smiled as Frederick entered the room. 'Professor good to see you, thank you for coming.' Rothschild shook Frederick's hand. 'May I present a distinguished colleague of mine, Professor Albert Einstein.'

Frederick froze as Einstein appeared in front of him. He felt like a small boy meeting one of his literary heroes.

'Professor Frederick it is an honour to finally meet you.' Einstein greeted shaking hands. 'I have read much of your work, impressive.'

Frederick had to summon all his strength just to say something back. 'I'm sorry but I'm feeling a little overwhelmed.'

Rothschild chuckled. 'We'll go easy on you Professor. I called you here today concerning the incident in Scotland a few weeks back. I would have contacted you sooner but I thought it wise to let the dust settle. Fellow member Alex Pavlov sends his regards and wanted to thank you for the information you helped uncover on those stones and regrets the actions of Colonel Konev.'

'I wouldn't be standing here if it weren't for him.'

All three men gathered around a large circular table on which were laid out large pieces of paper as well as photographs of all the stones. Frederick recognised the markings which were on the stones.

Einstein began to speak. 'Pavlov managed to make copies of what he took from the stones and the tablet recovered from the Viking burial site. I'm fascinated by your theory Professor Frederick that these circles on each stone represent planetary systems.' He picked up a photograph of the largest stone. 'You say this one represents our solar system.' He picked up another picture. 'And this stone which bears the constellation of Cassiopeia has a planetary system.'

'Yes, but can I just point out Professor that this is all speculation, as I told Pavlov.' Frederick explained.

Einstein smiled at him. 'If you are worried about treading on my toes Professor then you needn't. For some time I had suspected that we might not be the only creatures inhabiting our universe. And my speculations were confirmed during the Roswell crash.'

'You must have learnt much from your experiences.'

'The Americans granted me access to the wreckage of the ship in the hope that I could figure out how it works. I have studied the technology in detail. Unfortunately I learned that there are limits to my knowledge.' He looked back at the photographs. 'The information here is very intriguing, especially if this is a representation of the constellation that our own sun is part of.' He pointed to the photograph of the tallest stone.

Frederick noticed the three armed spiral pattern at the base of this stone. 'I told Professor Pavlov that I recognised this symbol.'

'This symbol is present on many ancient monuments around the globe. The Order has had teams of archaeologists scouring our planet looking for ancient monuments which could hold clues to the identity of visitors from other worlds.

'It's also carved onto the door of Ripley castle in North Yorkshire. The owner of the castle revealed to me that extraterrestrials have been taking women from the village for centuries.'

Rothschild nodded. 'This symbol is prominent on many ancient structures throughout the world. It appears everywhere from Egypt to Easter Island.'

'Whoever created these markings had advanced knowledge of the stars.' Frederick said.

'Or were from the stars.' Rothschild stated. 'It's the only plausible explanation as to how this information got onto these stones.'

'Which shatters my theory of relativity.' Einstein pointed out.

Frederick looked at him. 'I wouldn't go as far as to say that Professor.'

'Again Professor you assume I will be disturbed by such allegations. Over the years I have learnt that nothing is certain. And relativity is subject to change. My theory is merely a benchmark for science. To help others understand the universe as we see it in our time. But what about in five hundred years or a thousand years? How will men view our universe then? To state that the theory of relativity will always be and can never be changed is foolish. After we have left this mortal plane of existence, science will continue to develop in ways we cannot imagine. If mankind survives the twentieth century he will go on to discover what lies beyond the boundaries of what I have contributed to science. Create machines capable of reaching out to the stars. My only regret is I won't be around to see it. But at least I know there are men like you Professor Frederick who will carry on my work and expand on it.'

'Expand on it.'

'My time is but a brief presence on this world, as with all of us. What I have done is far from finished. I am passing the torch to you Professor Frederick. I want you to carry on the work and rewrite relativity for the next generation of scientists.'

Frederick leant against the table; his heart raced. 'I don't know what to say Professor Einstein.'

'There is no need to say anything. The Order of Galileo was established to push the boundaries of understanding. Given what you have contributed so far to this Order I feel that you are the right man to carry on my work.'

A knock on the door alerted all three men that the meeting was drawing to a close. The door opened and the tall man walked in. 'Professor Einstein, Doctor Rothschild it is time.'

'I'm afraid I cannot stay Professor.' Einstein said. 'I must leave for Berlin immediately. It has been a pleasure to make your acquaintance. I hope to see you again in the future.'

'Goodbye Professor.' Rothschild said. 'We shall see each other again soon.'

The tall man gathered up the scrolls and photographs and all three left the room leaving Frederick alone with his thoughts.

Chapter 82

The American Embassy – London – 12:01pm
Friday 27th November 1953

Agent Cones opened the dossier in front of him and started to read. Frederick, Dr Alan Good and Sir Malcolm Chambers were present in the room. A meeting had been organised with the Majestic Twelve representative at the embassy.

Dr Good opened up the meeting. 'Last week a colleague of mine contacted me regarding the only survivor from the Stoke Lacy incident.'

'The young farm hand.' Cones said. 'Jimmy.'

'Yes, since the events last January and because of his disabilities he's being cared for at a mental institute in South Wales. My colleague phoned claiming that on two occasions this individual was able to get out of a locked room and disappear for two days at a time before suddenly appearing again. The incidents in question have happened within the last six weeks. The patient started to exhibit extreme anxiety at night and has had to be sedated on a number of occasions.' Dr Good produced a number of sheets of paper and slid them over to Cones. 'He has also been drawing.'

Cones looked at the sketches before looking back at the three men. 'What the hell?'

The series of sketches depicted the events that occurred at Stoke Lacy where he and Frederick had encountered Janus. One of the sketches showed Cones facing Janus with the shotgun he had tried to fire. Another sketch depicted Agent Cones on his knees wearing what appeared to be a straight jacket in a small room with barred windows.

'We want you to accompany Professor Frederick to the hospital where you are to interview this individual and find out how he's been getting out of his room.' Chambers explained. 'You are to leave on Monday.'

Emneth – Norfolk – 7:28pm
Sunday 29th November 1953

'You look tired sweetheart.' Frederick noted.

'I am ok I have just been a little under the weather. Doctor Davies has given me something.'

'If you don't want me to go on this trip I'll cancel.' Frederick offered.

Elizabeth shook her head. 'No it's ok Ralph, you go I'll be fine.'

'Are you sure.'

Elizabeth nodded as Frederick scooped his wife up in his arms.

Chapter 83

Pen-y-Fal Psychiatric Hospital – Abergavenny - South Wales – 10:23am
Tuesday 1st December 1953

Frederick and Cones were led down a long corridor by a hospital orderly. Patients could be heard all around shouting and screaming, which made Frederick feel uneasy.

Cones also looked about nervously at inmates who wandered up and down the corridor.

A woman clutching what appeared to be a scruffy looking doll approached the three men.

'Have you brought any milk for baby?' She asked the orderly.

'For Christ's sake Rosie go back to your room.' The orderly snapped.

'Baby wants milk!' The woman demanded blocking their path.

The orderly snatched the doll out of her arms and hurled it down the corridor.

The woman started to scream lunging out, striking the man across the head. 'Baby needs milk!' She screamed lashing out again.

'Mental bitch, here's your fucking milk!' The orderly shouted before punching her in the side of the face.

The woman fell backwards onto the floor and started to cry.

'Now piss off back to your room you mental cow!' The man ordered.

'Was that necessary?' Frederick said with growing concern.

'Listen, you don't have to deal with these head cases day in day out!' The orderly complained. 'I bloody well do!'

Frederick didn't say anything more and followed the orderly to the doctor's office.

Dr James Baxter poured a glass of whiskey. 'Would you care for some?' He offered.

'Don't mind of I do.' Cones accepted the glass.

'None for me thank you Doctor.' Frederick declined.

'Wise man.' Baxter said sitting down. 'Alan told me you were coming. But I am surprised to see an American in these parts.' He said looking at Cones.

'I'm here on request of Jimmy's family. I'm an old friend stationed here during the war.'

'Well as I told Alan Good, there's not that much to tell. Jimmy has vanished twice in six weeks before mysteriously turning up. Last time he was found wandering the hospital graveyard.'

'Any witnesses?' Frederick asked.

'No, well unless you count Rosie.'

'The woman with the doll.' Cones said.

'We let some of the less serious patients wander but our orderlies keep an eye on them.'

'When was the last time Jimmy vanished?'

'About two weeks ago. He went missing for two days before just turning up.'

'Why has it taken so long for you to contact anyone about it?' Frederick asked.

'I didn't feel the need until last week, when he started to draw.'

'I take it we can see the patient.' Cones requested.

Baxter got up from his chair and finished his whiskey. 'Of course.' The doctor led Frederick and Cones through a series of corridors lined with patients. 'Good morning Captain.' Baxter greeted one of them.

The man dressed in a stained white robe stood to attention and saluted. 'Sir, good morning sir.'

'This is the Captain; he's been with us since just after the war. Helped liberate some of the death camps. Proved all too much for him poor fellow.'

Cones walked by the man and made brief eye contact.

Without warning the Captain grabbed Cones with ferocious speed and pinned him against the wall. 'Frank we have to get off this beach, otherwise we're all dead.'

'Captain, let the man go.' Baxter ordered.

'We are Fucking dead anyway!' The Captain screamed.

Cones shuddered as images of Omaha beach flooded his mind. Paralysed he stared into the eyes of the Captain.

Baxter grabbed the Captain's arm. 'Let the nice man go Captain!'

'You should have stayed where you were, you shouldn't have left him.' The Captain began to cry. 'Why did you do it Frank?'

An orderly helped Baxter pull the Captain away. 'Take him to the shock room. Have Doctor Dale administer a small dosage.'

Cones remained where he was while the doctor walked calmly down the corridor as if nothing had happened.

'Agent Cones are you ok? Agent Cones!' Frederick waved his hand in front of the American's face.

Cones snapped out of his trance. 'Yeah.' He nodded. 'I'm fine.'

'Are you sure.'

'I'm ok Professor!' Cones snapped.

Both men joined Doctor Baxter who was looking through a small square window. 'He's been misbehaving today so we've had to put him in here.' The doctor unlocked the door and opened it.

Jimmy was sat on a chair with his knees hunched up to his chest. Frederick and Cones stepped through the door into the padded room.

Jimmy looked up at the three men before fixing his stare on Cones. 'Mr Cones!' Jimmy jumped to his feet. 'Mr Cones you shouldn't be here.'

'Hey buddy, how you doing?'

Jimmy walked up to Cones and put his arms around him. 'Mr Cones what are you doing here?'

'I wanted to see you of course.'

Jimmy started to cry. 'They're all dead Mr Cones.'

'Who Jimmy.'

'Mum, dad, Stephen and Andrea. It was the nasty man from the church Mr Cones, he killed them.'

'Have you seen the nasty man from the church Jimmy?' Frederick asked.

Jimmy nodded. 'He visits me.'

'Clearly delusional.' Baxter mocked.

Cones ignored the doctor's comments. 'What does he say to you Jimmy?'

'He says he wants to give us medicine, make us all better.'

'What medicine Jimmy?'

'I don't know.' He sobbed before returning to his seat and curling up in a ball.

'You won't get any more from him. He'll stay like that for hours. We've given him some electric shock therapy.'

'This man doesn't need therapy he needs to be with family.' Frederick seethed.

'We are his family now and I suggest you keep your opinions to yourself.' Baxter replied dryly. 'I think that's it for today gentlemen. As you can see the patient is doing well. The doctor will be doing his rounds later to check up on him.'

'The doctor?'

'He's a specialist, comes in from up north somewhere.'

Cones and Frederick exchanged glances. 'Do you have a name?'

Baxter stood deep in thought for a moment. 'I'm afraid I don't. Look if there's nothing else gentlemen I suggest you come back tomorrow when Jimmy's more responsive.'

The Angel Hotel – Abergavenny – 8:32pm

'You haven't been very talkative since we left that hospital today.' Frederick commented.

Cones stared at his dinner plate before looking at Frederick. 'How the hell did that guy who grabbed me know my name? Let alone what happened on Omaha Beach in forty four.'

'I've no idea but I suspect there's more here than meets the eye. I didn't find Doctor Baxter very cooperative.'

'We shouldn't have let them just dump Jimmy at that hospital.'

'The committee didn't say anything about putting him in a psychiatric hospital.' Frederick stopped in mid stream and looked up. 'What on earth?'

'What is that?' Cones asked listening to the sound.

'It sounds like an air raid siren.' Frederick guessed.

A waiter walked past their table.

'Excuse me but what does that siren mean?'

'It's a warning siren; it usually goes off when one of the nut cases from Pen-y-Fal escapes.'

Chapter 84

Pen-y-Fal Psychiatric hospital – 8:59pm

'I told you to come back tomorrow!' Dr Baxter growled.

'We heard the siren.' Frederick explained. 'I didn't expect to see you still here Doctor.'

'I have a room in the hospital grounds.'

'Who's escaped?' Cones asked.

Baxter remained silent.

'Is it Jimmy?'

'I suggest you gentlemen return to your hotel.' Baxter advised.

'Not until we see Jimmy.' Cones demanded.

'I'm afraid that's not possible.'

'Why?' Frederick asked.

An orderly suddenly appeared at the door of the doctor's office. Blood streaked down the side of his face. 'Doctor Baxter.' He panted. 'The patients are out of control.'

The sound of screaming and shouting could be heard in the distance.

'I've telephoned for help they should be here soon.' Baxter revealed

'Is there anything we can do?' Frederick asked the orderly.

'You could help me secure the doors. The more we lock the more we can contain the patients out of control.'

Baxter looked at the orderly for a few moments before nodding.

Frederick and Cones followed the man down the corridor.

'Where are the other orderlies?' Asked Frederick.

'Most of them have buggered off. I don't blame them. Four went to try and restore order in the canteen. That was the last I saw of them.'

'How many patients are loose?' Cones asked.

'A couple of dozen, most of them are in the main canteen smashing things up.'

'That cut looks rather serious.' Frederick commented, indicating to the cut on the orderly's head.

'I will be ok. The most important thing is to contain the patients, watch out!' The orderly shouted.

A Wooden chair came hurtling down the corridor narrowly missing Cones who barely had time to jump out of the way.

The young woman they had encountered earlier stood in the centre of the corridor clutching her doll. 'They took Jimmy again.'

'Rosie sweetheart go back to your room.' The orderly said calmly.

'They took him.'

Frederick stepped forward. 'Rosie, my name is Ralph. Can you tell me who took Jimmy?'

'Them.' She simply replied.

'Who is them Rosie?'

Rosie smiled back at Frederick. 'You're a nice man, I like you.'

'Thank you, now could you tell me who took Jimmy?'

She continued to smile pointing at the ceiling. 'The angels of course silly billy. Such a beautiful light.'

Frederick looked at Cones and noted the sweat running down his face. 'Are you ok Agent Cones?'

Cones listened to the screaming in the distance.

'Agent Cones!' Frederick said louder.

Cones seemed to jump. 'Sorry I'm feeling a little out of focus that's all.'

'Do you want to go back to the hotel?'

Cones shook his head. 'No I'm fine Professor.'

'They won't be coming back this time.' Rosie said. 'They've taken Jimmy to heaven.'

'Rosie could you please go back to your room.' The orderly said more firmly.

Rosie looked at him smiling. 'Will you come and visit me later. I like it when you visit me late at night.'

'I can't tonight Rosie I have work to do.' The orderly replied giving Frederick and Cones a nervous look.

Rosie looked at the doll she was cradling before walking towards her room.

The orderly shut the door and locked it.

The shouting continued as the three men drew closer to the canteen. The sound of crockery being smashed grew louder.

'Well at least they've stayed in the canteen.' The orderly tried to sound optimistic.

'When did all this commotion start?' Frederick asked.

'About an hour ago.'

'Is that when you noticed Jimmy was gone?'

The man nodded. 'I can't understand I checked on him earlier and locked his room but he still managed to get out.'

'You set off the siren.' Cones guessed.

'I was hoping it would attract the local police. But they're useless this time of night.'

The three men made their way down a long dimly lit corridor. When they turned a corner the damage that the patients had caused was clearly evident. The main door to the canteen had been smashed off its hinges. The noise had died down but patients could still be heard inside.

The Captain suddenly appeared in the doorway clenching a broken chair leg. He looked straight at Cones and smiled. 'Hey Frank, come on you dopehead lets go, we don't want to be late.'

Cones stepped back shaking.

Frederick clasped his arm. 'Agent Cones ignore him; focus on the task in hand.'

A Tear trickled down Cones' cheek as he stared at the man in the doorway. A cold breeze enveloped him causing him to shiver and close his eyes. When he opened them again he looked around.

Army Recruiting station – New York – USA
Friday 12th December 1941 10:45am

'Come on Frank.' His younger brother Michael grabbed his arm. 'We don't want to be late.'

'Are you sure we are doing the right thing Mikey? When dad finds out we've enlisted he's going to blow his stack.'

'Stop worrying you dopehead, besides you heard the radio last night. The President says every able bodied man has to enlist. We will teach those Jap bastards for messing with us. After we enlist we'll go down to Benny's and shoot some pool. You and Debbs can smooch in the corner.'

Cones smiled at his younger brother.

Frederick waved his hand in front of Cones' face. 'Agent Cones!'

Cones ignored Frederick's attempts to bring him back.

'What's the matter with him?' The orderly asked.

Frederick shook his head. 'He's in some kind of catatonic state.' He grabbed the American's arm. 'Agent Cones listen to me!' Frederick's tone became aggressive as he shook Cones' arm.

Cones smiled at the man stood in the canteen entrance. 'Hey Mikey wait up will you!' He shouted wrenching himself away from Frederick's grip and making a dash for the canteen. He joined the Captain and disappeared inside.

'Bloody hell!' Frederick seethed. 'I need to use the telephone.'

Malcolm Chambers massaged his brow and picked up a glass of brandy taking a sip. 'Where is he now?'

'In the main canteen as far as I know.' Frederick replied. 'Malcolm there's something more going on here in this hospital than meets the eye. How soon can you get help?'

'The local police won't be of any use this time of night. I'll make a phone call and see what I can drum up. There's an army camp a few miles outside Abergavenny. In the meantime old boy you're on your own.'

'Ok, I'll try and get Agent Cones away from the patients then find some kind of safe haven.'

'Where's this Doctor Baxter you mentioned?'

'I don't know he's not in his office anymore.'

'Ok Ralph, sit tight and help will arrive.'

Frederick put the phone back on the receiver and looked at the orderly. 'I'm afraid we are on our own for now. We need to get my colleague away from the canteen. Is there somewhere safe we can stay for the night after we reach him?'

'The laundry block would be our best bet. It's warm and the food stores are there.'

'Let's go.' Frederick urged.

Minutes later Frederick found himself staring at the entrance to the canteen. A few patients had left and were wandering the corridors. Doctor Baxter suddenly appeared in the doorway.

'Doctor Baxter thank god.' The orderly said.

Baxter seemed to look right through the orderly and Frederick. 'The doctor will soon be here. He will put everything right.'

'Doctor Baxter are you ok?' Frederick stared at the man with suspicion.

'The doctor will make things better you'll see.' Baxter vanished back into the canteen.

Frederick and the orderly walked cautiously towards the entrance and peered in. Tables and chairs were scattered about. Broken crockery littered the floor as well as tinned food the patients had found.

One patient had managed to break into a tin and was scooping out the contents shoving it into his mouth. Blood streamed down his arm as a result of cutting himself on the jagged edges of the tin. A group of patients sat in a circle.

Standing in the centre was Doctor Baxter who was staring at the ceiling. 'The doctor is coming!' He yelled.

Frederick spotted Cones who sat on his own, arms folded staring at the floor rocking back and forth. 'Agent Cones.' Frederick called out cautiously.

Cones didn't respond.

'Agent Cones it's me Professor Frederick.'

Still no response.

Frederick walked over to Cones and tapped him on the shoulder.

Cones leapt off the chair without warning.

Frederick failed to notice the chair leg he was clutching which came crashing down on his shoulder.

Frederick leapt back stumbling over the unconscious body of an orderly the patients had knocked out. He lay on his back.

Cones was about to rain another blow down on him.

The orderly dived at Cones. Both men crashed into a stack of wooden chairs. The orderly managed to disarm Cones and held him in a half nelson lock.

Frederick scrambled to his feet out of breath and winced as pain stabbed at his shoulder. 'We have to get him somewhere safe.'

'I know just the place.' The orderly said.

Frederick looked on in shocked silence at Cones sitting cross legged in the middle of a padded room. They had managed to find a straitjacket and had wrestled the American into it. The sketch that Jimmy had drawn dominated Frederick's thoughts. He now realised that the sketch Jimmy had drawn was not for Agent Cones, but was for him.

The orderly locked the door of the cell and looked at Frederick. 'What do we do now?'

Frederick rubbed his sore shoulder. 'We need to get Doctor Baxter away from those patients.'

The orderly shook his head. 'No, we've rescued your

friend. We need to hold up in the laundry block until help comes.'

'I'm not sure when that will be.' Frederick said grimly.

'Then it's over, I'm off.'

'You can't just leave.' Frederick protested.

'Look, I've only been here a few months. I didn't sign up for this, sorry but you are on your own.' The orderly looked at the cell door he had just locked. 'Your friend is safe inside. I suggest you get to the laundry and stay there until help comes.' He tossed a bunch of keys towards Frederick. 'Good Luck.' He said before turning and sprinting off.

Frederick stood alone in the corridor watching as the orderly disappeared.

Chapter 85

10:32pm

Frederick found himself alone staring at the entrance to the canteen. More patients had dispersed and had managed to find their own way back to their rooms. Frederick walked into the canteen and stared at the group of patients sat in a circle with Baxter still stood at the centre.

'The Doctor is coming!' Baxter shouted.

Frederick walked over to an unconscious orderly and knelt checking his pulse, which was steady. Frederick then noticed a static discharge building up around him. He stood up and looked all around, the crackling of static electricity grew more intense.

'The doctor is here!' Baxter screamed staring at the ceiling.

The circle of patients also looked up.

A blue light streamed through the windows from outside illuminating the canteen. A fire exit door opened and the light intensified. Frederick looked towards the door shielding his eyes.

A figure appeared in the doorway and walked into the room.

Janus was dressed in a doctor's coat with a stethoscope around his neck. He looked at the circle of patients and then directly at Frederick. 'It seems Professor you and I are starting to develop a relationship, people will talk.'

Frederick felt no fear this time, he glared back at Janus. 'What are you doing here?'

'Still demanding answers to questions you don't fully understand.'

'What have you done with Jimmy?' Frederick demanded to know.

'Jimmy is safe, he is away from here.'

'Where?'

'I think Professor you should be more concerned with what I have shown you.'

The image of Susan on her knees crying flooded back into Frederick's mind. The Professor holding Elizabeth's dead body in his arms.

'You seem determined to go forward despite what you see.' Janus said. 'Let me show you more.'

Frederick suddenly became aware of another sound. The crying of another young child. He looked up and stared at a young boy of about three years old standing next to Susan. Hovering over them was a huge shadow. But Frederick could not make out who or what it was. Frederick summoned all his strength. 'The future has yet to be written.' He stated.

'Spoken like a true physicist, you have a strong will Professor.'

'What exactly do you want?'

'I already have what I want Professor.'

'Which is what exactly?'

'Control.' Janus replied. 'Your species has much to offer Professor. It can be easily manipulated to suit my purposes.'

'What purposes?'

'A new beginning.'

'What new beginning?'

Janus smiled. 'Your species has only just discovered that you are not alone in the universe. There are other creatures who have been travelling the stars for millennia and who possess knowledge your species would take eons to comprehend.' Blue light started to fill the canteen again and Janus turned towards the exit. 'My work here is complete, but we will meet again Professor you can count on that.' Janus' outline seemed to melt into the intense light that lingered for a few seconds before vanishing.

Frederick looked at Doctor Baxter who had a confused expression on his face.

The patients that sat in a circle started to stand one by one.

Frederick walked over. 'Doctor Baxter are you ok?'

Baxter took a few seconds to nod. 'I think so, what the hell am I doing here?'

Frederick thought for a moment. 'I don't know I just walked in here to find you amongst the patients.'

Baxter rubbed his forehead and spotted the orderly who lay on the floor. The man started to move. lifting his head off the floor.

Frederick looked down at the set of keys the orderly had left. He then ran towards the canteen exit.

'Hey!' Cones shouted. 'What the hell's going on? Let me out of here, Hey!'

Frederick unlocked the door to find Cones wrestling with the straight jacket. 'Thank god you're back to normal.'

'Get me the hell out of this monkey suit Professor!' Cones demanded.

Frederick pulled at the straps. 'I'm sorry I had to do this to you Agent Cones, you weren't yourself.'

'Where the hell am I?'

'You are at the hospital.'

'What? The last thing I remember is that siren going off.' Cones said throwing the straight jacket to one side.

'You don't remember returning with me to investigate the siren.'

Cones shook his head. 'No.'

Baxter appeared at the cell door. 'The patients are returning to their cells. Now would someone please tell me what's happened here tonight.'

Chapter 86

Pen-y-Fal Hospital – Abergavenny – South Wales – 12:09am
Wednesday 3rd December 1953

'Thank you sergeant.' Frederick said removing the Velcro strap from his arm.

'Your shoulder isn't too bad you'll have a bit of bruising but it'll fade in a few weeks.'

Agent Cones walked up to Frederick. 'I'm sorry I wacked you.'

Frederick shook his head managing a smile. 'It's ok you weren't yourself.'

'What the hell happened tonight Professor? Why did that Janus show up again?'

'I don't know but I've a feeling we haven't seen the last of whatever he is.' Frederick checked his watch. 'I suggest we head back to London the committee members need to be briefed on the situation.'

Emneth – Norfolk – 7:20pm
Friday 5th December 1953

Elizabeth Frederick flushed the toilet for the fourth time that day. The morning sickness she had been suffering from the last week had gained momentum and started to plague her throughout the day. She walked into the kitchen to find her husband reading the evening paper.

'Everything ok sweetheart?' Frederick asked without looking up.

Elizabeth smiled at him. 'That depends on what kind of mood you're in.' She joked.

Frederick looked up from his paper looking at his wife slightly bemused at her comment.

Elizabeth continued to hold her smile. 'I'm pregnant.'

Frederick drew a deep breath staring into space.

'Ralph did you hear me?' Elizabeth said. 'I'm expecting our second child.'

Frederick got up and walked over to his wife forcing a smile. 'Darling that's fantastic news.' He put his arms around her kissing her on the cheek, while forcing the image Janus had planted out of his mind.

Chapter 87

Canterbury – Kent – 12:02pm
Monday 11th January 1954

Professor Wilks poured a small glass of brandy for his friend before handing it to him and sitting down. 'I can understand your reluctance to go forward Ralph. What this Janus has shown you is enough to put anyone off.'

'Janus is able to project images into my mind. I can control them to some extent, but it casts a shadow of doubt on whether I should carry on with The Angel Committee.'

'I wouldn't make rash judgements just yet.' Wilks sipped from his brandy glass. 'What do you think he wants with us?'

'Control was one word he used.'

'For what exactly, it's not like we're a technologically advanced race capable of interstellar travel.'

'He also mentioned a new beginning.' Frederick explained. 'I've been thinking about that for the last few weeks.'

'Some kind of invasion.' Wilks suggested.

Frederick shook his head. 'No I don't think so. But I have been thinking about Edith Jones and the woman I encountered in the East End last year, Rosemary Smith.'

Wilks pondered Frederick's words. 'Rebirth, do you think he's somehow introducing his species into the human race through some sort of genetic manipulation.'

'It's a good theory Richard but there is no way to back it up. We know very little about the molecular structure of the human body or whether he is involved with Edith or Rosemary.'

'Do you know Maurice Wilkins?'

'Yes, I worked with him briefly during the war. He worked on improving the function of our radar system, why do you ask?'

'He and another scientist.' Wilks thought for a moment. 'Doctor Rosalind Franklin discovered something called DNA last year. It's all very frontier science at the moment but both are convinced that this DNA could well be the building blocks of life. More to the point the element that makes up all of us.'

'What's your point?' Frederick sipped from his glass.

'An advanced race of beings could have knowledge of DNA and could alter it to suit their genetic state.'

'Like a cross breed, half human, half whatever species this Janus belongs to.'

'Exactly.' Wilks nodded. 'Which would explain these so called abduction cases. Edith Jones was pregnant before she was abducted and then returned minus the baby. The woman last year from London was pregnant with no knowledge of how she got into that state.'

'A pattern.' Frederick said.

'A pattern.' Wilks repeated.

'We need to track down another pregnant woman in the hope that we can catch whoever or whatever is behind these abductions.'

'Do you think this Janus could be linked?'

'That's what I plan to find out.'

'How's Liz?' Wilks asked changing the subject.

'She's fine.' Frederick smiled. 'Her parents are over the moon that she's pregnant again.'

'You said it yourself Ralph. The future has yet to be written. Despite what Janus has shown you. I don't believe anyone has the capability to see the future, no matter which part of the universe they originate from.'

Frederick smiled as he sipped some brandy.

Chapter 88

**Old Manor Guesthouse – Abbotsbury – England – 4:23pm
Wednesday 20th January 1954**

Professor Wilks yawned and stretched like an old cat. Both men had set out early from London that morning and had made it to their destination before total darkness set in.

'I hate these long winter nights. I'll be glad when the clocks go forward.' Frederick grumbled looking out of a window at the fading light on the horizon.

'I second that.' Wilks agreed.

Grey cloud drifted in from the sea, masking the low lying hills around the quaint English village. An icy chill dominated the late afternoon.

Wilks tapped the bell at the reception desk and stood to attention.

A short woman in her sixties appeared from an open doorway looking the two strangers up and down. 'Can I help you gentlemen?'

'Good evening madam.' Wilks greeted politely. 'We would like two rooms for three nights please.'

The woman looked over the top of her spectacles. 'I see, and what manner of business brings you to Abbotsbury may I ask?'

'We're just taking in some of your lovely scenery.'

'A bit early for holidaying isn't it.' The woman questioned.

'We are both Cambridge professors.' Frederick said. 'Analysing the local wildlife, the beach along the front was used extensively during the war in preparation for the Normandy landings. We are here investigating the impact it had on the wildlife.'

Wilks added to Frederick's story. 'It had a huge impact on the great spotted worm population.'

The woman drew breath and opened up the guestbook. 'It's three shillings a night. We have a room with two single beds. I see no point in spreading you out.'

'Excellent.' Declared Wilks.

'There are a few guest rules we have.' The landlady revealed. 'No drunkenness or taking the lords name in vain.'

Wilks shook his head. 'Wouldn't dream of it madam.'

'The doors to this establishment shut at ten o'clock.' She turned and opened a key cabinet behind her. 'The King's Galley up the road will serve you supper.'

'Thank you madam you've been most hospitable.' Wilks said as she handed him the room keys.

'I seem to be having an acute case of déjà Vu.' Frederick said as he rested his suitcase on the bed.

'Really.' Wilks glanced at him.

'Stoke Lacy last year, the locals there weren't too fond of strangers either.'

'Yes but they were under Janus' control. You'll find most villages in rural England like that Ralph. Emneth probably has its share of people who don't like outsiders.'

Frederick laughed. 'Not unless you count Reverend Awdry. He's not been there long but he's already made a mark on the village. Gave a local boy a good clip across the ear last year for scrumping apples. Apparently he's writing a series of railway books featuring a character called Thomas.'

'Sounds charming.' Wilks commented clasping his hands and wringing them. 'Well let's not sit here talking about trains all evening, The King's Galley awaits.'

7:09pm
Frederick looked across the bar from the dining area at the locals who seemed oblivious of the two strangers chatting happily amongst themselves.

Wilks mopped up the last of the gravy with a piece of bread and munched on it contently. 'I have to say that is the best shepherds pie I have had in ages, even better than my wife's.'

'Better not tell her that.' Frederick smiled. 'Otherwise you'll be joining that small band of people getting divorced.' He indicated to an article in the Times he had just read on growing divorce rates in England.

A young girl in her late teens walked over. 'Are you gentlemen finished?'

'We have young lady.' Wilks replied.

The girl picked up Frederick's plate and then reached over for Wilks' plate. 'I take it you are here to pick up Mary tomorrow.'

'I beg your pardon.' Frederick stated.

'It's no good denying it. That old battleaxe from the guesthouse probably called you. The Church should keep their noses out of matters that don't concern them.'

'I can assure you young lady we are not from the church.' Wilks explained.

The girl's attitude changed abruptly. 'I'm so sorry I thought you were here to cart Mary away.'

'And who might Mary be?' Asked Frederick glancing at Wilks.

'Just a local girl who's got herself into a spot of bother.'

'Any chance you could point us in the direction of this young Mary.' Wilks said.

The girl eyed him with suspicion. 'Why?'

'I'm a doctor.' Wilks replied quickly. 'I don't expect you have a doctor in such a small village. I thought I might go out and examine her. You know, make sure she's in fine health.'

'Ann!' A loud voice shouted across the bar. The landlord approached. 'Don't bother these nice gentlemen. There's plenty of washing up to be done in the kitchen.'

The girl scurried off. 'Sorry dad.'

The landlord walked over to where they were sat. He towered over both Wilks and Frederick. 'Pay no attention to my daughter gentlemen, she can be too chatty sometimes. You know how these teenagers are.'

Wilks smiled. 'Of course.'

'We close at nine tonight so make sure you get yourselves off to the guesthouse. The street lamps go off just before ten. You don't want to be caught out after dark. I'm sure Mrs Brown has already told you this.'

'Sounds a bit spooky.' Frederick joked smiling at Wilks.

The landlord maintained a straight face. 'It's no laughing matter.' His eyes darted about nervously. 'A witch lives in these parts.'

'A witch?' Wilks said.

'A powerful one at that. She put a curse on one of the local girls.'

'A curse, a bit Middle Ages for this day and age wouldn't you say.' Frederick commented.

'Say what you will.' The landlord replied. 'I'd heed my warning if I were you.'

'Thank you we will.' Wilks said.

'You're right about the villagers they are a bit odd.' Wilks said as they made their way back to the guesthouse.

Frederick nodded. 'These people seem cut off from the rest of the world.'

'Hey.' The young woman from the pub called out as quietly as she dared.

Frederick and Wilks glanced behind to see her running towards them. 'Are you really a doctor?' She looked at Wilks.

'I am.'

'Mary lives in Stavordale Wood just over the way there.' She pointed towards the coast.

'Do you know this girl well?' Frederick asked.

'Mary Trembles, she's a friend of mine, or was. I'm not allowed near her anymore. We used to bother with Sarah, the woman who lives in a cottage in the middle of the woods.'

'This Sarah is whom your father referred to as a witch.'

Frederick assumed.

'She's not a witch.' Ann argued. 'She's just into her herbal remedies that's all, natural healing stuff.'

'I take it when you mentioned this Mary got herself into trouble, you meant she's Pregnant.' Wilks said.

Ann nodded.

'Who's the father?' Asked Frederick.

'That's just the thing, there isn't any father. I know Mary you see. She's never had a boyfriend.'

'Has Mary ever gone missing?' Asked Wilks.

'Yes, last spring she disappeared for two days, and then turned up in the woods. Several weeks later she found out she was pregnant. That's when her parents threw her out. So she went to live with Sarah.' Ann paused.

'And that's why the locals think this Sarah is a witch.'

'If you are a doctor then what are you going to do?'

'As I said earlier, I just want to make sure she's ok.'

'That old cow from the guesthouse called the church. I reckon they'll be here tomorrow to cart her off somewhere to have her baby.'

'It's ok.' Wilks assured. 'I'll make sure these people don't just cart her away.'

Ann looked back at the pub. Her dad was calling out her name. 'I better go.' She turned and headed back.

Wilks looked up and scanned the clear night sky. 'What do you reckon?'

'It's got to be her.' Frederick said. 'The marker on the map we created from the Roswell device is quite accurate.'

'We'll head out in the morning to check it out.'

'I'll give Malcolm a ring first thing and warn him of the possibility of officials from the church showing up.'

Chapter 89

**The Old Manor Guesthouse – Abbotsbury - 9:56am
Thursday 24th January 1954**

'And where are you off today?' The landlady appeared out of nowhere as Frederick and Wilks were about to walk out the front door.

'We are off to the beach.'

'Make sure you stick to the road away from the wood. The landlady advised. 'And stay away from the travellers.'

'Travellers?' Wilks said.

'Gypsies.' The woman replied. 'They come to these parts this time of the year and are usually trouble. They camp near the beach.'

'Thank you for the warning, we will be careful.' Frederick tipped his hat politely to the woman.

Twenty minutes later both men found themselves on a footpath leading into the woods. 'Should have brought some breadcrumbs.' Frederick suggested.

Wilks laughed. 'Hope we do come across a gingerbread house, it's my favourite.'

The two men navigated the narrow path through the woods until they came to an old stone cottage. Smoke snaked its way out of one of the two chimneys on the top of the thatched roof. An old wooden fence surrounded the cottage. Most of the garden was taken up by herb bushes. An apple tree stood at the centre, devoid of any foliage looking like a naked skeleton.

Frederick knocked on the door loudly.

'Who is it?' A woman's voice called from inside.

'We're sorry for bothering you but we are looking for Mary Trembles.'

More voices could be heard inside. Frederick was unable

to make out what they were saying.

'Go away!' The woman called out.

Wilks stepped forward. 'My name is Richard Wilks, I'm a doctor. I merely wish to see if the young girl living with you is in good health.'

'She doesn't need anyone she's fine. You can tell those do-gooders from the clergy to bugger off.'

'Madam we are not from the clergy. We were sent here by Ann the girl who lives at the pub. She just wants to know if her friend is ok.'

Eventually the door opened to reveal a short woman with greying hair wearing a black shawl which she wrapped around her. She glared at Frederick and Wilks. 'Ann sent you did she?'

Frederick nodded. 'She mentioned her friend last night, so we offered to help out.'

The woman eventually beckoned them in.

Mary lay on an old sofa that was padded with blankets and cushions. Wilks walked up to her kneeling. 'Mary.' He smiled at her. 'Ann sent me, she's concerned for your wellbeing.'

'I'm fine, Sarah has taken good care of me.' She winced in pain.

'Do you mind if I have a look.'

She looked at Sarah who nodded.

Four other people occupied the spacious living room of the cottage. Two men and two women sat on the floor around the fire, which gave off a lot of heat.

Frederick wandered over to warm his hands.

'Are you here to take Mary away?' One of the two women asked looking up at Frederick.

He shook his head. 'No, my colleague merely wants to examine her to make sure she's in good health.'

'We can take care of her, she'll be fine with us, she is better off with us.'

'And who might we be?' Frederick glanced at the group.

'I'm Paul.' The man stood up and offered his hand. 'This is

my wife Jane, and our friends David and Theresa.'

Frederick looked at the group noting how scruffy they appeared. 'You're travelling folk.' He guessed.

'We are travellers yes. We come here once a year through December and January to celebrate the winter solstice.' 'He looked at Mary. 'This year is special. Mary is about to give birth to her sky child.'

'I am sorry, sky child?' Frederick quizzed.

'This is why we come here, to communicate with the sky people who come this time of year.' Paul explained. 'We all gather up on the hill over yonder at Pendragon's table.'

'And you believe that Mary's child is one of these sky people.'

'Surely Ann must have told you about how Mary became pregnant.' Paul said.

'She mentioned that she vanished for a couple of days last spring.'

'Yes, she was in the company of the sky people. They gave her a special gift.'

Frederick looked at Wilks who stood and walked over. 'Well there's no doubt about it, she's in labour.'

'How long until she gives birth?' Frederick asked.

Wilks shrugged. 'About as long as a piece of string.'

'We will take her to Pendragon's table this evening to perform the ceremony.' Sarah said.

'You cannot move this girl unless it's to a hospital.' Wilks warned. 'The cold outside could kill her.'

'She will be safe with us.' Theresa assured. 'Once the baby is born we'll take her away and look after her.' She indicated to the group.

'I cannot allow you to take this girl out into the freezing cold it's too dangerous.' Wilks protested.

'And I say we can take better care of her than some fancy hospital.' Theresa argued back.

'Perhaps she's right Richard.' Frederick sided with the

group.

Wilks looked at Frederick with discontentment.

'We will stay for however long it takes. You can help Sarah administer whatever treatment she needs.'

'I don't have any medical equipment with me.'

'Some doctor you are.' Paul mocked.

Frederick looked at the traveller. 'Can you show us where this Pendragon's table is?'

'If you don't mind the trek.' Paul said.

'Have you taken leave of your senses?' Wilks' tone was dark as they stood outside waiting for Paul. 'We're in way over our heads here Ralph, I cannot help this woman. This girl needs to be in a hospital. I was just a lowly medic during the war. My skills are limited. A hospital is the best place for her.'

'I know that, but if we take her to the hospital then too many questions will be asked. Besides I have a theory. We will drive into Weymouth later on and telephone Malcolm updating him on the situation. Perhaps he can organise transport so we can take Mary to a safe location. If this girl is about to give birth to a child conceived by whatever abducted her then it could be the breakthrough we have been looking for. It could give us a bargaining tool with the Americans to share more information. While in Weymouth we may be able to pick up some medical supplies.'

Wilks eventually nodded, looking at Frederick. 'What exactly is this theory of yours?'

'You'll see.'

Paul appeared out of the cottage entrance.

Chapter 90

11:12am

Frederick stared at the stone monolith which lay flat on the ground facing inland. Paul was gathering wood for six pyres which had been constructed and set out in a circular fashion around the stone. The stone was similar to the standing stones in Scotland which Colonel Konev had destroyed.

Frederick climbed on the stone and looked at the constellation marked out on the top. 'Pegasus.' He said.

Wilks looked at the eleven circles spaced out towards the bottom of the stone. 'These are like the stones you described in Scotland.'

'Yes.' Frederick looked at the circles and noted three of them had lines pointing towards the tip of the nose of Pegasus. 'Incredible, if I'm reading this correctly the star here has three planets which may harbour life.'

'Three planets.' Wilks repeated. 'The possibility of a planetary system with three life sustaining worlds is too incredible to imagine.'

Frederick looked back at the stone. At its base was the familiar spiral pattern he had encountered before. 'This is the third time I have encountered stones like this with this symbol. First at Ripley Castle, then in Scotland and now here.'

'And your point being Ralph.'

'On two occasions the stones seem to be located in an area where people have been taken. Edith Jones in Ripley and now this girl. Both have become pregnant.'

'I still don't see what you're getting at.'

'Don't you see? These stones could be markers like an ancient version of that device Vannevar Bush demonstrated last year. This spiral pattern seems to be a constant on all these stones I have seen.'

Wilks smiled. 'You're right.' He looked at the stone. 'You realise that there are hundreds of stones up and down Great Britain similar to this one. And those are just the ones that have been discovered. There could be hundreds more buried or overgrown.'

'Yes, and they could hold the key to all that has been going on.'

'Finally information the Americans might not have.' Wilks said.

Frederick smiled. 'Which means we might not need them as much as they think.'

Wilks frowned. 'But what about the circle in Scotland. The one that Konev destroyed there was no one living in that area.'

'Not now perhaps, but we did find the remains of a Viking burial site. There could have been a settlement at some point. There was also a ruined cottage near the beach. The English uprooted a lot of Scots during the highland clearances.'

'And the woman in London, the one that was taken away by Vatican officials.'

'London is old and has expanded over the centuries. Who's to say there wasn't some kind of ancient monument where she lived.'

'True but if it's no longer there why are these beings still taking people.'

Frederick inhaled. 'Another missing piece of the puzzle.'

'You shouldn't stand on Pendragon's Table, it can bring bad luck.' Paul called out returning with a handful of wood.

Frederick jumped down. 'I'm sorry I was just examining the markings. Why do you call it Pendragon's Table?'

'It is told that King Arthur himself used to frequent these parts with his knights.'

Wilks looked at the stone. 'This is hardly the Round Table I've read about.'

'No, but there are those of us who believe a great castle once stood here and this is all that remains.'

'What do you think these markings represent?' Frederick pointed at the etchings.

Paul just shrugged. 'Decoration.'

Frederick and Wilks glanced at each other with a smile. 'My colleague and I are going to Weymouth to pick up supplies.' Frederick revealed. 'We'll be back later.'

'How do I know you are not going to bring the fuzz back?'

'Because we want what's best for Mary, just like you.'

'And what exactly do you get out of helping us?' Paul questioned again.

'Peace of mind dear fellow.' Wilks replied.

Chapter 91

7:43pm

Wilks smiled at Mary and mopped her forehead. He managed to pick up a stethoscope in Weymouth and some more blankets.

Frederick had phoned Chambers and explained the events of the past few days.

Malcolm offered to send help as soon as possible.

Frederick and Wilks did not return to the guesthouse, returning to the cottage instead.

The group of travellers had spent the afternoon preparing the pyres and converting an old cart to accommodate Mary.

'It is time.' Sarah said. 'We must get her to Pendragon's Table to prepare for the Birth.'

Wilks helped Sarah escort Mary to the front door where she was carefully placed on a cart which was padded with quilts and other soft material. More blankets were piled on her once she was on the cart. The two travellers Paul and David took up a cart handle and the small band of people made their way to Pendragon's Table.

'Mr Frederick!' Sarah called out from the front door of her cottage.

Frederick turned and saw her beckoning him back. 'Is there something wrong Sarah.'

'I know this is going to sound strange but last night I had a dream.'

Frederick felt frustration and looked back to see Wilks and the others making their way towards Pendragon's table. 'Can't this wait, Mary needs our help.'

'Listen to me!' She ordered. 'I have seen death, terrible death.'

'Look we haven't got time for this.' Frederick said walking

away.

Sarah grabbed his arm. 'I have seen him, he will kill me.'

'Who?'

'The coloured man.'

Frederick smiled. 'Perhaps you should lay off the mushroom tea Sarah. Now please come along we need to join the others.'

'I have seen you.' Sarah continued. 'I have seen your wife in your arms, dead!'

A shudder bolted through Frederick's body. The image that Janus had seeded flooded his mind. He thought back to the hospital where he had encountered Janus. The huge shadowy figure standing over Elizabeth's broken body.

'Beware the giant man, he will bring you nothing but tragedy.'

How do you know this?' Frederick asked.

Sarah seemed to stare into space. 'He will come for me. I will welcome death.' She wrapped her shawl tightly around her closing the door of the cottage. 'Perhaps you are right, Mary's child is important now.'

'I'm starting to have doubts.' Frederick revealed wrapping his jacket around him and looking at Sarah who had joined with the main party. Her words played over in his head.

'It's a little too late for that now old boy. Besides Malcolm said help will arrive in the morning. Until then we have to go through with this ritual.'

The pyres were already lit when they arrived at their destination. Without a wind the fires created a comfortable heat. The stone had been covered with blankets and cushions and Mary had been lifted onto the flat stone surface.

Paul took up position at the head of the stone and was dressed from head to toe in a white tunic with a hood covering his head. He looked up into the clear night sky raising his hands. 'We are in the presence of the Sky People and welcome them with open arms.'

Frederick looked up into the night sky at the glistening stars.

'Sky People we await your arrival and present to you your child.'

'Stop!' A voice shouted from outside the circle.

Frederick spun around and saw a group of people with torches. Three men stepped into the stone circle and walked up to Paul. 'This blasphemous ceremony must end now!'

Frederick recognised the three individuals. They were the men he had encountered in London with Agent Cones.

'You have no right to interfere.' Paul stood firm.

'We are taking this woman with us. You are to leave this area never to return.'

Wilks reluctantly stepped forward. 'You cannot move this woman. She is about to give birth.'

'To an abomination.' The priest stated. 'And who are you.'

'I asked you that question last year in London.' Frederick said.

The priest stared at Frederick before recalling where he had seen him. 'You are once again dealing with matters that don't concern you.'

'What concerns me is this woman's safety, you cannot move her.' Frederick spotted three more villagers stepping into the circle. 'Your so called Brotherhood has no authority here.'

The priest grinned. 'We have authority everywhere.' He looked back at Paul. 'I'll ask you once more to stop this ceremony.'

'Piss off!' Paul hissed.

The two cardinals walked up to Mary and grabbed both arms.

Paul rushed towards one of them but was stopped by more villagers who now poured into the circle of pyres.

Mary began to scream as the two cardinals began to pull her to her feet.

Sarah was also screaming at the priest calling him names.

A rush of air suddenly descended from above snuffing out the fires instantly, leaving the area in darkness.

Frederick became aware of a static discharge building up around the group.

Paul was the first to sight the object. 'Look!' He shouted pointing skywards.

The crowd looked towards the sky at the glowing circular object descending bathing the area in a blue light. A low pitch humming noise filled the air.

Wilks and Frederick looked on as the object descended.

'This is incredible.' Wilks said with wonder in his voice.

The priest stepped back making the sign of the cross. His companions let go of Mary and dropped to their knees with their hands clasped in prayer.

The object stopped its descent and hovered about twenty feet off the ground. For several seconds the group of people stared at the UFO.

Suddenly a brilliant flash of light emanated from the object.

Frederick shielded his eyes.

Without warning the object shot skywards and disappeared.

The pyres suddenly burst into flames again and the crowd of people were left stunned by their experience.

Frederick walked calmly up to the priest. 'Would you call that an act of the devil?'

The priest looked at him and shook his head.

'Go back and tell your brotherhood Her Majesty's government will not tolerate the random kidnapping of British citizens.'

'Mary's gone!' Sarah announced, pointing at the stone.

Everyone looked at the stone. Paul looked at the priest smiling.

'She is with the sky people now.'

The priest glared back but said nothing.

Whitehall – London – 12:47pm
Monday 1st February 1954

Malcolm Chambers put down the report he had just read looking at Wilks and Frederick. 'And there is no sign of this Mary?'

Both men shook their heads in unison. 'No.' Frederick said. 'We spent the next day searching but no trace was found.'

'It's my guess that whatever took her is long gone.' Wilks said.

'We need to find out why these creatures are abducting people at random. Vannevar Bush will be flying in from the United States next week. He'll be bringing a specialist who has had experience with these so called abductions; hopefully he will be able to provide answers.'

The Vatican – Rome – Italy
Wednesday 3rd February 1954 – 1:04pm

The cardinal looked around the table at the fourteen other men. 'Our suspicions have been confirmed. The British government have a group who has a vested interest in these so called UFO abduction cases.'

'We will deal with them in the same manner as we dealt with the Americans.' A man sat opposite said.

The cardinal shook his head. 'This is different, the man who confronted me during our recent encounter in England, mentioned the Brotherhood.'

Glances were exchanged around the room.

'Do you have a name for this man?'

'Professor Ralph Frederick.'

'How does he know about the Brotherhood?'

The cardinal thought about the question for several seconds. 'He must be a member of the Order of Galileo.'

'The prophecy is unfolding we should monitor events and

Professor Frederick. If he has been recruited by The Order then Rothschild would have no doubt told him about us.'

'The Brotherhood of the Holy See and The Order of Galileo have had their dealings in the past.'

'What of Agent Cones?' One of the group asked.

'I have encountered Agent Cones and Professor Frederick a while back in London. They have yet to be permanently assigned to each other. We know the day will come when they will work together. We will keep an eye on Professor Frederick and make sure he stays on his current path. I will brief his Holiness on recent events in England.'

The group of men nodded in unison.

Chapter 92

Highclare House – Surrey 1:08pm
Friday 5th February 1954

'As you can see we have two distinguished guests with us today.' Chambers began. 'I know that we are familiar with both of them so introductions aren't necessary.'

Professor Archie Watson and Doctor Henry Forbes had been handpicked by Chambers and Stanford as two new additions to the Angel Committee. Watson an aeronautical engineer had worked closely with Frank Whittle during the war developing the jet engine while Forbes had served with Morris Stanford in Europe. Forbes was the lead scientist examining the horrific treatment of prisoners of war by the Nazis and Japanese.

After a brief meeting lunch was served in the main dining room.

'How's Elizabeth.' Watson asked. 'I heard she's expecting.'

'She's very well, and she'll be pleased to hear I'm back in contact with you.'

'I'll have Joan give her a bell; do you remember what those two were like during the war?'

Frederick laughed out loud. 'All too well.'

Professor Watson surveyed the room. 'So this is the Angel Committee the old man put together. I thought all this flying saucer stuff was nonsense.'

'That was my point of view until my encounter at Church Fenton. Since then it seems a world I had no idea existed has opened up before me.'

Watson held up his glass. 'Well here's to getting to the bottom of it all.'

Chapter 93

Whitehall – London – 2:43pm
Thursday 11th February 1954

Doctor Henry Forbes glared at the man sitting across the table casually smoking a cigarette gazing out of the window as if in a world of his own.

Vannevar Bush looked around at the assembled members flashing a brief smile. 'I have read the recent intelligence you have provided us with. Which has prompted me to call on an expert who has had experience in this so called abduction phenomenon. Doctor Victor Klaus has studied many casefiles involving these so-called abductees and is here today to give us insight into how we might deal with this problem.

Klaus stood up. 'Thank you Doctor Bush.'

Frederick noted the thick German accent.

'I have been studying cases like this since the early thirties. I have reached the conclusion that whatever is taking these people must be running some sort of breeding program. It is my opinion that the reason for this is to create a part human, part extraterrestrial hybrid.'

'We already know that these creatures are taking people for experimental purposes.' Wilks said. 'What we need to find out is what method they are using to track these people.'

Klaus opened a briefcase sat on the desk and produced a glass jar which contained a small metal fragment which looked more like shrapnel. 'Over the years I have managed to extract many objects from test subjects which appear to be foreign to the body. Most of these objects are located in the nasal cavity of the subjects. I believe these objects act as some kind of homing beacon allowing these extraterrestrials to locate test subjects and take them at will.'

'Test subjects.' Forbes mentioned.

Klaus looked at him. 'Yes, last year since Professor Frederick was able to determine that the red and green markers on the Roswell device are people. We now know the location of people who have been abducted by these extraterrestrials. We have been tracking down some of these people.'

'You just mentioned you've been analysing cases since the thirties. Where would that have been exactly Doctor?' Forbes pressed.

'Doctor Forbes.' Bush interrupted. 'It would be beneficial if you could stay on topic please.'

'As I have just stated.' Klaus continued unfazed by Forbes' tone. 'I believe most of these objects recovered from subjects emit some kind of electrical signal. At this moment we cannot detect this signal because it is beyond our current level of technology. Our scientists are working to break this technology so that we may learn its secrets.'

'If and when you crack the signal.' Frederick said. 'Then how does that benefit us. From what I have seen of these UFOs they have the capability to just come and go as they please.'

'We will attempt to interrupt the signal in an effort to disrupt the plans of these extraterrestrials.'

'Is that wise?' Admiral Berkshire asked. 'Given what Professor Frederick has just said these beings not only possess craft which are faster and can out manoeuvre any aircraft we have. If we suddenly interfere in their plans to take people at will it might be seen as an aggressive act on our part. We have yet to see if these creatures have any weaponry on board their ships.'

'Which is why we will take every precaution Admiral.' Bush said.

'Do you know if the craft recovered at Roswell had any kind of weapon system?' Harold Bates asked.

'We believe that it did. Although no weapons system we

are familiar with. Let's not forget this is a technology centuries ahead of anything we have. We have theorised that any space faring species would not have weapons of mass destruction. The craft we recovered in New Mexico was not carrying any sort of ordinance we would be familiar with.'

'It is possible.' Klaus took over. 'That their weapons maybe energy based.'

'Some sort of death ray.' Wilks offered.

Klaus nodded. 'In most abduction cases especially where technology is involved there have been reports of a total loss of power with motor vehicles and aeroplanes. Not so much of a death ray but a device capable of knocking out our electrical systems rendering them powerless.'

'A non-destructive weapon, or as we have nicknamed it NDW.' Bush said. 'Such a device would be useful in bringing down enemy bombers the Soviets would use to destroy our cities.'

'What we need to do is combine our collective knowledge in tackling this technology.' Klaus said.

Doctor Forbes stood suddenly and marched out of the room.

Frederick made eye contact with Klaus before standing. 'Excuse me.' He said politely before hurrying out after Forbes.

'Henry are you ok?' Frederick asked.

Forbes pointed back towards the room he had left. 'Do you have any bloody idea who that man in there is?'

Frederick shook his head.

'Doctor Victor Klaus.' Forbes said. 'Klaus was one of the Nazi doctors on the most wanted list. Up there with the likes of Josef Mengele who managed to slip through allied fingers.'

Frederick glanced back at the meeting room. 'I don't understand why would the Americans be harbouring a wanted Nazi fugitive?'

Chapter 94

Whitehall – London – 4:30pm

'It is known as Project Paperclip.' Morris Stanford revealed. 'We have been trying to acquire information regarding the full extent of this operation but the Americans have been keeping tight lipped.'

'I bet they have.' Forbes scoffed.

'We believe that Victor Klaus is just the tip of the iceberg, a Nazi iceberg.' Chambers added. 'We did have our own version of Paperclip, called Operation Surgeon and an army unit known as T Force. We managed to round up about a hundred scientists. But it was the Americans who got the cream of the crop. It was a mad scramble to get our hands on German technology before the Russians moved in. We were lucky to get anyone. If the Yanks had their way they would have got everyone.'

'I know about Operation Surgeon.' Forbes said. 'I seem to remember a notorious doctor called Alfred Keller escaping the hangman's noose at Nuremberg. He managed to squirm his way out of facing justice.'

Stanford noted the expression on Forbes' face. 'I was there at Belzec as well Henry. I saw what that bastard did. Along with other doctors like Alfred Keller.'

'And yet Klaus is being paraded in front of us by the Americans. It makes a mockery of what happened during the war.'

'Believe it or not this could play to our advantage. Especially with what Vannevar Bush requested this morning before the meeting.'

Frederick looked at his friend. 'Which was what exactly?'

'The Americans have invited two Angel Committee members to the US to view their research facilities and to look over some of the wreckage they salvaged from Roswell. They are willing to give us unprecedented access.'

'In exchange for what exactly?' Forbes asked.

'Complete control and removal of any craft which may crash land on our territory and anywhere else in the Commonwealth.' Chambers said. 'They also want to secure long term airbases over here. Doctor Bush claimed that it was to strengthen NATO's position in Europe.'

'Who do you have in mind to go over to the States?' Frederick asked.

Stanford and Chambers looked back at him smiling.

Frederick shook his head. 'No, I can't, not with Elizabeth expecting our second child. What about my position at Cambridge. Osborne and Hinshelwood will have a field day.'

'It won't be for long, besides Liz and Susan have been allowed to go along with you.' Chambers assured. 'The Americans seem quite accommodating at the moment. I suggest we take advantage of their generosity. We will make sure your position at Cambridge is kept. Archie is going along with you with his family so at least Liz will not be on her own. I know she and Joan used to be the best of friends when they worked at the war office.'

'When do we leave?'

'March the fifteenth.' Stanford revealed. 'You are being temporarily assigned to the Majestic 12 group.'

'You realise that Janus is still out there, he needs to be dealt with.'

'Agents Cones and Baker have just returned from the United States. They will try and pick up the trail again.'

Stanford looked at Forbes. 'In the meantime I suggest we extend Doctors Bush and Klaus every courtesy.'

Chapter 95

Palm Springs – California – USA – 1:32pm
Thursday 18th March 1954

Frederick looked out of the large window at Elizabeth and Susan as they played in the swimming pool with Joan and her two children. The sun shone down from a deep blue Californian sky and despite being early in the year the temperature was in the eighties.

Professor Watson appeared from the kitchen of the spacious six bedroom house which was to be both his family and the Frederick's home over the coming weeks.

'Looks like they've settled in nicely.' Watson said.

Frederick smiled and looked beyond the swimming pool at the dry arid desert landscape dotted with greenery where houses had sprang up. He had taken a tour of the house when they had arrived the day before. 'I have to admit these Americans know how to live the high life.' He said.

'I'm sure there's another side to American society than swimming pools and golf courses. Did you know black people are made to sit on the back of busses and trains. And I'm sure there's plenty of poverty when you scratch below the surface. We Brits are only now starting to demolish the Victorian slums. There are plenty of people who have protested against the mass migration of people from the West Indies. They've nicknamed them the Windrush generation.'

'The war displaced many people. A lot of places were bombed out of existence. The people who were left behind had nothing.'

Both men looked up at the sound of a doorbell.

Vannevar Bush shook hands with the two British guests. 'Gentlemen, welcome to California I trust everything is to your liking.'

'You've been a most generous host.' Frederick said. 'This house is incredible, very spacious and modern.'

'We started to build luxury apartments here a few years ago. Some of our staff from our facility in Nevada like to come here to relax. I'm sorry where are my manners.' He said turning to the uniformed general standing next to him. 'May I present General Thomas Power of the United States Air Force.'

Frederick noted that General Power had an iron grip as he shook his hand. 'Been looking forward to meeting you Professor Frederick. Doctor Bush has filled me in on some of the casefiles you've been involved with.' The general turned to Watson shaking his hand. 'Frank Whittle's right hand man. I think you will find the new breakthroughs we are making in jet engine propulsion very inspiring.'

'I look forward to gaining first-hand experience. I'm sure we have a lot to benefit from each other's knowledge.' Watson replied.

'I expect you gentlemen will be eager to get started.' Bush said.

Frederick glanced outside at his family. 'There's no rush, thought I might enjoy the pool first.'

'Sure thing Professor.' General Power laughed.

'We were going to leave you until Monday anyway.' Bush stated. 'Then you will be picked up bright and early. There's an air strip a few miles from here. You will be flown out to White Sands in New Mexico first.' Bush glanced outside to make sure no one was within earshot. We still have a small amount of wreckage left over from Roswell we would like you to examine.'

'Look forward to it.' Frederick said.

Chapter 96

White Sands Missile Range – New Mexico – 2:01pm Monday 22nd March 1954

Despite the desert heat an icy chill seemed to envelop Professor Watson as he stood in the shadow of the German Built V2 Rocket. Its distinctive sleek design and striking black and white chequered pattern reminded him of darker days. Frederick had been escorted under armed guard to another building where Vannevar bush had accompanied him.

Dr Jerome Hunsaker a member of the Majestic 12 group stood next to Watson. 'We managed to put together quite a few of these after the war. Ingenious design and packed hell of a punch.'

Watson turned to Hunsaker. 'Yes it did, it's a shame my sister and her entire family were on the receiving end of one.'

'I'm sorry; I sometimes forget what their original use was for.'

Two men approached.

'Professor Watson may I present our lead contractor Sanford Moss and one of our lead scientists on our long range rocket program Doctor Hermann Jodi.'

'Contractor.' Watson said.

'General Electrics.' Moss replied shaking Watson's hand.

'We have invited a number of civilian companies to invest money in military projects saving the American tax payer.' Hunsaker explained.

'Something we need to do back home.' Watson glanced back at the V2.

'We have moved on a few generations since this design. We have three new rockets the Atlas one and the Jupiter one. And the Phoenix Four which will carry mankind into outer space and beyond.' Hermann Jodi looked up at the V2 smiling.

'Such a marvellous feet of engineering don't you agree Professor Watson?'

'It depends from which point of view you are coming from.'

Jodi looked at him. 'Come now Professor we are all allies now, fighting against a common enemy.'

Watson stared at him. 'Funny how quickly you Nazis changed sides when you knew the game was up.'

Hanger 18 – Laboratory 1A – 2:45pm

'The craft recovered at Roswell was remarkably intact, what you see here Professor Frederick are fragments of the fuselage which we believe broke off on impact. The bulk of the craft is now at our new facility in Nevada which you will be visiting.'

'And the bodies.' Frederick asked Bush.

'Stored at Wright Patterson. We have them on ice at the moment. We have another facility set up at Dugway Proving Grounds in Utah. Many of the information devices which the craft contained are stored there.'

'You're spreading yourselves around a bit.'

'We feel it's necessary. Since the Rosenbergs a few years ago and in case of a soviet surprise attack.'

Frederick picked up a wafer thin piece of wreckage noting it had almost no weight.

'We believe that it's a similar material to the device I demonstrated in London last year.' Bush held out his hand. 'May I.'

Frederick handed over the fragment and watched as Bush was easily able to scrunch it up like tin foil. 'Watch this.' He said putting the fragment back on the table.

'Good lord!' Frederick watched the fragment unfold returning to its original shape. He picked it up and examined it for signs of creases.

'It's self-repairing as you can see.' Bush said. 'How this is happening we don't know. We have theorised that the technology these creatures use operates on a sub atomic level, too small for our current microscopes to see.'

'An aircraft with this type of metal would be a giant leap in aviation.' Frederick said.

'We were thinking more on the lines of space travel.'

Frederick looked at Bush who smiled back at him before catching sight of two military police guards approaching from behind the doctor.

Chapter 97

Hanger 14 – 3:32pm

Hermann Jodi glanced nervously at Professor Watson who rubbed his sore wrists which had just been released from the handcuffs.

Frederick stared at the sight in front of him. A massive rocket lay on its side in four parts. Dozens of technicians scurried about like ants over a captive insect. Parts of the outer shell had been removed to reveal its inner parts. One panel was propped up against a large examination table still baring the mark of the German Iron Cross.

Jodi began his lecture. 'What you are looking at gentlemen is the Phoenix Four Rocket. I designed this model in 1938. We built eight in all, four of which are still intact and are in Antarctica. We are also working on a further five which will be completed within two years. The rocket stands at approximately two hundred and twenty feet in height with an extended height of two hundred and ninety feet with the lunar explorer.'

'Lunar explorer.' Frederick stated feeling a little sceptical.

Jodi nodded. 'This rocket was designed to reach the moon, three of which have been successful in reaching their goals.

Watson stepped forward watched by two military police officers. 'Are you saying that you've sent men to the moon?'

'No landing has been attempted yet but we have achieved orbit. The next step is to attempt a descent to the surface.'

'Are we advanced enough to take on such a venture?' Frederick asked.

Bush nodded. 'You will be surprised what the Germans achieved in such a short space of time Professor and what we've managed to develop thanks to men like Von Braun and Professor Jodi. If you'll step this way gentlemen we've more to show you.'

A few minutes later Frederick and Watson found themselves seated in front of a projector screen. Two guards stood outside while Jodi organised the projector. Dr Hunsaker and Bush sat next to the two British scientists.

'What you are about to see.' Jodi began. 'Is footage taken from an earlier mission to breach the outer atmosphere of our planet. In 1935 the German government began Project Constellation which focused on the manned exploration of space.'

Watson leaned across and whispered in Frederick's ear. 'German government, more like Nazi thugs.'

Frederick did his best to conceal a smile.

The projector started and displayed a picture of a rocket on a launch pad. 'This is the Phoenix One which was an early attempt to launch a rocket into space. This vehicle was launched in December 1939.'

Everyone looked on as the rocket lifted off the launch pad. The camera followed as it lifted into the sky. The picture then changed. 'We believe this footage was taken at approximately one hundred miles up. The rocket was fitted with a television camera and antenna which was able to broadcast a signal to our team on the ground. As you can see the earth is a perfect sphere in what looks like a protective bubble we all know as our atmosphere.'

'Unbelievable!' 'Frederick stated.

The film stopped and Jodi turned on the lights. 'Unfortunately our broadcasting equipment failed due to the conditions of space.' He then picked up another film reel and loaded it on to the projector. 'After some modifications we were able to successfully launch another space vehicle, six months later.' Once again the screen came to life. An image of the moon appeared at the centre of the screen. 'This footage was taken at over two thousand miles outside our atmosphere. As with our earlier attempt we eventually lost contact with the craft.'

'Incredible!' Watson stated.

Jodi returned to the projector and loaded a third reel of film. 'This was taken on our first lunar mission. Project Lunar was initiated at the end of 1941. Production of the Phoenix Launch Vehicle had already begun and was ready to launch by August of 1942. Although the crew made it back safely they died a few days after. My theory is that it was cosmic radiation or different atmospheric pressures that killed them.'

Watson glared at Jodi noting his lack of empathy for the dead pilots.

The screen once again came to life. 'What you are looking at here gentlemen is the lunar surface from approximately one hundred miles up.'

Frederick shook his head in wonder. 'I never thought I would see the moon so close up in my lifetime. It's startling to say the least.'

'Preparations are being made for a manned mission led by the USA.'

'When do you plan to launch this mission?' Watson asked.

'We have a scheduled launch for May of next year.' Dr Hunsaker replied.

'Plans are also being drawn up for an orbiting space platform which would be permanently manned of course.' Jodi added. 'Werner Von Braun one of our lead scientists at White Sands is currently designing such a platform.'

Frederick stared at the projector screen. 'I must admit I am overwhelmed by what you have shown us. When do you plan to announce to the public that you have rockets capable of reaching the moon?'

'At this moment there is no plan to reveal what we are doing. The base we have in Antarctica is concealed and is far from any commercial shipping lanes so any launch will not be visible with the naked eye. We also monitor all newspaper and TV broadcasts just to ensure no pictures reach the public domain.'

'What about the Russians? It's only a matter of time before they stumble on to your little operation.' Watson commented. 'British intelligence has sighted Russian ships in the south Atlantic.'

'Yes we are aware there are Soviet Naval vessels in the area. We make sure they don't get close enough to get a look.'

'Nevertheless.' Frederick added. 'There are countries that have shown interest in setting up scientific research stations in Antarctica.'

'Any country who wishes to conduct research has to go through the United Nations which is immediately brought to us to evaluate whether it will interfere with operations.'

'You can't keep this secret space program hidden forever. Sooner or later someone will see something.' Frederick said. 'Talk of missions to the moon and orbiting space stations will eventually leak out. You have thousands of personnel alone who work on this base. Something is bound to slip out.'

'We have a number of counter measures in place to ensure no one talks.' Jodi said.

'Such as.' Watson replied.

Bush clapped his hands together loudly. 'I suggest we break for lunch, after which Frederick and Watson can take a closer look at the Phoenix Four rocket. Since you will be here for the next three days some quarters have been prepared for you.'

Chapter 98

10:49pm

'I don't know about you Archie but I'm bloody knackered.' Frederick let out a loud yawn, stretching his arms as far as they would reach.

Watson sat on his bunk mulling over the day's events. 'As much as it's been an interesting day, there's a lot that doesn't add up.'

Frederick yawned again. 'How do you mean?'

'How is it possible the Americans have advanced so far in such a short space of time. Rockets to the moon, orbiting space stations. I feel as if I am in a weird science fiction film. What do the Yanks call them? B Movies.'

'I think we can assume that the Germans had much to do with advancements made by the Americans.'

'Exactly my point.' Watson said. 'I was with T Force during the closing stages of the war. Our job was to hunt down and capture advanced German weaponry and technology but we never heard anything about this Professor Hermann Jodi or any base in Antarctica let alone a Nazi space program. Von Braun was widely known as the scientist behind the V1 and V2 but this Jodi fellow wasn't on the most wanted list.'

'Some of the V2 rockets achieved an altitude which many would consider as space.' Frederick remarked.

'I'm not saying that the Germans didn't breach the upper atmosphere. What I'm saying is that the Nazis didn't acquire the technology all on their own. Even by our standards today it would take decades of research to do what the Nazis seemed to do in less than a decade.'

'They did spend the better part of five years rampaging through Europe stealing everything. Perhaps they came across information which aided them in their quest for dominance.'

'That's exactly what I was thinking. It still doesn't explain why the Americans have only now just opened up to us. We gained the spoils of war but not as much as what the Americans captured.'

Frederick thought for a moment. 'Are you suggesting the Americans made some sort of deal with the Nazis?'

'Take a look around at this place Ralph. It's crawling with Krauts. I have lost count of how many I have spoken to. There are literally hundreds of them running around on this base and I suspect that is just the tip of the iceberg. Thousands of wanted Nazis slipped through allied fingers during the war. Buying their way out of Germany with stolen wealth from holocaust victims. If you ask me Nuremberg was nothing but a show trial.'

'It's an interesting theory Archie, but I'm afraid you've already rocked the boat today. If we were to start accusing the Americans of siding with the Nazis during the closing stages of the war then we will be shipped back home. I suggest we gather all the intelligence we can and report our findings to the committee.'

'I don't know about you Ralph but I'm finding myself very homesick.'

Frederick lay down on his bunk, his thoughts turning to Elizabeth and Susan.

Chapter 99

Groom Lake – Nevada – 10:42am
Wednesday 7th April 1954

'Gentlemen welcome to our Groom Lake Facility.' General Thomas Power greeted.

Frederick and Watson looked out across the salt flat. Two Bulldozers were cutting their way across the dry lake bed.'

'As you can see we are busy extending the site runway with additional runways being drawn up. We've already constructed several large scale aircraft hangers, storage facilities and research labs. Unfortunately the accommodation is still rudimentary but we are used to it.' He said pointing to a few hastily constructed huts. General Power quickly surveyed the surroundings. 'Several miles over to the west beyond those range of mountains is our nuclear testing facility.' He noted the look on Frederick's face. 'Relax Professor the prevailing winds usually carry the fallout to the north. As a matter of fact we have a scheduled test for the day after tomorrow. Our engineers are also working on an underground facility capable of withstanding a direct nuclear assault. We estimate it should take about three years to hollow out the mountain side and convert the surroundings. We are already eight months into the project which is proceeding at remarkable speed.'

'This is impressive to say the least.' Watson remarked.

'You will understand gentlemen that this will be more of a whistle stop tour for you, as there is so much to see. But in time we hope there will be British scientists permanently based here in the United States working side by side.' Vannevar Bush said. 'We'll get you settled into your quarters before you can begin.'

2:32pm

Frederick stared at the object from behind the glass window. It was approximately nine feet wide and twelve to fifteen feet in height. Several men in special silver suits worked around the object which was shaped like a church bell. The bell shaped object was attached to four chains which were fixed to the floor.

'This is one of our prized possessions captured from the Nazis in the closing stages of the war.' Bush explained. 'We believe that the Third Reich was on the verge of discovering a new energy source. Thankfully we were able to obtain this technology before the Russians got their hands on it.'

Frederick watched as the men in silver suits headed for an exit.

'This room that we are standing in is lead lined and offers considerable protection from the effects of the device.'

'Which are?' Frederick asked.

'Once activated the bell emits gamma radiation. The few records we obtained from the Germans revealed that some of the technicians and scientists who came in direct contact with the device died due to exposure.' Bush indicated to the men leaving the hanger. 'Which is why we have taken precautions to limit any casualties.' He then nodded to a technician sat at a control panel. 'Fire her up.'

A low pitched humming noise started to fill the room, and Frederick noted static electricity building up around him. 'I have experienced these effects during encounters with UFOs.' He remarked.

'Yes. Something which we have found is common in many UFO encounters.'

As Frederick watched from behind the glass, light started to emit from the bottom of the object which seemed to be composed of two cylindrical parts spinning in opposite directions. After about ten seconds the whole object lifted off the ground. 'I don't believe it.' Frederick stated. 'Professor

Watson needs to see this.'

'He will, we have another demonstration this afternoon.'

'How on earth did the Germans come up with this?'

'Despite extensive intelligence operations in Europe our people have yet to discover how the Nazis were able to devise this technology. Most of the men we acquired through project Paperclip were unaware this device existed. But they had heard rumours of ultra-secret laboratories scattered throughout Europe. Our intelligence agencies also heard rumours the Nazis had more than one of these devices.'

'Do you think the Russians might have got their hands on this technology before you were able to obtain information on other devices which the Germans built?'

'No.' Bush replied. 'We believe that information regarding this technology was taken elsewhere. When our forces raided the facility close to the Czech border where this device was held they found a mass grave containing around sixty corpses.'

'Slave labourers.' Frederick said.

'No, scientists and technicians, all executed on the orders of Hitler himself. It was part of his scorched earth policy. To destroy everything the Nazis had built to prevent the allies getting their hands on new technologies. When questioned one of the SS guards revealed that the men were executed the day before. Documents relating to this device had been shipped out. But he didn't know where to. By that time the Nazis knew the war was lost. Information was strictly need to know. Our team even discovered that every member of the SS team on site had a cyanide capsule which they were to use in case of capture. I guess at the end of the day they realised the Third Reich wasn't worth dying for. When we stormed the facility they were preparing to load everything onto trucks and ship it out. They were to meet up with a high ranking SS general in Budweis for further orders. The SS commanding officer revealed the name of bell's project leader who escaped execution the day before, a Doctor Hermann Fritz.'

'Do you know where he is now?' Frederick asked.

Bush shook his head. 'We believe the Russians might have got their hands on him.'

The object seemed to dance tethered to the chains which stopped it from flying off. 'We have had several years to advance from this. If you'll follow me Professor.' Bush invited.

The aircraft hangar Frederick was being shown around was split into two sections of equal size and identical in look. Dr Bush showed Frederick through to another control room with a large glass window overlooking the main work area. The object on the floor of the hanger was approximately fifteen foot across and ten foot in height, cylindrical in shape and tapered at the top, on which sat a spherical component. Bush nodded to the technician sat at his post who immediately started to flick switches and turn dials. Once again a low humming sound came from the object. This time there was no static discharge. The object took half the time to lift off the floor. Unlike the German Bell there were no chains attached. A thick wire trailed away from the object directly towards the window and under the viewing room. The object hung motionless in the air.

'We've fitted magnetic gyros for control. As you can see the object is stable as it floats.' He nodded again at the technician who grabbed a control stick on the console in front of him and pushed it to the left.

The object drifted slowly without tilting and then in the opposite direction as the technician pushed the control stick to the right. The object then settled back on the floor.

'We've also discovered that the energy this utilises is limitless.'

'Which is what exactly?'

'Helium three.'

Frederick stared at Dr Bush. 'Impossible, helium three is one of the rarest elements on earth and almost impossible to synthesise, it's not limitless.'

'Another pie the Nazis had their finger in Professor. Something they discovered while constructing their Antarctic stronghold, which of course is now ours. You are correct it is extremely difficult to create. This is why we have small quantities. The amount we do have is enough to fuel our new rockets we're planning to use for space exploration. The Nazis however, believed that helium three is abundant beyond earth's atmosphere. There could well be huge deposits on the moon, as well as the smaller proto planets that exist in the asteroid belt. German astronomers have also theorised that the rings of Saturn could well be comprised of asteroids which have huge quantities of Helium three. This is why we are eager to get things moving with the space program.'

'This is incredible; it could render conventional aircraft obsolete overnight. Added to that Helium Three has almost no radioactive waste.' Frederick said. 'Do you realise what you've discovered here? The energy it creates could effectively make every fossil fuel redundant.'

'Let's not get ahead of ourselves here gentlemen.'

Frederick turned and saw a man enter the viewing room.

Chapter 100

'Professor Frederick, this is Senator Jacob Barnes.' Bush introduced.

Barnes grabbed Frederick's hand shaking it. 'Professor Frederick, a pleasure. I have been looking forward to meeting you. Doctor Bush has told me all about your little adventure last year concerning the woman rising from the dead, fascinating.'

Frederick recalled the incident involving Edith Jones.

Barnes stared at the object in the hanger bay. 'You're right it could solve all our energy problems and dependency on fossil fuels. But for now Professor I'm afraid this kind of technology isn't ready to be unleashed on the world.'

'Why not?' Frederick asked.

'We are in the middle of a cold war Professor. If we suddenly announce that we have an inexhaustible energy supply the Russians would launch everything they have at us in an attempt to get their hands on our knowledge.'

'You don't know that. Helium Three could advance science by decades overnight. Keeping it under lock and key is ridiculous.'

Barnes shoved his hands in his pockets. 'Ok then Professor; say we do release this new source of energy on the world. It powers our electricity grids and cars, who will profit?'

'I beg your pardon.'

'You have to realise Professor Frederick, the American and the British government generate hundreds of millions of dollars in oil and gas revenues every year. As time advances those millions of dollars will become hundreds of billions. If an energy source such as Helium Three were to be put on the market millions of dollars would be lost. Millions more who work in the oil industry will lose their jobs because of this.

Whether you like it or not Professor this helium three will be kept secure until the right time. Our dependency on oil and gas helps fund projects like this facility here at Groom Lake.'

'Until the oil runs out is that what you are saying Senator? When will that be exactly? A hundred years from now? The damage we are causing to this planet through industrialisation could be halted overnight if we started using this.'

'And both our economies will collapse Professor.' Barnes' tone was agitated. 'You scientists are all the same, dreamers. Never considering the bigger picture, always with your heads in the clouds. This is why you need men like me, to ground you. Profit before progress Professor Frederick, that's the American way. I suggest the British adopt this ideology.' Barnes then turned and walked towards the exit.

'That could have gone better.' Bush sighed.

'Surely you don't agree with him.'

Bush hesitated. 'No, but at the end of the day Professor Frederick Jacob Barnes is holding all the purse strings. He may call us a bunch of dreamers, but our dreams help create the future. One day professor the tables will be reversed and men like Barnes will be obsolete. You are right about everything you have said. We are damaging our world and ignoring the consequences. At our level of development our natural resources will be depleted within a hundred years.' Bush looked towards the door Barnes had just walked through. 'If men like Senator Barnes are still in charge, then the human race will have a hard time in the twenty first century.'

Chapter 101

6:12pm

Archie Watson marched up and down the room talking about what he had been shown earlier.

Frederick had issues plaguing him, particularly the attitude of Senator Barnes.

'It's just incredible what they have here. The rockets they are designing or have captured during the war. What the Germans were doing was even beyond my dreams. As for that antigravity device they were constructing. I feel like a boy at Christmas looking through a toy shop window.'

Frederick glanced at Watson. 'Funny, just a week ago you gave one of those Germans a bloody nose.'

Watson looked at his friend. 'What's the matter?'

Frederick looked at him. 'I take it you never met Senator Barnes.'

Watson shook his head.

'Don't worry you will. All this technology they're developing here means nothing if the Americans don't plan to share it. Senator Barnes wants to keep it hidden away because he is paranoid the Russians will attack the United States. I have never heard anything so ridiculous.'

'If it's any consolation I did encounter a bit of flak off General Power today when I mentioned sharing technology. He stonewalled me stating that it's best if what the Americans have is kept away from the rest of the world.'

Frederick picked up his jacket. 'We will get plenty more chance to argue at this dinner they have laid on for us.'

7:47pm

Frederick wiped his mouth savouring the taste of the large steak he had managed to get through. 'I have to say that is the best steak I have had in a while.'

'That's cornbread fed beef from my ranch in Texas Professor, I'm glad you liked it.' Senator Barnes boasted before raising his glass. 'A toast to our new friends all the way from England. To quote Bogart; I think this is the beginning of a beautiful friendship.'

All five men in the room raised their glasses. 'What do you think of our set up here Professor?' General Power asked.

'You've accomplished so much in the last few years. I was particularly impressed with the Helium three device demonstrated earlier.'

'Just one of many projects in development Professor. The work we are doing here at Groom Lake will have repercussions for decades.'

'Providing anyone gets to hear about it.' Frederick added.

A tense silence followed before Power spoke. 'You must understand the importance of secrecy Professor given the times we live in. You know the Soviets are poised to attack the west.'

'Do you know this for certain general?' Watson asked.

'We have people in the Kremlin who are adamant the Russians are planning a surprise attack on the United States.'

'And yet British Intelligence suggests otherwise.' Watson said.

Power smiled at Watson. 'British intelligence doesn't employ as many as our intelligence organisations Professor. Communism is everywhere infecting every corner of the United States. If we allow them to take hold then everything we are doing here will be lost forever, democracy will be lost.'

'Democracy comes in many forms General. Your government segregates coloured people denying them the right to vote and social interaction with white Americans.' Frederick stated.

'Exactly what point are you trying to make Professor?' Barnes challenged.

'The point I'm trying to make Senator is despite all that we have achieved over the centuries as a species. We are still bogged down with issues of race. What is the point of advancing scientific understanding and achievement if at the end of the day no one is going to hear about it?'

'We do not intend to keep everything locked away forever Professor.' Vannevar Bush explained.

'But you do plan to keep it from public view as long as possible.'

'No, not as long as possible but until such a time when the people understand scientific progress a bit better. You know Professor the average American is not very smart. I don't mean that in a bad sense but your average Joe on the street isn't interested in quantum physics. Unleashing the technical achievements we are making will only serve to confuse people.'

'But people can be educated Doctor Bush.' Frederick said.

Bush nodded. 'Plans are being drawn up to educate the population in matters of science. But before that happens we need to be sure they can understand what we are trying to tell them. And when the time is right we will deliver an education program designed so that even the less intelligent will be able to grasp the basic concepts of science.'

'We also want to examine the areas in which we can profit from what we have learnt so far.' Senator Barnes added.

Frederick looked at him. 'Yes you explained profit before progress earlier today senator.'

'You still don't see the bigger picture do you Professor. You are still annoyed at what I said. I don't think your government would share your view when they find out we intend to share the benefits of our knowledge with them.'

Chapter 102

Groom Lake – 9:26am
Friday 9th April 1954

Doctor Nathan Rosen and Professor Frederick shook hands as if it was the first time they had encountered each other. Dr Vannevar Bush had led Frederick to a large aircraft hanger that stood on its own under heavy guard. The building had been split up into several sections. Directly at the centre of the hanger was the main examination area which was a perfect square and windowless. A square spiral corridor surrounded the area arching outwards. Several doors lined the spiral corridor leading off into small research labs, again with no windows.

'Doctor Nathan Rosen is our lead physicist looking into the drive system of this craft recovered from the Roswell crash site in forty seven.' Bush explained. 'Because of the secrecy that surrounds this particular hanger only two people at a time are allowed to work in this area. I will leave you in Doctor Rosen's capable hands. I will be back shortly, enjoy the show Professor.' Bush left the examination area.

'Good to see you again Professor. I spoke to Rothschild last week who sends his regards.'

'I am a little surprised to see you here Doctor.'

'I was appointed to a similar project in 1945.'

'Similar project?'

'All I can tell you at this moment is that you are being fed half-truths by Majestic. Professor Einstein worked with me when they recovered the craft from Roswell.'

'Why did Bush say you've been here since forty seven?'

'It's the way the system operates. Each scientist or engineer is given instructions to limit the information they are allowed to reveal. The people who run this place are obsessed with communist infiltration. Have you noticed that you and Professor Watson have been split up ever since your arrival at Groom Lake?'

Frederick thought for a moment before nodding.

'Professor Watson is a new member of The Angel Committee and although he has probably been briefed on the UFO situation. Unlike you he has yet to gain first-hand experience with this phenomena. Which is why you have been given access to this area.'

Frederick looked at the circular craft in the middle of the examination area walking towards it. A hole in its side revealed the inner compartment. The object was approximately thirty feet in diameter by ten feet at its tallest point. He walked around the craft which was perfectly smooth on the outer shell with no visible windows.

'This is the third craft I have examined for our government.'

'The third.' Frederick responded with surprise. 'Where are the other two?'

'At our main research facility on the Midway Atoll.'

'In the Pacific Ocean. Why all the way out there?'

'it's thousands of miles from the nearest continent. A perfect spot for secret research. No commercial ships are allowed within a hundred miles of the area and the skies are constantly being monitored for soviet aircraft. There is also a facility on Wake Island which is being converted into another launch site. You already know about the base we have in Antarctica. Our government believes that it's not sustainable over the long term because of the extreme climate. So they are dismantling the main launch complex and shipping the whole lot out to Wake Island.'

'But I was told that they're preparing a launch next March by Hermann Jodi at White Sands.'

'Yes, they are keeping a scaled down launch pad out there. One which they plan to launch rockets with artificial satellites.'

'A man by the name of Dmitri Kirov defected last year and revealed that the Russians are also working on a program to launch an artificial satellite within three to four years.' Frederick revealed.

'The Order knows this and is monitoring the situation in the Soviet Union.'

Frederick looked around the hanger. 'Where an earth is all the money coming from to pay for all this?'

'You've met Senator Jacob Barnes no doubt.' Rosen said.

Frederick nodded.

'A man with deep pockets and very influential in Washington. Needless to say he has Eisenhower's ear. He set up the funding for the Majestic 12 group. Every member is in his pocket. I also suspect your group haven't been given the full story of what has transpired over the last several years.'

'Senator Barnes' pockets can't be that deep.' Frederick stated. 'The amount of money you are piling into this place alone must be phenomenal, let alone the other research facilities you have.'

'I can assure you Professor the senator's pockets are bottomless. He has fingers in almost every major US corporation. From banking, oil, electricity, defence, Pharmaceutical, Motion Pictures, Newspapers and television. He has lunch with Senator Joseph McCarthy on a regular basis, and plays golf with Walt Disney. Senator Barnes is a dangerous man. There is so much more you need to be aware of concerning this man, but I am afraid it will have to wait. In your stay here how much of this facility have you actually seen?'

Frederick gathered his thoughts. 'Not as much as I would have liked to. There are dozens of buildings which we haven't been allowed near. And we've been under armed guard everywhere we've been.'

'I have been here a total of eight times and I have only

been allowed where the bell is or in here. Myself and Professor Einstein have also seen other technology recovered from the Roswell craft. We were tasked with giving a demonstration of the Roswell device you and your team were shown last year to President Truman back in 1947. There are a number of defence contractors who operate out of Groom Lake, Aerojet, Boeing, General Electric. Vannevar Bush is joint head of a company called Raytheon. I do know one thing, it's senator Barnes who decides who sees what.'

Frederick looked at the craft. 'So you examine the drive system that makes these things fly.'

'Yes, my particular field is the Einstein Rosen bridge theory, we developed back in 1935.'

'Linking two points in space, a wormhole.' Frederick said.

Rosen nodded. 'Given the vast distances between solar systems it is the only theory that stands up as to how these beings are able to navigate the vastness of space.'

'How much have you learnt?'

'Of the three craft I have examined, not much and it's not through lack of trying. I have estimated the technology this craft utilizes is at least two hundred years ahead of our own, give or take several decades. So you can understand it's slow progress.'

'Doctor Bush is optimistic that it's possible to reverse engineer some of this technology. He gave an impressive demonstration of a storage device last year in London.'

Rosen smiled. 'Doctor Bush is a bit of a dreamer I'm afraid Professor, what we like to call a futurist. I am not saying it's not possible to duplicate this technology, but like I just said, it's slow going. It is very compartmentalized here at Groom Lake. Different scientists and engineers are assigned to different jobs. No one is allowed to roam freely. They even have guards for the guards to make sure they don't stray into any areas they're not supposed to be in. Jacob Barnes employs his own security company here. They're nothing more than a bunch of thugs with guns.'

'You say that the other two craft you've examined have been shipped out to the Pacific atolls, any idea where they came from in the first place?'

'I wasn't told where the first craft that I examined came from. Due to the limited information they give me. I do know the second craft I examined at the end of forty five was exported out of occupied Germany, I came by this information via the Galileo Order.'

'Did it crash land?' Frederick asked.

'No, it was handed over to the Germans in 1940.' Rosen replied.

'By who?'

'The Vatican.'

'Why would the Vatican have links to Hitler's thugs?' Frederick asked.

'To be precise The Brotherhood of the Holy See. I was informed of a deal between the Nazis and the Vatican. The Holy See already knew Hitler wasn't to be trusted. A plan was implemented in order to prevent the Third Reich from marching into St Peter's Square and stripping the Vatican of its priceless treasures. The Pope ordered his top Cardinals to unlock the secret Vatican vaults and find anything that might be used as a bargaining chip.'

'I take it that's when they found the craft.' Frederick said.

'They found a great many other things, including a diagram drawn up by Leonardo da Vinci resembling the German Bell you examined yesterday. I have also examined the bell, when they first shipped it back here. The Vatican persuaded Hitler that a great many technological advancements supposedly lost throughout history would be of great use to the war effort. The Vatican promised to release information if it was spared the onslaught.'

'It makes sense why the Nazis didn't just march into the Vatican and take what they wanted.' Frederick said.

'I'm afraid we don't have a lot of time Professor. There is too much to explain here and now. I can tell you that our government has implemented a new drive. To extend its research operation which is why they have opened up to the British Government. Senator Barnes plan is to use every allied country in exchange for UFO technology. The allies are stepping up plans to fortify Western Europe. Both McCarthy and Barnes are paranoid that the Russians will try and invade. This is why we are experiencing these communist witch hunts at the moment.'

The door opened to the examination area and Vannevar Bush appeared. 'Time to go I'm afraid Professor.'

Frederick and Rosen shook hands and said their goodbyes.

Chapter 103

Palm Springs – California – 6:12pm
Monday 19th April 1954

Frederick looked out of the Window at Elizabeth and Susan with Archie, Joan and their two children as they played in the pool. Also by the pool were Senator Barnes' wife Jennifer and their two teenage sons. Barnes had shown up with Vannevar Bush and his wife to say goodbye to the visiting British scientists and their families. He had organised a barbeque and had spent the afternoon hosting the gathering by cooking most of the food. Both Susan and Joan were taken back by the American's charm, and were eager to maintain a friendship with Jennifer Barnes. Elizabeth even offered to accommodate them the next time they were in Great Britain. Senator Barnes was all too eager to accept the invitation.

'Your wife is a delightful lady Professor Frederick and your daughter is the pinnacle of politeness.' Barnes said, joining Frederick alone in the spacious living room.

'Thank you Senator, you've been a most generous host this afternoon.'

Barnes looked out of the patio windows at the families. 'I feel that we have accomplished much over the last few weeks. No doubt what you have seen has given you plenty of food for thought.'

'Plenty.' Frederick remarked dryly.

Barnes looked at him. 'I know you are not happy with the way we run things out here Professor. You feel that the people we employ deserve to be put on trial for things they may have done in the past. Like you I had reservations about employing these men. When I first found out about Operation Paperclip I strongly opposed it. There were many concentration camp survivors who moved out to the United

States to escape the memories of the horrors of what had happened to them. Yet here we were letting Nazi war criminals in the back door. I couldn't find a way to justify it, until that is, I saw the full extent of what the Russians are capable of. Stalin may be dead but the legacy of his brutality lives on. Every year we receive intelligence reports revealing the full extent of Soviet atrocities against their own people. Millions dying of starvation, while millions more are worked to death on the Soviet war machine. You have to ask yourself Professor Frederick. What would the world be like if the Russians would have got their hands on the likes of Hermann Jodi, or Werner Von Braun and all the other prominent scientists that worked on Hitler's Atom Bomb project.'

'Your argument is compelling Senator.' Frederick said. 'But there are those who fought against Nazi Germany and lost loved ones in the process. My own parents were killed during the London Blitz. So you see I have no love for the men you employ. Great Britain was on the front line and stood alone for a few years against Nazi Germany.'

Barnes seemed unfazed by Frederick's words. 'I sleep soundly at night knowing full well that we were able to beat the Russians to most of the scientific and military hardware the Nazis built. When I became involved in Project Paperclip I encountered a German banker. He told me that prior to Germany invading Poland in thirty nine, he tried to convince Hitler and the Third Reich to hold off for two years before attempting to break out of Germany. He said that more advancements in science and warfare needed to be developed if Germany was to claim a total victory over Europe. If they would have taken his advice we would not be stood here having this conversation. Two years Professor, to develop the V1, V2, the jet propelled aircraft, Heavy Water and a host of other wonder weapons that could have single handily won the Germans the war. When our boys were pushing into Germany they found an installation developing a new type of long range German Bomber capable of reaching the Eastern seaboard. We raided shipyards with submarines designed to carry and launch the V1 and V2 rockets. Two years Professor that's all it would have taken them. There would have been no glorious Battle of Britain. Goose stepping German troops would have marched on Whitehall sweeping away any resistance. Then they would have marched on Capitol Hill.' Barnes stopped talking allowing time for Frederick to digest his words. 'Thank god that crazy bastard didn't listen.'

Chapter 104

Whitehall – London – 12:39pm
Friday 23rd April 1954

Malcolm Chambers stared at the report contemplating the information Frederick had detailed in the dossier. 'I have to admit Ralph what you and Archie were shown during your time in America has shocked me somewhat. A base out in Antarctica, rockets capable of reaching the moon. Hundreds if not thousands of former Nazi scientists and engineers working for the Americans.'

'So many Nazis escaped during the closing stages of the war. It was a total mess trying to capture the ones responsible for so much atrocity.'

'The ratlines out of Europe helped a lot of those bastards get away. Which leads me to one of the reasons I called you here today.' Chambers looked back at the report. 'You mention here a man called Jacob Barnes.'

'Yes he's a prominent figure over there. He tried to convince me the positive aspect of employing all those Nazis.'

'He's a man of many traits.' Chambers continued. 'In 1929 he was a prominent New York Banker. Despite the Wall Street crash Barnes seemed invulnerable and survived. At the time he was pulled up by the FBI in connection with missing bearer bonds allegedly worth in excess of one hundred million dollars.'

Frederick listened to Chambers.

'Unfortunately the FBI couldn't find the missing bearer bonds so they let him go.' Chambers reached into a drawer in his desk and pulled out a file which he handed to Frederick. 'I compiled this file on him, dug it out yesterday when his name cropped up in your report. After the crash of twenty nine he went to ground for a few years until 1935. He turned up in

Hollywood spreading a lot of money around and investing heavily in the film industry. He had a lot of return from his investments.'

'I take it no one questioned where the money was coming from.' Frederick said.

'No.' Chambers replied. 'After that he started to branch out. Oil, gas and now it seems he has his fingers in Americas most top secret research facilities.'

Frederick noted the look on Chambers' face. 'Something tells me this Barnes character is going to be a problem. How is it you are familiar with him?'

'Nearly seven years ago British intelligence intercepted a German businessman in London making his way to the USA. A man by the name of Joseph Frank. Myself and Morris Stanford interviewed the man. He confessed to being a former Nazi who was being smuggled out of Europe to the USA. When searched he was found to be carrying half a million dollars in American bearer bonds. He claimed they had come from the pocket of Jacob Barnes. While in our custody Jacob Barnes turned up and carted Frank away without as much of an explanation. A few days later Joseph Frank's body was found drifting face down in the Thames estuary.'

Frederick listened with interest.

Chambers indicated to the file he handed Frederick. 'As you can see his file is quite extensive. I suggest you read it thoroughly. You are going to have to familiarise yourself with Jacob Barnes.'

Frederick looked up at Chambers.

'I received a telephone call this morning concerning a conference being held in just over a week.'

'What kind of conference?'

'Apparently to discuss the matter of the existence of beings from other worlds, among other things. This Senator Barnes is heading the meeting, and it's him who phoned me this morning.'

'Really.' Frederick remarked.

'I want you to listen to me very carefully Ralph. This meeting, that file is to be kept between the two of us. No one else must know of its existence, not even fellow committee members.'

'Of course.'

'Jacob Barnes is dangerous. He has the ability to find a person's weakness an exploit it. If I would have known he was involved with the Majestic 12 group last year I would have never have agreed to set up a partnership. The device shown to us from the Roswell crash last year, your invite out to the USA are all part of a plan. It is obvious Barnes has access to all the files we have shared with the Americans. He is a thorough man. It is highly likely he will know everything that has happened over the last two years. Operation Mainbrace, the Edith Jones casefile, Janus, everything. He was explicitly adamant that you should attend this conference which is being held in the Netherlands.' Chambers looked down at a piece of paper he had scribbled on. 'At a place called the Hotel de Bilderberg, near Arnhem.'

'Another trip abroad.' Frederick commented his thoughts turned to Elizabeth and the child she was expecting.

'The conference itself only lasts one day so you won't be gone too long. But you will be going alone, Barnes was insistent on this. This is how he operates. He will try and isolate you from the committee and put you in a position where you won't be able to say no.'

'From my experience Malcolm I think saying no is quite easy for me but I will heed your warning.'

'Good, we will meet up after the conference and try and guess what Barnes' strategy is.'

Chapter 105

Hotel De Bilderberg – Arnhem – Netherlands – 11:01am Monday 3rd May 1954

Frederick quickly swept the room glancing at the nine other men who were in attendance. Professor Albert Einstein was sat opposite and greeted Frederick as soon as he walked through the door of the conference room. Vannevar Bush and Jacob Barnes sat at each end of the large oval table. The scale of security surrounding the small meeting room was immense. Over a hundred secret service agents stood guard at every entrance to the hotel, as well as patrolling the grounds. Even the local police had been assigned to patrol a radius of three miles from the hotel.

On arrival Frederick was unaware that anyone else had arrived. He was escorted straight to his room and given a memo with instructions to read through it. His evening meal was brought to his room, which had an adjoining bathroom.

Even though just ten men resided in the conference room, every room in the hotel had been booked and paid for. No outsiders were allowed within three miles of the hotel.

'Good morning gentlemen.' Barnes greeted. 'Thank you for attending this meeting today. Our hosts have been gracious enough to hand over this splendid hotel for a few days so that means room service is all yours.'

Chuckles resonated around the room, while Einstein and Frederick remained straight faced.

'You all know me of course.' Barnes smiled. 'And the man at the other end of the table, Vannevar Bush. To my right Mr Walt Disney well known movie producer, along with Louis B Mayer another prominent movie producer. Astrophysicist and Cambridge Professor Ralph Frederick. Next to Professor Frederick well known astronomer Doctor Martin Steinberg.'

Barnes paused to catch his breath. 'Sat to my left is General Frank Stacy United States. A man who needs no introduction Physicist Albert Einstein. Next we have Cardinal James Macintyre, our representative on religious matters. And Last but no means least William Randolph Hearst Junior. Son of the late newspaper baron William Hearst.' Barnes looked directly at Vannevar Bush. 'Doctor if you please.'

Bush Stood. 'I take it you have all read the report we gave you last night, The Road to Disclosure.' Bush picked up a glass of water and took a sip. 'We are here today because we all have one thing in common. We are fully aware that our planet is being visited by beings from another world. Besides the ten of us in the room there are probably another hundred people or so who have access to this knowledge, including President Dwight D Eisenhower.' Bush looked across at Frederick. 'And British Prime Minister Winston Churchill. However as time progresses it is obvious that we cannot keep this knowledge to ourselves. Our operations out in Groom Lake, White Sands, The Pacific atolls and, Antarctica have thousands of personnel. All of whom have access to materials that have come from the remains of the craft that crashed at Roswell. Whether we like it or not information is bound to come out sooner or later. We've all read the newspaper reports and seen TV interviews regarding flying saucers. There is no denying it, as time progresses more and more people will start to ask questions. This is why I have come up with this agenda to educate the public not just in matters concerning flying saucers but also in the progress of science. As we start to explore outer space people will be curious to know more and more. Therefore it is our goal to educate the public. First in the matters of space travel then eventually the possibility of life existing elsewhere. Our colleague Mr Disney has details of how we can educate the public on matters of space travel and technology.'

Walt Disney stood. 'A series of documentaries are being

produced at the moment to promote space travel and the science involved in making this possible. We hope to keep this series an ongoing feature which will be broadcast into the homes of every American who has a TV set.'

'Excuse me.' Frederick interrupted. 'We are dealing with a worldwide phenomenon here not just something which is happening in America.'

'True.' Disney replied. 'We will be making these documentaries for a global release to television networks in developing countries. In fact we have a documentary coming out later this year entitled Man in Space. It focuses on the development of the rocket. From man's earliest attempt to the rockets being tested today. And also what the future will hold for mankind. I will be presenting this documentary. We are also producing another documentary about the possibility of life on Mars.'

'We feel that Mr Disney's involvement in these documentaries will make it more appealing to the public. A friendly face so to speak that everyone is familiar with.' Barnes said.

'I don't see how a documentary is going to prepare the general public for what lies beyond our atmosphere.' Einstein commented.

'This is just one of the strategies we are planning.' Bush replied. 'Another strategy is to promote the science fiction genre, to make it part of everyday life. Reruns of Flash Gordon and Buck Rogers are already being shown on TV. We especially want to promote the subject of life elsewhere.'

'The science fiction genre has been around for years.' Frederick said. 'People still take it with a pinch of salt. And very few people read science fiction books.'

'I believe that will change.' Bush stated. 'Mass markets will be encouraged so that more people are exposed to the science fiction genre. Books and TV shows, toys, comic books and games will also be developed to educate people. We want to inspire the current generation of youngsters who will grow up and encourage their children and so forth.'

'The movie industry is also doing its bit.' Louis B Mayer added. 'There are over a dozen films Hollywood studios are churning out this year alone containing the science fiction theme. They may not all be about space, but the idea is to promote the fantastic. This will get people used to the idea that anything is possible.'

'And how long do you suppose this road to disclosure will take effect.' Asked Frederick.

'Generations Professor.' Bush answered. 'Nothing happens overnight. As science progresses so will public understanding of the world around them. I predict by the end of the twentieth century the general population on this planet will be educated to accept the possibility of life elsewhere. When we do announce we have found life on other planets no one will be surprised.'

'That's if there are other planets out there.' Cardinal James Macintyre added.

'I think we can be certain of that, given what happened at Roswell in 1947.' Doctor Steinberg said. 'The fact that we cannot see them doesn't mean they are not there. Based on what we know about our own solar system, we can assume there are other planetary systems similar to the solar system we inhabit. Development of radio telescopes and more powerful optical telescopes is the key to proving the existence of other earth like planets. But as Doctor Bush pointed out it will take time. Decades perhaps to develop instruments that could theoretically discover distant planets. Of course the key is to gradually disclose information concerning the possibility of life elsewhere in our universe. As our technology progresses we will be able to send probes to planets such as Mars and Venus to look for life. Once we establish that life flourishes on these planets we will inform the public. But again this will be done in stages. Microorganisms will be the first to be announced, before we reveal more complex lifeforms.'

Frederick looked across at James Macintyre. 'What is the church's view on what's happening?'

'The different religions of the world have always told stories of heavenly beings descending and interacting with various people.'

'True, but we are talking about something quite different. From what I have experienced over the last two years, these beings are anything but friendly. We are talking about technically advanced civilizations interacting and abducting human beings for experimentation.'

'The church has believed for some time now that some of these stories may well be first-hand accounts with creatures from another world. It has even been speculated that the Virgin Mary herself may have experienced an encounter with such a creature.'

'The virgin birth.' Barnes stated, before looking across at Frederick. 'The woman you encountered Professor Frederick, Edith Jones. Her story is not unlike something from the bible. A woman who has an encounter with a strange being and becomes pregnant as a result.'

Macintyre paused for thought. 'Of course I only represent one religion, Christianity, Buddhism, Jewish and Islamic faiths have to come to terms that we are not alone.'

'How many species do we suppose are visiting this planet?' Steinberg asked.

'With what crashed at Roswell and Professor Frederick's experience with this entity Janus we have had direct contact with two separate species.' General Stacy replied. 'But we believe the figure could be higher. There are witness reports of all kinds of creatures which people claimed to have encountered. Our two main operatives Agent Cones and Baker have also had their fair share of close encounters over the years. The United States government is looking into a way to monitor UFO activity. We have space radar stations based throughout the continental United States and working with our allies in setting up installations throughout Europe.'

'We are also monitoring information being fed to the press.' William Hearst said. 'Any stories that come in involving UFO encounters will be scrutinised before any article is written. Our approach to the way we publish articles involving UFOs will be in a manner that no one will take them seriously. Television news programs will also follow suit.'

'That's just the American Press.' Frederick pointed out. 'The press back in Britain seem to love a good flying saucer story.'

'I think we should break for a spot of lunch gentlemen.' Barnes suggested. 'After we will go in to detail about what we've already discussed.'

Chapter 106

7:46pm

Frederick opened the door. 'Professor Einstein!' He said with surprise.

The 75-year-old physicist slipped in as quietly as possible. 'I'm afraid time is of the essence Professor Frederick. We are not supposed to have any contact with each other outside the conference room and all of us are returning home first thing tomorrow.'

'Of course.' Frederick replied.

'The Galileo Order has concerns concerning Senator Barnes. It seems he is trying to manipulate whoever he can to keep information from UFOs escaping into the general population.'

'I have to admit I had doubts about him the first time we met. Doctor Rosen warned me, as well as one of my colleagues back in England. He warned me of the dangers of getting involved with him.

'The Order have many misgivings about this man. This conference today was just to test the water with your government.'

'What do you mean?'

'Senator Barnes wants a gateway into Europe and he sees Great Britain as his way in. Unfortunately as with Doctor Rosen my knowledge on his plans are limited. What the Order needs is someone to gain his trust.'

'I take it you have me in mind.'

'From what I have heard Professor Senator Barnes is interested in you because of your personal encounters with the entity who calls himself Janus.'

'I'd hardly call them personal encounters. I've run into this Janus by accident.'

'Maybe so Professor, but Barnes wants to gain your trust in order for you to gain him access to this Janus should you encounter him again.'

'I don't see how that could be possible.' Frederick said. 'I have noticed that Barnes has shown an interest in my work.'

'Jacob Barnes interest in you goes back several years.'

'Really!' Frederick remarked.

'When the Majestic group was established in 1947, one man opposed Barnes at every turn. Former Secretary of Defence James Forrestal. President Truman appointed Forrestal to pick the men who make up Majestic. In 1949 he committed suicide.'

Frederick looked at Einstein. 'Something tells me that this man was aided on his way.'

Einstein nodded. 'I was in a meeting with Vannevar Bush and Jacob Barnes just after Forrestal died. Barnes asked us if we had ever heard of anyone called Janus or Frederick.'

Frederick felt an icy shiver race down his back. 'How could Barnes have known about me in 1949?'

'It was when you were awarded your Nobel Prize was it not.

'Yes.'

'Barnes said nothing else, but the Order believes that Forrestal may have encountered Janus before his death. I know you have reservations Professor but we need you to gain the trust of Jacob Barnes. We need to know what he's planning.'

Frederick looked at Einstein, eventually nodding. 'Ok, but it will take time, we have our differences.'

'I understand Professor, Rothschild will contact you soon enough.' Einstein shook Frederick's hand before turning and heading back towards the door.

Chapter 107

Hotel Bilderberg – Arnhem – 8:26am
Tuesday 4th May 1954

'Well Professor I hope you found yesterday interesting.' Senator Barnes said.

'I admit your plan to educate the population is ambitious. However, over time I believe people can be educated in matters of science and of course what lies beyond.'

Barnes smiled at Frederick.' 'You and I are alike Professor.'

'I seriously doubt that Senator.'

'We both like to say what's on our minds. It's a quality I admire in a man with your stature. I'm sure we can work together on future projects.'

Frederick thought about what Einstein told him the previous evening. 'Yes senator I think I am beginning to understand you now.' Frederick offered his hand. 'Until next time.'

Highclare House – Surrey – 2:04pm
Wednesday 5th May 1954

'Educate the public.' Chambers remarked.

'It is a bold plan, and will take years for people to become familiar with science.'

'Do you think it will work?'

'From what I have seen people get really excited when they read stories of UFO encounters in the newspapers. This is a new aspect of the press that people are getting used to. Perhaps after many years of exposure people will get to the point where they will read such stories and shrug their shoulders.'

Chambers nodded slowly taking in a lung full of air looking at Frederick. 'Good work Ralph.'

'Thanks.'

'I want you to take time off from the Committee. You've been active for a few months now. You to take a few weeks to catch up with Elizabeth and Susan and the child you are both expecting.'

'Ok.' Frederick replied.

'You are very important to the Committee so it's best if you have a break so that you can recharge your batteries. Keep hold of that report I gave you last week and keep it safe.'

Chapter 108

RAF Buchan – Aberdeenshire – Scotland – 8:49pm
Monday 14th June 1954

David Bride had been staring at the object on the radar screen for several minutes. It was moving fast, coming in off the North Sea. Bride mulled the situation over in his mind. He dreaded having to pick up the phone and call it in as a UFO. The Radar operator had attended a briefing a few weeks earlier about such occurrences. His commanding officer gave a strict talk on unidentified radar contact protocol.

'If you pick up anything which you think is out of the ordinary.' Squadron Leader Robert Mason rumbled. 'And you are sure it couldn't be some sort of aircraft, natural phenomena or some other man made aerial object. Only then, are you to call me. I will not have this base brought into disrepute, or have us labelled as a bunch of flying saucer loonies, is that clear.'

Finally, Bride reached over and picked up the telephone dialling quickly.

'Mason.'

'Sir we have unidentified air traffic coming in over the North Sea.'

Mason clenched the receiver for several seconds. 'I'll be right there.'

Bride continued to stare at the radar failing to notice his commanding officer enter the room until he was stood behind him.

'I'm sorry to call this in as unidentified sir but I have checked and double checked. There's no way it's one of ours.'

Mason nodded slowly.

'It's been descending at a fast rate for a few minutes now, just passed over Inverness, shit.' Bride seethed. 'It's just dropped below radar.'

Trinity College – Cambridge – 1:24pm
Tuesday 22nd June 1954

Frederick looked up from the paper he was reading to see Morris Stanford and Malcolm Chambers stood in his office doorway. He smiled and stood. 'Gentlemen what brings you to my humble place of employment?'

Both men stepped into the office. Chambers closed the door behind him and sat down wincing.

'Everything ok Malcolm?'

'Yes I am fine Ralph, just been getting a few twinges that's all.'

Stanford wasted no time in getting to the point. 'Just over a week ago our radar net in Scotland tracked an object coming in from over the North Sea. It descended rapidly and dropped below our radar net.'

Chambers produced a newspaper and handed it to Frederick. 'We thought that was the end of the matter. However this newspaper article was published in the London Evening Examiner the day before yesterday.'

Frederick looked at the headline on top of the article.

'Mysterious lights spook local residents'

People living around the Loch Ness area have reported strange lights. Hotel owner Mrs Jean McCloud told journalists that strange lights have been seen beneath the surface of the Loch. Which has also been credited as being the home to the famous Loch Ness Monster.

Frederick looked at both men who were already smiling back at him. 'You can't be serious. If you think I'm going all the way up there on some sort of wild goose chase you can forget it.'

'I told you he'd say that.' Stanford jibed, looking at Chambers.

'Don't think of it as a wild goose chase old boy.' Chambers

said. 'Think of it as the first serious scientific investigation into the Loch Ness Monster. Besides Morris has offered to go along for the ride.'

'Yes, I thought it was about time I stretched my legs.' Stanford added with a dry tone.

'Aren't we better off sending Agent Cones. This sounds like his sort of thing.'

'Agent Cones is in America at the moment.'

'You know this is going to turn out to be a load of old codswallop don't you. Not to mention the fact that the loch will be swarming with Nessie hunters.' Frederick complained handing the paper back to Chambers.

'Probably, and normally I would agree with you. But there's still the matter of the radar contact. If something has gone down in that loch then we need to be there.'

'Ok, but you owe me if this turns into a farce.'

'Good.' Chambers said. 'You'll both fly up to RAF Buchan the day after tomorrow and interview the ground crew who reported the sighting, before heading up to Loch Ness.' Chambers smiled at Frederick. 'Make sure you come home in one piece Ralph. We wouldn't want old Nessie making a snack out of you.'

Chapter 109

Loch Ness – Scotland – 2:23pm
Thursday 24th June 1954

Frederick took in a lung of highland air and looked across the Loch. Surrounded by high mountain peaks. Frederick found himself wishing Liz and Susan were there. He thought it over for a few seconds before deciding that he would bring them both here for a summer break together with their new baby.

'Ten shillings.' Stanford grumbled as he returned from a boathouse. 'It costs for the hire of a boat.'

'With all the fuss these sightings are attracting the locals are bound to cash in. Did you see how many idiots were back at the hotel?'

'I saw, which is why we have to maintain a low profile, remember your cover story.' Stanford reminded. 'You are a writer and I'm your research assistant. We are here at the loch investigating the Loch Ness monster phenomena.' Stanford counted the coins he had. 'Ten bloody shillings for that boat.' He moaned again.

'You and Malcolm were the ones who wanted to check this out so there's no point in complaining about the cost of things. I bet that ten year old bottle of brandy I have sitting in my office back in Cambridge says this turns out to be a wild goose chase.'

'You're on.' Stanford beamed. 'Our vessel is called the Rival three. Fortunately me being an old Navy hand I was able to convince the owner to take the boat out alone.' He glanced at the change again in his hand. 'Which is probably why it cost ten shillings.'

'Now that we've secured a boat we'll head back to the hotel and have a little chat with Mrs McCloud. The sooner we get this over with the sooner we can go home.'

Highlander Guesthouse 3:45pm

Mrs McCloud sat across the table from Frederick and Stanford staring at them intently over her turtle shell glasses.

Stanford smiled at her. 'Now Mrs McCloud why don't you tell us the first time you saw these lights.'

The 67-year-old widow composed herself. 'Well now let me see.' She said with a quiet and soft Scottish accent. 'It would have been a week and a half ago. I was out walking Bess, that's my dog, along the Loch shore. I like to go out just as it's getting dark. My late husband used to do it, but now that he's not here, I do it. The first time it happened Bess started to bark at the lake. I looked across and saw nothing at first, and Bess stopped barking so we carried on along the shore.'

Frederick looked at his watch and noted the disapproving look on Stanford's face.

'A short time later.' Mrs McCloud continued. 'Bess started to bark again. As I looked across the loch I saw that the water was glowing.'

'Glowing.' Frederick stated.

'Yes, something just below the surface. It was hard to make out the shape. Bess continued to bark, and I felt a strange tingly sensation. The hairs on the back of my neck stood on end.'

Frederick and Stanford glanced at each other.

'Then all of a sudden the object just shot off.' Mrs McCloud continued. 'Bess stopped barking and we finished our walk.'

'And did you see this object again.' Frederick asked.

She shook her head. 'No, but the water horse has been seen about. I caught a glimpse of her last night under the full moon. Which is unusual because she doesn't usually like the full moon. She likes things nice and dark. Robert McFadden saw her last night. I was talking to him this morning at the post office.'

'Well thank you for that account.' Frederick said quickly before Mrs McCloud had time to say anything else. 'Do you know anyone else who has seen these lights?'

She thought for a moment. 'Willy Tennant, and Tom Clemance. You will probably find them both at the local inn just down the road.'

'Thank you Mrs McCloud you've been most helpful in our research.' Stanford said.

'Well I suppose I better start dinner for you gentlemen and the other guests.'

'Thank you.' Frederick smiled.

Mrs McCloud got up and left the dining room.

'Still think it's a load of old codswallop.' Stanford asked, his mind clearly on the brandy Frederick had bet him.

'Yes I do and I know where you're going with this. The static discharge she describes has been a constant factor with flying saucer encounters. But she also added the bit about.' Frederick paused. 'The Loch Ness monster or the water horse.' Frederick said in a mocking Scottish accent.

'Well I suggest we wash up for dinner then head down to the pub for a chat with the locals about what they have seen. Then we'll charter the boat later on for a spot of late night fishing.'

'Ok but if I have to listen to any stories about Nessie all night long then the bets off.'

Stanford frowned at the thought of not getting his hands on that brandy.

Chapter 110

The Weighed Anchor Inn – 8:13pm

Stanford and Frederick met outside the guesthouse and made their way down to the local pub. A mixture of locals and visitors mingled. The atmosphere was lively and laughter was the order of the night.

Frederick and Stanford fought their way to the bar. 'I didn't expect it to be this packed!' Stanford shouted over the din of the crowded bar.

Frederick looked behind him at Stanford. 'There's no way we'll find the men Mrs McCloud mentioned in all this.'

The barman placed two pints of locally brewed Highland beer on the bar in front of Frederick who handed over the money. Stanford picked up his glass and took an approving sip. 'I suggest we go back outside. I noticed some benches overlooking the loch.'

Frederick around and walked straight into a short man who had his back to him. The man stumbled forward a few steps spilling his drink.

'I'm so sorry.' Frederick apologized as the man turned to face him.

'You!' The man exclaimed.

Frederick felt his heart drop into the pit of his stomach. 'Uh.... hello there.' Is all he could manage.

The man excitedly tapped the shoulder of the man standing next to him who turned.

Fred Barnet grabbed Frederick's hand shaking it rigorously. 'What happened to you last year at Mildenhall?' He asked with a young child's enthusiasm.

Frederick struggled to get in character. 'I was released by the Americans. They gave me a slap on the wrist and told me not to be naughty again.'

'So were we, we couldn't believe it.' Barnet laughed. 'Albert was shot in the leg, but he's fine now.' He then looked at Stanford. 'Are you with him?' He said, offering his hand.

'Yes I am.' He replied shaking Barnet's hand. 'We were about to step outside, it's a bit too crowded in here.'

'Excellent idea, we'll join you.' Barnet announced.

All four men seated at a table overlooking the Loch.

Fred Barnet stared at Frederick with a mischievous look on his face. 'I know who you are now.'

'I beg your pardon.' Frederick said.

'It's obvious; I pegged you last year when you sneaked in to Mildenhall with us. There is no way you were just there for the fishing. And it's more than a coincidence we should bump into each other again all the way up here.'

'I'm sorry I don't quite follow.' Frederick said innocently.

Barnet smiled. 'Still playing us are you Mr Frederick.'

'Obviously.' Frederick replied taking a good swig from his pint glass.

'You and your colleague here and the two you were with last year are part of another UFO research group.' Barnet wagged his finger. 'Don't deny it. I know it to be true.'

Stanford decided to take advantage of Barnet's ignorance. 'You know what Mr Frederick we have been rumbled.'

'I knew it!' Barnet announced triumphantly. 'What's your group called?'

Stanford gathered his thoughts quickly. 'We uh... represent the Flying Saucer Working Party.'

Barnet looked almost disappointed. 'Hmm, the Flying Saucer Working Party.' He repeated. 'Not a very creative name I must say.'

'It was all we could come up with at the time.' Frederick explained glancing at Stanford.

'Have you found out anything interesting about our UFO friends or as we call them USOs?' Albert Atkins asked.

'USOs.' Stanford queried.

'Unidentified Submarine Objects.' Atkins said. 'It's a new term. I thought of it myself, due to the fact that these objects seem to be operating underwater.'

'I'm impressed.' Stanford complimented. 'We only arrived today. We haven't had much time for any proper investigation.'

'We arrived two days ago.' Barnet revealed. 'And we've spoken to quite a few locals who have told us some fascinating stories about the strange goings on in the loch. Most of the USO encounters have a common feature.'

'Which is?' Stanford asked.

'A static discharge.'

'Fascinating.' Frederick added.

'Yes, our group members believe that it's created because of the propulsion system these craft use.'

'And what means of propulsion would that be?'

'We have yet to come to any conclusions but we think it's an exotic form of nuclear propulsion. Far more advanced than what science of capable of.'

Stanford finished the rest of his pint and set it down. 'Sounds like you chaps are well up on your research into this phenomena.'

'Well we are the top UFO investigation group in the country.' Atkins boasted. 'Our members are dedicated to investigating the unknown. I'm currently writing a book on the subject of UFOs.'

'A writer as well, you appear to be a man of many talents.'

'We feel that the public deserve an explanation of what these UFOs could be. We are about to begin a campaign to lobby the government into releasing top secret files regarding flying saucers.'

'Dear lord, we should have thought of doing that.' Stanford said.

'Clearly your group lacks expertise on the matter of flying saucers.' Atkins mocked.

'Clearly.' Frederick said.

'Anyway, we were down at the loch this morning looking for signs of our USO friends and found a considerable amount of diesel oil washing up on the shore.'

'Fishing boats operate up and down the loch day in day out.' Stanford suggested.

Barnet shook his head. 'Not recently, not since the first sightings. The folk around here are very superstitious. Since the sightings began there hasn't been a single fishing boat out on the loch.'

'Have you any explanations regarding the diesel oil spill?' Frederick enquired.

In a low voice, Barnet started to speak. 'We believe that there are government investigators up here looking into the matter of these sightings. And they're going out onto the loch in the dead of night looking for USOs.'

'That's going out on a limb isn't it.' Stanford said.

Atkins shook his head. 'Not really, considering what we learned from our experiences at Mildenhall last year. We believe that the British Government is actively involved in clandestine operations looking into UFOs.'

'Now you're really going out on a limb. I'm sure her Majesty's government have better things to do with their time.'

Barnet grinned. 'We have first hand information and the name of someone who is involved in a highly classified research group. We have yet to learn the name of this group unfortunately.'

'And who is this someone exactly?' Frederick asked.

Both Barnet and Atkins looked at each other.

'If we tell you.' Barnet said. 'Will you promise us you will not take credit for knowing such information.'

'Cross my heart.' Frederick promised.

Barnet remained silent for a few seconds. 'Henry Tizard.' He finally said.

'The radar pioneer.' Stanford said.

Barnet nodded. 'Think about it. Who better to head up such a group than the man who helped develop one of the greatest technological achievements of the twentieth century. And that gentlemen is all we are prepared to share with you.'

'And we are grateful for the information. Our fellow group members will be most fascinated to hear this, won't they Mr Frederick.'

Frederick finished the rest of his pint. 'Indeed they will Mr Stanford.'

'Are you chaps having another one?' Barnet asked holding up his empty glass.

'That's very kind of you, yes please.' Stanford said offering up his glass.

Atkins stood grabbing Frederick's glass. 'We'll be back in a jiffy.'

Frederick and Stanford watched the two men disappear through the pub's main entrance. People were starting to spill out onto the pub's courtyard. 'What do you think?' Frederick said.

'I think we need to find out how those two know about Tizard.' Stanford replied. 'His group is not known in any public domain.'

'Last year Barnet mentioned that they have some sort of newsletter. The Duke of Edinburgh is one of its many subscribers.'

'That's more than a coincidence, considering that you encountered Peter Horsley while investigating the Edith Jones case. I have a bottle of scotch back at the hotel I packed. Why don't we invite them out onto the loch later tonight? The scotch should help to loosen their tongues a little.'

Frederick nodded. 'Agreed.'

A few minutes later Barnet and Atkins returned.

Stanford held up his glass. 'A toast.' He gestured. 'To

brothers of a noble cause, the search for truth.'

'Here here.' Atkins said clanking his glass against Barnet's.

Stanford took a good swig before setting his glass down. 'How would you chaps like to come out with us onto the loch later on?' Stanford invited.

'You managed to hire a boat.' Barnet stated, suspicion evident in his tone. 'How? The locals have not been hiring.'

'We found a local who was. Although I had to give him a considerable amount of money.' Stanford looked at both men. 'You were kind enough to share information with us a few minutes ago. It's only fair that we return the favour.'

'We were planning to return home tomorrow, but I'm sure we can manage a little boat trip.'

'Excellent, I have a fishing rod back at the hotel I'd like to grab.' Stanford said. 'Even if we don't see anything spectacular we're guaranteed a sumptuous breakfast in the morning.'

Chapter 111

Loch Ness – 10:56pm

The full moon shone down on the Loch's mirror like surface creating a mesmerising reflection of the star filled sky above. The four men had been out on the loch for just over an hour and had yet to see anything. Stanford had already caught four good sized salmon and had just thrown his line back. Frederick operated the sonar. All he had sighted so far were shoals of fish that passed under the boat.

Albert Atkins sipped from the tin cup which Stanford had just handed him and gazed at the heavens. 'You know considering the amount of stars there are in our night sky it's impossible to imagine that we are the only planet with life on it.'

Frederick glanced up taking in a lung full of air. 'How many planets do you think have life on them?'

'Dozens perhaps, or even hundreds. All of them inhabited by beings who are probably wondering the same thing as we are right now.'

'It's an interesting hypothesis.' Stanford said giving the sky a quick scan. 'Let me ask you chaps this. Why do you believe in UFOs?'

'That's easy.' Barnett answered. 'For me it's a fundamental drive. Life has formed on this planet and has spread all over. Why can't the same be true with the rest of our universe? In nature we see patterns all the time, repeating all over the place. That fact alone demonstrates that the same must be true out there amongst the millions of stars that exist. Besides anything has got to be better than this planet.'

Frederick fixed his stare on the sonar. An object was showing up below them.

'How so?' Stanford asked with puzzlement.

'Look at us.' Barnet stated. 'The way we act towards each other with all our wars and other methods we use to happily kill each other. It almost makes you ashamed to be human.'

Stanford sipped from his cup.

'I'm not sure but I think we have something.' Frederick announced breaking the silence. The sonar started to ping steadily. 'It's below us moving quite fast, four hundred feet.'

The other three men were now looking over the side of the boat and were aware of a shimmering blue light coming up from the depths of the loch.

'Incredible.' Atkins gasped.

'Three hundred feet and closing fast.' Frederick announced glaring at the sonar which quickened its ping. 'Two hundred and fifty feet and closing.'

The blue light below began to expand beyond the fishing boat in all directions. 'Two hundred feet.' Frederick shouted. 'One hundred feet....'

The light engulfed the small fishing boat bathing it in a sky blue aura. 'Brace for impact!' Stanford screamed.

All four men grabbed what they could to stop themselves being flung over the side.

After what seemed an eternity Frederick looked at the sonar. 'It's stopped twenty feet below us.' He said.

Stanford could feel his heart beat again and looked down into the loch. The object glided effortlessly to the side and moved down the loch. 'There's no way we'll be able to keep pace in this bloody tub.' Stanford cursed.

The sonar continued to ping ominously. 'There's something else below us, one hundred and fifty feet and closing fast.' Frederick revealed.

The shimmering blue light had gone leaving nothing but the reflective surface of the loch.

'I can't see anything!' Atkins shouted as he stared into the black water.

'Seventy five feet and closing.' Frederick barked.

'Shit.' Stanford seethed. 'Here we go again, hold on to something!' He ordered.

The water under the boat started to surge causing the vessel to lurch to one side.

Atkins and Barnet clung to the side rail.

'Hard to bloody starboard!' Stanford yelled.

Frederick grabbed the boat's wheel and spun it pushing the throttle. The boat's idle engine roared into life and the boat surged forward.

'We're clear!' Barnet announced looking over the side of the boat.

'Clear of what exactly?' Stanford demanded to know as he looked behind.

In the light of the full moon Frederick could make out the black lifeless silhouette of a submarine which had just surfaced a few dozen yards behind.

Stanford grabbed a torch and shone it along the side of the submarine. His heart skipped a beat as a Russian Red star came into view. A hatch was flung open and several heavily armed men appeared pointing their guns at the small fishing boat.

Chapter 112

11:47pm

Frederick, Stanford, Atkins and Barnet were hauled aboard the submarine and had been taken to a cramped compartment. Frederick reminisced over his experience on board the Russian submarine during the Operation Mainbrace incident. This sub was much smaller, but as with the other submarine the smell of diesel oil hung thickly in the air. 'Well that clears up that mystery.' He said looking at Atkins and Barnet.

'What mystery?' Barnet said despairingly.

'The diesel oil at the loch shore you mentioned earlier tonight.'

'I think the bigger mystery is how a Soviet submarine is able to penetrate British waters and find its way into a Scottish Loch.' Stanford said.

'They say that these Lochs are linked by underwater passageways which open out into the North Sea.' Atkins said quietly. 'It's only theory at the moment but there is ongoing research to prove this. They also say that's how the Loch Ness Monster gets about.' He stopped talking after noting the disapproving look on Frederick's face.

Stanford looked at him. 'And you know this because.'

'I'm a geologist. I teach out of Leeds University.'

'I thought you were a UFO investigator.' Frederick said.

'Only in our spare time.' Atkins answered. 'Mr Barnet here is a bank manager. We set up our organisation because we have a common interest. Mr Barnet happens to be my financial adviser. We met a few years ago when I was sorting out my mortgage. We got talking and discovered we both had an interest in H.G Wells and other things including UFOs.'

'Charming Story.' Stanford said dryly.

'What do you suppose they plan to do with us?' Barnet asked.

'I have no idea.' Stanford answered. 'Perhaps they will drop us off at the next port.'

The bulkhead door suddenly swung open and two armed guards took up position either side. A few seconds later the sub's senior commanding officer marched in. For the second time that day Frederick's heart fell into the pit of his stomach.

Colonel Yuri Konev glared at Frederick and Stanford before breaking out into laughter. 'Well well we have caught some big fish tonight. Professor Ralph Frederick, Nobel Prize winning physicist and none other than Morris Stanford head of British Intelligence.' Konev shook his head and then eyed Atkins and Barnet who virtually cowered in the corner. 'And who might you gentlemen be? More members of the infamous Angel Committee.'

'Never mind that Colonel.' Stanford said with defiance. 'I would like to know what gives you the right to infiltrate British waters. You've committed an act of war.'

Konev waved his hand. 'Please Mr Stanford save your pointless banter.'

'Exactly what do you plan to do with us?' Frederick asked.

'You will be taken back to the Soviet Union for interrogation. After the incident last year in these parts and what happened at operation Mainbrace my superiors are most anxious to meet with you.'

'We've done nothing wrong. I demand you release us immediately!' Stanford shouted.

Konev walked up to him. 'You will be released eventually, into a gulag.' He then turned to face Frederick. 'You will be of great use to us in Siberia.'

The Captain of the submarine appeared in the doorway. 'Colonel, we have made contact with the craft again.'

Konev looked at Frederick and Stanford for a few seconds. 'Bring them, but leave the other two here.'

A few minutes later both Stanford and Frederick found themselves on the bridge of the Russian submarine. Frederick surveyed his surroundings.

'We have sonar contact sir.' The Captain said. 'Two hundred yards out.'

'Hold our position Captain I want to see if it tries to move off again.'

'What exactly is going on here?' Stanford asked.

Konev smiled at him. 'If you are expecting me to share intelligence with you Mr Stanford then you are going to be very disappointed.'

'Why not?' Stanford replied candidly. 'Like you said we'll be hauled off to Moscow for interrogation anyway.'

Konev looked at him for a few moments before speaking. 'Very well, Soviet Radar stations tracked an unidentified object over Russia. We were able to scramble planes to intercept it and were actually able to engage.'

'You shot at it.' Frederick said.

'And we damaged it.' Konev boasted. 'Unfortunately it was still able to evade being shot down. Our radar tracked its trajectory to this area, so we despatched a small taskforce to locate the object and take it back to the Soviet Union for study.'

'A small taskforce.' Stanford said.

'Yes, we have two other submarines at our disposal.'

'All operating in British Waters no doubt.' Stanford added.

Konev laughed. 'Your precious island isn't as protected as you would like to think Mr Stanford. You may have kept Hitler's dogs at bay during the war. But since then you have become arrogant. And arrogance breeds complacency.'

'It still doesn't explain how you managed to get this boat into a Scottish Loch.' Frederick joined in.

'Our expedition last year revealed fruitful results. We were able to locate a subterranean passageway which led from the ocean and connected to this loch, which is in fact the remains of an old Lava tube. We were able to navigate it within several hours before it brought us out here.'

'Still you took quite a risk coming out here Colonel.'

'There is no reward in playing things safe Mr Stanford.'

'Sir the object has started to move again.'

'Arm tubes two and three.'

'What!' Stanford exclaimed. 'You're not serious, you have no idea what will happen if you hit it. Not to mention the fact that we are in a loch, not open sea.'

'I'm aware of the risks Mr Stanford.' Konev shot back. 'Fire tubes two and three.' He ordered.

'Firing tubes two and three.' The Captain repeated, as the sonar started to ping. 'One hundred and fifty yards and closing. One twenty five yards. One hundred yards. Seventy five yards, fifty yards.' The Captain stepped back from the sonar swallowing hard. 'The object has accelerated away sir. It no longer appears on the scope.'

Konev glared at the officer before stepping over to the sonar. 'Shit.' He seethed. 'Bring us about.'

'What about the torpedoes you just fired where are they?' Stanford asked.

The captain peered into the scope shaking his head. 'They're no longer active. They have a limited range so they'll just sink to the bottom.'

At that moment the sonar started to ping again.

'Colonel we have movement again.' The captain announced.

'Is it the craft?'

'I'm not sure this is different.'

'Another sub.' Frederick suggested.

Again the Captain shook his head. 'No, our other subs are holding position at the mouth of the passageway in a bid to stop the craft from escaping. This is larger and moving quite fast.'

'If it's not the craft and not another sub then what the

bloody hell is it?' Stanford demanded to know.

'One hundred yards and closing. Seventy five yards.'

'Arm tubes one and four!' Konev screamed.

'No time!' The Captain shouted. The collision alarm echoed throughout the submarine.

Frederick clamped on to a pipe which was above him, just in time. The whole submarine lurched violently to one side. A Russian sailor who had not managed to hold on to anything was tossed from his seated position, his body smashed into the bulkhead.

'Damage report!' Konev screamed.

'The front compartment is taking on water.' A sailor shouted back.

'Seal it off, or we're all dead.' The colonel ordered.

The captain lay on the floor unconscious.

Frederick looked across to see Stanford scrambling to his feet and rushed over to help the sixty four year old. 'Are you ok?' He said over the din.

'Yes, a little bruised but still here.'

The sonar continued to ping, a sailor picked himself off the floor and manned the station. 'It's coming back!' He yelled.

'Sod this!' Stanford cursed grabbing a hand rail.

'Brace!' Konev yelled again.

Frederick had no time to grab anything solid. For a few fleeting seconds he felt total weightlessness as the submarine once again lurched violently. The whole scene became slow motion as Frederick sailed through the air, but suddenly came crashing down. A sharp pain shot through Frederick's body, he tried to yell out, but blackness descended over him.

Chapter 113

Friday 25th June 1954 – 2:34pm

The smiling face of Stanford looked down at Frederick as he opened his eyes. 'Thank god for that Ralph.' Stanford said. 'I thought you were a goner there for a moment old boy.'

Frederick looked around and noted he was back in the compartment they had been held when they first arrived. He also noticed that Barnet and Atkins were missing. 'What happened, where are the other two? Are they ok?'

'They're perfectly fine. In fact they're better than that. It turns out our two UFO experts are old navy engineers and have been busy helping out with repairs. Which as just as well the Russians lost three men. You on the other hand took a nasty bump on the head and have been out for over twelve hours.'

Frederick rubbed his head and sat up. 'What's our situation?'

'We were stuck at the bottom of the loch for a few hours. Whatever attacked us moved off, probably because we lost power and sank to the bottom. But thanks to the ingenuity of Mr Barnet and Atkins we are on our way again and have been for several hours. My guess is that we're in open sea again. Looks like Konev is cutting his losses and heading home.'

'You mean Russia.' Frederick said, feeling regretful as Elizabeth and Susan's faces flooded his mind. 'All this has been for nothing.' He said despairingly.

The bulkhead door opened and Konev marched in. 'I'm glad to see you are awake Professor.'

'Where are we?' Stanford asked.

'We cleared the passageway about an hour ago and are heading back to Russia. Where you will face questioning.'

'Kidnapping us will be considered as a provocative act. Our

government will not stand for it.'

Konev smiled. 'All but a few in your so called government is unaware of the existence of your little group Mr Stanford. I doubt they realise you are even missing yet. And we are not going to tell anyone we have you in our custody, so you see in the eyes of your people.' Konev looked at Frederick. 'Your loved ones, you simply disappeared, never to return.'

At that moment the submarine's General alarm sounded. *'Battle Stations!'* The Captain shouted over the tannoy system.

'For Christ's sake what now.' Konev groaned.

A dull thud rocked the submarine.

Stanford smiled. 'Looks like the game's not over yet Colonel.' He said as another dull thud hammered at the hull. 'If I am not mistaken those are depth charges. They will keep going off around us until wreckage floats to the surface. Then all your efforts will be for nothing.'

Another explosion shook the Submarine.

Colonel Konev steadied himself glaring at Stanford.

The Captain appeared in the doorway. 'Sir we're taking on water again. We must surface.'

The standoff continued for several more seconds before Konev nodded. 'Take us up.'

After two more impacts the submarine began its ascent to the surface.

Frederick, Stanford, Atkins and Barnet were hauled out of the sub's main hatch. Frederick gulped down the fresh sea air savouring every mouthful. Royal Navy personnel swarmed over the deck of the submarine.

The Russian crew knelt with their hands behind their heads. As he looked across from the stern Frederick spotted four Royal navy destroyers and six frigates blockading two other Russian submarines.

'Well Colonel.' Stanford said to the kneeling Konev. 'It looks to me as if you will be our guest for a while and believe me. We have many questions for you.' 'Stanford started to walk away.

Konev stood. 'I wish to make a trade.'

Stanford turned to face him. 'What an earth do you think you can possibly bring to the table at this moment Colonel?'

'Information.' Konev said.

'I'm listening.'

'My government is working on a top secret project.'

'As are many governments Colonel.'

'Do you honestly think that the Americans are the only ones to have flying saucer technology? You British have The Angel Committee, and the Americans have the majestic group. In Russia our project is known as Orion.'

Stanford stopped and turned again to face the Colonel. 'We already know about Project Orion Colonel. It was revealed to us by a defector last year.'

Konev grinned. 'And we know all about the crash at Roswell New Mexico and a great other things about what the Angel Committee has been up to.'

Stanford said nothing.

'You have a mole Mr Stanford, a mole that has unprecedented access to all your research. He has given us information regarding the device you were shown from the Roswell Crash.'

'What do you want?' Stanford asked.

'I want to be able to return to Russia.'

'Forgive me Colonel but it sounds like you would tell us anything to save your own skin.'

'And yet I have saved yours. We could all be lying at the bottom right now.'

'True but I'll have to talk it over with my fellow committee members.' He said.

Chapter 114

3:32pm

The familiar smiling faces of Lord Admiral Anthony Berkshire and Sir Malcolm Chambers were there to greet Frederick and Stanford as they boarded the HMS Vanguard. Barnet and Atkins were taken below to the infirmary to be looked over before being assigned quarters.

'Well I'm glad to see you two are none worse for wear after your little adventure.'

'How on earth did you know we were on that sub?' Frederick asked.

Stanford started to speak. 'I telephoned William just before we went out onto the loch and mentioned the diesel oil that Mr Barnet and Atkins had told us about.'

'Most of the fishing boats in the lochs are petrol powered.' Berkshire added. 'And just over a week ago naval intelligence got wind of a Soviet submarine sighting in Loch Alsh which opens onto the North Sea. The navy were sent to investigate but were unable to find anything.'

Chambers took over. 'When I telephoned the hotel you were staying at early this morning Mrs McCloud had told us that your fishing boat had been found without you on it.'

'So we alerted the navy and flew up here ourselves to help coordinate a search. This morning our fleet picked up two Russian subs steaming out of Loch Alsh, so we managed to intercept them. Their commanding officers were more than happy to oblige and told us your sub had gone down in Loch Ness. We were about to list you as missing in action when you showed up. What an earth happened in Loch Ness?'

Chapter 115

Fort William – Scotland – 10:56am
Saturday 15th June 1954

Fred Barnet and Albert Atkins jumped off the small boat onto the quayside. Frederick and Stanford had accompanied them. 'Well gentlemen I cannot tell you how grateful we are for your help. If it weren't for you old naval hands we would have been food for the fishes. We have arranged transportation to take you home, so I guess this is farewell.'

Barnet folded his arms glaring at Stanford. 'So you're head of British intelligence.' He stated before turning to Frederick. 'And you're a renowned astrophysicist. Then I take it this Flying Saucer Working Party you say you represent is a fabrication.'

Stanford smiled and nodded.

'I should have known with such a ridiculous name like that.'

'You were at Loch Ness investigating the USO.' Atkins said. 'Which would mean the government does have people who investigate flying saucer sightings.'

'I'm afraid gentlemen that information is highly classified.'

'Well one thing is for certain. I am going to be plastering this story all over our newsletter. I shall be ringing the London Evening Examiner when I get back home.' Barnet said with a smile on his face. 'You gentlemen are going to be front page news.'

'Based on what evidence.' Stanford shrugged. 'Have you any pictures or anything that proves your story to be fact?'

'Well we have, um, well.' Barnet reluctantly shook his head. 'No.'

'Exactly.' Stanford returned. 'As for you telephoning The Examiner. Your story will never see the light of day.'

'But we have our newsletter.'

'You do indeed.' Stanford said. 'But how many subscribers do you have? A mere handful.'

'We have his royal Highness the Duke of Edinburgh.'

'So I've heard, but we have plausible deniability on our side. You see, you chaps are just a couple of enthusiastic flying saucer investigators that will do anything to get attention. I think his Royal Highness will simply shrug off your story.' Stanford smiled as he walked away.

Atkins and Barnett looked on as Stanford boarded the boat.

'I will say this gentlemen.' Frederick said. 'You still have one mystery that no one has mentioned. What exactly was it that attacked the sub in Loch Ness?'

Atkins and Barnet looked at each other and smiled. 'My dear Professor, I hope you are not suggesting that it was the Loch Ness monster.'

Frederick shrugged. 'You told me during our little adventure last year your group is based on scientific understanding and research. Perhaps you need to expand your field of expertise beyond flying saucers. Whatever it was that attacked us in Loch Ness brought us precious time.'

A thoughtful Barnet considered Frederick's words. 'Perhaps we can investigate other matters of the unexplained.'

'That's the spirit.' Frederick said looking at Stanford who stood watchfully on the boat. 'Despite what Mr Stanford said, don't lose heart. He wouldn't like to admit it, but we need people like you to spread the word on flying saucers. The public may not be ready to know the truth at this moment. But in time they will, and it will be people like you who will pave the way.'

'Before we part company Professor. When we were in the submarine, that Russian Colonel asked if we were members of The Angel Committee. What exactly is that?' Barnet asked.

Frederick smiled back. 'Once again gentlemen it's been interesting.'

Atkins shook Frederick's hand. 'Until next time Professor Frederick.'

Frederick shook his head smiling. 'I sincerely hope not Gentlemen, I sincerely hope not.'

Chapter 116

Southport – Lancashire – 2:57pm
Wednesday 7th July 1954

Agent Cones and Frederick looked out across the coastline. The sky was deep blue, cloudless and the sun gave off a fierce heat. People walked up and down England's second longest pier enjoying the summer sunshine. Frederick looked across the shoreline and could see the Blackpool Tower shimmering like a desert mirage in the distance.

'I have to admit you British have wonderful towns. In America we just build in square formation.'

'I do love the seaside.' Frederick remarked.

A man walked by clasping a bag of fish and chips. The aroma drifted over to the two men. Frederick smiled remembering times he had spent in the seaside town of Hunstanton with Elizabeth and Susan on the Norfolk coast.

Cones reached into his pocket and pulled out a small piece of paper. 'Ok who's our lucky contestant? According to this her name is Lucy Williams.'

'Providing the information is correct.' Frederick added.

'Trust me it's correct. We have accessed information regarding pregnant women in the area and she shows up where one of the red markers appears. She lives in Bold Street.'

Both men started to walk in the direction indicated on the piece of paper. 'You know this is our first assignment together since the hospital in Abergavenny last year. How have you been?'

Cones smiled. 'You mean have I lost it since then?'

'You didn't lose it.' Frederick remarked. 'Janus played with your head.'

'He played with your head as well Professor but you seem

to be able to cope more than me.'

'Don't blame yourself Agent Cones. Janus is a dangerous individual.'

Ten minutes later both men arrived at the location. Frederick knocked loudly on the door.

'Can I help you?' A large man growled on opening the door.

'Good afternoon sir we are looking for Lucy Williams.'

'And who might you be?'

'We are from the ministry of health and wish to check on her progress. We are currently working with local district surgeries, it standard these days.' Frederick looked at the man feeling slightly unnerved by his bulk.

'I don't remember Doctor Brown saying anything about strangers calling.'

'He wouldn't have, we only arrived yesterday.' Frederick replied.

'The midwife is due to show up soon to take her away. I'm afraid you've wasted your time.' The man began to back away from the door.

Cones stepped forward shoving his foot in the door before it shut. 'We need to see Lucy now sir otherwise we will come back with senior health officials.'

'You're a Yank, what's a Yank doing with the ministry of health?'

'I'm a specialist sir, now I suggest you let us see Lucy Williams or we will be back with more people.'

Frederick and Cones were escorted to a back room. A young teenage girl was sat in a rocking chair staring out of the window. Tears welled up in her eyes as she nursed her heavily pregnant stomach.

'Lucy, you have some visitors!' Her father barked.

The girl looked up at the two strangers, her face racked with fear.

Frederick walked over and knelt. 'Hello Lucy my name is

Ralph Frederick. I'm here to check if you are ok.'

'Of course she isn't.' Her father said sternly. 'She's got a bloody bun in the oven.'

Lucy looked away shamefully.

'It's ok, we are here to help.' Frederick reassured. 'Can I ask you how old you are?'

'Fifteen.' She replied, her voice almost a whisper.

'Aye, fifteen bloody years old and pregnant.' Her father complained. 'And she still refuses to tell me who the father is so I can wring his bloody neck.'

'Why don't you go and put the kettle on, so we can talk to your daughter alone.' Cones suggested.

Williams hesitated for a few seconds before disappearing into the kitchen.

Lucy started to cry. 'I don't know who the father is, it's not my fault.' She sobbed wiping away tears.

'We know it's not your fault Lucy. How far are you into your pregnancy?'

'I'm not sure, but I think I'm almost full term. The midwife said she will take me away today to have my baby, then I can come back home.'

A loud knock on the door interrupted the meeting. 'That will be the midwife thank god.' The girl's father said walking towards the door.

Frederick gathered his thoughts searching for an explanation for the midwife who now appeared in the doorway. As he made eye contact with the woman his mind thrust back almost two years to where the whole UFO affair started with the pregnancy of Edith Jones. Who now stood in the doorway staring at Frederick.

Silence enveloped the room, Frederick stared at the woman who had risen from the dead in the surgery at Ripley. 'Why are you here?'

'Professor Ralph Frederick.' Her voice was devoid of emotion.

Frederick nodded.

Edith looked at the American. 'Agent Frank Cones.'

Cones took a step back. 'Yeah.' He said cautiously.

Edith looked back at Frederick. 'Your presence here is unexpected, but it does not interfere with our plans.'

'I could easily say the same about you.' Frederick replied. 'Where have you been all this time?'

'I have been preparing the way.' She replied.

'The way for what?'

Edith looked at the young girl. 'Her.'

'What's going on here?' Lucy's father demanded to know. 'Who the hell are you people?'

Edith looked at him and held out her hand touching his cheek.

Williams dropped to the floor like a lead weight.

Cones instinctively drew his gun. 'Hands where I can see them lady, now!' He demanded taking another step back to distance himself from her.

Frederick looked at the man on the floor. 'What have you done?'

'He is not dead, he is neutralised.' She replied.

Lucy started to scream at the sight of her unconscious father, but suddenly stopped. Liquid began to pour onto the floor directly below her. 'It's coming.' She sobbed.

Edith walked over to her, stroking her hair.

Lucy stopped crying immediately and closed her eyes.

Cones blocked doorway pointing his gun at Edith. 'There's no way you're getting out of this room lady. Now back away from the girl, slowly.'

Edith looked at Cones. 'There is no need to fear for her Agent Cones. We are not here as your enemy. We seek answers. Your species is unique.'

'We.' Cones replied.

An intense burst of light suddenly filled the room for a few seconds before dissipating.

Frederick's heart skipped a beat as he looked around.

Four tall slender looking creatures stood looking down at Lucy tending to her. Another intense burst of light followed. Lucy and the creatures were gone.

'What the hell just happened?' Cones said.

Edith stood looking at Frederick. 'It is time.' She said.

'Time for what?' Frederick replied.

'Contact.'

Chapter 117

The Kremlin – Moscow – Soviet Union – 10:23am
Friday 9th July 1954

Colonel Yuri Konev bolted down a shot glass of vodka placing it heavy handed back on the table. He had just read the report in front of him. 'Is there any way that we can interrupt this meeting?'

Lakatos shook his head. 'No, my source in London has told me any intervention would compromise him, and would stall our intelligence gathering.'

Bulganin thought for a moment. 'What about exposing the Americans, telling the rest of the world about what they are doing.'

'Impossible.' Lakatos said. 'The western press have a tight leash around their necks. Such a story wouldn't see the light of day.'

Konev looked at him. 'We are losing this race, we must do everything we can to jump ahead of the Americans. If you have another solution then say something. Your pet research project in Siberia is going nowhere since Kirov deserted us last year. Perhaps you should consider allowing Doctor Vilenko back onto the program. She made progress and solved a lot of problems your team were incapable of.'

'Gentlemen.' Bulganin held up his hand. 'Now is not the time for division in our ranks. The meeting about to take place is a setback yes, but the game is not over.' He looked at Lakatos. 'Inform your contacts in England and the United States that they must obtain information or artefacts that is of use to Project Orion and your project in Siberia. If they do not comply then we will cut them lose and expose them to British and American intelligence.'

Lakatos nodded slowly.

Chapter 118

Mildenhall Air Force Base – Suffolk – 10:56pm
Saturday 10th July 1954

Frederick looked beyond the edge of the runway at the area that had been lit up by gas powered flood lamps. Edith Jones had given him a map grid reference a few days earlier. The map reference was located on grassland beyond the main runway on Mildenhall Air force base, a secluded spot surrounded by woods. Security had been maximized; both guards and dogs patrolled the outer perimeter fence. Frederick smiled recalling his experience at the base the year before with the two ufologists.

Cones had contacted the Majestic 12 Group informing them of the incident in Southport. Four members of the group had flown in. Vannevar Bush, Roscoe Hillenkoetter, Donald Menzel and General Nathan Twining. Accompanying them was Senator Jacob Barnes and General Frank Stacy.

Other Angel Committee members included Malcolm Chambers, Morris Stanford, Richard Wilks and Ian Morgan. Edith Jones was also present, despite the protest of Barnes who wanted her under lock and key. Chambers felt that if any meeting was going to take place then Edith would be used as mediator.

Only four soldiers were assigned to guard the group of men. One soldier was armed with a film camera to capture the event.

'Gentlemen.' Barnes said. 'We are about to take part in what probably is the greatest moment in human history, direct contact with an extraterrestrial intelligence. Both President Eisenhower and Prime Minister Churchill have given their approval for this meeting. There are those who would say that we are touching the hand of god right now, but we know that isn't true.'

The group waited patiently scanning the skies beyond the trees. Frederick checked the time on his watch, 10:58pm.

'Look!' Richard Wilks called out.

Beyond the tree line a light could be seen approaching the group skimming over the treetops. The familiar static sensation that Frederick had experienced filled the air, followed by a low pitched humming noise.

Barnes quickly looked at the group. 'Gentlemen, this is it.'

The object touched down several metres from the group of men and the static discharge dissipated. The craft that had just landed was approximately thirty foot across dull silver in colour and shaped like a giant smartie. There was no landing strut. The object hovered approximately two feet off the ground. As the group looked on a section of the craft dissolved revealing an opening in which stood a tall figure who stepped down from the craft. Four other creatures followed, dressed in ultra-thin skin tight jump suits. The creatures walked towards the group of humans.

Senator Barnes stepped in front of the group to greet the visitors. For several seconds no one spoke. Finally Barnes held up his hand. 'On behalf of the United States of America I welcome you to our planet.'

Chambers and Frederick shot each other a disapproving glance.

Edith Jones stepped forward. 'We acknowledge your greeting.'

Barnes looked at her then back at the extraterrestrials. 'We hope this is the beginning of peaceful relations between us. I'm sure we have much to offer each other.'

The front alien bowed its head.

'Our time here is brief.' Edith translated. 'This encounter is intended for the benefit of your species. To show you that you are not alone.'

'We are grateful for your gift of knowledge.' Barnes

answered. 'What can we offer you in exchange?'

'We have no need for material substances. Our species has evolved beyond the emotional challenges that is bestowed on human beings.'

'I see.' Barnes almost sounded frustrated. 'Then why come to our planet?'

'Your species is spreading across your world rapidly consuming the planet's natural resources. If your population continues at its current rate of growth then you will face collapse within the first few decades of the twenty first century.'

'Is there anything we can do to prevent this?' Barnes asked.

'You are already taking your first steps beyond the boundaries of your world. This is the way forward for your species. But your progress is slow and there are other lifeforms who wish to see humanity's destruction.' The alien looked at Edith. 'Our species believe that mankind has a promising future and has been aiding your species.'

Frederick looked at Edith Jones recalling her story. The kidnapping, the pregnancy and the return.

Edith walked up to Frederick. 'There are those among you who now understand our purpose here. If the human race collapses then it will endure elsewhere which is why we have been taking individuals.' She then looked at Senator Barnes. 'But there are still those among you who are interested in self-preservation and the acquisition of material items. This is what is preventing your species from evolving to its potential.'

Frederick looked back at her. 'The other day when you took that young girl. You said you seek answers and that our species is unique. What did you mean by that?'

'We seek a cure for a disease that has ravaged part of this galaxy. Entire star systems have fallen because of this disease. Your species has an element that is resistant to infection. We wish to know how this is possible.'

'That's why you have been taking humans.' Frederick speculated.

Edith walked towards the extraterrestrials, then turned and faced the group of men. 'You still have a choice, but this will not last if you continue down your current path.'

Together with the group of creatures Edith retreated towards the entrance of the craft, which started to glow.

The group of men looked on as the ship lifted into the air. Then in the blink of an eye it accelerated away.

Chapter 119

10:27pm

'Goddamn it.' Barnes cursed. 'We should have shot their craft down.'

'And what exactly would that have achieved Mr Barnes?' Malcolm Chambers asked before breaking out into a cough.

'We could have had their ship, that's what it would have achieved. The technology would have increased our advantage over the Soviets.'

'You already have the craft recovered from Roswell senator.' Frederick pointed out. 'And I know you have other craft recovered from earlier crashes.'

Both groups exchanged stares for several seconds.

Chambers continued to cough, clutching a handkerchief to his mouth.

Frederick looked at his friend who seemed to struggle for air.

'I see you and Doctor Rosen had quite the chat at Groom Lake Professor.' Vannevar Bush commented staring at Frederick and ignoring Chambers' constant coughing.

'Yes we did, he also told me about your other projects out in the pacific atolls. But before you put him in chains for betraying your trust, there's the matter of our trust you have betrayed.'

Chambers continued to struggle for air.

'We would have given you full disclosure of our other projects in time.' Bush answered.

'Providing we would have been of use to you.' Ian Morgan remarked.

Barnes glanced at Chambers who seemed in considerable pain. 'You Brits are lucky we let you in on anything. We could have kept everything to ourselves.'

'Exactly what is America's intentions Senator?' Frederick asked.

'To spread democracy across the globe.' Barnes answered.

'Not everyone wants democracy Senator.' Frederick stared at is ailing friend.

Chambers winced in pain clutching his chest.

'They will have it whether they like it or not. Unless of course you prefer communism gentlemen.' Barnes looked at the Angel Committee members present.

'Forgive me Senator but you sound like a certain German dictator who tried to spread Fascism a decade ago.' Professor Wilks said.

Barnes looked at him and smiled. 'Unlike that crazy bastard Professor Wilks, we won't be using gas chambers to get our point across. Our way is far less painful. I suggest we part company for now gentlemen we have a lot to digest.'

Chambers slumped forward.

Frederick Jumped up and rushed to the aid of his friend.

Chapter 120

Whitehall – London – 1:09pm
Monday 12th July 1954

The Angel Committee members sat around the large table in silent prayer remembering Sir Malcolm Chambers. The heart attack he had suffered was massive and at seventy six he was too frail to survive.

'Funeral arrangements have been made for next week July 19th.' Frederick said.

'His Birthday.' Stanford replied.

'The Prime Minister has given instructions that this committee is to cease all actions until further notice. He explained to me that he is due to talk with Eisenhower over our future.' Frederick revealed.

'You don't suppose he plans to shut us down.' Admiral Anthony Berkshire said.

Frederick shook his head. 'At this point Admiral I cannot be sure of anything. The Majestic members have flown back to the United States. For now we return to our normal working lives until the Prime Minister contacts us.'

Chapter 121

Trinity College – Cambridge – 2:13pm
Wednesday 14th July 1954

'Come in!' Frederick called out hearing the knock on his door.

Ian Morgan Entered the room smiling at Frederick. Two men followed behind him and closed the door. 'Ralph, hope we are not disturbing you.'

Frederick glanced at the men behind. 'No not at all, what is it I can do for you gentlemen?'

'You know Sir Arthur Barratt.' Morgan said. 'And this is an old friend of sir Barratt's, General Martin.' He introduced.

General Martin shook Frederick's hand. 'Pleasure Professor Frederick.'

'We were wondering if you would attend a talk which will be taking place tomorrow night.' Sir Barratt invited.

'What kind of talk?' Frederick replied.

'Flying saucers.' General Martin took over. 'I was impressed with your television interview last year with that chap, Patrick Moore, and was wondering if you would offer your scientific opinion to our little group.'

Frederick looked at Morgan. 'I have no real interest in UFOs and I am extremely busy at the moment with end of term dissertations.'

'I promise you Professor it won't interfere with your duties here at Cambridge.' Barratt assured.

Frederick sighed. 'I could spare a few hours, who will be attending this talk.'

'Myself and General Martin as well as Peter Horsley and his Royal Highness the Duke of Edinburgh.'

'Of course I will be delighted discussing matters with his Royal Highness.'

'Splendid.' Barratt said. 'We shall see you tomorrow night Professor.' Both General Martin and Sir Arthur Barratt left Frederick's office.

Frederick fixed his stare on Morgan. 'What was all that about?'

'Believe me when I say this Ralph I had no idea they were going to spring that on you. They showed up this morning first thing and started babbling on about flying saucers, before mentioning you.'

'And you mentioned nothing about the Angel Committee or the events of last weekend at Mildenhall.'

'Not a word.'

'Who was that General Martin?'

Morgan shook his head. 'I have no idea, and I like to think I know every general at the Ministry of defence.'

'Well I cannot let His Royal Highness down. This will give us an opportunity to see what Horsley has been up to these last few years.'

'My thoughts exactly.' Morgan replied. 'How are you coping?'

Frederick shrugged. 'I still can't get over the fact that he's gone.' His thoughts turned to Chambers. 'But I know he would have wanted us to carry on.'

'Which is why I brought those two along. I know you would be open to such a meeting.' A short silence followed. 'Any news from the Prime Minister.'

'No,' Frederick shook his head. 'I don't even know if he has talked to Eisenhower yet.'

'I guess all we can do is wait.'

Chapter 122

13 Smith Street – Chelsea – London – 7:56pm
Thursday 15th July 1954

Frederick waited patiently at the door of the three storey Victorian building. He was greeted by a woman who introduced herself as Mrs Markham the resident housekeeper. She led him through a narrow hallway and up two flights of stairs. 'A gentleman is already here.' She said opening a door to a second floor drawing room.

Frederick stepped inside spotting a man staring into a fireplace.

The door shut and the figure turned to face him.

'Good evening Professor.' Janus greeted. 'Thank you for accepting my invitation.'

Frederick glared at Janus recalling the events that had brought them together. Stoke Lacy in Herefordshire. The psychiatric Hospital in Abergavenny. Then the image of himself cradling Elizabeth's body flashed through his thoughts.

'There is no need for apprehension Professor I am not here to harm you.' Janus indicated to one of two tall armchairs. 'Please sit down.'

Janus handed Frederick a cup of tea and sat opposite. 'I expect you have many questions for me.'

'Just one.' Frederick's tone was blunt. 'Why are you here?'

Janus sank back into the chair pondering Frederick's question. 'Same reason those other creatures you met with the other night are here.'

'The beings we met made it quite clear that their role on this planet was one of preservation.'

Janus smiled. 'The term you are searching for Professor is self preservation. Any species that has the capability to travel from one galaxy to another is out for more than just helping other species.'

'Are you saying they're here to harm us?'

Janus remained silent for a few seconds. 'Not exactly.'

'What's that supposed to mean?'

'From what I know of these beings they come from a place far away from here. Even with their level of technology it would be impossible to go back to where they came from.'

'Which is where exactly?'

'The edge of your known universe and beyond.' Janus replied. 'A place of infinite distance staring out into the abyss that exists between universes. The species you encountered the other night are so old that they would be considered as immortal by any man. God like creatures with god like powers. They are the first known intelligent lifeforms in the universe. But they are just like you and I Professor, making their way through the journey which is life.'

Frederick sipped from his cup. 'Is there a reason you are telling me all this.'

'There is.' Janus nodded. 'I merely want to inform you that they are just one of many civilisations which have discovered your world and are using its inhabitants to advance their own evolution. There are billions of intelligent species in this galaxy alone. If you were to compare your most advanced telescopes with a window looking out onto a garden then you have only seen a few millimetres beyond the windowpane. There are wonders out there that would make you believe that anything is possible. And terrors your worst nightmares couldn't even conjure up.'

'If what you say is true.' Frederick asked. 'And there are many species who have visited this planet. Then why not just waltz in and conquer us.'

'What a pointless question for a man of your intelligence Professor.' Janus mocked.

'Humour me.' Frederick replied.

Janus hauled himself out of the armchair and walked over to a globe which stood near the fireplace. He looked at the United Kingdom and then spun the globe staring at it. 'There have been many men throughout your history who have tried to conquer this world, most recently Adolf Hitler. Currently both America and Russia are locked in a silent war busying themselves with creating weapons of mass destruction. It seems that your species has a knack of forgetting history so quickly. Alexander the Great, the Romans, and the Nazis are but a few conquering nations that eventually fizzled out because their armies became over stretched. It became impossible to hold on to land which they conquered. Imagine a race of beings who wanted to conquer the galaxy using what you would call conventional means. The amount of foot soldiers they would need to conquer this planet alone would be in the hundreds of millions, perhaps billions given that there are currently two and a half billion people on this planet. Imagine if they wanted to conquer ten planets, how many soldiers would they need. Tens of billions, twenty planets, trillions of soldiers. So you see Professor conquest on a galactic scale is a pointless gesture even for the most advanced species.'

Frederick thought about Janus' explanation and found himself agreeing with the mysterious stranger.

'Most of the civilizations that have achieved interstellar travel have moved beyond material needs. They have achieved such a level of advancement they have the means to create anything they want. The goal of any civilization when it reaches maturity is to find the answer to the ultimate question, who created them?'

'I would have thought that even the most advanced civilizations would have moved beyond religious matters.' Frederick pointed out.

'True, but even the most advanced civilizations have a longing to return to their mother's womb.'

'What's your opinion on creation?'

'I accepted long ago Professor that the universe is like a force of nature. It does what it does to survive. There are an infinite number of universes out there. Some so big that mathematics being the universal language cannot calculate their size. Then there are universes that are so infinitely small they are invisible. There are universes that are ageless and there are universes that come and go in a blink of an eye. But in that brief moment of time life evolves and thrives.'

Frederick stared at Janus. 'You appear human, are you wearing some kind of disguise?'

Janus smiled at the question. 'No, I am as human as you Professor. Although my race is a little more down the evolutionary timeline than yours.'

'And your purpose in visiting our planet?'

'My purpose Professor along with other visiting species is because we are threatened by a more aggressive species.'

'How so?'

'Thousands of years ago our planet was ravage by a disease released by a species that has devastated other worlds. Their goal was clear, to populate our planet by infecting us with a disease which changed the population into them.'

'I don't understand.' Frederick said.

'The race of beings which spread this disease to not procreate through natural process like human beings. They release an organic pathogen that infects the indigenous population transforming into them. When they arrived my people had already mastered interstellar travel and had colonised several other planets. The pathogen they released devastated our homeworld. Before we could do anything three quarters of our population had been turned. Billions were infected, while the rest fought to survive. For those of us who escaped we found a suitable world to rebuild. We were fortunate to make allies in surrounding star systems including the beings you encountered at Mildenhall. Exchanging knowledge for advanced warning of another attack.'

'Did they attack again?'

Janus shook his head. 'No, but I believe that it is just a matter of time before they find what is left of my people.'

'If you are a more advanced form of human then that means the human race is not unique.'

'There are hundreds of billions of galaxies that make up our universe Professor. Some species evolve in unison in different parts of the galaxy. There are humans scattered throughout the Milky Way galaxy that have followed the same evolutionary path. Some humans have developed more abilities than others have. My people are able to access thirty percent of our brains which has given us an advantage over you.'

'Those creatures we met with the other night claimed that they had seeded other worlds with humans taken from this planet. Why, if there are already human populations spread throughout the galaxy?'

'It's an attempt to expand the human race. They have also seeded planets who's native inhabitants are human to strengthen their immune system. Your species has one unique property not found in other forms of humans.' Janus closed his eyes briefly. 'They mentioned the disease didn't they? They also revealed that the human race has a unique property.'

'Yes.' Frederick admitted.

'DNA which your science has only just discovered. It contains an element which is the key to saving my people, as well as other species that have been wiped out by the disease.'

'And this element is not within your DNA?'

'No.'

'This is why you and other species take humans.' Frederick

stated.

Janus frowned. 'You see us as barbaric.'

'You are not unlike the Nazis. Experimenting on human beings for the so called advancement of science.'

'I have not killed anyone Professor. The villagers from Stoke Lacy, Jimmy from the hospital are still alive.'

'That's not what Jimmy said when we encountered him at the hospital. He said that you killed his entire family.'

Janus took a few moments to answer. 'If I were to explain everything to you Professor then I would jeopardize my mission and a great many other things including your destiny and the destiny of others.'

'Others.'

'I see many things Professor. My species has the unique ability to see the future. I have already demonstrated this to you, along with Agent Cones. Although I am limited in what I can see, my ability gives me an advantage.'

Frederick thought back to their first meeting. 'When we first met you told Agent Cones you had met him many times before.'

Janus shook his head smiling. 'Careful Professor if you know too much you will unravel time itself.'

'What is that supposed to mean exactly?'

'The only thing I can tell you at this point Professor is that Agent Cones will play an important part in your future. Beyond that I cannot reveal anything else.'

Frederick felt disappointed. 'I'm puzzled, why invite me here tonight and reveal your plans.'

Janus looked towards the door smiling. 'Believe me Professor you are not the only person I intended to snare this evening.'

The door suddenly burst open and three men rushed in with their weapons drawn. The three men fixed their guns on Janus who remained remarkably calm.

Senator Jacob Barnes stepped into the room.

Chapter 123

'What is the meaning of this?' Frederick demanded to know.

'I might well ask you the same question Professor.' Barnes looked at Janus. 'Interesting company you keep, just as well we've been keeping tabs on you these last few days.' He nodded to one of the men. 'Kill him.'

Janus stared at the man with the gun. 'I've already explained to Professor Frederick Mr Barnes you cannot kill me.'

The agent stepped closer to Janus pointing his gun directly at his head.

'Tell me Agent Wells are you as eager to pull that trigger and end my life as you did with your brother.'

Familiar with Janus' tactic Frederick stepped between him and the agent. 'Janus, don't do this.'

'Too late Professor.' Janus remarked coldly looking at the agent who had just dropped to his knees. He glanced at Senator Barnes. 'A demonstration is in order.' He looked back at the agent who knelt looking at the revolver. 'Your father died hating you Agent Wells. Knowing that you were responsible for the death of his first born.'

The agent started to sob. 'No it was an accident. I didn't know the gun was loaded.'

'Your excuses won't bring Mark back. From now until the day I die I will never forgive you.'

Agent Wells looked up at his father's ghost. 'Please dad, I'm sorry, it was an accident.'

'The only accident here, was your mother giving birth to you.'

Frederick knelt down waving his hand in front of Wells' face. 'Agent Wells can you hear me?'

'His mind exists in another time Professor.' Janus said.

Barnes signalled to the other three agents. 'Gun him down!'

All three men stood like statues oblivious to the command Barnes had just given. He stepped towards the nearest agent reaching for the gun he was holding. All three men suddenly trained their guns on Barnes. 'What are you doing?' He cried out.

'I am in control of your men Mr Barnes. I can make them do whatever I choose.'

The man kneeling stared at his revolver before turning it on himself. He put the barrel of his gun into his mouth.

Frederick jumped to his feet. 'Janus, you've proved your point, end this now.' He demanded.

'My thoughts exactly Professor.'

A single gunshot rang out and the agent keeled over, knocking over a small table.

Mrs Markham let out an ear-splitting shriek.

'Have you seen enough Mr Barnes or shall I continue with this demonstration?' He glared at one of the men pointing his gun at the Senator.

The agent cocked his gun.

'What do you want?' Barnes stared down the barrel of the gun.

'The same things as you Senator Barnes, power. And I am willing to give you the means to dominate this world.'

'In return for what?'

'Unprecedented access to the human race.' Janus revealed.

Frederick looked at Barnes. 'You cannot accept the offer you don't know what it will lead to.'

Janus laughed. 'You're wasting your time persuading him otherwise Professor. Senator Barnes has already made up his mind.' Janus walked up to the American. 'I can offer you anything you desire Senator. Technology to defeat your enemies, I can show you how to utilize the technology you already have. Advancing your own technology hundreds of years in a matter of a few decades. I can make you the richest and the most powerful man on this planet.' Janus held out his hand. 'How about it Senator, do we have a deal?'

'This is madness.' Frederick protested. 'Senator Barnes, if you accept his offer then you are selling out the human race.'

Barnes looked at Frederick and smiled. 'No Professor, I am ushering in a new era.' He reached out and shook Janus' hand. 'Mr Janus, I look forward to working with you.'

Static discharged started to build up. An intense white light filled the room for a brief moment before vanishing. Janus and Mrs Markham were gone leaving just the six men including the dead Agent.

'Do you have any idea what you've done?' Frederick rumbled.

'I know exactly what I have done Professor. I've single handily won the cold war.' He looked at the other agents then at the body of Agent Wells. 'Clean this mess up.'

Chapter 124

St James' Park – London – 2:01pm
Monday 19th July 1954

Dr Rothschild sat down beside Frederick.

'It's over.' Frederick's tone was one of remorse and grief. 'Janus has been given complete access to whatever he wants.'

'The Order knew this day would come.'

'Senator Barnes flew back to America yesterday. The committee is clueless on how to proceed without Malcolm.'

Rothschild reached into his inside pocket and pulled out an envelope handing it to Frederick.

Frederick looked at the front of the envelope which had his name on it before opening it and unfolding the letter it contained.

My Dear Ralph,

You know me well enough to know that I hate clichés, but to quote an old one; if you are reading this then I am probably dead.

I knew this day was approaching. Our encounter with Janus last year revealed more than memories from the Great War. I wanted to tell you everything but I couldn't risk being discovered. I gave Doctor Rothschild instructions to give you this letter after I am gone. I have been a member of the Galileo Order for many years.

It was no accident that you encountered Doctor Rothschild two years ago at Downham Market station. When the Prime Minister came to me and asked me to select members for The Angel Committee I knew then you had to be part of it. Myself and Rothschild have followed your work and were adamant that you should become a member of the Order.

I know how much your life has changed these past two

years. You have seen things that challenge every scientific theory known to man. But I know you will meet this challenge and come to understand that this is not the end, but the beginning of man's next great adventure.

There are dark days ahead for you my friend. Senator Barnes would have already put the wheels in motion to gain control of everything. He is a dangerous man and will stop at nothing to get what he wants. I also know that there are indeed spies in our ranks. Who they are still remains a mystery. So therefore the only advice I can offer, is to trust no one.

Whatever is ahead you must stay on the Angel Committee despite the difficulties that will plague you. You have also encountered The Brotherhood of the Holy See, which is an organisation that will stop at nothing to conceal secrets that have been hidden away for centuries. You must uncover these secrets no matter what the cost.

I wish I could be there to guide you through the difficult times ahead, to advise you. But I know you well enough to know that you will meet any challenge head on. You have been a good friend Ralph and I know you will watch over William at Cambridge and pop in on Agnes to make sure she's ok. I'm sorry I won't be there to see Elizabeth give birth to your son.

Do not grieve for me my friend, a lifetime is just a blink of an eye in the ocean of time. The memories we leave behind are there to comfort others and remind them that those who have been lost are never far away.

So no goodbyes, just good memories.
I wish you well on your journey.
Your Friend
Malcolm.

Chapter 125

Whitehall – London – 10:06am
Wednesday 21st July 1954

Frederick hesitated in front of the large oak door to the meeting room before opening it.

'Good morning Professor.' General Frank Stacy greeted.

Frederick sat next to Professor Wilks who managed to force a smile.

'I have just been updating the committee on the latest developments.'

'Latest developments?' Frederick said.

'Both President Eisenhower and Prime Minister Churchill conducted talks yesterday concerning the future of The Angel Committee. I know some of you may be reluctant to carry on, especially with the loss of Sir Malcolm Chambers. But both the President and the Prime Minister feel that the Committee should continue under new leadership and guidance.'

Frederick stared at the American.

'It is with great pleasure that I assume the role of Sir Malcolm and take charge of the Angel Committee.'

Looks were exchanged around the table.

'I have an executive order from both the President and the Prime Minister. From this moment The Angel Committee is to operate under the guidance of the United States authorities. All information and investigations will be submitted to the Majestic 12 Group and senator Jacob Barnes.' General Stacy swept a gaze around the table. 'Welcome aboard gentlemen, and god bless the United States of America.'

The story continues in The Angel Conspiracy.

Help an independent author.
Many thanks for buying a copy of Codename Angel.
Before you take to Amazon and hammer me about grammar please stop to pause.
Please e-mail and tell me if there are any problems with the book. If you want to be added to my mailing list please e-mail me at the link below.
Many thanks
Jason Chapman

Jasonchapman-author@hotmail.com

Other books by Jason Chapman

The Angel Chronicles
The Fallen
The Angel Conspiracy
The Angel Prophecy

Speculative fiction series
Dystopia
Avalon Rising
Signals
Project Genesis